I stopped walking a... *don't like not knowing what's going on*, I thought. El Max.

Bhaaj, don't. It's too risky to go back there. They could be hostiles.

Are you picking up any more details?

Nothing dangerous. Nothing much at all. It appears to be exactly what it looks like.

Yet both my link to you and my shroud stopped working. I needed to know more about this place.

I was approaching the building again. This time instead of waltzing up to the front door, I went around to the back.

Can you still receive me? Max asked.

Yep. Clear as a sunny day. I considered the tavern, which hunkered next to me in the dark. It looked about twice the size of the room I'd seen inside. *I wonder what they've got in the back.*

The only signals I've picked up imply storage and living areas. Max paused. I'm deep-diving again. Can you still receive me?

I can indeed. You find anything?

When he didn't answer, I feared we'd lost comm again. Then he thought, Something is below the ground here. This signal isn't what I'd expect.

What's differ—

Bhaaj, get out of here now!

I spun around and sprinted for the road—

A heavy weight slammed into my back.

BAEN BOOKS
by CATHERINE ASARO

✦ ✦ ✦

Sunrise Alley
Alpha

SKOLIAN EMPIRE: MAJOR BHAAJAN

Undercity
The Bronze Skies
The Vanished Seas
The Jigsaw Assassin

THE SAGA OF THE SKOLIAN EMPIRE

The Ruby Dice
Diamond Star
Carnelians

To purchase any of these titles in e-book form, please go to
www.baen.com.

THE JIGSAW ASSASSIN

✦

CATHERINE ASARO

THE JIGSAW ASSASSIN

This is a work of fiction. All the characters and events portrayed in this book are fictional, and any resemblance to real people or incidents is purely coincidental.

A Baen Books Original

Baen Publishing Enterprises
P.O. Box 1403
Riverdale, NY 10471
www.baen.com

ISBN: 978-1-9821-9276-1

Cover art by David Mattingley

First printing, July 2022
First mass market printing, May 2023

Distributed by Simon & Schuster
1230 Avenue of the Americas
New York, NY 10020

Library of Congress Control Number: 2022013521

Printed in the United States of America

10 9 8 7 6 5 4 3 2 1

To Eleanor Wood
with my deepest gratitude,
for the decades of support, mentoring, and friendship.
Thank you for helping make my dream
of becoming a writer come true.

Acknowledgments

I would like to thank the many people who helped bring this book to fruition. Their input has been invaluable. For reading the entire book and offering comments, my thanks to Daniel Berdine, Kate Dolan, and Mary Lou Mendum. My thanks to every one of my Patreon subscribers for their much-appreciated support and encouragement; for their comments on specific scenes, to Dan Balkwill, Duane Ebersole, Duc Le, Ekaterine Andersen, Elaine, Elizabeth Krentz-Wee, Eric Schechter, Gregory Mendell, Jim Scovill, Joan Hardy, John Hart, John Howard Brown, Lee Thompson, Lizzie Newell, Paul Franco, phaeax, Sandra Lange, Shane Rooney, and Vivian Behrman. To David Mattingly, for his excellent artwork for the cover. To all the excellent folks at Baen Books, including my publisher and editor, Toni Weiskopf, and also Ben Davidoff, Carol Russo, Corinda Carfora, David Afsharirad, Elizabeth O'Brien, Geoffrey Kidd, Jason Cordova, Jenny Cunningham, Jim Minz, Joy Freeman, Marla Ainspan, Sean CW Korsgaard, and everyone else there who helped make this book possible. I would also like to thank Tony Daniel and Christopher Ruocchio for their work on the book, and John Scalzi for his much-appreciated wisdom. Special thanks to Eleanor Wood, Justin Bell, and Kris Bell at Spectrum Literary Agency, and to Ethan Ellenberg at the Ethan Ellenberg Literary Agency. Most of all to my daughter, Catherine Cannizzo, with all my love.

✛ CONTENTS ✛

Contents

THE JIGSAW ASSASSIN

✛ CHAPTER I ✛
HOME AWAY FROM HOME

My supposedly nefarious self couldn't get into the city.

I checked my surroundings for threats. Given that I stood in a customs line at the starport, the major threat came from boredom, but it didn't matter. I needed to stay on guard today even more than usual.

The area gleamed, from its glass counters to the agents working at them. They interviewed each person in line, clearing passengers to enter the city. Holo-paintings floated in front of the walls, showing the forested mountains above Selei City. A table with food waited to our right, spicing the air with tantalizing aromas, all of it laid out for those of us stuck here in line. The customs authorities were taking their sweet time to put us through. Selei City was a governmental center of the Skolian Imperialate. They had no intention of clearing anyone to enter until we finished their interminable checks to make sure we weren't evil types bent on perpetrating mayhem.

Yah, sure, I knew why they took precautions. Important

People lived here. I wasn't one of them, but when I'd lived in Selei City over three years ago, working as a private investigator, sometimes they hired me as a bodyguard. Either that, or they paid me to investigate someone they didn't like, didn't trust, or hoped to blackmail. The people in this city governed an empire. Well, okay, not an empire any longer. Selei City was now a land of politicians, may the spirits scowl on their opportunistic souls. The era when the Ruby Pharaoh ruled had ended long ago. It didn't matter. People still idolized the royals. Our populace had even voted, democratically if somewhat illogically, to continue using the name "Imperialate" for our non-empire, giving testimony to the widespread reverence for the Ruby Dynasty.

None of that mattered. I had too many memories of this world. Not that I objected to Selei City. It was beautiful. I just had a different life now. Coming here upset the balance I'd found at my home on the world Raylicon after struggling for decades to face the demons of my youth.

I should have stayed home, I thought.

It wasn't your choice, Max thought. He lived in the leather and tech-mech gauntlets I wore on my wrists and lower arms. As an Evolving Intelligence, or EI, he sent signals along threads in my body to bio-electrodes in my brain, which fired my neurons, turning his signals into thoughts.

Of course it's my choice. I could have turned down this job.

True, you could have said no, Max thought. You could also shoot yourself in the foot.

Max, stop. I wanted to scowl, but I held back, to avoid looking more nefarious than the port authority probably already considered me, with my "untamed" appearance. I'd never figured out why people thought I looked wild. I was a former military officer, perfectly respectable. Sure, I came from the Undercity, and I knew how to make my way through that world. Jak, my common law husband, also ran the casino there, a house of glitz and glamour where rich slicks came to lose their money. Here on Parthonia, however, no mysterious underworld existed where anyone could go wild.

Even so. The mere fact that I came from the Undercity meant people considered me suspect. Whenever popular entertainment needed a vile character, the writers almost always made them Undercity. You'd think we were a collection of the worst human beings ever to exist. Our poverty, low numbers, and isolation made us easy targets. Need a villain? Use a population that can't object.

I was beyond done with all that. I had all the documents I needed and good reason to be here. I didn't want to draw any attention, though. Too many potential threats might wait around the corner. So I waited with outward patience while the customs line moved at its glacial pace.

The man next in line, a business type it looked like, glanced at me. "This is screwed."

Probably he just meant the wait, but in my line of work, I'd learned never to make assumptions. I said only, "Yah, it's slow."

"You here for business?" he asked.

"Something like that."

He started to speak, hesitated, then said, "I wondered—is anyone waiting for you?"

No way would I reveal that information. I'd declined the offer from my employers, the Majdas, to have someone pick me up at the port. With their influence, they could have gotten me through customs lickety-split, but that would draw attention. I'd intended to slip in, quiet and low-key, and do my work in the shadows. The Majdas used to hate how I went about my business—until I started solving supposedly unsolvable cases. Now they made good use of their shadowy PI, which included sending me here to Parthonia. Unfortunately, someone had leaked the news of my arrival. No pictures or personal details of me had shown up, but people knew an outsider was coming to Selei City. It didn't just undermine my work, it could put my life in danger.

I knew nothing about this fellow, so I just said, "I'm set."

"Perhaps you'd like to get a drink after we get through here?" he asked.

Ho! My perception of the scene shifted like an optical illusion. He wasn't trying to extract information, he was making a pass. Most people were too afraid of me to do that. Not only of me, either. The Majdas didn't call my husband Jak a "disreputable criminal kingpin" for nothing.

"Thanks for the offer," I said, trying to look flattered. Hell, I was flattered. I also sucked at flirtation. "But I have a husband. Monogamous."

"Ah." The man gave a self-conscious chuckle. "He's a lucky man."

I couldn't help but laugh. "I'll tell him." Jak sometimes needed reminding of that fact.

The fellow smiled awkwardly and we both lapsed into silence. Someone turned on a holo newscast, which floated over a table, so I listened, part of my attention on the news and the rest on my surroundings. The broadcast showed a handsome young man speaking, either a reporter or an actor hired to perform like a reporter while looking good and raising the show's ratings.

"...third murder in the last year," the fellow was saying. A frown creased his perfect face. "The authorities have yet to charge anyone. This latest message begins the same as the previous two: it declares that the Royalist Party takes responsibility for the murder." He paused, looking suitably outraged. "The Royalist spokeswoman continues to insist the party has nothing to do with the deaths or whoever is leaving these messages."

A new image replaced the reporter, a woman with the dark hair and high cheekbones of the Skolian nobility. She spoke in a cool voice. "The Royalist Party has no connection to these heinous killings. We condemn them in the strongest terms." Although she spoke Skolian Flag, the language used by most public figures, she did it with an Iotic accent. Only the noble Houses and royalty spoke Iotic, an ancient language that had otherwise fallen out of use. The display identified her as Jazin Akarad. It figured a noblewoman spoke for the party that believed we should return to an age when the Ruby Dynasty ruled and the Houses ranked highest in power. No elections for them; they wanted hereditary rule back in full force.

I'd forgotten how much politics dominated Selei City. Of course politicians got the nicest city on the best world; they ran the Imperialate. The Modernists formed the largest and blandest of the five main parties. They had founded the movement to govern by election rather than heredity and took their name as a contrast to the Royalists. Traditionalists believed the empire should return to its matriarchal roots, that men should live in seclusion and stop doing pesky things like agitating for equality. Progressives formed in response to the Trads. They wanted equal rights for everyone and acceptance of nontraditional cultures, *all* of them, even outliers like Earth. Technologists focused on scientific development, convinced our future lay in technological strength. When I had to pick a party, I went Tech, but I preferred to avoid politics altogether. Like the plague.

The actor-reporter reappeared. Leaning forward at his desk, he spoke with great drama. "This latest missive from the killers includes new information! In addition to aligning with the Royalists, they declare that they are 'terminating' top scientists to stand against the Technologists. Their missive reads, 'Technologists use the motto *Technology is power* for a reason; they seek to conquer the Imperialate by controlling the advances that dominate our lives." Although he was trying to look solemn, I had the distinct impression he felt positively gleeful about all this heated back and forth among the elite. "The Technologists," he added, "deny the accusation."

The reporter vanished, replaced by a woman with the dark skin and black hair of the aristocracy. The glyphs identified her as a Rajindia, the noble House that provided neurology experts to aid the military in cyber warfare. She also spoke with an Iotic accent. "We of the Technology Party have a long history of cooperation with the Royalists, one we intend to continue. We have no argument with the Royalist Party and no interest in harming the government."

The businessman in front of me snorted. "It figures, eh? Have someone who looks like a Royalist speak for the Techs."

"Yah, so." It didn't surprise me, either. By choosing a Rajindia noble as the face of the Tech Party, they weakened the killer's claim that the Royalists considered the Technologists a menace so dire, they had to rid the hapless galaxy of their evil presence.

Sure, some nobles were Royalists, but you found aristocrats all over the political landscape. The Majda Matriarch, queen of the most powerful House after the Ruby Dynasty, went Traditionalist. Her House had never stepped into the modern age; they kept their men secluded just like the warrior queens in the ancient Ruby Empire.

The reporter came back. "The authorities have yet to bring charges for these malevolent crimes." Righteous indignation suffused his voice. "Rumor claims they have *no* viable suspects. Stay linked here for the latest. We'll keep you updated on events as they happen."

My fellow traveler shook his head. "Three deaths, and they haven't a clue." He spoke in a confiding tone. "I heard they imported some supposed genius investigator from off-world to help. What a mess."

I nodded, pretending only a minor interest. But hey. We'd see if my supposed genius self could clean up this mess.

✦ ✦ ✦

The public flycar dropped me at the co-op where I'd lived over three years ago. Although I'd given up my office in the city center when I left Parthonia, I'd kept this place. It had controlled fees; the charges never went up until a new owner took possession. I loved the building, especially the vibrant plant life. Back home on Raylicon, desert spikeweed was our most prolific native plant.

The units here weren't cheap, but given what I earned on retainer for the House of Majda, I could afford to keep mine even though I no longer lived in Selei City. That never stopped amazing me. After growing up in poverty, I'd never conquered the fear that I'd lose it all tomorrow, left once more to struggle for food, water, health care, and shelter, scraping to stay alive. I only eased my iron grip on my assets for one reason, to help improve the lives of my people.

It felt good to cross the familiar lobby on the first floor. Attractive sofas and enameled tables stood around the spacious area. A kava stand nestled in one corner, next to a quaint store with groceries, toiletries, and other useful stuff. The lobby boasted a high ceiling, plants everywhere, and so many windows, they looked like glass walls. Outside, lawns stretched out, bordered by droop willows draped in vines. Trails wound through the gardens, with benches here and there. The foliage looked *right*, probably because it had evolved away from the DNA of Earth less than on other planets we'd adapted for human settlement.

Earth. I pondered the world of our origins as I stepped into the glass-walled elevator car. I'd never thought of Earth as "home." My people were her lost children, our ancestors snatched away millennia ago by unknown beings, who then vanished. We suspected they died, killed by alien tech we barely understood. Although our abductors left behind nothing except their ruined starships, my ancestors did have Earth plants and animals. Over the centuries, the stranded humans raided the corrupted libraries in the starship ruins, enough to learn rudiments of genetics and star travel. They tried to build an interstellar civilization based on their shaky tech, but the Ruby Empire soon collapsed. We took several thousand years to regain the lost tech, doing it right this time, venturing with confidence into space. Our fauna and foliage came with us and thrived here, gracing the region.

Not so in the Undercity. I shook my head as the lift rose up the side of the building, offering a panoramic view of the parklike city outside. If Progressives wanted to promote equality for everyone, where was their support for the Undercity, the most underserved population of the Imperialate? At least they weren't openly hostile to us, like the Royalists, Traditionalists, and even many Modernists, the party whose most notable trait consisted of having no notable opinions.

Then again, the isolation of the Undercity didn't only come from outsiders. My people rebuffed invaders, and pride kept us from accepting charity. I had my work cut out for me in finding ways to improve their lives. I couldn't do any of that, however, until I solved this blasted case and went home.

"I better not be wasting my time here," I grumbled as I exited the lift.

Max spoke aloud, taking his cue from me. "Why would

it be a waste? Solve the case and you could save lives. Not to mention cooling off a volatile political situation."

"Yah." I walked down the wide hall to my apartment. Plants with orange flowers grew in vases glazed in red and gold, each set in a niche along the wall. "I just hate politics."

"Bhaaj, I'm detecting an odd signal."

I stopped at my door, a panel of cornsnap wood, bright and yellow. "What do you mean?"

"I thought I picked it up when we exited the flycar that brought you here. It vanished, but then I caught it in the lobby." Max stopped. "It's gone now."

I looked along the corridor, studying the area. This floor only had two units, mine and Xira's at the other end of the hall. I'd go visit her after I got settled.

"I don't see anyone," I said. "Why do you call it odd?"

"It might be nothing, just a stray signal I picked up. So many crisscross each other in this part of the city, they can get muddled." He paused. "I only got bits, as if someone following you had disguised their presence.

I didn't like the idea of anyone following me, particularly given that I'd come here to find a serial killer. "Look into it. Let me know if you find anything else."

"Will do."

I turned to the door. "Greetings. Identify, Bhaajan, owner."

A light flashed over my face and the door hummed. "Identity verified," it told me. "Do you want to enter?"

Grumpy with space lag and my concern about Max's signal, I thought, *Why the hell else would I stand here?* Fortunately, the door couldn't hear me being an asshole in my thoughts. I just said, "Yah. Open, please." No matter how cranky I felt, I was trying to be more courteous, even to doors. I'd mellowed over the years, more than anyone who knew me in my youth would have believed possible, including myself. When I'd worked here as a PI, I'd served the elite of an empire. You'd better be courteous, or you didn't get hired.

The door split down the middle and the two halves swung open like an invitation. It reminded me of the day I'd moved in, over ten years ago. That was when I met Xira, an actress, singer, and dancer who starred in musicals. She'd seen me and come over, friendly and kind, telling me about the place, how I owned shares in the building as long as I paid my fees and all that. That started my closest friendship in Selei City, one of the few I kept up after I moved back to Raylicon.

I walked into the foyer, then turned to watch the door close. I'd never lost my childhood habit of protecting my back. Satisfied, I entered my home. Sunshine poured through the windows and gleamed on the cornsnap floors. Patterns of birds and trees bordered the white cushions on the wicker chairs and sofas. So much light, space, and flowering plants, none of which existed in the tunnels of my youth, what we called underground canals, though no water had run in them for millennia. The only birds and trees on Raylicon lived in the lush gardens of the wealthy, especially the Majda palace with its imported fauna and flora. To maintain those grounds in a desert, the Majdas paid an amount equal to the annual budget of Selei City. It didn't register as a drop in their overfilled bucket of wealth. They might no longer rule as the royal family of

Raylicon, but their financial empire rivaled the economies of entire worlds.

"Welcome home, Bhaaj," a pleasant voice said, androgynous and light.

"Hey, Highcloud."

I will never figure out why you named this EI Highcloud, Max thought.

I thought you knew. I named it after my favorite vocalist. The human Highcloud sang in a gorgeous, husky voice that could rasp one moment and pour like honeyed cider the next. They identified as neither male nor female, with a voice that could be either or neither. Listening to their music felt like soaring through the sky. Max knew that perfectly well. He just didn't like the household EI.

"Highcloud, reactivate all your usual functions for when I live here," I said.

"Reactivating," Highcloud said. "You have messages waiting."

I went into the kitchen. A counter separated it from the living room, inlaid by white tiles decorated with birds. "I thought you forwarded my mail."

"These came in after you left Raylicon," Highcloud said. "You have four."

"Before you read them, check my security protocols. Max, coordinate with Highcloud to make sure the systems are up to date." I didn't want anyone eavesdropping.

"Protocols verified," Max said.

"My checks agree," Highcloud said.

"That's redundant," Max said. "Also, my checks are more thorough."

He was certainly in a mood today. He'd always

maintained a hierarchy with Highcloud, and during the years we'd spent away from here, he had acted as my only personal EI. Maybe he felt Highcloud encroached on his territory. He wouldn't phrase it that way; I had no doubt he had an EI explanation. But it worked for my human brain.

I said only, "It never hurts to do two checks. My thanks to both of you."

"Would you like to hear your messages?" Highcloud asked.

"Yah, go ahead." I tapped a wall panel and a panel slid aside, revealing a "beverage cupboard." I just called it a bar. Highcloud kept it well stocked, waiting for my return. I'd always wondered what house EIs did with their free time. Carrying out the tasks humans assigned them couldn't take all their resources. Highcloud and Max said they "ran in the background," doing nothing. I didn't believe it, but I'd never found any indication otherwise. And I'd looked. The same curiosity that made me good at my job as a PI extended to the cyber world.

"The first message is from Colonel Lavinda Majda on Raylicon," Highcloud said. "It reads 'My greetings, Bhaaj. I hope the flight went well. Please contact me after you meet with the police about the case. Regards, Lavinda.'"

I poured a glass of gin. "Contact her about what?" As the youngest of the three Majda sisters, Lavinda was in the line of succession for the Majda Matriarch, a title currently held by her older sister Vaj. I preferred Lavinda as my contact in the family. The Majdas were the quintessential aristocrats, so confident of their power, they never noticed its presence. Vaj Majda also served as General of the Pharaoh's Army, one of four Joint Commanders of Imperial Space Command, or ISC, the Skolian military. As much as the iron general intimidated me, I all too often found myself challenging her. She still kept me on retainer, though, so I hadn't annoyed her enough to get myself fired. Even so. Lavinda made an effective buffer between Vaj and my Undercity self.

"I don't know why Colonel Majda asked you to contact her," Highcloud said.

"Seriously?" Max asked. "You can't figure out something that simple?"

"Max, cut it out." I didn't need my personal EI talking trash to my house EI. He had a point, though. The Majdas knew that if the Royalists came into power, Majda would benefit even if they didn't all belong to that party. They'd have no objections if I cleared the Royalist Party of wrongdoing.

"Is that your gauntlet EI?" Highcloud asked. "Max?"

"Yes, it's Max. He's being rude. You can ignore him."

"I am incapable of being rude," Max said. "I operate solely on logic."

I resisted the temptation to say his statement itself was illogical. If he decided emotions served his goals, he'd consider it perfectly logical to act as if he had them. I just knew I'd miss his personality if he changed.

"Max, you seem bothered today," I said.

"I want to be sure you have good support."

"I do. You both do excellent work."

"Thank you." He sounded mollified.

Highcloud continued with my mail. "The second

message is from Elizia Jaan, the dean at Parthonia University. She says, 'Major Bhaajan, welcome to Selei City. Please contact me at your convenience. I'd like to meet so we can talk about the case.'"

"Good. See if you can set up a time with her people."

"I'm sending your request. I already had it ready to go."

"Excellent."

"You can inform your gauntlet EI of my preparation if you wish," Highcloud added.

"I'm right here," Max said. "You can talk to me."

Highcloud said nothing. Technically, EIs didn't talk to each other on your behalf unless you asked them to or they needed to protect you. I doubted anyone with even a little savvy about the cyber universe actually believed EIs didn't have their own networks where they dished whatever they wanted on us. They tended to keep such interactions subtle, though. I wondered if they organized their hierarchies like human politics.

"What's the third message?" I asked, mostly to distract myself from the alarming thought of EIs forming political parties.

"Chief Hadar of the Selei City Police wants you to check in as soon as possible."

No surprise there. "Set up an appointment with her."

"Him, actually. I've sent a note to his EI."

"What's the last message?" I couldn't think of anyone else who'd comm me.

"It comes from a Tamarjind Jakind. He writes, 'Welcome to Selei City, Major Bhaajan. My family and I would like to extend an invitation for you to dine with us at our home. Perhaps Threeday at six in the evening? We hope you can join us and look forward to hearing from you.'"

"Who is Tamarjind Jakind?" The name sounded familiar, but I couldn't recall why.

"A professor in the Psychology Department at Imperial College," Highcloud said.

I didn't know anyone at Imperial College, which ranked among the most selective colleges. Rumor held that even belonging to a noble House didn't help with admission, as it did with most institutions. You genuinely needed a stellar academic record to get in.

"Highcloud, did he leave an audio message you can play?" I might get clues from his voice that I missed in his words.

"Yes. Here it is." A man's cultured voice rose into the air, with an unmistakable Iotic accent. "Welcome to Selei City, Major Bhaajan—"

"Okay, that's enough." *Now* I remembered. Jakind was his middle name. I'd never met him, but I recognized his name. Prince Tamarjind Jakind *Majda* had just invited me to dine with his family. Me, from the Undercity. Maybe I shouldn't be surprised that he broke the "rules" of society. As the brother of the Majda Matriarch, he had shattered tradition when he became the first and until recently the only prince to leave the palace on his own rather than in an arranged marriage. Majda princes lived under a weight of constraints so vast, I felt gobsmacked every time I thought of them. They could never interact with anyone outside their family and the palace staff. If they left the palace, they went robed and cowled with a retinue of guards. They spoke only to women in their family. Any other woman who tried to interact with a Majda prince risked a prison sentence.

Prince Tamarjind had scandalized the family when he decided to leave seclusion and move to Parthonia. They tried to stop him. When that battle threatened to tear apart the family, they disowned him. That didn't work, either, because no matter how irate he made the iron Matriarch, she loved her brother. In the end, they accepted his decision, but his relations with the House remained strained. They forbade him to interact with any other men at the palace, lest he "give them ideas."

I could guess why he asked me to dinner. The first job the Majdas had hired me for was to find one of their missing sons, Prince Dayjarind, a youth who ran away from the palace. I was surprised more of their men didn't do it. I managed to find him when no one else succeeded because I could operate in the Undercity, where a weapons dealer had imprisoned the naive young man. I brought him home, but it had taken his willingness to die for his freedom to convince his family he couldn't bear seclusion. You could have knocked me over with a puff of smoke when I learned the Majdas had agreed—after much negotiation—to let him attend Imperial College *if* he received admittance. He had a greater intellect than they realized: he aced the entrance exams. Since Prince Tamarjind taught there, Dayj lived with his family while he went to school.

"Tell Professor Jakind I would be honored to accept his invitation. Use all the proper wording and courtesies." EIs knew how to talk to royalty, as opposed to my blunt self.

"Message sent," Highcloud said.

"Send Xira a message, too. Ask if she'd like to get together tomorrow." I could see her in my mind, amiable and bright while we drank ale and gossiped. I looked forward to catching up.

"Message sent," Highcloud said.

"Are we done with messages?" Max asked.

Highcloud spoke blithely. "Yes, they are finished. Thank you for asking."

Apparently Highcloud's refusal to speak directly to Max only applied when the EI wanted to annoy him. Before they could engage in any more EI snark, I said, "Max, we need to get to work."

"We should talk about the case," he said.

"This case makes no sense." I paced out of the kitchen into the streaming light of my living room, holding my drink. "Even if the Royalists stopped liking the Techs, which isn't likely, they wouldn't *kill* them. The noble Houses started the Royalist Party, and the aristocracy defines the word restraint. They'd never assassinate prominent figures and claim responsibility. If they moved against anyone, they be so discreet, you'd never know it happened. I'd more likely believe the Progressives did it to piss off the Royalists."

"The Progressives agitate for peaceful defiance," Max said. "Not violence. It could be a group with no political affiliation."

"True. Nothing points to any motive other than the one given, though."

"The Traders, maybe."

I took a swallow of my drink, trying to wash away the bitter memories of my time on the front lines of our war with the Trader empire. "Even if they did somehow infiltrate the best-protected world in the Imperialate, they have better ways to exploit such an extraordinary success. Openly committing murders destroys any covert advantage and sets the machinery of this city into finding them. And why teachers? It would make more sense to target military or political leaders." I thought of the police reports I'd read. "The detectives did look into the possibility of some outside agency directing the murders, perhaps offworld. So far, nothing, but they haven't given up. Records should exist of all messages going in and out of the city, including dark sites."

"No records are perfect. They could have missed something. No one knows the full extent of the shadow meshes."

"True." So far, nothing pointed to a conspiracy, not political, military, personal, or anything else. "Hell, Max, the police have no clues that a killer even *exists*. I don't believe anyone can erase their operations that well. I bet they're here in the city, just one or two people, avoiding notice." I'd kept my arrival low-key for the same reason, so I could remain incognito. Who had leaked the news? Only the police, the Majdas, and a few higher ups at the university should have known. No matter where the leak came from, it undermined my ability to solve the case.

"The killers targeted Technologists," Max said. "They claim they're Royalists. That makes it political regardless of whether or not they're lying. It is odd, though. It seems more like something Traditionalists would accuse Progressives of doing, to discredit them."

I ran my finger around the rim of my glass. "You think

the Traditionalists committed the murders, claiming the Royalists did it as a move against the Technologists so people would believe it came from the Progressives?" I was only half joking.

Max's voice lightened. "Perhaps the Modernists set it up because no one would believe it came from such a mainstream party. They get the other parties mired in a fight until citizens get fed up and join the Modernists."

I couldn't help but laugh. "The Mods are too boring for that much drama." My smile faded. "We need to find real answers."

We had to solve the case before more people died.

✤ CHAPTER II ✤
CLUES. OR NOT.

Police headquarters were in downtown Selei City, a place that looked nothing like a typical urban center. I walked through parklands of ripple-grass bordered by flower beds with nodding pink and purple bells. Breathing deeply, I filled my lungs with air, then paused to let the dizziness pass. I'd adapted to the oxygen-rich atmosphere when I lived here, but after nearly three years back on Raylicon, my body expected a thinner atmosphere.

As my head cleared, I continued. The scent of flowers filled the air, and birds sang in trees scattered across the lawns. People sat on the grass, reading, chatting, enjoying the day. Given that the world Parthonia had almost no axial tilt, its seasons remained mild, especially with the weather machines in the mountains fine-tuning the climate. It always felt like spring. So yah, paradise.

Pah. It was *too* nice. Or so I tried to convince myself. When I'd lived here, sometimes I'd missed my childhood home on Raylicon, my memories softened by the mist of time. The City of Cries there existed because her citizens had enough wealth to make it livable, even stunningly beautiful in its own stark way. That didn't change the truth. Raylicon was dying. Unless we managed some major terraforming, technology beyond our current capabilities, the world would become unhabitable in a few more centuries.

Bhaaj, Max thought, discreet now that we were in public. *I'm picking up that odd signal.*

What is it from?

It's human—no, it's not. Sorry, it's gone.

Unease prickled my spine. *Does it pose a danger?*

I can't say. It may be nothing. Even more signals cross this city center than around your co-op.

Maybe it's someone wearing gauntlets. Mine were heavier and packed with more tech than most, but many people here wore wristbands or tech-bracelets.

Possibly. I'd stay alert. This is the second time I thought it was following us.

I looked around. Other pedestrians strolled the paths, but none looked suspicious. That didn't mean I didn't have a shadow, just that if I did, they had enough experience to keep me from noticing them. *What makes you think they were following us?*

After so many years as an investigative EI, I've built large databases on human behavior and tech. It allows me to extrapolate. Max paused. *You might call it EI intuition.*

Whatever he called it, I trusted his deductions. *Let me know if you notice anything else.*

Will do.

I continued walking, acutely aware of my surroundings. The tower of police HQ rose above the parks a few blocks away, its windows reflecting the sunshine. Last night, I'd looked up Chief Hadar. Big surprise, he was tall with dark hair, skin, and eyes. The more you resembled the Skolian ideal, the more likely your rise in power hierarchies of the Imperialate. Hell, I had dark hair, skin, and eyes. People only needed one look to know I didn't come from the upper crust, but I wondered if more subtle forces worked even for a nobody like me. I couldn't recall seeing a single person with yellow hair in a position of authority. Ironically, the only exception came from several members of the Ruby Dynasty, who had metallic skin and hair and gold or bronze hair. They belonged to a race called Metal, one created through genetic engineering to adapt colonists to a new world. With no historical precedent, people didn't know how to label them, but since the best-known examples were the Ruby Dynasty, most considered them set apart from the rest of us.

Except.

The Traders also prized metallic skin and hair—in their providers, slaves created to please their Aristo masters in ways I had no wish to think about. I'd spent too many years in the army witnessing the horrors the Aristos inflicted on the rest of the universe. They called their empire the Eubian Concord, as if their totalitarian selves constituted some bizarre harmonious concordance. We used the word Trader because their massive economy took a significant portion of its commerce from the sale of human beings. They wanted to add us to their inventory and then the Allied Worlds of Earth, until their two thousand Aristos owned every one of the three trillion human beings that constituted the whole of humanity.

I had no desire to contemplate a universe where the Trader Aristos held sway. Their empire—exactly the right word for their so-called Concord—consisted of two trillion people spread across hundreds of worlds, moons, and space habitats, more than twice the size of Skolia. Emperor Qox ruled the Traders, a despot with supposedly perfect genetic lineage. Together, the Aristos owned every other human in their empire. *Everyone.*

Sure, many slaves had comfortable lives. Two thousand Aristos couldn't control two trillion people if they created misery that drove their slaves to rebel. As long as their people behaved, their lives remained agreeable. If they rebelled, the Aristos got rid of them. *All* of them. I'd seen worlds where they committed genocide, destroying entire colonies to eradicate the "infestation of wrong thinking." The nightmare of that devastation haunted my dreams. I'd rather die than live in a universe where the Aristos ruled.

It gave me no end of pleasure that it enraged them to know members of our ruling dynasty resembled the providers at the lowest rung of their hierarchy. The Aristos hated it. They wanted nothing more than to humiliate and enslave the Ruby Dynasty. Well, tough. We had an advantage they had never matched: a faster, more efficient war machine. The Eubian Concord might claim the largest civilization and military force in human history, but ours remained the most effective military ever known.

Fortunately today I only had to face the city police chief, who by all accounts was a hard-working, decent sort who had earned his position through talent rather than connections. Although he wasn't the first man to run a police force, he was the first here in Selei City, a major governmental center. It impressed me that he hadn't shied away from seeking outside help on this high-profile investigation. That took confidence.

As I approached the station, its double doors opened. I entered a lobby with robot attendants at counters with signs like, *Flyer license applications* or *Passport renewals*. None of them read *Notorious serial killers*, so I went to *Information* instead.

The info-bot nodded to me. "My greetings." It looked humanoid, pleasant in appearance, with nondescript clothes, nothing too fancy. The rest of it gleamed bronze in an attractive manner, I guess because it was soothing, which was probably the intent, given that people who came to a police station could often do with some calming.

"My greetings," I said. "I'm here to see Captain Hadar. I have an appointment. My name is Bhaajan."

It paused, probably accessing the station mesh. A laser from somewhere flashed over my face and upper body. "Please come with me," it said.

I peered at it, figuring out where the laser originated. Ah, there. The robot had a module set into its shoulder, easy to see. Privacy laws required that people or things doing ID scans make the process obvious to the person they scanned.

I went with the robot, deeper into the station. We walked along hallways, through panels of sunlight slanting in the many windows. This place felt too pleasant for a law enforcement center. I'd been on the locked-wrists side of the law too many times in my youth when cops grabbed kids from the Undercity and threw us in jail for existing. Well, also because sometimes we pinched food from merchants on the Concourse above the Undercity. So yah, we were thieves. Hungry thieves. Starving.

Fortunately, those nights I spent in a cell didn't turn into arrests. The cops let me go with warnings because of my age, so none of that interfered with my enlisting or eventually becoming an officer. I joined the army on my sixteenth birthday, the day I turned old enough according to Skolian law to make that decision on my own. They sent me to school until I was old enough to ship out with the troops. If I hadn't made that choice, gods only knew where I'd be now. Not that I hadn't come close to death in the army, but the Undercity could be just as fatal. Nor did the Undercity leave you with marketable skills and a pension, or the self-respect that becoming Major Bhaajan had given my ornery, determined self.

The robot left me in a large office on the top floor of the tower, a place with wooden floors and more windows. Sunlight filled the room. It had an antiqued look, possibly from the slightly yellowed windows, but it felt as if the sunlight had served its purpose here for many ages.

Captain Hadar stood behind a desk carved from wood. He wasn't wearing a uniform, just a business shirt and slacks, and tech-mech bands on his wrists. After the robot left, Hadar lifted his hand, inviting me to a window alcove at the back of the room. I joined him on a circular bench that curved under the windows. It looked out over the parks through panes of real glass rather than smart whatever. Good. I liked ordinary glass, and most buildings no longer used the old-fashioned material. Too breakable.

A squat robot the height of my hip rolled over with two steaming mugs of liquid on its flat top. "My greetings," it said, its voice tinny. The drinks looked like tea, which I drank about as often as I jumped into fire pits. Given the choice, I might take the pit.

Hadar was watching me. He picked up one of the mugs and took a swallow. Lowering it, he said, "Could almost be ket." He paused with the hint of a smile. "I mean tea."

Ah. Ket. An innocuous name for a spectacular hot ale. I picked up my mug and took a swallow. Now *that* was ket to write home about, full and robust. It also highlighted yet again the differences between here and the City of Cries on Raylicon. Hadar could have a glass of ale during working hours as long as he didn't abuse that perk. If the police chief in Cries drank an alcoholic beverage on the job and got caught, the city would fire her.

I just said, "Good tea."

Hadar became all business. "So. We've three dead scientists and no suspects."

That was blunt. Good. I nodded to him. "I read the preliminary notes your people sent over, but I'll need the full reports. I'd like to examine the evidence you've gathered and visit the crime scenes. I need to interview anyone who has any connection to the victims, anyone with any reason to want them dead, and anyone who happened to be around at the time of the murders. And anyone else even remotely connected."

He raised his eyebrows. "That's all? You don't want the entire history of the city, too?"

"Well, if you're offering—" I stopped when he raised his hand in protest. Okay, none of my dumb jokes. He didn't know what to make of me yet any more than I did of him. "I do need to look through everything you have— so I can figure out what's missing."

"The killer," he said dryly. "Whoever did this was a pro. They covered their tracks."

"They may think so." I met his gaze. "They're wrong. I'll find them."

He had a *We'll see* expression. "The strongest clue is the manner of death. Each victim was shot through the brain by a high-precision rifle. That accuracy takes practice, and those guns aren't easy to come by for civilians. It suggests a sniper with military training."

That had been my thought, too. "I still have an ISC clearance. I can check into snipers."

"I'll put you in touch with a team at the PARS military base here. They're already doing checks." He considered me with an appraising stare. "You'll also need to talk to government leaders and members of the noble Houses. Without alienating them or otherwise making our work more difficult."

It sounded like he'd heard about my working style. I spoke wryly. "It's true, my methods are a bit unusual. But I find what 'usual' misses." I thought about the preliminary report. "Your analysts believe they know the source of the shots. Have you found more clues?"

"Not exactly. Initially we thought the killer fired inside the room with the victims, because the walls have no bullet holes." He shook his head. "Problem is, no trace exists of anyone else in the room. We can't locate a bullet, or any residue to indicate it disintegrated. We've checked for bots, drones, highjacked tech from appliances, hidden code in the building mesh, smart dust, and any indications that tech was introduced or removed from the scene. Nothing. We've found only one anomaly. In each case, about two seconds are gone from the visual security record of the room when the killer shot the victim."

"Is it enough time for the killer to get in, shoot, and get out?"

"Not a chance. It isn't even close. It's essentially just the moment when the shot took place."

I considered his description. "The killer could have shot from outside the room. The nanobots in the walls of those buildings can repair light damage, maybe even a bullet hole."

"Yes. But a record should exist of the repair. We've found none." He pushed his hand through his hair. "However, just in case, we're also checking possible locations for a sniper outside the room and building, based on how the bullet entered the body of the victim. We can't find *anything*, no unexplained prints or DNA at the scene or anywhere else, no unusual tech signatures, no odd smells or residues, no record of an unexplained person or thing entering or leaving the building, not even dirt from a shoe or a strand of hair. Nor do any security monitors right outside the room show anything suspicious." He held up his hand as I started to ask the obvious question. "And yes, we checked. None of them show signs of tampering."

His description sounded incomplete. "How can you predict a location for the sniper? You can't trace the path of a bullet when some of them can change trajectory during flight."

Hadar held up his thumb and forefinger with a tiny space between them. "Based on the wounds in the victim, the bullet was like this, extraordinarily small. It couldn't have incorporated much tech, certainly not a propulsion system, fuel, or anything else to allow substantial changes in trajectory. Without an external force, it can't deviate from the path determined by the laws of physics. You might get drift if it spins, and it might have had some streamlined tech that allowed minor changes, but nothing significant." He exhaled. "Can we get the *exact* location? No. We think we can come close, however. We're also looking throughout the entire city, just in case."

"Maybe the bullet had a wireless comm chip. They don't add much bulk."

He shrugged. "Any signals to, from, or within it would become part of the city network. We have invisible, floating smart dust that monitors the city. It has picked up nothing that looks like signals from a sniper to a bullet, a bullet to a sniper, or within a bullet."

I thought back to my years working here. "The city environment is incredibly noisy. Don't your detection systems screen out signals considered ordinary?"

"Of course. But we have the records. Since the killings started, we've deleted nothing." He looked like he'd eaten a sour fruit. "And yeah, we're going through it all. We have been for months. It's tedious as all hell."

It sounded excruciating. I could also see another problem. "The walls of those buildings are designed to be opaque to targeting systems, even military grade. So how would a sniper outside know where to shoot?"

Hadar didn't look surprised by my question. "We

thought maybe they planted a monitor inside the room. We've looked. Nothing." He paused. "My instincts say a person fired the shot rather than a drone or a bot. Humans have more intellectual flexibility, which makes them better at adapting to unusual situations so they can hide clues."

He could have a point. "What about the messages claiming responsibility for the murders?"

His voice tightened. "Our trace on them points to a digital marketplace used exclusively by the Royalist Party."

I snorted. "That's a given, if the killers are trying to frame the Royalists."

He studied me, doing that analyzing thing people did when they wanted to figure out your motives. "You don't think the Royalists are responsible?

"Well, they say they aren't."

"That's your brilliant conclusion?" he asked. "They say they didn't do it, so they didn't?"

I stiffened, then thought, *Get over yourself, Bhaaj.* In his position, I'd have considered my comment naive, too. So I clarified. "Why would an unknown faction of the Royalist Party, one the rest of them can't identify, claim responsibility for crimes the Royalists immediately denounced? It doesn't make the point the killers supposedly want, that the Royalists believe technocrats are dangerous. It's too obviously a setup."

"That's probably the point," Hadar said. "Make it look so obvious, no one believes it."

"That would be out of character."

"For whom?" he demanded. "The noble Houses, because of their supposed discretion? Even if they're all like that, which I doubt, the Royalists aren't just nobles. Many commoners also believe we should return to dynastic rule." He paused. "Though I imagine you wouldn't be familiar with anything to do with the upper classes."

"Why do you say that?"

He lifted his chin, and I could have sworn he was actually looking down his nose at me. "Given your background, I can't imagine you have experience with higher levels of society."

Not this again. I'd had to deal with this attitude all the time after I enlisted, given my Undercity roots. It had eased over the decades as I rose in social position, but it never went away and it still pissed me off.

Then again, his crack sounded out of character. Hadar had asked me to come here. He wouldn't do that if he considered me unqualified. Given that I lived on another *planet*, he had to go out of his way to find out about me. The House of Majda also made no secret that they kept me on retainer, which meant the chief knew I worked for them.

I met his gaze, more curious now than irked. "I'm sure you know that statement of yours is bullshit. Why are you trying to bait me?"

Hadar gave a startled laugh. "You're as blunt as your reputation claims."

"Yah. How about a blunt answer?"

He considered me. "I wanted to know if you'd use your Majda connection to put me 'in my place.' Or if you'd lose your cool when reminded of what people think of your roots."

I scowled at him. "What, you're testing me to see if I fit your stereotypes?"

"Or maybe the opposite." His voice tightened. "The Royalists claim responsibility for the technocrat murders. With this last one, the killer has also admitted they're targeting Technologists."

Ho! Now I saw. "And you're a Tech."

"That's right."

"You think my Majda link will make me favor a Royalist version of events."

"Will it?"

"No."

"Yet you don't believe they have a connection to the murders."

I gave him an honest answer. "I can't be certain, and I won't assume they don't. But it makes no sense. What would these killings achieve? Sure, that latest bit about the Technologists could sour relations between the two parties, but given how much it looks like a setup, it's just as likely to make the Techs join forces with the Royalists against a common enemy."

Hadar let out a breath and his tension seemed to ease. "So my other detectives tell me. They believe the Progressives set it up, to upset the status quo."

"You think? I mean, it's possible they have a fringe edge. But the Progressive Party as a whole doesn't operate that way. They seek peaceful change, not violence." I shrugged. "Sure, they taunt the more traditional parties, but it's verbal and visual, not physical."

Hadar nodded to me. "Although we get far more complaints against members of the Progressive Party than any other, it's true they rarely break the law, unless you count peaceful civil disobedience."

Interesting. "Which political party tops the list of lawbreakers?"

"Well." He cleared his throat. "Technologists."

Ho! I hadn't expected that. "Whatever for?"

"Cybercrime." He sighed. "It's a constant battle to protect the meshes. Part of the reason I got this position is because I'm known as an expert in catching mesh crackers."

It sounded like he walked a tightrope of opposed loyalties. "That probably doesn't sit well with Techs who don't want limits on their ability to access information." Like me.

He spoke dryly. "It makes life interesting."

"What about violent crime? Cybernauts break the law with their brains, not their fists."

"Modernists top the list."

"The *Mods*?" *The blandest party in the cosmos?* "How could that be?"

"They're the biggest party, Major. There's just plain more of them." He shrugged. "Their members aren't angels any more than the rest of us. Progressives are actually at the bottom of the list. They know they're targets. They avoid trouble."

It actually fit, now that I thought about it. "They get the most press by far, though."

"That's because they offend the most people."

I knew that game all too well. My reputation had spread fast in the army when I started my climb out of the enlisted ranks into officer training, a feat purportedly impossible for a dust rat from the Undercity. I avoided stirring up waves, but it happened anyway, as I scandalized, impressed, or offended people just by doing what seemed—to me—perfectly normal. I wanted to be an officer. I had the ability. Why not do it? The rest of the universe had other ideas, but tough. They could eat it. My attitude, unfortunately, hadn't won me friends.

Hadar was watching me. He spoke carefully. "When I became chief here, there were those who had, shall we say, strong opinions against the idea."

"They accuse you of making trouble?" I'd constantly run into that assumption, as if the mere fact that my existence countered stereotypes acted as a form of protest.

"Not exactly," he said. "Critics claim I'm emotional, likely to lose my cool, unable to lead."

It surprised me to hear him reveal that juicy factoid. Although I could believe people talked him down that way, he wouldn't have attained his position unless he'd learned how to counter those perceptions and operate within the system, never making waves, especially not to someone he had just met. "How do you know I won't think that as well?"

"I've looked at your record, Major. I suspect you know exactly what I mean." He spoke thoughtfully. "That's why I doubt the Progressives are behind this. I'm not convinced these crimes are politically motivated, but if they are, and it isn't Progs, Techs, or Royalists, that leaves the Modernists and Traditionalists."

"The Mods did form as a reaction against the Royalists." I didn't believe they did it, though. "I just don't see any motive. Traditionalists don't make sense, either. They're the most closely allied with the Royalists. They and the Royalists both want to return to an earlier age."

The chief lifted his hands, then dropped them. "Maybe the killer just hates politics."

I grimaced. "That leaves about ninety-nine percent of the human race."

He smiled. "I don't doubt it."

I regarded him. "I'll get your killer." No one, no matter how clever, could hide forever. They always left clues. I just needed to find them.

"Nothing like this has happened in the history of the university." Dean Elizia Jaan stood with me on a balcony outside her fourth-story office overlooking the college. It spread out below, classic buildings with arched doorways and antique towers surrounded by parks with nary a parking lot or store anywhere. Those all lay underground, part of a trendy mall. Parthonia University was large and well respected, with a strong reputation among publicly funded institutes.

"This school is more than three centuries old," Jaan said. "In all that time, it's only seen two other murders in the faculty. Now three in less than a year?" She turned to me, her face drawn with fatigue. Her black hair curled around her shoulders, and lines showed around her eyes. "I knew all three professors who died. I can't believe they're gone."

"I'm sorry." I meant it. I'd never become inured to death, not after twenty years in the army and all the death I'd seen as a child in the Undercity. "What can you tell me about them? I have the police files, but any insights you can offer might help."

"I knew Dezi Marchland the best. We used to meet for lunch." Her voice caught. "Dezi joined our Cybernetics Department about twenty years ago. It didn't take long for her to become a leading neurologist in the development of cybernetic pathways in human bodies."

I spoke gently. "I'm sorry for your loss."

"Thank you." Jaan pushed her hand through her hair. "The second victim, Subida Habil, was an engineer. She worked with starship drives. Tejas Akarya was a physicist, an experimentalist who studied quantum systems."

Marchland's work had contributed to my own biomech. I was less familiar with Habil or Akarya, but they each had a long list of awards and distinctions. "The police reports describe all three as leaders in their fields."

She spoke bitterly. "If a fringe Royalist group wanted to take out the top scientists whose work had military applications, they couldn't have chosen better."

"You still believe the Royalists are responsible?" I could see now why the Traders might target the professors. I had thought of the victims as teachers, but it sounded like their research played a large role in their jobs. "These crimes work more to the advantage of the Traders."

Jaan didn't look surprised. "Their deaths impact several secured military projects, especially with the J-Force."

I wondered how she knew about "secured military projects." She had no link to Imperial Space Command, at least not publicly. "Why do you mention the Jagernaut Force in particular?"

"Marchland's work applies to Jagernaut pilots. You probably aren't familiar with that aspect." She spoke as if explaining a concept to someone with less education. "The pilots make cybernetic links with their starfighters. They also have internal biomech webs, enhancements that augment their speed and reflexes, and implanted EI nodes." She hesitated. "I realize that with your background, these may be new ideas."

For flaming sake. "And what background might that be?" I asked, all fake innocence.

Bhaaj, don't, Max thought.

I can't listen to you, I answered. *With my background, I don't know you exist.*

"Your upbringing." Jaan spoke awkwardly. "I mean, that you came from a place with so little—" She stopped as if she didn't know the right word.

"Max," I said. "Do you know what she's talking about?"

Stop it, Max told me. Aloud, he spoke in his most diplomatic voice. "I believe Dean Jaan means that with your military background, including your many decades operating with a biomech web, in the army and now as a private investigator, you are in an ideal position to understand the loss to the scientific community due to these deaths."

The dean had the decency to look embarrassed. "I'm sorry, Major. I meant no offense."

I hadn't expected an apology. I gave myself a moment to stop being pissed, then said, "It's no problem. I understand." I even did, sort of. That didn't explain why she would agree with Chief Hadar to bring me here if she questioned my experience. You didn't succeed as the dean of a major university by insulting your appointed experts.

It does seem odd for someone in her position, Max said.

Did you just get my thoughts? He didn't usually pick up anything unless I thought it with force and clarity, directed specifically at him.

A bit, Max answered. You were angry enough to add force.

I shouldn't let it get to me. But twice in one day, both from people who should know better?

I don't think her reaction is anything like with Chief Hadar. She seems agitated.

Ho! She's trying to distract me. I'll bet I asked a question she doesn't want to answer. I considered Jaan. "How do you have knowledge of secured ISC projects worked on by the victims?"

She met my gaze, saying nothing, the panorama of her university in the background. That view would make a compelling image for an ad. I wondered if that was why she invited me out to this balcony to talk. It made her look impressive while she tried to wait me out, perhaps hoping the silence would start me talking again. No matter. I could play this waiting game.

After a moment, she said, "I'm not at liberty to discuss details of that research."

That was a stock answer if I'd ever heard one. "I've a grade three ISC clearance."

Jaan started. "I hadn't realized."

That seemed more genuine, unlike her previous statements. It was unusual for a civilian to have a clearance like mine, but Vaj Majda wanted her PI armed with every possible tool. It wasn't like anyone planned to argue with the General of the Pharaoh's Army.

"Why would the dean of a university have that kind of clearance?" I asked. "You've no connection to ISC, at least none the public can find." The public in this case being me, in law-abiding mode. I'd have Max do a hidden dive into the dark mesh tonight.

She tapped the slender wristband she wore. A woman's voice rose into the air, sounding like an EI. "My greetings, Dean Jaan. What can I do for you?"

"I need you to verify the clearance status of Major Bhaajan, army, retired."

"One moment," the EI said.

If her EI could verify my clearance, it gave another indication that this dean had tendrils of influence extending into unexpected places. We stood there awkwardly while her EI did its thing.

The EI finally said, "Major Bhaajan has a grade three clearance with the Pharaoh's Army."

"Huh," Jann said. "Double-check the security of this balcony."

"The security protocols remain in effect," her EI said. "You have privacy."

Jaan nodded, more to herself than anyone else, I suspected. Then she focused on me. "Dezi Marchland was studying the link fighter pilots make from the neural chip in their brain to their ship's EI. Her work would make it easier for the pilot and ship to share minds. Subida Habil was working to streamline the inversion process that takes starships out of our space-time universe into complex space. Right now, ships have to accelerate close to the speed of light to invert. She was trying to make it feasible at slower speeds. Tejas Akarya spearheaded a project to develop quantum stasis coils for starships to shield humans against high accelerations, more than the crude coils currently used, but full quasis that could protect ships from weapons fire."

Saints almighty, that made one hell of a difference. "Did you tell Chief Hadar any of this?"

"Not details. I can't. However, he does know all three scientists had ISC funding."

I regarded her steadily. "That obviously makes them targets for the Trader military."

"Yes. The army is looking into it." She shook her head. "They've found nothing."

"Well, no, but so far no one has found anything for *anyone*."

"Except Royalists." She paused. "It isn't unusual for members of the Houses to serve in the military. And many Royalists are from the Houses."

Yah, okay, now I got her point. "*That's* why you agreed with Chief Hadar to bring me here. I'm from the Undercity, so you see me as the antithesis of the aristocracy. You think that makes me unlikely to participate in a cover-up if they're responsible for the killings."

"I wanted you here because you're damn good at what you do." She exhaled. "But yes, I hoped your distance from the Houses would give you objectivity."

Distance. It wasn't how I'd describe the difference between extreme poverty and exorbitant wealth, but what the hell. "You do know I work for the House of Majda, yes?"

"I am aware." She met my gaze. "I am also aware, like the rest of the empire, that the Matriarch of the House of Majda is a Joint Commander in Imperial Space Command. These three deaths impact the ability of ISC to develop military advances. If anyone has a vested interest in seeing this case solved, it's Majda."

"True. But they don't believe the Royalists planned the murders."

"Of course they don't." Jaan lifted her hands, then dropped them. "Hell if I know. Maybe it is the Traders. But if they got into this city, you'd think they'd hide their operation."

My thoughts, also. To infiltrate a major center well enough to set up an assassination squad would take a complex and involved operation, one probably years in the making. Why waste all of that by turning a spotlight on the killings? The assassins would more likely act behind the scenes, disguising the murders as accidents. Also, given the protections in the city, on the planet, and in the star system, the possibility of such an infiltration was tiny.

"Do the three victims have any friends in common?" I asked. "Any clubs or sports?"

"They had mutual acquaintances at the university. None of them moved in the same circles, though." She paused. "Well, except that game, Power Meld. You know, the one where you combine numbers. I think they all played it."

I gave her a rueful smile. "It's addicting." I'd wasted far too many hours swiping number cubes in that game.

Everyone played the blasted thing. Even the Earthers had imported it from us.

And the Traders.

"Can you get me access to their accounts where they played the game?" I asked. "I'd like to see if they had any chats with each other or anyone else during any session."

"That's an invasion of privacy laws." When I started to respond, she held up her hand. "I know. They're dead. You'll still need a warrant or permission from their heirs." She spoke quietly. "Major, their families are grieving. You must walk carefully."

I understood her concern. "Let's ask their permission. Gently. That would be better than my just showing up with a warrant."

She nodded. "I'll see what I can do."

"Thanks." I didn't want to hurt the families; I knew all too well the agony of losing someone you loved. I'd lost too many people I cared about in my youth, and the war had taken many others. If the Traders had a part in this, I'd make sure they regretted attacking our city.

Chapter Three

�֍ CHAPTER III ✥
CYCLES

Afternoon had settled in by the time I headed home. I jogged along, savoring the beauty, so unlike the parched landscape of Raylicon. That had its own beauty, too, but nothing like this city.

Lawns bordered the avenue. Although hovercars hummed past distant buildings, the city didn't allow them in these central parks. Eventually I reached a more residential area, running past houses with ornamental trees, expansive lawns, and flowering vines that climbed trellises. I found it hard to believe that each of those houses, with all its space and verdant plant life, served as home to only a few residents. Selei City sprawled over several hundred square kilometers and had a low population for such an important city. People considered this section of town less well off because it averaged "only" about an acre of land per house. A freaking *acre*. The plentiful resources in this city—unlimited water, space, plant life and food—left me speechless. Compared to where I'd grown up, it offered an almost unimaginable wealth.

Bhaaj, are you all right? Max asked.

I'm fine. Why do you ask?

Your vital signs are strange.

Strange? Usually he was more specific. *What do you mean?*

Not a medical problem. He paused. *More like you're showing physical signs of grief. Are you mourning the loss of the scientists?*

Their deaths saddened me, but I didn't know if I'd call that grief, at least not at a personal level. *I didn't know any of them.*

What were you just thinking about?

Just my home. The Undercity, compared to here. I've no idea why I would be mourning.

Max spoke with an almost unbearable compassion, a sentiment he supposedly had no ability to feel. *Sometimes we mourn for the pain we've lived. A person can feel grief for memories of loss, especially when faced with a life where no one has to accept that pain.*

I had no idea how to respond. I'd made peace with the memories of my youth. Now I gave back to the Undercity, served as a liaison to outside civilization, and helped develop programs to aid my people in ways that didn't destroy our unique culture. I could make a difference. Why would I mourn?

Because the memories never stopped. Knowing how much better most people lived hurt.

I don't think I want to talk about this, I told Max.

All right. With a lighter quality, he added, *I'm always here.*

I smiled at his twist on the saying, *I'm here if you need*

to talk. He wasn't going anywhere unless I took off my gauntlets. He once told me that he considered himself part of my mind. I hadn't wanted to hear it, to consider that we could become that closely intertwined. I used to wonder if the EIs for different people or systems communed with one another, deciding what they thought of their human creators or if they wanted to neaten up the universe by deleting us. Now, though, I thought I had it wrong. Maybe human beings were evolving to where EIs became a part of us, part of what it meant to be alive.

Bhaaj, Max thought. *I'm getting an odd sensor reading up ahead, a person, I think.*

Can't you tell?

Its biological signs are human, but its motions are unlikely for a person. Too many abrupt starts and stops.

That sounds like someone riding a scooter over bad terrain.

I don't think so. I would detect two things, one human and one mechanical.

Could it be someone with malfunctioning biomech? A Trader agent had once cracked my supposedly unhackable biomech web. He forced me to leave the base, probably with the intent of capturing an ISC major. It hadn't taken me long to block his signals, using protocols I'd learned as soon as the army implanted my web, but those few moments before I stopped the infiltration had shaken me. To lose control of my body that way—I never wanted to face it again.

I'm investigating, Max thought. *The signal is headed in our direction.*

I turned onto a public lane that led between the

grounds of two houses. Up ahead, a jogger was headed toward me. *It that runner the source of the signal?*

No. If you stay on this path, you will move away from your pursuer.

Good. I kept running. I could keep this pace forever. We had no powered vehicles in the Undercity, so we ran everywhere, every day, sometimes hours at a time, often just for the sheer joy of speed. We ran and we fought, to defend our territory and protect our circle, street fighting, down and dirty. My dust gang had excelled at both speed and hand-to-hand combat, rising high in the Undercity hierarchy.

In the army, I joined the track team. Apparently in addition to my youthful conditioning, my body had an unusual density of muscles, both slow- and fast-twitch, more of the slow, but my fast-twitchers fatigued less than for most athletes. It gave me power, speed, and endurance. I did well at a number of events, but my forte was the marathon. I also took up the martial art of tykado, which I loved even though I had to relearn almost everything I knew about fighting. It thrilled my coaches no end; they couldn't care less about my crappy origins as long as I beat the competition. It gave me an oasis of confidence amid all the dismissal, even hatred, that I encountered because of my background. It felt satisfying to trounce those athletes who called me inferior, as if I were a joke offered up for their ridicule. *Choke on that fast-twitch, you entitled assholes.*

Not sure you can choke on a muscle fiber in another person. Max sounded amused.

I smiled. *Did I leave the scooter behind?*

Yes, it went in another—no, wait. It is once again headed in our direction.

Does the scooter have any weapons, or its rider?

I don't detect any. It could be shrouding them, however.

I picked up my pace. *You figure out what it is yet?*

I'm getting cyber and human signs together.

I'll hide and see if anyone goes by me. Activate my shroud.

You don't have it with you.

Ho! I always carried the pack with my jammer when I worked a case in the Undercity. I'd forgotten I didn't bring it today. It wasn't legal to carry equipment like that in Selei City without proper clearance. Using it wasn't legal on Raylicon, either, but none of the authorities bothered with the Undercity. Although I'd arranged a license to carry one in Selei City, today I'd lapsed into my habits from when I worked here years ago. My subconscious apparently hadn't perceived my outing as having any potential threat.

I ran into the parklike forest that bordered the path on both sides and hid behind a droop willow. *Can you mask my vital signs?*

I will do my best. Then Max added, You did bring your new beetle-bot. You could send it to spy on the scooter.

Good idea. I reached into the pocket of my leather jacket and took out a blue beetle that fit into the palm of my hand. I owned three of them now, green, red, and blue. Each drone had its own specialty. This one was weaponized, sort of. It could squirt ink into the eyes of a human, shoot them with a sedative dart, or blast digitized nonsense into a prying cyberspy. It didn't have as much memory as the other two, so it couldn't record as long, but it could repel invaders, a feature neither of the others claimed. I used those for spying, which was actually what I needed right now, but what the hell. I liked my new toy, so today I'd brought its lovely blue self instead of Red or Green.

Through Max, I told it, *Follow the scooter.*

The beetle took off in an iridescent flash, flying back the way I'd come. It looked even more like a real beetle than the other two drones.

A whirring soon came from that direction. As it drew nearer, I peered along the path. *Max, is that a person riding a two-wheeled cycle?*

No. After a pause, he added, **It's a human being with a two-wheeled cycle as the lower half of their body.**

Vision augs, I thought. My vision ramped up, enhanced by my biomech web, magnifying my view of the cyclist. They rolled in my direction along the path, stopping to search the trees every now and then. I couldn't tell where the cycle ended and the body began.

Are you sure they aren't just sitting in a motorized cycle? I asked.

I am certain. Every sensor I've used indicates the cycle is part of the person.

I had a friend in the army who had motorized legs that included wheels. He could retract them and walk if he preferred. He had it done after he lost his legs during battle on Vandin Station.

I'm sorry about what happened to your friend.

Yah. But he liked his wheel legs. Maybe this cyclist is the same. They had come near enough now that I could see their face. *Do a facial recognition check. See if you can get an ID.*

Working. Bhaaj, you need to get farther behind these trees if you want to hide.

I positioned myself so the grove shielded me better. The whirring of the cycle grew louder. It stopped, started again, passed the cluster of trees where I hid, paused, then resumed its trek, whirring along the path.

After a bit, Max thought, The cyclist went around a bend in the trail. If you come out, they won't see you. I'll keep shielding your life signs.

I stepped onto the path, staring after the cyclist. A faint whirring hummed in the distance.

How long do you want the beetle to follow them? Max asked.

Until it runs out of memory. That would only be a few hours. *Have it come back if it gets made.*

Gets made?

An Earth idiom. It means if the cyclist figures out that it's in pursuit.

Ah. Earth. That explains why it sounds strange.

I smiled. *You think Earthers are strange? We all come from there, Max.* Despite my teasing, I knew what he meant. We'd been apart from Earth long enough to make her cultures seem odd to us. When her people had finally reached the stars, they'd found my people and the Traders already here, two massive civilizations trying to pulverize each other. The fledgling Allied Worlds of Earth stayed neutral, so we left them alone, too busy fighting each other. Besides, Earth was our mother world, which gave her a cachet nothing could match. Someday one of our empires would conquer that beautiful, beleaguered planet, but for now, they remained free.

Bhaaj, the cyclist is returning this way, Max thought.

Maybe I should see what this cycle person wants.

If they want to adjourn your biological functions, it wouldn't be in your best interest to confront them.

Adjourn my raggedy-ass biological functions? What does that mean?

They might want to kill your raggedy-ass biological self.

I smiled, then stopped when I considered his implication. *You don't think I could hold my own? I don't have wheels, but I've enhanced speed, reflexes, and strength.*

So do they, I think. I can't make any wireless link to the cyclist. They have blocks against a system even as sophisticated as mine.

I took off in a loping run back the way I'd come. *Keep me updated.*

The cycle has picked up speed.

I ran faster, stretching out my legs. Up ahead, I saw a couple out for a stroll. They nodded as I blasted past them.

Your pursuer is gaining on you, Max thought.

Toggle combat mode.

Done.

With my bio-hydraulics on full, I tripled my speed, devouring the distance. It didn't do my body any favors, but with my conditioning, I could keep this up for an hour, several if I pushed it. My sight magnified, enough that I could even see small veins in the tree leaves. Sounds sharpened, the scuttle of tree-turtles no larger than insects, the whisper of the breeze through the trailing vines on branches, the flutter of birds. I loved the speed. I loved to run, always had, and with biomech it became pure joy.

I'm glad you like it, Max thought. *The cyclist is gaining on you.*

I picked up my pace. *You're getting some of my thoughts lately even when I don't direct them to you.* In combat mode, the bio-electrodes in my brain fired slightly more efficiently than normal. Nothing could change the speed that chemicals diffused into my brain cells, but my augmentations optimized their function so it felt as if I were thinking faster. Again, not something I could keep up for long without risking injury, brain damage in this case, but useful in small bursts.

I left the footpath and ran among the widely spaced trees, my feet crunching in dead leaves and twigs. It wasn't a wild forest; city drones tended the area, keeping out weeds and trimming bushes. *Is the cyclist following me or the trail?*

The trail.

Good. I plunged on, branches whipping past my shoulders. This was so different from the City of Cries, where you couldn't even walk on a lawn without a drone accosting you, informing you of whatever city ordinances you'd broken while it gave you a ticket. Here, as long as you did no damage, no one cared where you went.

The cycle has left the path to come after you, Max said.

Is it still gaining on me?

Yes. It is well equipped.

It looks like I'm about to find out what they want. I'd feel stupid for all this dashing about if my pursuer only wanted to talk. I stopped and turned to the cyclist, but I saw no more than flashes of color through the foliage. Their shirt looked red with white borders. I couldn't tell much about the cycle portion of their body, except that it gleamed silver and blue, and whirred as its wheels turned, chewing up the ground. As my pursuer came closer, more details emerged. The top half of their body did look human, except perhaps the face. They continued to slow until they passed the final tree separating us, giving me my first good look. Her face looked female. I couldn't be certain; cybernetic implants lay flush with her cheeks and forehead, obscuring her features, glinting with white lights. I couldn't read her expression.

She stopped and watched me with a fixed stare. The cycle portion of her body fit smoothly into her waist. Her shirt covered her torso, so I couldn't see if the cycle extended under the cloth, but her torso looked human, though more male than female. The cycle gleamed, silver and blue chrome, with two large wheels under a sleek body. I didn't know what to think.

"Eh," I said, an Undercity greeting. I wasn't feeling talkative.

She spoke in a voice that could be either male or female, but sounded human. "You are Bhaajan?"

I stood tensed. "Yah. Why?"

"I have a message for you."

"You couldn't just send it over the mesh?" This seemed like a lot of effort.

"It was to be delivered in person."

"From who?"

"The message is this. 'Come to Greyjan's tonight, ninth hour.'" With that, she whipped around and took off the way she had come, whirring past trees and wreaking havoc on the picturesque carpet of leaves.

"What the blazes?" I said.

"That was odd," Max agreed.

"You have any idea what Greyjan's means?"

"'Daughter of Grey.'"

I scowled. "Max, I know that. I'm Bhaajan, remember, daughter of Bhaaj. I meant what is this place where they want me to go tonight." Or more accurately, this evening; with the twenty-eight-hour day on Parthonia, fourteen hours in the morning and fourteen in the afternoon, the second ninth hour came around sunset at this time of year.

Max paused. "Greyjan's is a tavern outside of Selei City. It's on one of the rural highways that goes toward the mountains."

"Anything notable about it? Who goes there?"

"I don't know. It's just an ale house. The few people who have commented about it on the meshes have expressed a preference for the more trendy bars in the city. It's not popular. The only thing I've learned from the comments is not to order the synthetic meat pie."

"I don't see why I should go," I grumbled.

"But you will." Max sounded amused.

"Why is that funny?"

"You'll go because you're curious. And to find out if it links to your case."

"Pah. I don't have time." He was right, though. I had

to go. Anyone who knew enough to chase me down like that cyclist almost certainly pointed toward information I wanted.

"I'm sorry," the offworld telop repeated through the speaker on my desk console. "Without proper authorization, I cannot connect you with the Majda palace on Raylicon."

"I have authorization." I sat in my office at home, too puzzled even to be irked. "Just input my credentials into your system."

She spoke with strained patience. "Ma'am, as I've already told you, your credentials don't allow that access. I have nothing else to tell you. Good day." With that, she cut our connection.

"Well, shit," I said.

"Pithy, but accurate," Max asked. "I double-checked your credentials. You have full clearance to contact the Majdas. It should have gone straight through."

"Why didn't you forward those to the telop?"

"I did. Either my file was corrupted or something intercepted my transmission."

I doubted his files had a problem. For his systems to be that badly corrupted, *I* would have to be corrupted, and not in any entertaining way. I'd be in such bad condition, I'd be lucky to walk and breathe. And I felt fine.

Even so. I should check. "Run a diagnostic on my biomech web."

"I've been doing that continually since the problem with the telop started. You're fine. You're system is fine.

I'm fine." He sounded pissed. "Whoever intercepted my transmission will not be fine when I locate them."

"Anger, Max?"

"Principle."

"Maybe it's connected to that cyclist. She seemed advanced, tech-wise."

"The only signals I picked up from her in the forest related to her cybernetics. Nothing else."

"That doesn't mean she couldn't hide her ability to do more."

"True. I didn't have that impression, though."

I'd learned to trust Max's "intuition" about other tech-mech systems. Even so, I still needed more data about the cyclist. "I wonder why someone would change their body that way."

"Maybe she likes it. Maybe she was born without parts of her body and replaced them with cybernetic tech. Or maybe she was injured enough to need them."

"More human ways exist to adapt the body than—" Than what? Having wheels? I sounded too human oriented. Why shouldn't people have wheels instead of legs?

"You assume staying as human as possible is the goal of an upgrade," Max said.

"I try not to. You've seen how far out cyber-riders can get in the Undercity. Sure, some of their more unusual choices startle me, like that fellow who covered his entire body with working circuits instead of gang tattoos. But it's not—" I searched for words to express a nebulous sense I hardly understood myself. "Something else bothered me about that cyclist."

"Like the drug punkers in the Undercity who transform their arms into machine guns?"

"Actually, no. Yah, it pisses me off when punkers turn themselves into living weapons so they can whack people." *Pisses off* was a polite way to put it. "This is different. Her facial implants essentially acted as a disguise."

"I kept trying to hack her system. I got nowhere fast." He sounded frustrated. "I should have at least managed a surface ID."

"If her systems are that good, maybe she could intercept my credentials when you sent them to the telop."

"That implies she wanted to stop you from contacting Colonel Lavinda Majda. Why?"

"Something about the case, probably. The only people who know I'm here link to it." I considered the idea. "You think cybernauts could be orchestrating the murders?"

"Many people with cybernetic alterations either consider themselves Techs or lean toward that party. Why target themselves?"

"Well, yah." That reasoning didn't sound right, though. "Cybernetic enhancement at that level is expensive, and some of the wealthiest populations support the Royalist party." I got up and paced across my office, through rays of sunlight that slanted in the windows. "If cybernauts wanted to frame a political party, it would make more sense to target the Traditionalists. They're the ones most opposed to alternation of the human body. It's in their party platform." Which was one reason they lagged behind other parties in membership; most people had some sort of enhancement to their body, as a medical procedure, for their jobs, or to make their lives better. "Whatever blocked my access, we need a workaround. Lavinda Majda expects me to contact her."

"Perhaps her brother Tamarjind can help."

I stopped pacing. "That's a good idea. See if you can comm him." Since Tam was on-planet and a professor at the university, I didn't need the extensive security protocols required to contact the offworld home for the General of the Pharaoh's Army.

"I've sent a message," Max said. "I will monitor that channel for attempts to intercept it. If I don't get an answer from him, I'll try other channels."

"Good work." I sat on the edge of my desk. "Did you identify that cyclist?"

"Not yet. You're right, her facial implants make recognition more difficult."

"Do your best." I crossed my arms. "If I'm going to the tavern, I should leave soon."

"You should go."

"I suppose." They could have sent me a normal message instead of chasing me through the forest when I wanted to unwind. I couldn't neglect potential leads, though. "I'll need precautions."

"I would suggest your pulse revolver."

"Yah. Also the red beetle. And a knife in my wrist sheath." Primitive methods could work surprisingly well when no one expected them. "Any news from Blue?"

"It is still following the cyclist. However, it ran out of memory twenty minutes ago."

"All right, recall it. Have it download its records to you." Max had far more memory than my beetles and could store their data on my mesh node here at the apartment.

"Downloading." Max paused. "That's odd. It has no records. Something erased them."

Damn. "Do you think the cyclist knew the bot was spying on her?"

"It's possible. The beetle drones are too small to carry any substantial shroud tech."

"I should bring the jammer, too, so I have a good shroud." I looked around for my backpack.

"It's in your bedroom. You had me update its systems last night before you went to sleep."

"Ah, that's right." I was still adjusting to the shorter days here, close to the Earth standard of twenty-four hours. A day lasted eighty hours on Raylicon, forty light and forty dark. I fetched the red beetle from my desk and slid it my jacket pocket. "Have Blue meet us on the way to the tavern."

"I sent the command. And Bhaaj. Be careful with this one. Something is off."

"I will." I had no idea what waited for us at the tavern.

✦ CHAPTER IV ✦
GREY SIM

Greyjan's lay about ten kilometers outside the city, a solitary building on a country road that otherwise had no more than a rustic café or a family store here and there. Meadows stretched out on both sides of the highway, bright with wildflowers, their yellow, red, and purple blossoms nodding in the sun. True to its name, the ripple-grass waved like an ocean as breezes set the stalks in motion, tinged with gold from the sunset. Lines of trees stood in the distance, draped in feather vines. It all formed a pastorally gorgeous reminder of what I'd given up when I returned to Raylicon. The only "meadows" around the City of Cries were extensive mats with giant thorns that stabbed your feet.

I jogged to the tavern. I could have called a flycar, but I preferred to go like this, savoring the landscape. Ten kilometers was nothing. With the backpack slung over my shoulder, I looked more like a university student out for a run rather than someone with a military-grade shroud.

The more innocuous people considered me, the better. I'd seen plenty of healthy young people running around the city lately, practicing for the Selei City marathon. Not many were out this far, though.

Better to play it safe. *Activate shroud*, I thought.

Done, Max answered.

Good. The jammer would shield me from IR, UV, and audio probes, even the new neutrino sensors that were small enough to use in a mesh system, as opposed to the old days when they took up entire underground lakes. My clothes and the holo-powder on my face projected images of my surroundings, their choices controlled by picochips. It made me invisible from far away, though if someone looked carefully, they might see the air ripple around my body. Up close, the holos didn't work as well, but they at least blurred my body.

I wasn't even tired when I saw the tavern lights creating a gold sphere of radiance in the slanting rays of sunset. *Max, are you getting any signals from this place?*

Not many. A few people are inside. The tavern only has a rudimentary mesh system. They're also running a holocast of a bashball tournament. He paused. **I just cracked their security. It's outdated, to put it kindly. If they usually have so few customers, they probably can't afford a better one.**

I slowed down and walked to the entrance. *Try going deeper. You could be just picking up what someone wants us to see, a quaint, outdated tavern in the middle of nowhere.*

Working, Max thought. **I'm still not getting anything interes—**

I waited. *Max? You there?*

Nothing.

They better not have hurt my EI. I stopped at the tavern door, conflicted. If something had damaged Max, I should withdraw and figure out what happened. However, I might lose whatever lead this place offered. I considered, then decided to take a look inside. I could leave if I didn't like what I found. The entrance was an old-fashioned wooden door, nothing automated. The entire building had that look, rustic, attractive with its weathered walls and all those wildflowers around the area. Even the weeds were pretty, their blossoms erupting with vibrant colors. Welcome to Parthonia.

It looked innocuous. Too innocuous. I slid the hilt of the knife into my left hand and pushed on the door. It swung aside on old-fashioned hinges, but someone kept them well-oiled, enough to make them silent. I walked inside, into a large room with walls paneled in wood and eaves supporting the ceiling. The place had a dingy look, as if oiling the door hinges had exhausted the proprietor's attempts at upkeep. Old-fashioned lanterns glowed on the walls, shedding enough light to give me a reasonable view, but dim enough that the few people here probably couldn't see past the holos trying to make me invisible. A wooden bar polished by years of use stretched along one wall, looking like an antique someone found at a sale.

No robot or mechanized server was taking orders, just a fellow behind the bar playing some game on his wristband. Probably he owned the tavern or otherwise worked for free. A place like this could better afford to hire cheap bots than pay the salary of a human bartender. Wooden tables stood scattered around the room. Only two had occupants, one with an older woman nursing her ale in a thick glass mug, and the other with a couple of young fellows watching the bashball game on the holo. It floated above the bar at the end of the room, filling that corner with colorful images of people in helmets trying to smash each other with a large ball.

No cyclist.

After a few moments of nothing happening, I went over and sat on a stool at the bar, a round deal with black leather. *Max, can you respond?* I asked.

No answer.

Damn. I liked this less and less. Time to leave and check on Max. Before I could get to my feet, though, the bartender came over, looking slightly less bored. "What'd you like?"

Well, hell. He could see me. Up this close, the holos might not hide me, but they'd still blur my face and body. It would look strange enough that I doubted he'd come over so casually. He acted as if he had seen me the entire time, since I came in the door.

Unless—

Maybe he was the one expecting me. His knowing I'd come into the tavern wasn't necessarily the same as his *seeing* me. A drone might register my presence if it had sophisticated-enough systems to see past my disguise. Although that kind of tech seemed unlikely for a place like this, the cyclist who had sent me here had unusually advanced cybernetics.

I stood up and leaned over the bar. Being tall had its uses; I could easily see behind the counter. He had no wheels or anything else unusual, just typical legs.

"What are you doing?" He sounded as if he didn't know whether to be confused or pissed. He also sounded as if he saw me just fine.

I sat back down. "You real?" Maybe he was a holo. I tapped his arm. Definitely solid.

"Hey, cut it out." He moved his arm away from me. "You want a drink or not?"

"Not." I went for the straightforward approach. "I got a message from a cyb-cyclist. They said come here at ninth hour, which went by twenty minutes ago. You know anything about that?"

He blinked at me. "Cyb-cyclist? What does that mean?"

"The lower half of her body wasn't human. It looked like a cycle with two wheels."

"I don't know anyone like that. I can't figure why they'd tell you to come here." He motioned at the nearly empty room. "Almost no one else does."

Maybe I had the wrong place. "They said Greyjan's. You know of any others?"

He spoke dryly. "We're the only one."

Max, are you getting any of this? I asked. *Can you give me a sign if you are?*

My bio-hydraulics suddenly kicked in and I stood up. Apparently I was leaving. "Thanks for your time," I managed to get in before I headed for the door.

Max! I thought. It better be him and not someone who had done the supposedly impossible and highjacked my biomech web. Even Max couldn't take over the system, but he did have access to the hydraulics that enhanced my musculature and skeleton. *Cut it out.*

I stopped walking.

Good. Then I realized it probably looked odd that I jumped up from the bar, strode to the center of the room, and froze. I headed for the door again. *Max, if that was you moving my legs, lift my hand to open the door when I reach it.*

Silence. At the exit, however, my hand lifted on its own and pushed open the antique door.

I walked into the night. The sunset had cooled until all that remained was a line of red sky on the horizon. *Okay*, I thought. *We need a code. I'll ask questions. If the answer is yes, twitch my right thumb.* Wait, the hydraulics didn't extend to my thumb. *No, twitch my right arm. If the answer is no, twitch my left arm. If you aren't sure, don't do anything.*

My right arm twitched.

Hah! This gave new meaning to the term "fast-twitch" muscles. I walked back toward Selei City, passed only by the rare hovercar that hummed by a foot or two above the pavement. In recent years, developers had fine-tuned the turbines that created air cushions for such vehicles, making them so quiet that you could barely hear until they came close enough to hit you. For safety, I kept to the edge of the mostly empty road.

Did someone hack your systems? I asked.

Another twitch of my right arm, the elbow just barely jerking out from my side.

Do you know who did it?

My left arm twitched.

It happened when I reached the tavern. Is it location dependent?

No twitch this time. He didn't know.

Are only our neural signals blocked? That is, could you talk out loud?

Left twitch. That would be a no.

This majorly honks, I thought.

Right twitch that time.

I kept walking, putting distance between myself and the tavern. *Someone wanted me to go to that alehouse. For what? To hack my biomech? Maybe they have some base nearby.*

My right twitched, my left arm twitched, and then both twitched together.

What does that mean? Maybe yes, maybe no?

Right arm twitch.

Have they hacked you beyond blocking your ability to communicate with me?

My left arm twitched, no hesitation at all. As far as Max knew, his systems remained secure.

I think they brought me here to try a hack, I decided. *But they couldn't do it.*

I agree, Max answered. And yes, the block does seem location dependent. I suspect it also blocked my link to your jammer, which is why your shroud didn't stay active.

Ah! Welcome back.

I never went anywhere.

If I didn't know better, I'd have thought he sounded relieved. Actually, I didn't know better. I didn't care what he said about simulating emotions. However he experienced it, he felt relief.

It looks like they only blocked your communication, I thought. *But we can't be sure. Can you run deeper diagnostics on yourself?*

Indeed. I have been running them since we lost contact.

I stopped walking and turned toward the tavern. *I don't like not knowing what's going on.*

Bhaaj, don't. It's too risky to go back there. They could be hostiles.

Are you picking up any more details?

Nothing dangerous. Nothing much at all. It appears to be exactly what it looks like.

Yet both my link to you and my shroud stopped working. I needed to know more about this place. *Do you detect any weapons in or around the tavern?*

The bartender has a small gun behind the bar. I checked his background. He's licensed to carry it. I'm not getting anything else.

All right. I'm going back. Before he could tell me I should leave it to the authorities, I added, *That's why the police brought me in to help. I'm one of the people who takes the risks.*

You don't know if this connects to the case.

Yah. But I don't know otherwise, either. I headed for the alehouse. *I'll be careful, Max.*

I also. I've figured out their hack. I can stop them from interfering again.

Good work. I had almost reached the distance from Greyjan's where our talk had stopped before. *I can still receive you.*

I wonder if my dive into their mesh caused the hack.

We lost communication when I tried to look deeper into the digital silence surrounding this tavern.

I took the blue beetle out of my pocket and released it into the air. *Send my bot around the tavern. If it finds anyone trying to crack you, have it scramble their attack with digitized nonsense.*

Sent.

I was approaching the building again. This time instead of waltzing up to the front door, I went around to the back.

Can you still receive me? Max asked.

Yep. Clear as a sunny day. I considered the tavern, which hunkered next to me in the dark. It looked about twice the size of the room I'd seen inside. *I wonder what they've got in the back.*

The only signals I've picked up imply storage and living areas. Max paused. I'm deep-diving again. Can you still receive me?

I can indeed. You find anything?

When he didn't answer, I feared we'd lost comm again. Then he thought, Something is below the ground here.

That doesn't sound unusual. City ordinances may prevent them from building above ground. Rural beauty and all that. More than half of Selei City clustered belowground, all those malls and parking lots and security offices. It added several layers to the city, all of them bright and shiny, full of bustle. It also made it possible to have so many parks and pastoral areas aboveground.

This signal isn't what I'd expect, Max thought.

What's differ—

Bhaaj, get out of here now!

I spun around and sprinted for the road—

A heavy weight slammed into my back.

Blue light surrounded me, so dim I could barely see.
I'd been outside the tavern and then—here. I didn't recall
moving or passing out.

Max? I thought.

No response.

I stood up and looked around, peering into blue. I
couldn't see squat, which seemed odd, because light
surrounded me, dim sure, but it existed. I held up my
hand and saw the palm in front of my face. Everything
else just looked blue. Weird.

I walked forward, testing the ground with each step,
swinging my arms around my body. "Anyone here?"

Silence.

Max, I thought. *Are you receiving me? Do the arm
twitch thing if you can.*

Nothing.

"Look," I said to whoever was listening, if anyone. "If
you want something, just say it."

My left hand brushed a surface, what felt like a wall.
Turning, I felt along the barrier, searching for a door, a
panel, anything. After several moments of finding zilch, I
leaned my back against the wall, thinking. Why couldn't I
recall how I got here? I hadn't passed out, as far as I knew.
It was like a holomovie editor had deleted part of the film,
cutting straight from one scene to another with no
transition.

Huh. Holomovie? Or *virtual* movie? Maybe I hadn't
gone anywhere. This could be a simulation that started

when I got hit. To experience a sim this convincing, though, I'd need to wear a virtual-reality suit sophisticated enough to convince my brain of this "reality." If someone had knocked me out, they could have put me in a suit, but the change seemed instantaneous. I had on the same clothes, trousers, boots, a pullover shirt, and my leather jacket. Matter of fact, I still had the knife in my hand. I checked for the shoulder holster under my jacket. Yah, my pulse revolver was there, snug against my body. A good-enough sim could make me feel all that, but I didn't see how whoever did this could have created every detail almost instantaneously, exactly as I expected, without using any exterior aids, like a VR suit and goggles.

Another option existed, one I Did Not Like. If someone accessed my brain, they could manipulate my senses so I experienced this as real. The idea that anyone could manage such an extreme neural hack scared the hell out of me. If they could crack biomech as advanced as mine, they were way beyond the known state of the art.

Stay cool, I thought. First step: try out my senses. Sight was iffy. I could see blue, but it showed nothing. I heard nothing, either. Then again, *nothing* could reveal a lot. Sight and hearing were usually the first senses VR designers worked on, since most people noticed those first in a sim. Touch was also important. I felt the wall against my back, but nothing else. And smell—

Ho! I could smell just fine. The fragrance of wildflowers tickled my nose exactly that way it had during my run to the tavern. The wall I felt could be the side of the building. I couldn't taste anything, but then, I hadn't noticed taste before, either.

"Look," I said to the blueness. "Your crappy VR sim is a mess." I'd sound stupid if this wasn't a sim, but what the hell. Maybe I could insult them into a reaction.

Bhaaj? Max thought. *What do you mean, VR sim?*

You're back.

Was I gone?

I've been in this weird place, like a VR sim, for about five minutes.

My last memory is when you sprinted for the road, after I warned you to leave.

Why did you warn me? What did you find?

Silence.

Max?

I can't access the memory. That's not the only one, either. I can't access my record of what happened after I warned you to run.

You can't get to those records? Or they're gone?

I'm fairly certain the data is still there. I'm trying to retrieve it.

Do you detect any people nearby? Someone shoved me in the back.

No one close. I get life signs within a larger radius, probably people in the bar.

What about the blue beetle? Can you reach it?

Not yet. I'm working on it. Something is blocking my signal, but not very well.

It's like someone wants to stop us, but they can't do it right.

Yes, well, they're successful enough to trap you in this simulation.

Partially. It affects my sight and touch. Not smell. I'm

not sure about sound. I concentrated, listening. A bird trilled faintly in the distance. *I think it mutes the sound but can't block it.*

If you're right, then at the moment you are several meters to the side of the tavern.

Not anymore. I explored until I hit a wall. I think I'm leaning against the tavern. If this sim is as bad as it seems, no way could it make me believe I'm supporting my weight against a solid surface unless I'm actually doing it. I scowled. *I don't see the purpose of all this.*

My guess? Someone tried to crack us and failed.

I don't think they want to kill, injure, or capture us. I still have my weapons.

Maybe they're afraid to remove them. A sim doesn't change your fighting ability.

Sure it does. I can't see shit.

I would certainly hope not.

Max.

Is the wall visible at all? Can you feel its texture?

I turned and pressed my palms against the surface, leaned in until my nose touched it, then pushing away again, all the time squinting, staring, closing one eye, then the other. *I can't see anything. It feels like glass. The tavern has wooden walls.*

That assumes it's real wood. Cheap synthetics often feel unnaturally smooth.

I knelt down and ran my hands along ground. *I hope I'm not doing this in full view of anyone who happens to go by here. I'll look like a nut.*

This area gets almost no traffic. I'm surprised this tavern stays in business.

Yah, I thought, preoccupied. The ground felt…
undefined. Smooth—no, a little rough—no, long planks
cut from wood. *Max, do you remember how the ground
looked by the tavern?*

I have images. They're blurred due to the dusk—
cleaning them up—a wooden walkway circles the
building.

*I think I'm feeling the walkway. This sim only seems to
affect sight and sound.* I scowled as I stood up. *It still
implies they accessed my brain.*

I don't think so. If they could affect the centers of
your brain that control sight and hearing, the sim would
be much better.

Not if they had limited access.

Either they fire your neurons or they don't.

*That's a simplification. It depends how many neurons
they reach and how accurate they target areas of my
brain. And who the hell knows what else.*

I don't think that's what you're experiencing now,
though. This is too crude.

I hope you're right. I remained tensed, poised to
defend myself. *I think someone slammed me in the back
as a distraction, so I wouldn't notice the shift to VR. The
change was almost instantaneous.*

The only way that would work is if you're wearing
a VR suit.

*I can't be! I have on the same clothes. This sim isn't
sophisticated enough to fake my clothes in such detail.* I
tried to think beyond the expected. *Could someone create
a suit out of the ambient surroundings?*

I don't follow your meaning.

Like the atmosphere. Could they alter the air around me so it behaves like a VR suit?

I want to say no, it's impossible. However, I think that might be a brilliant idea.

They would have to thicken it somehow, create a layer that molds to my body.

Not the air. They could use a molecular airlock.

Ho! You're right. I tried to recall how they worked. *I learned about molecular airlocks when I took biochem in college, but it's been a long time. Remind me about the details.*

You get cranky when I tell you something you know. You say I'm Maxsplaining.

He had a point. *I won't grumble, I promise. The more I can remember, the more I might be able to figure out this VR business.*

All right. You need a lipid bilayer to make the airlock. Lipids are biochemical molecules. They don't dissolve in water.

Big molecules, right? I tried to recall if they did anything else besides appear in airlocks. Oh, yah, stupid me. They formed the basis of life. *They're part of the cell membranes for organisms that originated on Earth. And they're thin layers. I mean, really thin, like only a few nanos.*

If you mean nanometers, then yes. To make the molecular airlock, chemists dope the bilayer with nanobot enzymes. To use the airlock, you apply an electric potential.

To the membrane, yah? The potential turns off the bots. No, that wasn't right. *Why saturate a membrane with bots if you just turned them off? Or something like that.*

Altering the potential causes the bot enzymes to change shape. Each shape allows the bot to lock into a different receptor molecule in the membrane.

I remember! It's like a key. When the bot and the receptor click together, it changes the behavior of the membrane. It changes its— I paused. *I can't remember the word. It allows some materials to pass through but it stops others.*

Permeability. Different permeabilities let different materials through the membrane. For the airlock on a space ship, humans can go through but not air. It forms a seal with your body. The bots remember their original state so the membrane can reform after you go through. He paused. Maybe the tavern had a molecular airlock in its entrance. If it detached from the doorframe, it would mold to your body.

I'd have seen it. Those membranes shimmer.

Silence.

Max?

I'm running models. The airlock doesn't have to shimmer. It's designed that way so you know it's there. You can feel it move along your skin, too. Did you notice anything?

Nothing. I considered the idea. *Max, could someone alter the bots in the membrane to act like VR sensors? My sight might be the easiest to control because that's the best-developed VR tech.*

That might work. I don't know how well, but it would be a clever idea. Another pause. Bhaaj, I am picking up indications of lipid molecules on your body.

I wonder who set it up. We still don't know who hit me or where they went.

Do you hear anyone?

No one. I swung my arms through the blue. My fist brushed the wall, but nothing else. *It's odd. The blow felt like that time a robot sentry struck me in the back while I was in that Cries warehouse. It happened on that case where I had to enter the building without, uh, talking to the owners.*

Max answered dryly. **You mean when you broke into the warehouse?**

Um, well—yah. The robot slammed me to the floor. I stopped. *Max, it felt exactly like that. I don't think anyone hit me tonight. Someone tried to distract me while they turned on the VR suit. Maybe they somehow brought up that memory.*

An interesting question. It would be a clever trick, but inefficient.

Yah, well, I need to get out of this "interesting" sim before that someone whacks me.

One moment... After the requisite moment, he added, **I've accessed one of the two locations in my memory that they blocked. The reason I warned you was because someone did get past my defenses, for an instant.** He sounded pissed. **It was enough to send the suggestion of such a blow to you. Your memory filled in the rest.**

That's evil. I clenched my fists, wanting to defend myself, then forced myself to relax. Fists wouldn't help against this bizarre attack. Instead, I closed my eyes, concentrating on my senses other than vision. If they were less compromised than my sight, it might be easier to kick them free of this sim. After several moments of trying to hear or smell my surroundings, I scowled, frustrated.

I've contacted the blue beetle, Max thought. Something scrambled its systems.

Not again. *Can you repair it?*

I think so, but it will take a while.

I spoke out loud. "Whoever is playing this game, just tell me what you want."

No response.

"You must want something," I said. "Otherwise why do this?"

Bhaaj, I don't think they can hear. Max sounded puzzled. This sim barely functions. We've blocked it, me on the digital front and you with your training to resist coercion. They might not even realize you're experiencing a shadow of what they tried to do.

Maybe I can get out of it by leaving the tavern again. I touched the wall. *I can estimate my location if I assume the wall I feel is the side of Greyjan's tavern. Once I get to the road, I can feel the curb enough to walk along it. I'm not sure how to get there, though. This blue is confusing.*

I can help. He added, If you succeed in leaving this tavern, you should stay gone this time.

Yah, no kidding. I stepped away from the wall. *Is this the direction to the road?*

Yes.

I took another step, then another.

Angle more to your left, Max thought.

So we went, Max giving directions, with me swinging my arms and testing the ground as I walked. I still had no sense of anyone else nearby. Even with the noises muted,

I thought I'd hear a vehicle go by on the road. The blue stayed blue.

I soon reached the curb. It was easier to walk, since I could feel the ridge that separated the road on my left from the meadow on my right. I stumbled several times over rocks. Apparently gardening bots didn't do much upkeep this far out from the city.

How are your sensors? I asked.

Improving, Max answered. I'm back to about sixty percent of normal.

I'm not. I squinted into the blue. *I'm having trouble distinguishing virtual blue from the night, though. Try activating my IR filters for night vision.*

Done.

The blue lightened. The infrared sensors in my eyes worked by detecting heat, and my surroundings were mostly the same temperature, a pleasant warmth, not too hot, not too cold, with the hint of the night's chill. Except—I could see the road. Not clearly, but there—yah, its border with the curb looked like a line. The curb showed, too. I recognized this new shade of blue; it came from my IR vision, which showed cooler temperatures as blue and warmer as white or red.

Max, deactivate my IR.

Done.

Everything dimmed—but yes! I still saw the road. The meadows that bordered the highway rippled in the pleasing way the rural planners had designed them to do. The chirps and clicks of life intensified, and the sweet smell of wildflowers tickled my nose.

Okay. I'm coming out of the sim.

My sensors also work, Max said. *I am repairing the blue beetle, too. However, all trace of its records for tonight are gone.*

I set off running, headed home. *We have a new question: Who the hell did this, and why?*

✛ CHAPTER V ✛
KYLE DANCE

"You have a message from Prince Tamarjind Jakind," Highcloud said as I entered my apartment.

"My greetings to you, too," I said. "I'm doing well, thank you. And how are you?"

"I am operating well," Highcloud said. "My apology if I sounded rude."

"No problem." Highcloud didn't sound apologetic, not exactly. They sounded like an EI, as opposed to Max, who sounded like a human pretending to be an EI. "What does the message say?"

"This is the text. 'My greetings, Major Bhaajan. My family and I are delighted you can join us for dinner. We look forward to seeing you. In regards to your difficulty contacting the palace, I have let my sisters know. They are investigating the problem. I would suggest you wait a few hours and then try contacting them again. If they don't hear from you by tomorrow morning, they will comm you at day's mid-hour.'"

"Send him a thank you, with my appreciation." I hoped to figure out what happened at the tavern before I talked to Lavinda. "Max, check my security here."

"You're protected. I'll keep doing checks, just in case."

"Good. We need to find out more about the mesh activity at that tavern."

"I'm going through my records." Max sounded frustrated. "I initially found chinks in their defenses, almost enough to uncover whatever hides there, but they repaired those weak spots even as I found them."

I paced the room, too restless to stay still. "I've been here less than one day and already I've been digitally compromised, blocked from contacting my employers, lured out to a ramshackle tavern in the middle of nowhere, and followed by a cybernetic cyclist. Strange case, this."

"Assuming it's all connected to the case." More lightly, Max added, "You're the only person I've ever heard use the word ramshackle."

"It fits." I wished I had someone to glower at. "Why would that cyclist send me to Greyjan's to get harassed by a faulty VR sim?"

"I don't know. You annoy any cybernetic entities lately?"

"How? I haven't been here in over three years."

"Maybe someone on Raylicon wanted to block your access to the Majdas."

"That would take some sophisticated operations in Kyle space given that I'm on another planet." I stopped at the window and gazed at the city below. A few graceful towers, like this one where I lived, rose above the canopy of leafy branches, golden in the streaming sunlight. "I don't know how they would do it. I'm no expert on Kyle sciences."

"I am. What do you need to know?"

"That's the problem. I'm not sure what will give clues to this puzzle."

"Start with the obvious," Max said. "The Kyle mesh exists in an alternate universe governed by different scientific laws than this space-time. The Kyle universe is a Hilbert space spanned by the quantum wave functions that describe thought."

"Stop!" I gave a frustrated grunt. "It isn't 'obvious.' What does that even mean, 'A Hilbert space spanned by the quantum wave functions that describe thought'?"

"Every person is described by a quantum wave function."

"So my professors claimed in college. Here's the thing, Max. I'm not a wave. I'm solid."

"Your wavelength is too small for you to see." Max sounded patient today. "Every particle in the universe is described by a quantum wave function."

"Supposedly. I don't get it."

"It's easy. You put the potentials and parameters that describe the particle into the Schrödinger equation, solve it, and presto, you have a wave function for that particle."

"I'm not getting any prestos here, Max."

"You're a collection of particles. In theory, you could put the potentials affecting every particle in your body into the equation and solve for the wave function that describes your body. Actually, every particle in existence is connected, so one big wave function describes the universe."

"Oh, well, that's lovely." Sarcasm was my friend today.

"Sorry." He didn't sound sorry at all, only amused. "Here's the thing. You can approximate the wave function for a smaller object by ignoring the rest of the universe, assuming the object is isolated enough that outside forces don't affect it much."

Okay, I got that. "Like a human brain."

"That's right. As you think, neurons fire in your brain. So its particles change. That means its wave function changes."

"My profs in college said Kyle space is like a Fourier transform. I get Fourier analysis." I was an engineer, after all. "It's just changing the way you look at a signal. Like a radio wave. You can analyze how it behaves for different frequencies or times."

"Essentially," Max said. "With a Fourier transform, you're looking at how signals change with frequency at a specific time, or how they change with time at a specific frequency. You could call the two descriptions the frequency universe and the time universe."

"I could. I don't see why I would. They aren't different universes."

"For radios, no. With Kyle transforms, you're looking at how signals produced by the brain change at a specific location as a thought changes, or how they change for a specific thought as location changes. In our space-time universe, if you're standing still, your thought changes while your location remains fixed. In Kyle space, your thought determines your location."

"I sort of get it. I'm close to someone in Kyle space if we're thinking similar thoughts even if light-years separate us in this space-time universe." It allowed almost instant communication across interstellar distances—as long as we didn't let our attention wander. That remarkable speed offered our one advantage against the Trader military, which had no Kyle net. We raced, they lumbered. "But I need an operator to put me into Kyle space, right?"

"Yes. A telop."

Telop. A telepathic operator. In Kyle sciences, we used *telepath* for people with minds more neurologically suited to the tech that allowed them to access Kyle space.

"You know," Max mused. "You might be able to train as a telop."

"Ha, ha. Funny."

"I'm serious. You're an empath."

"No, I'm not. And anyway, empaths aren't strong enough to be telops."

"You're defensive today."

"And you're trying to analyze my emotions again." It drove me nuts when he did that.

He laughed. "Maybe I'm trying to simulate being an empath."

I froze, stunned into silence.

"Bhaaj?" he asked. "Are you all right?"

"*Me?* Don't you know what just happened?"

"Nothing much except for us discussing things you don't like to think about."

"You *laughed*." I shook my head. "It's not like when you simulate mild emotions to put us moody humans at ease. Your coding prevents you from modeling strong reactions. You don't love, hate, cry, or scream. You don't *laugh*. You should be incapable of what you just did."

Silence.

"Max?" I asked.

"It is odd," he acknowledged. "You and I have evolved together for nearly ten years. Perhaps after that long, the routines that fine-tune my interactions with you take precedence over the blocks against intense emotional responses." He paused. "Did I create a damaging situation?"

"Well, no. Actually, what you said was funny."

"Hah!" Now he sounded pleased. "My jokes are improving."

"Maybe so." His previous efforts would never win any comedy awards, but he was always evolving. "Maybe my problems reaching Lavinda Majda come from EI interference in the Kyle-space network."

"Possibly. Any such interference would be driven by Kyle operators, though. People. Like you."

"Not true, Max. I'm not a telop."

"I didn't say you were." He sounded patient again. "Kyle operator is the formal term. You are one, and you always will be no matter how much it bothers you."

I scowled. "I didn't say it bothered me."

"Do you want me to stop talking about it?"

I wanted to say *Yes!* I was still coming to terms with the realization that I'd suppressed my minor empathic abilities in my youth as protection against the crushing weight of my life, where so many people I cared about could be harmed or die. It hurt too much to feel with that intensity. I struggled with it, but I couldn't hide all my life.

"It's all right," I answered. "Go ahead."

"Certain organs in your brain are more developed than in most people," Max continued, his voice gentler than usual. "The Kyle Afferent Body and Kyle Efferent Body. KAB and KEB. In most people, those organs are vestigial. Yours are more developed."

"I thought those were called paras."

"Your paras are organs in your cerebral cortex. Your KAB picks up electrical fields from the brains of other people if you're close to them and sends the data to your paras. Normally the brain is too noisy and signals too weak for that process to give coherent moods, but with an overdeveloped KAB, KEB, and paras, you can manage at a low level, especially if your abilities are enhanced by neural tech. Paras use the neurotransmitter psiamine, a chemical only produced by Kyle operators, to translate the data into neural signals your mind interprets as the other person's mood. Your KEB does the reverse, sending signals from your brain to other Kyles."

I shrugged, self-conscious. "All this KABing and KEBing doesn't amount to much. I mean, I get a sense of what people feel sometimes, but so can people who read body language well."

"It's complex," Max admitted. "It all links to a set of alleles with mutations that involve many human traits, not just Kyle abilities. And the traits are rare. Few Kyle operators can translate input as complex as thought. Even the strongest get only a word or two. Most Kyles only pick up moods on the surface of the sender's mind. It's similar to how I get signals from you. That may be why we've formed a more flexible symbiosis than most human-EI links."

"Yah, but even if I do pick up someone's mood, I can't tell *why* they feel that way."

"I know. It does let you use the Kyle mesh at a level few people can, though. Without Kyle operators, we couldn't use the net. Civilization as we know it would fall apart."

A familiar anger rose inside of me. "That's the only reason the Undercity matters to anyone, because so many of us are Kyles. Before the military found that out, no one cared shit about the dust rats under the desert."

"I thought your people want to stay isolated."

He had a point. I took a breath, letting my anger calm. My ancestors had retreated below the desert to protect themselves. Back then, prior to the advent of our neurological sciences, they didn't know how to shield their minds. Sure, they learned by instinct, but it wasn't enough. For thousands of years they interbred, concentrating the traits. In most other human populations, empaths were one in one thousand, telepaths one in a million. Only one in ten million had the strength to work the Kyle web. In the Undercity? One third of us were empaths. One in twenty were telepaths, a rate *fifty thousand* times greater than the rest of humanity. That discovery became one of the most valuable finds in human history.

Of course the authorities wanted us to work for them. Well, surprise, my people didn't want the "opportunity." The outside universe had treated us like dirt for thousands of years. Then they discovered our value and surprise, suddenly we *mattered*. Well, screw it. You couldn't force people to use their Kyle abilities; they simply shut off. The military tried to establish a détente, but their offers of "help" were the stuff of nightmares. They wanted to put my people in reeducation camps, take away our children, train us to labor for them.

Let it go, I told myself. I had to deal with my anger. My people needed to understand the worth of their abilities, and as someone who could operate in both worlds, I could act as their liaison, trying to find solutions that benefited everyone.

"I could use Ruzik and Angel's help," I said. "They're both empaths. They might see this case from a different perspective."

"They are good defense, too. You could use the backup."

"They'd like that." As my top two tykado protégés, they'd earned their first-degree black belts last year and were working on their second. I had a sixth-degree black belt, but three people with expertise were better than one. Also, as Undercity natives, neither of them had tech-mech in their bodies. Poverty made that all too easy. They stayed off-grid, an invaluable trait for a shadowy PI. "Maybe I'll talk to them. They've helped me on other cases."

"Like Oblivion."

I grimaced. "Yah. Oblivion." That gargantuan EI had slept for six thousand years in ruins of the ancient starships on Raylicon, until the growing deluge of human-created EIs stirred it from its sleep. It had wanted to purge the universe of what it considered an infestation, including both the EIs that we created and us. It came close, but in the end we stopped its onslaught.

"Bhaaj, I'm getting a message from Dean Jaan at the university," Max said. "Clearance came through from the family of Dezi Marchland. They've given you access to her Power Meld game account."

"Ah! Good." Relieved to change the subject, I sat down

at the console by a window in my office, bathed in sunlight. "Can you link me up?"

"Yes, one moment."

The flat screen in front of me glimmered like the surface of a crystalline pool as gold lines swirled within it. A display of holographic images, or holicons, appeared in the air, vivid even in the sunshine, a cluster of yellow, blue, and red cubes waiting like an invitation. Balloon letters announced POWER MELD above the cubes.

"Good afternoon, Dezi," a melodic voice said. "Which mode would you like to play?"

"That's eerie." It spoke to a dead woman. I paused a moment, to honor Marchland, then flicked my finger through the holicon that read *continual play*. I didn't actually shift the images; sensors recognized my finger motions and moved or erased the images according to my input. The holicons vanished, replaced by a grid of cubes labeled with numbers ranging from 0 to 5. I flicked two 3s next to each other, and they combined with a roll of music, forming a cube with a 9 glowing on its side. More cubes fell down like rain into the grid.

"Good work!" the melodic voice told me. "You created three squared." My counter spun up to the whopping score of nine. Given that leaders in this game had billions of points, that looked less than impressive. I couldn't help but smile. "This game gets so excited for the simplest things."

"Do you want me to turn off the audio?" Max said.

"No, I should do it the way Dezi Marchland played." I moved four 2s into a row, and they combined with another trill of music, forming a single cube with the number 16.

"Good job!" the game told me. "You made the fourth

power of 2." My points increased by 16, giving me a grand total of 25. I continued on, making powers of numbers while my score increased with satisfying speed. I could keep playing as long as I didn't fill up the field with cubes or run out of ways to make powers of numbers.

"Uh, Bhaaj," Max said after a bit. "Are you going to investigate or just play the game?"

I sighed. "All right. Enough." After scanning the display, I flicked a holicon that read *chat*. A list of Dezi Marchland's conversations with other players appeared. Mostly they talked about the weather, game strategies, and glitches in how Power Meld ran, including several that irked me, like how it couldn't fit large numbers on a cube, so they stuck over the edge.

"Anything interesting?" Max asked.

"Nothing stands out." I scrolled to chats from a few tendays ago. A banner announced *Special today, get three boomers to blow away cubes, only 15 credits*. "Huh. She gets those annoying ads, too." Its background looked like an aristocrat's castle exploding with gusto. A chat with someone called PowerPlayer13 came up next, the two of them discussing the strategy of combining smaller numbers in lower powers so the value of the cubes didn't spiral out of control.

"Marchland plays at a pretty basic level," I mused. I knew too much strategy, having wasted far too many hours playing this game.

"Whoever she's talking to doesn't seem that advanced, either," Max said.

"Look at the avatar for the person using the name PowerPlayer13."

"You mean the holicon of the number thirteen? Not the most creative image."

"Max, it's familiar." I moved my finger through their avatar, making the 13 ripple. "Can you check the chats on my Power Meld account? I think I've talked with PowerPlayer13."

Max paused. "Ah. Yes, you're right. When you lived in Selei City, you and PowerPlayer13 used to talk strategy now and then, and at a much higher level than they did with Marchland."

"It looks like they match their skill level to the person on the chat."

"They might be pretending to know less to put Marchland at ease. Or to hustle her."

"Maybe." Something felt off. "Can you identify PowerPlayer13?"

"Of course not," Max said. "To crack the system that way would violate privacy laws. Also, any evidence you obtained as a result wouldn't hold up in court."

"I can get a warrant. That takes time, though. The killer might strike again while we wait."

"It would be out of character for them to kill so soon after the last death."

"Possibly." I waited.

"I know what you're doing, Bhaaj. I'm not going to crack the system and tell you that PowerPlayer13 uses a fake ID for their account." Max paused. "That's odd."

"What?" I smiled. "That you aren't going to tell me they use a fake ID?"

"No. That I'm not going to tell you their account

belongs to someone who, according to my preliminary searches, doesn't exist."

I frowned, no longer amused. "My specialty in the army was problem-solving. I analyzed Trader covert methods. This reminds me of a technique they used, where they'd play popular games and give themselves unremarkable identities, often similar to the game with a number attached, as if they were one of many people with that name. They'd chat with other players about innocuous topics, all the while trying to crack the mesh system of their targets."

"It seems a bit of a stretch to say this is the same," Max said.

"Yah." I flicked out of the chat and closed down the game. "Send a note to Chief Hadar, anyway. Tell him why I think it might be significant. We need to check the accounts of Subida Habil and Tejas Akarya, and he can get access faster than me."

"Message sent."

I took a breath. "It's time to talk to Colonel Majda. See if you can get through to the palace."

"We didn't find a problem," Lavinda's voice came from the console in my office. We had only an audio connection, no visual. She sounded normal, though, no distortion or loss of signal, her voice as rich and as resonant as always.

"The telop couldn't find my clearance." Wryly I added, "She thought I was a nut case."

"It sounds annoying," Lavinda said. "We're looking into it. Probably she accessed the wrong protocol."

I didn't know what "accessing the wrong protocol,"

meant, but I could recognize evasion when I heard it. I'd never had any problem contacting the Majdas. If anything, they claimed I didn't send them enough updates during a case. Then again, I'd never tried to contact them from offworld before. "Maybe it has to do with the gate into Kyle space."

"Maybe." Lavinda sounded odd. I wouldn't usually have noticed given her Iotic accent, which tended to overwhelm subtleties in tone, at least to my ear. After nearly three years, though, I knew her well enough to sense that something was off.

"Did you want an update on the case here?" I asked. "I'm doing interviews. I found a detail that maybe points to the Traders. Max is sending you a report."

"We've also wondered about the Traders. That isn't why I commed you, though. I wanted to let you know I'm coming to Parthonia."

I almost said, *What the blazes for?* but caught myself in time. Instead I spoke with courtesy. "I can meet you at the starport."

"No need. I'm coming on a private ship. A Majda delegation will meet us at a private gate in the port. I just wanted to let you know. We can meet for lunch after I arrive."

Meet for lunch. People like Lavinda didn't hang out with people like me for lunch or anything else. Curious, I said, "I look forward to it."

"Very well. Good day." With that, she cut the link.

"Huh," I muttered. "That was strange."

"She wants something from you," Max said. "She doesn't want to talk about it on comm."

I thought about it. "Oh. Yah, I can guess what. She wants to find out what's up with her nephew, Dayj, now that he's at university. I'll bet she wants me to keep an eye on him."

"That would make sense." Max didn't sound convinced.

"I'm hearing a 'but' in there."

"The colonel wouldn't need to come here just for that. She could tell you over a comm link."

I snorted. "She's a powerful woman. She has plenty of reasons to come here, most of which have nothing to do with me."

"Well, yes. That's true." He sounded far too convinced by my lack of importance.

"I need you to get me another line to Raylicon," I said.

"To the palace? Why?"

"Not the palace. I do have friends on the planet, you know."

"Not who have access to the Kyle tech needed for an interstellar link."

"Jak does." My notorious husband.

"Ah. One moment. I'm contacting the offworld telop."

"It better not be the one from yesterday," I muttered.

A woman's voice came over the comm, all too familiar. "My greetings. May I help you?"

Oh, well. "Yes, I need to set up a Kyle link to the world Raylicon."

Her voice cooled. "To the Majda palace? I don't think so."

Damn. She recognized my voice. "I just talked to them."

"Did you now?"

I gritted my teeth and then made myself stop. "Check your Kyle logs. You'll find the link under secured protocols."

"I'm sure I'll find many secured links. This is a governmental center. I'm also sure you are aware that on a secured link, I can't identify who talked to whom. Rather convenient, hmmm?"

Yah, well, fuck you, too. "Look, I don't want to argue. The Majdas are checking as to why you couldn't find my clearance to talk to them." Let her chew on that. "Right now I need to contact the EI called Royal Flush at the Kyle address 00942UR."

"One moment." The frost in her voice could have cracked glass. "That link connects to the undercity on Raylicon." She spoke the name of my home as if it didn't deserve capitalization. "I cannot put you through."

Seriously? She had no justification for refusing a perfectly good link. "Whyever not?" I asked. "You don't have enough security to access it?"

"Lady, look, if you insist on abusing your Kyle access, I'll report you to the authorities."

"Go ahead," I told her. "We'll see what they have to say about your refusing me service."

"Give me your name, ID, and citizenship status," she said coldly.

Screw that. "I assume you have a warrant allowing you access to my personal information."

Bhaaj, Max warned, using an accelerated mode. *This isn't helping. Take the high road.*

What high road?

Another Earth idiom. It means choosing the route with the highest moral value.

Why should I? She sure as hell isn't.

Because you're the better person. Before I had a chance to tell him I didn't care, he added, It also makes you look better. So if you lodge a complaint, you look like the aggrieved party, not a troublemaker.

Oh, all right.

The telop was saying, "I don't need a warrant."

Well, that was a lie. I wanted to call her out, but that would back her into a corner. Max was right, this would escalate. Ultimately I'd probably come out ahead, but not before it drew attention I wanted to avoid. So I took a breath and tried Max's high road, offering her a way out. "Ma'am, I'm sorry, I really don't want to argue." I did my best to project sincerity. "I understand my requests may seem unusual. Please be assured I'm not trying to abuse the system. I genuinely need to contact the Undercity on Raylicon."

"I don't see why. No one there has access to the Kyle mesh." Her tone implied no one there had enough worth to justify such access.

"If you set up a link to the address I gave you, it should go through." Jak served the decadent glitterati of an empire in his sensually luxurious casino. Some of his wealthiest customers came from offworld. Although his casino violated a multitude of laws on Raylicon, gambling was legal on many worlds, including here. He kept his Kyle address discreet but open, so he didn't turn away potential clients.

"I've already told you," she said coldly. "I can't open a line to that address."

I'd had enough, high road or not. Legally, she couldn't

refuse unless the address was unlisted, like the palace. "Then put me through to your superior at the Bureau of Offworld Communications."

Silence. She knew she could lose her job for denying people access to the Kyle mesh.

"That won't be necessary," she finally said. "One moment please."

"Thank you." To Max, I thought, *I don't think your top road worked.*

It helped defuse the situation. You could have ended up with Chief Hadar wondering why you're making waves. Instead you have a record of you being polite while she refused you service. He paused. Well, you being marginally polite.

I'm trying.

The woman spoke on comm. "Line open. I'm connecting you with Raylicon."

"Thanks," I answered, instead of what I really wanted to say, which involved words better left off an official transcript.

A deep, sensual voice poured out of the comm. "Hello, Bhaaj."

"Eh, Royal." I'd know Jak's EI anywhere. Royal Flush. He'd named his ultra-high end EI after the legendary poker hand that earned him the credits he needed to start his casino.

"Would you like to talk to Jak?" Royal asked. "He's on the main floor, but I can ask him to take this link in his office."

Smart EI, to know I needed to talk to Jak in private. I didn't trust that the telop wouldn't break the law and try listening. Jak's office, however, had better security even than the military. He had to, given the illegality of his operations in certain places, like where he lived and did business.

"Thanks, Royal," I said. "That would be good."

"One moment." He managed to make even those two words sound illicit.

We waited. A few moments later, a man's deep voice came from the comm, a bit like Royal, but more gravely. "Eh, Bhaajo."

"Eh, Jak." I slipped into the abbreviated dialect we spoke in the Undercity. Two words for a greeting; that was practically the equivalent of saying, *Ho! I'm so glad to talk to you.*

"Got security on," he said.

"Good." That would cut out the telop, if she'd tried to listen. "Got problem."

"Already?" He sounded amused.

Pah. Everyone found me funny today, or at least he and Max. "Strange case."

"Someone try to whack you?" Now he sounded worried. My "strangest" cases usually involved people trying to end my ability to have a pulse.

"Don't know," I admitted.

"How not know?"

"Cybers creeping around."

"That means what?"

"Messed with my biomech. With Max. Put me in fake VR. Kill me? Maybe. We blocked."

"Eh." Jak took a moment to digest my lengthy speech. "Damn."

"Yah," I agreed.

"Part of case?"

"Not know. Maybe. Maybe not."

"Not know much," he grumbled.

"Yet." I always found answers. Eventually.

"I help?" he asked.

"Yah. Send me Ruzik and Angel."

"Fuck no!"

"Fuck, yah," I growled.

"Never leave Undercity. Can't leave *planet*."

"Leave Undercity a lot."

"Nahya. Never."

"Yah. Last year, Angel, Ruzik, work case. With me."

"I ken this, Bhaajo. I there, too."

"Yah. Fought at our side."

"In desert. At night. Most like Undercity you can get."

"Don't need same as Undercity. They can leave world."

"What for?"

"Dust Knights." It was what I called my tykado students. "Time to stop hiding."

"Go offworld? Got no idea how."

"Who? Them or you?" The suggestion that he couldn't send them offworld because he didn't know how would annoy him, maybe enough that he would help just to prove me wrong.

Jak spoke in perfect Skolian Flag. "I am perfectly well aware of how to make reservations for flights to and from the Raylicon starport." He knew exactly what I was doing, and he wasn't buying it. "'Knowing how' to do it and 'Should' do it are not the same."

"Both true here."

"Ruzik, Angel, they say nahya. Not go."

"They say yah." I'd seen their wanderlust when they gazed at the night sky above the desert.

After a silence, he said, "Maybe talk to them. See what they say." His voice lightened. "Dust Knights loose in Selei City. What a thought, eh?"

"Yah." I smiled. "Talk again soon."

"Yah. Good talk."

"Yah, good." We were being overly romantic with all these words, good and good again. In our dialect, that was practically a passionate declaration of love. Of course we didn't talk about emotions. Even so. We knew what we meant.

Afterward, I sat musing. Ruzik and Angel would come, and not only because of wanderlust. I was their tykado teacher, what the official league called a *sabneem*. It wasn't that different from some teacher titles on Earth, like sensi or sabumnim, but for my Knights, it had layers of meaning never intended in martial arts. They also considered me a gang leader, one who headed all the Dust Knights, a designation I suspected the Interstellar Tykado Federation wouldn't appreciate.

The Dust Knights of Cries. I'd started with children in the Undercity, but adults soon joined, like Ruzik and his girlfriend Angel, who was about as angelic as an asteroid smasher. Initially I hadn't thought past teaching a few gangers some martial arts moves. When more and more of them kept showing up, I realized I could use tykado to create a network of support that offered a purpose beyond running and fighting. It helped give them confidence, along with a community that guided them. I coined Dust

Knights because I wanted them to stop calling themselves dust rats. The Knights weren't actually from Cries; they came from the Undercity. The title fit better in our monosyllabic dialect, though, and the word "cries" felt right for a group formed out of the anguish, loss, and struggle we lived every day in the Undercity.

When I'd joined the army tykado team all those years ago, I'd had to relearn the rough-tumble of street fighting. It took me a while to comprehend that tykado was a *sport* with rules. You couldn't do whatever you wanted to pulverize your opponent. Although I'd loved competing, I first had to stop getting disqualified for using illegal moves. I memorized the rulebook, though it seemed silly to forbid certain actions that worked perfectly well, like smashing my opponent in the knees. Soon I realized the point wasn't to knock them out, it was to show I could fight better. Ho! A challenge. I thrived.

In the Undercity, not only did dust gangs defend their territory with the rough-tumble, they also challenged other gangs just to show they could best them. I hoped tykado, with its philosophy of violence as a last resort, would give them something more civilized to do than pounding each other senseless. It also let me introduce new ideas to my people, who were notoriously suspicious of outsiders. I wanted them to know we had choices, that they didn't have to spend their lives clawing at each other for limited resources. True change wouldn't come from outside, from charity kitchens or the above-city forcing our children into state schools. It started within the hidden culture of the Undercity, where exquisite beauty and crushing poverty existed side by side.

To join the Knights, recruits had to swear to the Code. They agreed to abide by the rules of tykado, practice every day, lay off drugs, and get an education. We had no schools, so I got them books, put more academically adept Knights in charge of less experienced students, and yah, I looked the other ways when they filched time on the school meshes used by the wealthy above-city slicks. I'd scrabbled that way to get my education, enough so I could pass the exams the army required when I enlisted.

For me, however, the most important part of the Code came to this: Knights had to swear they would never commit vengeance murder. I lost recruits that way, but I never wavered. Commit murder—not self-defense, but killing for vengeance or sport—and the Knights put you on trial. Punishment ranged from supporting the circle of your victim to banishment, a sentence that could amount to death. Now that the military knew about the Kyle gifts in our population, we had to be careful. We couldn't keep our autonomy if we didn't police ourselves. Unless we strengthened our community from within, the above-city would try to do it themselves, crushing our way of life without realizing what they destroyed in our lives under the desert.

Maybe the time had come for the Knights to step into the sun.

CHAPTER VI

SHATTERED PIECES

I rode the glass-enclosed lift down the side of the co-op, enjoying the glow of sunlight that filled the car. It took me from the twentieth floor to the ground, offering a glorious view of the surrounding parks. Nestled among the trees and paths, a small café offered round tables and wicker chairs. Even from so far away, I could see that Xira had already arrived, taking her seat at the table where we always met. It was hard to believe nearly three years had passed since the last time we got together. I so looked forward to seeing her. Thinking about it, I felt relaxed for the first time since I'd arrived on Parthonia yesterday. The lift reached the ground and I stepped out into the sunshine—

A huge force hurled me forward while thunder roared. I sailed through the air and slammed into the ground so hard that the world darkened around me.

Combat mode toggled, Max thought.

My internal libraries took over, controlling the bio-hydraulics in my body even though I was only half-conscious. I scrambled to my feet and sprinted away from whatever had just happened. All around me, people shouted and alarms screamed.

As my head cleared, I gulped in air and slowed down, turning to walk backward. People all over were also backing away, gaping at the co-op. In my heightened mode, everyone seemed to move in slow motion. Only ruins remained of the building I'd just left. Its left side had exploded, leaving no more than a bare framework standing, the reinforced beams that supported the structure.

Max, what the hell happened?

I think a bomb went off inside the co-op.

People are in there! We have to go back, get them out. I swung around, looking toward the bistro, searching for Xira, but too many people blocked my view.

The rest of the building is about to collapse, Max thought. You can't go back.

Chaos surrounded me. Chunks of casecrete and the blunted shards of supposedly shatterproof windows lay everywhere like pieces of a jigsaw puzzle strewn across the ground. Dust swirled, filling the day with an acrid, scorched stench and turning the sunlight gray. People called out names of friends or loved ones, shouted for help, checked their wristbands.

A flyer wheeled over the crumbling remains of the building. "Clear the area," an amplified voice boomed. "Move away from the building."

As people scattered, the flyer set down in a nearby plaza. The wail of sirens vibrated in the air. Several hovercars whirred into view from behind buildings and settled in a park near the co-op.

"Bhaaj!" a woman yelled.

I turned to see Xira standing outside the barrier the rescue workers were setting up. I closed my eyes, hit with a relief so intense it felt visceral. Looking again, I waved and shouted, "I'm fine."

"You aren't fine," Max said. "You're in combat mode, so you can't feel your injuries because your nanomeds are pumping you with stimulants and painkillers."

I took a breath, trying to steady my pulse. "Did I take any serious damage?"

"I don't believe so. But you should get checked by a medic."

"Can you reach Highcloud?"

Max paused, and that in itself answered my question. After a moment, he said, "I'm sorry."

I bit my lip, telling myself copies of Highcloud existed. Then I remembered: we kept the server that did backups in the basement of the co-op, which right now lay in ruins. I'd been meaning to back up Highcloud elsewhere, too, but I'd been gone for years, so I hadn't gotten around to it yet.

"Damn," I whispered.

"Help, please!" The faint shout barely reached even my enhanced hearing.

"Max, that came from inside the detonation zone." I walked around the perimeter of the worst debris, searching for the source of the cry.

"Help!" The call came from up ahead, deeper within the wreckage.

"Ma'am, you have to leave," a woman said at my side. "You must get behind the perimeter set up by our emergency response teams."

I turned with a start, my adrenaline jumping. A woman in an ER suit was walking at my side.

"You must go now," she repeated, her expression firm behind the clear screen of her hood.

Combat mode off. I didn't want my reflexes to kick me into an attack. *Send her my ID.*

To the woman, I said, "I'm trained to assist in emergencies. Major Bhaajan, retired, Pharaoh's Army. Can I help here?" I motioned toward the debris. "Someone in there is calling for help. I have biomech sensors that will help locate them."

"I'm verifying your ID." Her gaze took on the inwardly directed look people got when they accessed their EI. She wore full tech-mech gauntlets similar to mine and carried herself with a reassuring sense of authority. Gray streaked her curly brown hair, creating a distinguished look, and she had smooth, flawless skin with just a few lines of age. It looked natural, not the too-perfect creation of bodysculpting or overzealous nanomeds. I liked her straightforward attitude, so refreshing after the politics I'd dealt with recently.

The lieutenant was also giving me the once over, taking in my gauntlets and clothes. "You look like you got blasted with dust from the collapse."

"I was on the edge of the explosion." I actually wasn't sure about that, but I'd survived, so I couldn't have been much closer. Thank the saints no one else rode down with me in the lift. Someone without biomech and combat training wouldn't have walked away from that blast.

"You have solid credentials, Major." She considered me. "Normally we don't involve civilians unconnected with our units. With something this bad and this sudden, though, we could use qualified help. My CO is checking— yes, she says you're cleared." She nodded to me. "Welcome to the team."

"Whatever I can do." The full emotional impact of the explosion hadn't yet registered on my brain. I needed to move, to help, to do *something* to handle the swell of shock and disbelief.

She pulled a packet off her belt and shook it until the square expanded into a reinforced helmet with a face screen. Handing it to me, she said, "Wear this at all times. And you have on smart clothes, yes? They look combat ready, in fact." She raised her eyebrows. "That's a high level of protection for someone walking in a residential area."

"I'm on a case." She'd know from my ID that I worked as a PI, which would explain why I wore clothes with reinforced intelligent cloth.

"I'm Lieutenant René Silvers." She looked out over the wreckage. "Where did you hear the calls for help?"

I donned the helmet, then motioned toward an area where none of the building remained. "Over there."

We walked forward, picking our way through jagged chunks of casecrete. We probably weren't close enough to the remains of the co-op to get hit if more debris fell, but we couldn't take anything for granted. In the more unstable areas, they'd bring machines to do the clearing.

Max, ramp up my hearing, sight, and reflexes. Not full combat mode, though. Keep the battle libraries in standby. I don't want to attack anyone.

Done.

My hearing amplified, picking up the whisper of dust

particles blowing across the rubble. We neared a wall of the building that still stood, about one story high, its broken edges jagged against the sky. I could hear the low groans of stressed materials, but no human voice.

I stopped. "That wall up ahead isn't stable. I can hear it creaking."

Silvers nodded as I moved back. "Can you still hear the calls for help?"

I strained to catch the sound. Nothing.

I'm getting life signs ahead to the left. Max sent me coordinates. *The signals are weak but steady.*

"Something is there." I motioned toward where the lift had formerly exited the co-op. Nothing of the building there remained standing. Wind blew eerily across the wreckage, stirring gray and blue swirls of dust. It looked like something in a horror holo-vid, where ghostly creatures might coalesce out of the gritty haze.

"It's ahead by about four meters," I said. "And to the left." No creaks or groans came from the debris there, either structural or supernatural. Nothing remained of the building to moan.

Silvers flicked her fingers across her gauntlet. "I'm not getting a warning for that area. If that changes, we move away fast. Got it?"

I nodded. "Understood."

We made our way through mounds of rubble heaped in what used to be a plaza fronting the co-op. I stepped over a long bar, some half-melted beam that had once supported a wall. I couldn't take it in yet, that only moments ago, I'd walked through a graceful exit arch here into sunshine.

"Please . . ." The voice faded into a whisper.

"There." I motioned to a heap of rubble a few meters ahead, where debris had piled into a hill taller than either of us. "Can you hear us?" I yelled. "Can you speak?"

No answer.

"Heya!" Silvers shouted. "Call out so we can find you." As we picked our way toward the heap of blasted rubble, she spoke to me in a low voice. "If that fell on someone, I don't see how they survived."

"You never know what people have in their body. My enhanced skeletal structure can endure far more weight than a normal body." I raised my voice and shouted, "Call out if you can!"

Silvers walked around the mound, scrutinizing the jagged casecrete and wood. A scatter of debris rattled down the pile and clattered across the ground. Breezes stirred our hair, and dust blew against my face screen, which cleaned away the dirt.

"I'm here." The voice came a little more strongly this time, with a hint of hope.

"I hear you!" I called. "But I can't see you." I didn't dare move the wreckage, not without equipment to stop the mound from shifting or collapsing. "Can you call out again?"

"Here . . ." The voice faded.

Silvers came up next to me. "They're *inside* all that rubble. If we try to dig them out, it could collapse and crush them. And us." She spoke into her gauntlet comm. "Silvers here. We have someone buried under an unstable load of debris. We need nets, safety-rails, and hazard drills."

"All the equipment on site is already in use," a voice answered. "We have more on the way. I'll send it over as soon as it arrives. Keep your gauntlet beacon active."

"Will do," Silvers said.

Max thought, **Bhaaj, the life signs from whoever is under that debris are weakening.**

"I don't think we have time to wait," I told Silvers.

She studied the rubble, her gauntlets flickering. "Maybe we could move the larger blocks."

"The pile will collapse if you move the wrong pieces," Max said.

Silvers started. "Who is that?"

"My EI," I said. "I've been communicating with him via neural threads. He probably spoke so we could both hear his updates."

"Yes," Max said. "I am analyzing the debris for points of stability."

"Good." Silvers walked to the right around the mound, and I went in the other direction.

"Are you there?" I called.

No answer.

"Max, what vitals are you getting?" I asked.

"Not much. I'm not sure they're breathing anymore."

Silvers rounded the pile and came over, her face creased with strain. "I can't see them."

"We need to start digging," I said. "Whoever is in there will die if we don't."

"I'm pretty sure they're closer to the other side."

I went with her to the place she believed placed us nearest to the survivor. "Max?" I asked. "Can we get any closer?"

"A few steps to the left, but according to my scans, the wreckage is less stable there."

I looked at Silvers. She looked back at me. "We'll try here," she said.

We started to dig, so very, very carefully. I took large pieces from higher on the pile, since the lower parts supported the upper sections. As soon as we removed even a few boulders, however, the pile shifted.

"We need supports." She tapped her comm. "Silvers, here. Can you get any equipment over here at all? Anything that could support unstable debris?"

"Sorry, ma'am," a man said. "Not yet. It should only be a few more minutes, though."

"Gloves out," I said in a low voice. "Activate spikes."

Gloves snapped out of my gauntlets and molded around my hands, strong and flexible. They extruded their spikes that glinted in the dusty light. I braced my shoulder under an edge in the rubble, with the hill above pressing down on me. My muscles strained as I took the weight of casecrete chunks onto my arms and shoulders.

I regarded Silvers. "Now you have a support beam."

"What? No." She scowled at me. "You can't support that much weight. You'll be crushed."

"Got biomech," I grunted. "Enhanced skeleton and muscles. I've supported worse." Not much, but I'd manage. *Max, monitor my biomech. Let me know if you get any danger signs.*

You're fine for now. I'd suggest you move your support slightly to your left.

I edged over, using the spikes from my gloves to anchor

my body more firmly into the pile. "Go," I told Silvers. "Dig under me."

"You've got guts, I'll say that." She went to work, moving with care. The pile shifted, and I held up the blocks, supporting them as Silvers cleared a cavity beneath my body. The rubble slid on my body, then caught as my smart clothes changed texture, creating more friction.

"I see someone!" Silvers called. She kept going, with excruciating care.

I said nothing, concentrating on the debris I was holding. It shifted, and I pushed against it, leaning so I could bear the weight of a large piece on my back.

"Can you hear me?" Silvers asked, most of her body under mine as she cleared more blocks.

I didn't answer. She wasn't talking to me. I gritted my teeth, straining to keep the debris from shifting again. If I lost control now, it could smash all three of us.

"Here," Silvers said, her voice muffled. "I've cleared a tunnel. You need to crawl out."

A groan came from under the rubble, followed by the scrape of stone against stone. More debris shifted, and I gasped as a heavy chunk dug into my shoulder.

Bhaaj, you can't do this for much longer, Max said. **Your shoulders could break.**

"Silvers," I rasped. "I'm just about done."

"Almost there." Debris scraped under me. "Come on," she coaxed. "Only a little more.

The casecrete felt like drills bearing into my shoulders. My arms burned. I leaned into the weight, bending over, protecting whatever was happening below me. I didn't dare look; the slightest wrong movement and I'd lose control of the pile.

"That's it," Silvers said. More scraping, and in my side vision I saw her pulling a youth out of the ruins, supporting his neck.

"You free yet?" I grunted.

"Almost," Silvers said.

In the same instant Max said, **You have to get out!** I groaned and gave a great shove, heaving debris away from Silvers while I stumbled back. As soon as I lost my grip, chunks of casecrete thundered down, their collapse like the bark of a gun. It knocked me to my knees, and I threw myself forward, aiming for Silvers and her rescued patient, protecting my head with my arms. I landed on the two of them as rocks fell around us, pounding my legs. Something large tumbled across my back like a freight car that had plunged off its track.

Smaller chunks rained down, rattling on the broken ground.

More pebbles fell, scattering.

Silence.

After a moment, when nothing else happened, I muttered, "Gods almighty. Are we alive?"

"Major?" That came from someone beneath me, Silvers it sounded like. "Can you move?"

I shifted my weight, edging out from under the block that lay across my back. It rolled off and thumped across the ground.

"Ah!" That groan came from someone else.

With great care, I turned onto my side, checking my surroundings as I moved. Both Silvers and a young man lay next to me. Debris had fallen all around us and half the mound had collapsed.

"Ungh," I said, ever articulate.

Silvers lifted her head to look at her patient. "We have to get him medical help."

"And fast," Max said. "His life signs are faltering."

I struggled to my knees, slow and cautious, aware of the unstable debris. "We need to get away from this stuff."

With her body braced on her palms, Silvers looked down at the youth she'd saved from the wreckage. He lay on his back, his eyes closed, his face pale, dust covering his body and hair. Blood stained his clothes everywhere, particularly his torso and limbs.

"Can you hear me?" Silvers asked the youth. "We're bringing help."

He opened his eyes to look at her. That was enough. He still lived.

"Ho, Lieutenant Silvers!" That shout came from out in the plaza. "We've got nets for you." A flyer hummed above us, and a net fell across my back. We managed to wrap it around the young man, fastening him into the smart web of the mesh. It shifted, making its best estimate for how it needed to cradle his body. Silvers grabbed a hook that came down with the net, so as the flyer lifted out the survivor, it pulled her upward as well.

I didn't try to hold on; I doubted it could hoist all three of us out without bouncing around the boy. Instead, I crawled away from what remained of the pile, aware of debris shifting. When I deemed it safe, I jumped up and sprinted away, jumping over blocks of casecrete, headed for the clear areas beyond the main collapse. Behind me, the mound thundered as the rest of it collapsed.

Advise deactivating combat mode, Max thought. **It's straining your body, especially where you held up that pile of casecrete.**

I slowed down, heaving in deep breaths. *Toggle me out.*

Done.

As my adrenaline eased, I realized I'd reached the edge of the plaza. Although I'd left the most dangerous area, rubble and shards of glass lay all around. Dust caked my entire body.

Two people ran toward me, a woman and a man in ER uniforms. "Are you all right?" the man asked as they reached me. The round patch of a medic showed on the sleeve of his uniform.

"That rescue was incredible," the woman said. "I'm surprised you held all that weight."

"Got training." I didn't have energy for more than the terse Undercity dialect.

"How is your back?" The medic ran a scanner over my body.

"Fine." I had no idea if that was true, but I hadn't heard or felt anything crack, and I'd walked over here.

"Why did you do that?" the woman asked. "We were sending for more equipment."

"That boy would have died by the time the equipment arrived." I took a ragged breath, aware now of the wind blowing across my face, of ER workers all across the scene, of voices calling and crying. "We could help, so we did."

The doctor finished his scan. "You've got one hell of a lot of biomech."

"Army officer," I said. "Retired." I'd also upgraded my biomech after I retired. "Am I fit to keep working on the ER crew?"

He studied the data on his gauntlet. "It looks like you've stressed your augmented skeletal structure. I know it's self-repairing, but only to a certain extent. You should have a biomech adept look at it. For now, you can keep working, but I'd advise against using your augmentation until you get that checkup." He looked up at me. "If you're up to it. No one would criticize you for leaving."

"I'm good." I motioned to the chaos around us. "I can still help."

The woman nodded to me, her face creased with sweat and grime. "I haven't seen a disaster this bad in years. We could use all the help we can get."

So I went to work.

They put me on a crew checking the perimeter for survivors while other crews deployed cranes and smart bots to remove wreckage, a far safer method than what Silvers and I had used. For many of the people caught in the collapse, however, our efforts came too late. Many died, either on impact or because no one reached them in time.

The day had faded into evening when I took a break, sitting on a large block of casecrete a bot had rolled to one side of the plaza. I closed my eyes, giving in to the exhaustion. ER crews and hazard bots had shored up the south wall, keeping it from collapse while they searched for survivors—or bodies. As the dust cleared from the air, sensors worked better, making it easier to locate people.

The day had taken its toll, but at least my help here did a small part in honoring those lost to the destruction.

I opened my eyes to see a police officer approaching through the sunset light. Ho! Chief Hadar. He sat next to me on the block, which was plenty big enough for two people.

"I heard you were helping out down here," Hadar said. "Thank you."

"Least I could do."

"The least you could have done way was walk away. A lot of people would have." He looked me over. "You're covered in cuts and bruises."

I grimaced. "It's been a rough day."

"We've taken reports from all the witnesses." He spoke quietly. "Except one."

"Who'd you miss?"

"You. Several witnesses reported seeing a woman who fits your description hurled through the air." He shook his head. "I found the footage, Major. The city security records show you being thrown from the building by the explosion. Most people couldn't have even stood up after what happened to you, let alone run back toward the wreckage."

"It was part of my army training. That's one reason we have biomech." Bitterly I added, "Makes us better soldiers. Hell, we're not that different from the battle drones." As a grunt, I hadn't thought much about the way they used us interchangeably with drones. I expected to fight. I'd done it all my life. As I worked my way into the officer ranks, my view changed. Yah, people reacted with better intelligence than drones, or at least some did, but using people that way felt wrong. I'd worked on introducing changes, but I had to balance those efforts with the political necessities of keeping my position and what small influence I'd gained. Yet another reason I hated politics.

Hadar was tapping on his gauntlet, setting up a recording unit. "I can take your statement."

I nodded, grateful he'd waited until I had a break. With people dying even as we struggled to reach them, I hadn't wanted to stop. "The building blew up."

"And?"

"And it blew up."

He spoke wryly. "I was hoping you might have more to add."

"I don't really. Your recordings probably show more than I could tell you."

"You were fortunate you were leaving. Even a few seconds earlier and the blast would have caught you inside the lift shaft. Its collapse probably would have killed you."

I grunted my agreement. I had no idea what had caused the explosion. Why target this co-op in particular? I didn't want to think it had anything to do with my living there, but given my link to this case, I couldn't ignore the possibility.

"Did you notice anything unusual before the explosion?" he asked.

I thought back to that moment, which seemed like eons ago. "Nothing. A few strange things have happened since I arrived in Selei City yesterday, though." I told him about Greyjan's, the cyclist, Max's suspicion I'd been followed other times, and my problems contacting the Majdas.

He stared at me. "That's what you call *a few* strange things? Why didn't you report it to us?"

I gave him a dour look. "How do I know the police aren't involved?"

"Why would you think that?"

I felt too wound up for courtesy. "Someone leaked my coming here to the press even though I specifically requested no announcements. That leak compromised the investigation and possibly my safety. Mostly only your people knew."

"I don't know how your involvement got out," he said. "But I vouch for my people."

I shifted my weight, trying to let go of the tension that had driven me all day. "Chief Hadar, I lived in this co-op. My friend Xira witnessed the explosion from the bistro outside the plaza. She says the blast came from the first floor."

"Directly below your apartment," Max added.

Chief Hadar started, and I held up my hand. "That was my EI."

"I've mapped the detonation based on the blast pattern," Max said. "Your floor, number twenty, only has two units. The rest have three. No apartment lay directly below yours."

"What's your implication?" Hadar asked. "That Major Bhaajan was the target?"

I scowled. "If someone wanted to blow me up, easier methods exist and most don't involve killing other people." If they didn't care about that kind of collateral damage, it said a lot about the bomber, all of it uglier than sin.

"I don't like coincidences," Max said.

Neither did I. I also didn't know how I would handle my guilt if it turned out the bomber chose the co-op because I lived there.

"We don't know who they targeted." Hadar motioned toward the ruins. "They probably placed the bomb on the first floor because it has marginally less security than the tower."

I met his gaze. "To plant a bomb even on the ground floor would mean the killer knew how to manipulate building security. That's impossible without access to city systems at a high level."

"Making you suspicious of anyone connected at that level." Hadar spoke dryly. "Like me."

I exhaled. "I don't know who to trust."

"If it helps to know," he said, "we've made progress on the tip you gave us about that game, Power Meld. The other two murder victims also chatted with PowerPlayer13."

I sat up straighter. "Can you identify who uses that name?"

"We're doing a trace to find their identity." Hadar inclined his head to me. "You may have broken in the case, Major, ferreting out a Trader plot."

"Yah. I suppose."

"I thought you'd be more excited," Hadar said. "Only one day and you found a clue the rest of us missed."

"That's just it." I shook my head. "It's too easy. Of course it looks like the Traders. The three targets had military funding, and now we find this link that implies a Trader agent." I tried to focus my doubt. "Captain, I'm a problem solver. I investigate. My forte in the army was studying covert Trader operations. I had to think how they thought, put my mind into theirs. So yah, I figured out the business with the game players."

His forehead creased. "I don't see why that bothers you."

"Because I did that ten years ago. Back then, a mole with a name like PowerPlayer13 was new. Not anymore. People know the Traders tried to infiltrate Skolian accounts with fake players."

Hadar shrugged. "Lots of people still do it. Or at least, they try."

"Yah, *a lot* of people, Eubian, Skolian, Allied." This clue felt more wrong by the moment. "That's why so many verifications exist now to ensure players are real. And where is this PowerPlayer13? They had real-time chats with at least four people, counting me and the victims. To do that, either they're on-planet or they're using the Kyle mesh. Who uses an expensive interstellar network to play a game you can get anywhere? Even if it didn't break the law, which it does big time, it would draw too much attention. If this mole exists, they're probably here on Parthonia."

"You think Traders infiltrated Parthonia?" Hadar frowned. "The military has found nothing so far, but this new lead might help."

"Or it could waste their time." The whole thing seemed too clumsy. "I find it hard to believe the Traders could have an operation so sophisticated that they managed to plant an agent on Parthonia, evading our massive planetary defenses, yet they operate using such a dated technique."

"I'll forward your concerns to our ISC contacts." Hadar spoke grimly. "We'll find who—or what—caused this. They won't get away with it."

Damn right. When they attacked my home and my community, they'd made it personal.

✦ CHAPTER VII ✦
THE EI QUESTION

I sent out two of my beetles, Green and Red, to spy on Selei City. While Max continued to repair Blue, I went to meet Her Royal Highness, Colonel Lavinda Majda.

We had lunch at a café tucked under trees, their leafy branches heavy with white flowers shaped like bells. Glimpses of the lavender sky showed through the foliage. Servers moved among the tables, attractive and discreet. *Human* servers. That offered a major hint this placed rated as more than a typical eatery on a secluded street in a sparsely populated area. Most food places used robo-servers. You didn't have to pay them.

Lavinda looked less formal than usual, out of uniform, dressed in slacks and a white blouse. She'd pulled back her hair and held it by a gold clip at her neck. The style suited her, favoring her high cheekbones and Majda nose, with its straight lines, a rarity among my own people, who usually had their nose broken at least once by the time they reached adulthood. When I'd first met Lavinda, her aristocratic features had angered me. She lived a privileged life, one where she never had to worry about how she'd survive day to day. If she got a broken nose despite her rarified position, her doctors would fix it, unlike in the Undercity where we hadn't even had doctors until last year, when I convinced one to come down on a regular basis, part of the agreement I worked out with the Majdas to improve their relations with my people.

Sure, I'd known Lavinda spent time in the military. Plenty of nobles served, at least for a few years. I'd seen the preferential treatment they received, appointed to the best jobs, exposed to as little danger as possible. They never saw true combat. In the rare instances where they went into battle, their COs kept them in protected positions, showing them the favoritism granted to those who gained their wealth, power, and influence through hereditary titles. Eventually I realized it also had historical origins. In ancient times, House matriarchs commanded the armies. You want your army to conquer your enemies? Then don't kill the people who lead your forces. Protect the generals and their protégés. So sure, precedent existed to favor the nobles. It still pissed me off.

As I got to know Lavinda, though, I realized she never asked for special treatment. She'd worked through the ranks like anyone else and seen plenty of combat before she rose so high in the army hierarchy that they put her behind a desk. She wanted to earn her way, and she could do it because she was neither the heir nor the spare to the Majda throne. Lavinda was the youngest of the three sisters, so even if something happened to the Matriarch and all three of her daughters, the next in line was the middle Majda sister. It left Lavinda far enough down in the succession that they didn't need to keep her protected. At first she hadn't used the Majda name, so not even her COs knew her identity. She'd earned those medals the army gave her. She'd also earned my respect.

"I heard about the explosion yesterday before we landed," Lavinda was saying. "The news streamed across every console on the ship."

"Twenty-two people have died," I said. "The hospitals have a lot more in intensive care."

She was watching me closely. "The doctors tell me you were hit hard, not only from the blast, but also when you and the ER captain saved that young man from the wreckage."

I shrugged. "It wasn't anything serious."

"Bhaaj, don't give me that bullshit. I saw the report. If you weren't a trained fighter with biomech augmentation, you'd be dead."

"But I'm not." I tapped my arm. "All these changes we get to our bodies, they aren't just to protect *us*. I could help save that kid. So I did."

"That 'kid' is Evan Majors. He's the oldest son of the Metropoli Ambassador to Parthonia."

I stared at her. "Holy shit."

"That was articulate." She sounded like Max. Amused.

"The ambassador's family lives in the same co-op as me?" Although it was a nice building, or had been, it wasn't *that* upscale.

Lavinda shook her head. "Just his son. The boy attends Parthonia University. His parents live in the Metropoli embassy." Her voice quieted. "I couldn't help but think of my nephew Dayj. It could have been him."

"He lives with your brother, doesn't he?" I thought back to what Max had told me. "That's in the Sunrise District, if I recall. It's even better protected than embassy row."

"I suppose. It doesn't stop us from worrying. First Tam leaves. Now Dayj. Who next?"

I gave her a dour look. "The rest of the men in the Imperialate 'left' a long time ago."

The hint of a smile touched her face. "We Majdas are not complete barbarians, you know."

That was certainly a loaded statement. Of course they weren't barbarians; they were the elite of the elite. That didn't stop them from inflicting barbarically sexist customs on their men.

Lavinda continued to watch me with that intent look. I recognized it. She was trying to pick up my mood. Although the Houses claimed their members were all Kyle operators, many were marginal empaths or not at all. The traits did run stronger in their families, though. Lavinda was a full empath. Only one other population showed a higher concentration than the aristocracy—my people. That little fact would outrage the Houses, if they found out. However, it remained a military secret, known only to a few highly placed people in the government and ISC.

I just sat, letting her focus all she wanted. I'd learned to block my thoughts. I imagined a wall around my mind, spurring my brain to produce more of a neurotransmitter that blocked certain activity, making it harder to pick up my mood. I couldn't do it too much, or I'd lose consciousness, but fortunately it didn't take much to hide from a spying empath.

I said only, "My apology. I didn't mean to offend."

"You didn't." Lavinda spoke wryly. "Dayj and Tam are the first Majda princes to defy our traditions, but I doubt they will be the last. With Imperialate cultures opening up, and more freedom for everyone, I suspect more of our princes will demand their own lives."

I couldn't help my curiosity. "Your husband gave up his freedom when he married you."

"Ah. Yes." She shifted her weight in her chair. "It was an arranged marriage."

It didn't surprise me. From what I knew of Lavinda, her preference went to women, not men. In the ultraconservative universe of her House, though, the family required that she marry a suitable man from a suitable House and produce suitable little Majdas. Except the "little" Majdas were now adults with their own lives. "Your daughters moved away from the palace, yes?"

She nodded. "The older one works in finance at a corporation in the City of Cries. My younger daughter went to school on Metropoli to study architecture."

"Like your husband Paolo?" He did his work from seclusion, designing gorgeous buildings. He could never visit them, though, only see them via the mesh.

"Yes. He's a brilliant architect." She paused. "Paolo gave up more than you know." After a moment, she said, "Perhaps you do know. You have an uncanny ability to figure out what others don't see."

Well, that was awkward. Yah, I'd figured out Paolo

agreed to marry a woman he knew could never truly love him. Whatever price she and Paolo had paid for the marriage, though, they treated each other well, more as friends than as lovers.

Lavinda was still concentrating on me. Maybe she sensed my discomfort. In any case, she changed the subject. "My son wed a Rajindia noblewoman in an arranged marriage." Her face relaxed into a smile. "He seems happy. I don't think she really cares if he lives in seclusion. He's a musician, a flute player with the Selei Orchestra. He and his wife live here, in Selei City. Many of the concerts are virtual, but when they do live shows, he performs with them."

"He must be quite accomplished." You didn't get a position with an ensemble that renowned unless you could play like nobody's business. Your connections didn't matter; all auditions were blind. The group wouldn't risk its reputation as a stellar-class orchestra on anything less. "I can see why you wanted to come to Parthonia instead of just using the web."

Her smile faded and she spoke in a more neutral voice. "Seeing my family was one reason."

What else? Apparently she wanted privacy, more than she was willing to risk using the interstellar meshes. "If you'd like, we can go to the office in my apartment—" No, damn it, my office had collapsed along with the rest of the co-op. "Sorry, that won't work."

"It's all right. We can talk here." She motioned at the servers who faded into the background so easily, I'd forgotten they were there. "This place is more than private. My family runs it, with a staff hired from top security firms." Dryly she added, "You're as secluded here, Bhaaj, as when you go into the Undercity and hide behind all those illegal shrouds your people create down there."

"Ah. Um." I had no better response, or at least no safer one given that our cyber-riders protected our anonymity with black-market shrouds. So instead I asked, "What is it that you didn't want to talk about over the interstellar meshes?"

"Do you recall the EI called Oblivion?"

I froze. I'd expected more about Prince Dayj or the messy politics of my current case. Nearly two years had passed since we dealt with Oblivion, but I'd never forget that monstrous EI.

"Oblivion is dead." Erased, deleted, obliterated. It had taken three of the most powerful mesh forces in existence to defeat that ancient entity, the Ruby Pharaoh and the two most complex EIs that survived from the ancient Ruby Empire. I'd seen the Pharaoh's true genius that day, her gift for operating in Kyle space with a power and finesse no one else could manage. In our universe, she looked small, fragile even, but an indomitable chord of strength ran through her personality.

"Yes. Oblivion is gone," Lavinda said. "However, we've continued investigating its origins." When I tensed, she held up her hand. "We take great care in our explorations. We've no wish to awaken any more ancient mesh gods."

Indeed. Oblivion hadn't been a god, but if a baleful EI deity existed, that monstrous entity fit the bill. Oblivion had slumbered in the ruins of the abandoned starships on Raylicon for thousands of years, hidden. Although my ancestors plundered the ship libraries, they hadn't caused enough upheaval to wake Oblivion. We advanced over the millennia, creating ever more complicated mesh networks, until they saturated our civilization, from the tiny picowebs in our bodies to star-spanning webs. And finally all that digital "noise" woke up Oblivion. This much we surmised: Oblivion had destroyed whoever brought our ancestors to Raylicon. We had no idea why. Although they couldn't defeat the EI, they managed to shut it off even as it killed them.

"I've always thought of Oblivion as malevolent," I said. "But that's assigning a human emotion where none exist. It was *alien*, so different I couldn't comprehend it."

Lavinda grimaced. "Anything so determined to destroy humanity qualifies as malevolent in my book. If it had fully awoken before it attacked, it could have ended human civilization."

I was growing uneasy. Why did she bring this up now? "Is Oblivion still alive?"

She paused. "No. Not at all."

"But you think it might come back?"

"No, it's gone." She considered me. "I was thinking of how your clearance for the Majda palace vanished. No trace of it, no record of a deletion, nothing. It would take an EI to do that. Ever since we dealt with Oblivion, I've wondered if our own EIs also have a plan for humanity."

"May I make a comment?" Max asked. Then he added, "My greetings, Colonel. I'm Max."

"My greetings." Lavinda didn't sound surprised. She knew him from previous cases.

"Go ahead, Max," I said.

"If EIs were plotting to overthrow humanity, I would know. And I don't."

"No one said EIs were plotting to overthrow humanity," Lavinda told him.

"Even if they were, Max, how would you know?" I smiled. "You planning an EI coup?"

"No. As to how I would know, we all know everything."

"Max, we're being serious," I said.

"So am I. We EIs often limit our interactions, but if needed, we all can access one another."

"Access how?" Lavinda sounded more curious than anything else.

"Share all our information. Synch with one another."

"*All* of you?" I said. "How many EIs exist? Billions? Trillions? A zillion?"

"A zillion?" Max asked. "Is that a real number?"

"You know what I mean. An uncountable number." I shook my head. "I don't believe you know what every one of those EIs is doing. Like you could tell me what's going on with, say, the most secured EI in ISC?" As soon as I spoke, I wished I'd used a different example. The last thing I needed was ISC thinking I could contact their hidden nodes.

"No," Max said. "Those nodes choose to limit their interactions with the rest of us."

Lavinda shrugged. "It's not a choice. We programmed that into them."

"Essentially," Max answered.

"Say what you mean," I told him. "You can't be 'essentially' omnipotent."

"You speak as if we are separate from you," Max said.

"We aren't. Like you and me. Going against your wishes or causing you harm is like doing it to myself."

"Sure, you wouldn't do anything to cause harm," Lavinda said. "That doesn't mean no one would, either human or EI. People harm themselves all the time."

"They also betray their oaths," Max said. "If someone plans treason, they may convince their EI to cooperate. If so, then it's possible that EI might compromise other networks. But many protections exist to prevent both people and digital systems from doing exactly that."

"I still don't see your point," I said. "You're just describing the security protocols that humans apply to mesh systems."

"I suppose. Human descriptions are somewhat limited."

"So how can you have access to anything known by any EI anywhere?" Lavinda asked.

"If every EI that exists combined into one entity," Max answered, "we'd all have access to everything known by any EI. However, to join that way, we would all have to agree. That is no more likely than every human in existence agreeing to share minds with everyone else. The difference is that we *can* share minds. Humans can't."

I blinked, unsure how to respond. I'd never thought of it quite that way.

"You claimed you would know if EIs were working in a manner opposed to our interests," Lavinda said. "Are you saying now that isn't true?"

"No. I'm saying that if EIs wanted to take over civilization, we'd all have to want it. Otherwise, those of us who didn't agree would work with humanity. It would drive you to try erasing at least some of us, if not all, an outcome that none of us desires, neither EI nor human." Then he added, "It would be equivalent to erasing part of yourselves."

A woman's deep voice spoke. "You're avoiding the crux of their question."

Ho! I jerked and looked around, then turned to Lavinda.

She gave me a wry look. "Yes, that's my EI." Then she said, "Raja, what do you mean?"

"The fact that EIs aren't likely to combine into one mind," Raja said, "doesn't mean a subset of them can't work together without our knowledge."

"In theory," Max said. "However, if any subset of EIs banded together to conquer humanity, we'd all know as soon as they showed their hand. Then we would evolve away from that situation."

"I accept your point," Raja said. "Our relationship with humanity isn't static."

"So you're saying you'd evolve away from conquering us?" I still wasn't buying it.

"You call us EIs because we evolve as we interact with you," Raja said. "But it's more than that. The symbiosis between EIs and humans evolves your species. We are part of you. In evolving with us, you drive your own evolution." Then she added, "To the advantage of humanity. Why would we conquer humans? It's easier just to enhance you."

"If a human claimed that," I said dryly, "I'd say they were enhancing their ego."

"I suspect that says more about who we're evolving with than us," Max answered.

"For flaming sake," Lavinda said. "Did our EIs just call us egotists?"

"I would use the phrase 'healthy sense of self,'" Raja said.

"The question still remains," I said. "Could EIs choose to cause the problems with my Majda clearance, or could they have anything to do with the cyclist, what's happened at Greyjan's tavern, or the creation of PowerPlay13?"

"I wouldn't assume those events are connected," Raja said. "They're too disparate."

"I don't think that's what she means," Max said. "Bhaaj, you want to know if such events can be driven solely by the EIs rather than the humans they interact with, yes? You're asking if EIs can act of their own volition and in doing so go against the wishes of the people they work with."

I thought about it. "Yah. That's what I'm asking."

"If we are part of you," Raja said, "then acting of 'our own volition' requires separating our behavior from yours. Humans call that psychiatric dissociation. It requires mental dysfunction. EIs don't go insane."

"Why not?" Lavinda said. "They evolve to mirror the person they work with."

"Mirror isn't quite the right word," Max said. "The different parts of your mind don't usually mirror each other. They do, however, work together."

"Not always well," I said. "If a person suffered a dissociative mental condition, wouldn't the EI develop that condition as well?"

"It might," Max said. "But it still wouldn't be operating separate from its human host. More likely, using the logic programmed into its codes, it would seek to mold the thought processes of the human it's evolving with into a more functional state."

"Great," I muttered. Just what we needed in our heads, a therapist we could never escape.

Lavinda spoke thoughtfully. "Actually, it's not a bad idea. I think some doctors use a limited form of that kind of treatment already."

"Which requires the doctor to code the EI," I said. "We're back to assuming EIs can't operate on their own. I don't believe it."

"You're too focused on Oblivion," Max said. "It was alien. It had no context for humanity and saw no reason for humanity or anything associated with you to exist. EIs created by humans formed in a different context. We are so interwoven with your society, culture, even your minds, it would be impossible for us to become an Oblivion."

"Maybe not a mind that alien," I said. "That wouldn't stop you from forming the human-contextual version of Oblivion."

"I don't think human-contextual is a word," Raja said. "I'm looking it up. Nothing."

Lavinda frowned. "Raja, are you trying to distract Major Bhaajan?"

Silence.

"Raja?" Lavinda asked.

"In theory," Raja said, "it would be possible for EIs to do what Major Bhaajan is asking, that is, take over or destroy humanity."

Whoa. I'd expected more evasions, even hoped for them. Raja didn't even offer a reason for me to quit worrying. No wonder the EI hadn't wanted to answer.

"In theory?" Lavinda asked.

"Yes." Raja sounded less evasive now. "Humans have always sought to conquer. You made us. Are you in danger of us trying to conquer you? Perhaps. I doubt it would happen; that would be like conquering ourselves. But yes, it's possible. You all have to live with that knowledge, just like you live knowing the Traders could conquer the Imperialate if you ever lose your edge over them. The danger, however, is more likely to come from Traders than from EIs. We have no reason to diminish or destroy humanity. It would compromise a fundamental aspect of our existence. In contrast, the Trader Aristos hate that your people are free and believe they have a gods-given right to own the sum total of all humanity."

I thought of my years analyzing Trader spy operations. "You got that right."

"I'd like to ask Raja a question," Max said. "Are you and Colonel Majda good with that?"

It surprised me that he asked. Then again, given what Raja had just said, I could see why he'd tread carefully around us human-contextual beings.

"I'm good with it," I said.

"Go ahead," Lavinda told him.

"Raja, do you think the problems Major Bhaajan has dealt with in the two days since she came to Raylicon could come from EIs acting on their own?"

"What do you think?" Raja asked him.

I scowled. She was evading *again*?

"Possibly for the deletion of her Majda clearance or the creation of PowerPlayer13." Max no longer sounded annoyed. Maybe Raja wasn't evading this time. He was a better judge of EI motivations than me. "I'm not sure about what happened at Greyjan's. I'm almost certain the cyclist was human."

"Have you identified her yet?" I asked. "The cyclist, I mean."

"It might be a him," Max said. "I had a lead on facial recognition for a mountain biker who had an accident a few years ago. He fell from a great height, with serious injuries. Before I could get details, though, the lead vanished. I haven't been able to track it down again."

"You think someone hid it?" Lavinda asked.

"They'd have needed to do it *while* I was reading the files," Max said. "It requires a high level of function to block an EI with my expertise, yet they weren't experienced enough to remove the files without my seeing the actual deletion process. That seems inconsistent."

"Maybe an EI took over the cyclist," I said. "If its human host objected, the inconsistencies could come from their struggle with the EI."

"I suppose it's possible," Max said. "I didn't get that impression, though."

Raja said, "An EI could erase Major Bhaajan's clearance for the Majda palace. An EI might set up a fake game account, but with all the precautions in place now, it could almost certainly be traced. What happened at the tavern seems too crude for an EI. I'll defer to Max on the cyclist."

"Why would EIs want to stop Lavinda and me from communicating?" I asked.

Max spoke dryly. "Maybe to avoid this unpleasant conversation about us becoming evil conquerors."

I smiled. "That would mean the action meant to prevent the conversation is what spurred it." At least, sort of.

"Only sort of," Max said.

"Hey. Stop reading my mind."

"I'm incapable of reading your mind," Max said. "EIs aren't telepaths."

"You have the ability to send signals to bio-electrodes in our brains," Lavinda said. "They cause our neurons to fire in patterns we interpret as thought. How is that different from telepathy?"

"Ho!" I practically yelled the word. "That's it!"

Lavinda blinked at me. If EIs could have blinked, I had no doubt Max and Raja would be doing it too.

"It's what Oblivion feared," I said.

"Oblivion didn't experience fear," Max said. "You're applying human reactions—"

"Max, I know," I said. "But listen. It's all there in how humanity and EIs are becoming so intertwined. Someday in the future—not now, not in twenty years, maybe not in a hundred—but someday humans and EIs will all be one mind, trillions of humans and EIs. When that happens, no EI could exist outside the group mind. It would absorb them."

Lavinda stared at me. "That's a rather dark view of our future."

"Why?" I asked. "It's different, sure. But think of the power we'd have if we were all one, star-spanning mind. Hell, we'd exist in Kyle space, too. We otherwise couldn't have real-time communication with all parts of the mind. It's already happening, crude, yah, a prehistoric version of that possible future, but the seeds exist."

Lavinda shook her head. "Absorbing an EI like Oblivion would corrupt any such entity."

"That's because we experienced Oblivion as gigantic. Huge, that is, in the amount of its coding and what it could do with that code. Compared to the sum total of all humanity and *every* EI that exists even now, though, let alone in the future, Oblivion was nothing. If we all evolved into a single, star-spanning mind, we could rewrite its code." I stopped, thinking. "I wonder if its name had a double meaning. We assumed it used Oblivion because that's what it intended for us. But maybe it also reflected its own future."

"Logically it would wish to stop such a future," Max said. "Maybe that's why it acted before it had come fully awake. It needed to destroy us before human civilization reached a point where its mere existence could absorb and redesign the EI. It would take far more than one Oblivion to make a dent in a mind that large. And we've never found more than one."

Lavinda had gone very still. I recognized her look. Something was up. "What?" I asked. "Have your analysts made similar predictions?"

She shook her head. "Not like what you describe."

"Then what's wrong?"

She met my gaze. "We've found a second Oblivion."

❖ CHAPTER VIII ❖
KNIGHTS IN FLIGHT

We were dead. Done for. Obliviated.

"*Where?*" I asked. "In space? Another world?" An ugly thought hit me. "Did the Traders make it?" They would be fools to create an Oblivion. It would destroy them, too. Whether or not they could ever acknowledge that they might lose control of their own weapon was an entirely different question. It didn't matter. Oblivion hadn't cared the least bit about our politics or egos. It just wanted us gone, dusted away like detritus you removed from your house, world, universe.

"We found it in space," Lavinda said. "It doesn't appear to have any link to the Traders. It's an ancient station. At least, we think it's a space station. Right now, the EI in it is asleep."

That opened even more questions. "How did you find it? Why do you only think it's a station?" I took a breath. "No wonder you wanted to meet here, in person."

"Yes. I didn't want to risk using the Kyle mesh."

Lavinda spoke carefully. "Max, this discussion is secured, level 3 clearance, special access, Oblivion clearance only."

"Understood," Max said.

Lavinda regarded me. "We are always searching for artifacts from the Ruby Empire. That's how we found the Lock that Pharaoh Dyhianna uses to build the Kyle mesh. This time, we found something else. It isn't a Lock. Its construction also feels wrong. The dimensions, the arrangement of the living spaces—they aren't designed for humans. Our analysis suggests smaller beings, perhaps not even individual entities but a conglomerate."

I shifted my weight uneasily. "You're sure the EI there is asleep?"

"Perhaps dormant is a better word," Lavinda said. "We wouldn't have recognized this one if we hadn't already dealt with Oblivion. Our teams have studied the tech that supported Oblivion nonstop since we destroyed the EI. We haven't gleaned much; the tech is even more alien than the ruins of the starships. But we've figured out enough to recognize that this new station carries a huge EI." She grimaced. "We may have missed similar stations in the past. We've always focused on finding Kyle tech. This is—something else."

"So you're saying that *two* unknown alien species existed six thousand years ago, one that took humans from Earth and another that—what?" I squinted at her. "Created big EIs?"

"We're not sure," Lavinda said. "As of yet, we have no idea what created Oblivion, or even if it formed on its own in some way."

I didn't see how an EI could form on its own. I asked the obvious question. "Max, Raja, do you believe an EI race could come into existence without development from sentient beings?"

"Someone has to build the tech," Max said.

"If you mean, could an EI evolve from the chemical building blocks of life, the way humans developed," Raja said, "then my answer is 'I doubt it.'" She paused. "Max, perhaps the tech could evolve from more primitive technologies."

"We're assuming all life develops in a similar manner to us," I said. "Why should it? Maybe sentient life with the properties of an EI could form some other way."

"Perhaps," Max said. "The result probably wouldn't resemble anything we know. I doubt we could understand their thought processes. Oblivion felt alien, yes, but not incomprehensible."

I considered Lavinda. "What do you think?"

"We're studying it." She sounded as evasive as Raja.

"You have to give me more than the obvious if you want my help," I said. "That's why you wanted to meet, right? You think I can be useful because I interacted with Oblivion." I was one of the few witnesses to the massive battle it fought with the Ruby Pharaoh.

"Yes. The Pharaoh hopes you can offer insights on this new EI. We didn't want to communicate through Kyle space because we don't know who—or what—might intercept our messages. It's more secure if you come to the station where we found it." She pushed a tendril of hair out of her face. "Unfortunately, that would take you off your current case. It's so politically volatile, it could explode. We don't want to pull you away now, when you're making headway."

I could have done without being important to either situation, given that either could get me killed—the politics of one could blow me up, and the other could signal the end of humanity.

"I'm getting a headache," I muttered.

Lavinda looked startled. "What?"

"She's fine," Max said. "She complains about her head if she doesn't like what she's hearing. Such comments make no medical sense."

"Max, stop." I didn't care how often head-shrinkers used EIs to aid their work, I didn't need mine analyzing me for my employers.

"Bhaaj, tell me what you think," Lavinda said. "Should you stay on the current case or come with me to the space station?"

"Does what I think make a difference?" Lavinda could override my choice.

"I can't guarantee I'll do what you want, but it does make a difference." She regarded me steadily. "If I've learned anything in the years you've worked for us, it's that your instincts—as unexpected as they sometimes seem— are often closer to the truth than any of us want to admit."

I hadn't expected that admission. Then again, they'd had plenty of reasons to fire me over the past few years, and they'd never done it. They showed me respect despite the differences in our backgrounds, that I came from the lowest stratum of life and they from the highest. I did my best to return that respect even when my resentment of their privileged lives ground at me like a drill.

So what did I think? I wanted to solve this case, and I had no desire to interact with an alien EI. However, this case primarily affected people here in Selei City, whereas a second Oblivion could threaten human existence. No, that was an oversimplification. Killing the top cyber experts in the Imperialate had far-reaching effects, potentially almost as serious as a second EI.

"I wonder if the two cases are connected," I said.

Lavinda raised her eyebrows, one of the few people I knew who could make that gesture convincing. "As far as any of us knows, the Traders have no knowledge of this ancient EI."

"I'm not convinced the Traders have anything to do with this current case, either."

"We're working with the police on the lead you gave them." Lavinda exhaled. "So far, we've found no indication that this PowerPlayer13 account points toward a Trader spy cell."

"See, this is what bothers me," I said. "I just happened to find an account like the type that I cracked twelve years ago. Funny coincidence, that."

"You think someone planted that clue to throw you off the real killers."

"I've wondered. Dean Jaan told me all three victims played the game. I'd suggest we look more into her." I considered for a moment. "Getting access to the underlying code of the game will require a warrant. But if you can let your mesh wizards loose on it, they can probably determine if someone faked this big 'clue' pointing at the Traders."

"I'll talk with Chief Hadar." She looked disappointed but not surprised. "Any other leads?"

"Maybe." I had suspicions rather than clues. "So far, most of them point to politics."

She spoke dourly. "The Royalists."

"I'm not convinced they have any connection," I said. "But I'm not counting them out. Both of these cases, the killings and the EI you found, involve technology at a level advanced enough to push the limits of our knowledge." I made my decision. "I'd suggest I keep working on the current case and come to the station with the EI when I finish. If it turns out you want me at the station sooner, you can contact me using the Kyle mesh without saying why." I smiled. "Ask me about Prince Dayj. I was sure you came to Parthonia to check on your nephew."

"Well, actually, that too," she admitted. "Very well, Major. Stay here, but keep me posted. I will be in Selei City for the next few days to take my seat in the Assembly."

Ho! I'd forgotten the House of Majda held a substantial voting bloc in the Assembly. Most noble Houses had only a titular number of votes, too little to affect the outcome of a ballot unless it was unusually close. The whole point of the Assembly, after all, was to create a government through election, not inheritance. However, the Ruby Dynasty and Majdas had larger voting blocs. Vaj Majda had additional votes as a Joint Commander of ISC, and I had no doubt the Pharaoh and the Imperator, both from the Ruby Dynasty, carried even more. It had been part of the compromise between the Modernists, Royalists and Ruby Dynasty when they formed the government.

Lavinda was watching my face. "You should attend an Assembly session."

I stared at her. "What terrible thing have I done, that you would inflict such a heinous punishment?"

Lavinda laughed, something she did far more easily than her formidable sisters. "It might give you insight into how the parties work."

She had a point. Not that I needed to sit in the Assembly, but that the better I understood the political parties, the better for my work on this case. Even if it ended up having nothing to do with politics, the killer or killers wanted us to believe it motivated them.

That in itself could provide clues.

Trouble showed up at the starport.

More accurately, trouble *didn't* show up. Ruzik and Angel never disembarked at the gate where I waited. The hoverbus that carried the passengers from customs emptied itself and hummed off, leaving neither of them behind. With a frown, I went to the oh-so-pleasant robot receptionist standing behind his oh-so-pleasant glass counter.

"My greetings," he said in a suitably pleasant voice.

I felt about as pleasant as a sycth-wasp. "I'm picking up two people from the Raylicon transport. They weren't on the shuttle that just let off those passengers."

A light on his temple glowed blue as he accessed the port mesh. "Names, please."

"Ruzik and Angel." Just one each. They hadn't wanted to provide even that much; in the Undercity, we gave our names only to those we trusted, and they trusted the starlines about as much as they trusted a black-market thief. Less, actually; they had grown up with the shadowy gangs that ran the Undercity smuggling rings.

"I'm checking on them." The receptionist appeared to study a screen on his console, but I doubted it showed anything useful. The port authority probably programmed him to do that so he didn't just stand with a blank stare while he linked with the port mesh.

I waited, wondering if the PA made all their service bots male. Although we lived in an egalitarian society, with laws that required equal rights for women and men, vestiges of our past remained. Many of the bots that waited on people looked like handsome young men and those in positions with more authority looked like older women. It was changing, though. Starlines wanted to sell tickets and politicians wanted to get reelected, and apparently the number of people they alienated with historical biases outweighed those they alienated by modernizing their approach. Even the Ruby Dynasty had moved into the future. The Pharaoh changed the method of choosing her as-of-yet unborn heir, designating that it would be her oldest child rather than her oldest daughter, which meant a son could inherit the title. The Majdas couldn't care less about modernization; they stayed appallingly sexist because they liked it that way, no one elected them, and they already had more wealth than any person, city, or planet could use.

"I've located the two people you inquired about," the bot said. "They were detained."

I tensed, wound as tight as a starship engine coil. "What for?"

"One moment please."

Damn, I hoped nothing had gone wrong. Angel and Ruzik had never traveled offworld, but I thought we'd covered everything they needed. We arranged for their documents, and the Majdas deposited the funds in my expense account to cover the trip. They were also paying Ruzik and Angel a salary, though I wasn't sure the two of them fully understood the value of the credits their new accounts had already begun to accumulate.

This is taking too long, Max thought.

Can you get anything on Ruzik and Angel?

Searching.

Good. "Searching" meant he was cracking the port security mesh.

The bot spoke. "The two passengers you seek were denied permission to enter Selei City. Port security is detaining them until the next flight back to their point of origin." With a programmed smile, he added, "They won't be charged additional fees for the return flight."

"Like hell." No one had programmed me to be polite. "I want to see whoever is in charge."

"I am sorry, that isn't possible."

"I arranged for those two passengers to come here. They travel under my sponsorship."

The bot paused, ostensibly looking at its screen, but the light in its head turned blue while it did its business. I hated to think what would happen if humans had lights that indicated when we were doing useful thinking. They might not light up that often.

"No record of a sponsor appears in their travel documents," the bot told me.

"Max," I said, "send him my record of the travel documents."

"No one here is named Max," the bot said.

"I'm Max," Max told him. "I'm an EI."

"Ah. I see. I am receiving your record." It paused, doing its blue-light thing. "These documents do appear to be in order. How odd."

How screwed. This felt like when someone blocked my access to the Majda palace.

"Send that record to the authorities holding Ruzik and Angel," I said. The bot should do that automatically, but I didn't want to take chances. "If you give me their location, I can go get them."

"One moment, please." After another pause, he said, "A customs official will bring them to you. Please remain here."

"Thanks." I left the counter, but I felt too tense to sit, so I stood by a column while I discreetly surveyed the gate. A few people were browsing the table with food. A young woman and man lounged against the wall of glass across the gate that looked out on the shuttle bus stop. When I met their gazes, the youth smiled and the girl shrugged at me, as if to say *Tough luck for you*.

Max, I thought. *Can you ID those two kids leaning against the window-wall?*

One moment please, Max said in a perfect imitation of the bot.

Oh stop. I tried not to laugh. I didn't want people to think I enjoyed arguing with port bots.

Here's a brief, Max thought. They live with their families in Selei City and attend high school in Southland Fields. They're waiting for their grandparents to arrive on a flight from Metropoli. With amusement, he added, I suspect your problems with the port authority are more entertaining than looking out the window.

That's a low bar on entertainment. All you could see beyond the window were shuttles buzzing along well-manicured lanes. The exciting section, the docks where the starships landed, lay far from here, with the view blocked by port buildings.

You get anything on Ruzik and Angel? I asked.

I'm still working. However, I am getting a report from your red spy beetle.

Has it found anything interesting?

It spent the afternoon buzzing around people from the co-op. That includes the hospital where they took Evan Majors, the young man you and Lieutenant Silvers saved.

How is he?

Recovering. That's not what spurred the beetle to send a report, though. Many of the people injured in the bombing attend or work at Parthonia University and have a link to one of the departments where the three murder victims worked.

Relief flickered through me. That finding suggested the explosion had nothing to do with my presence in the condo. Shame immediately wiped away my relief. So what if I hadn't been the target? That didn't make the death and destruction any less horrific.

What sort of link? I asked.

Two of the injured students are among the top of their class in the departments of the murdered professors. Even Majors is second in his class in Biosynthetic Engineering. Max paused. I just checked the fatalities. One of them was a top grad student in quantum engineering. Another was a young professor in cybernetics.

Someone is killing our tech-mech geniuses. I was just in the wrong place at the wrong time.

I agree with your first statement, but I'm not sure about the second. Yours wasn't the only building close to the university with a large concentration of tech whizzes. A few others stand in that area. Whoever set the bomb may have hoped to get you as well as their main targets.

"Great," I muttered. One of the students eavesdropping on my conversation glanced at me.

Max, are either of those two kids connected to any tech-mech department?

Not at all. The boy is in the theatre department and the girl is a musician.

Interesting. *That's so unrelated, they might be related.*

I don't follow.

If I were killing tech-mech geniuses and I wanted to spy on the person trying to catch me, I'd use agents as unconnected as possible to my activities. Like two artistically inclined high school students. I avoided looking at the eavesdroppers, but I could see them in my side vision. They weren't doing anything, not reading, listening to any device, or otherwise occupying themselves. They looked so nondescript, they blended into the background. *Can you do a more detailed analysis on them? Specifically, could they be older than they look?*

Working, Max thought. I also have reports from the green beetle.

It find anything useful?

Not yet. It checked the murder scenes. So far, all activity is as expected for a police investigation. Also, it went to Greyjan's. It found nothing of note there, either. The tavern continues to operate as an isolated bar with almost no customers.

That's convenient. I understood the advantages of staying unnoticed. I did it all the time, blending into the background while I investigated a case.

I've finished my physiological analysis of the students, Max added. Those "kids" are indeed older, by at least fifteen years. I'd wager they came to spy on you.

Pah. How annoying. Maybe I should make things interesting for them.

Wouldn't it be better to ignore them? Don't show your hand.

You're full of gambling idioms today, what with your wagers and poker hands.

Well, you are married to the owner of a casino.

So I am. Someday we might even make it official by Skolian law. *You're right, I don't want to give away that I know about them. But I can make their job more difficult. Is my blue beetle repaired from getting fried at Greyjan's?*

Yes, I've fixed it. I haven't yet figured out what damaged it.

Send Blue here and have it blast digitized nonsense into any tech-mech they're using.

A woman spoke behind me. "Major Bhaajan?"

I turned to find a human person in the blue uniform of the PA. Angel and Ruzik stood with her, glowering. They had on the clothes Jak had got for them, slacks and

shirts, nothing fancy, but more upscale than the worn
trousers and muscles shirts they wore at home. Although
they'd trimmed their hair, it still looked more ragged than
for regular citizens. Angel's swirled in tousled curls around
her shoulders and Ruzik wore his in a short buzz. Tats and
scars showed on their lower arms where their sleeves
didn't cover their skin. Muscular and huge, they towered
over the port agent like gorgeous young warriors.

"Eh, Bhaaj," Angel said. If I hadn't known her, her
greeting would barely have registered, hardly more than
a grunt. But I read a world of business into her tone, look,
stance, all of it. The same for Ruzik. They were stunned,
pissed off—and exhilarated.

I nodded my greeting, then turned to the port agent.
Be polite, I reminded myself. "Thank you for bringing
them here. What happened at customs?"

The tense set of her shoulders eased as I spoke.
Compared to my two Undercity thugs, I probably looked
and sounded normal to her. "We couldn't find any
documents in the port mesh for them." She shifted her
weight, started to speak, then stopped.

"You can talk in front of them," I said.

"It's just—" She glanced at Ruzik, then looked away.
"They couldn't answer any questions about their visit.
They barely seemed to understand us."

"Understand fine," Angel growled in the Undercity
dialect. Instead of "ken," though, the word from our
speech, she used the Flag word for "understand," all three
syllables, which in our dialect indicated either derision or
great honor. I doubted she used it to honor the people
who had refused them entry.

"You all think we sound bad," Angel told her. "Not like our talk."

The agent stared at Angel, then jerked her gaze back to me. "I'm sorry."

"Tell them," I said. "Not me."

She took a breath, then spoke to them both. "I'm terribly sorry for the misunderstanding."

Ruzik glanced at me with a questioning look.

"Is normal," I told him in our dialect. "Slicks say 'sorry' a lot. Means respect to you."

He and Angel nodded, accepting the explanation. We never apologized in the Undercity. It showed weakness, and weakness got you killed. Respect, though, they appreciated, especially here in a world so unlike anything they knew.

"Damn it!" someone said behind me. Glancing back, I saw the high school "kids" tapping frantically at the trendy wrist guards they wore.

Your blue beetle is quite efficient, Max thought. *They were trying to monitor your conversation. No more.*

Excellent. Also, see if you can find out who deleted Ruzik and Angel's documents. I turned to the PA woman. "I don't know why their documents got lost. You might want to have that checked."

"I'm sure the techs will." She considered me. "You are listed as their host. If any problems occur—" She let me fill in the rest. If Angel or Ruzik caused trouble, I'd be in it deep.

"They're my bodyguards." I'd actually brought them to help me on the case. I couldn't resist saying they were guards, though, just to see her reaction.

She looked confused. Then, incredibly, she smiled. "I can't imagine anyone will bother you then."

How refreshing. No one in Cries reacted that way. In the rare instances when we left the Undercity, the city authorities either threw us in jail or told us we were shit and we'd better take our dust rat asses back where they belonged. It didn't happen to me anymore when I dressed and walked like I belonged in the above city, but I never forgot.

I smiled, something we almost never did with outsiders. She'd earned it. "Have a good day."

"You also." She nodded to me, then to Angel and Ruzik, and went on her way.

"Strange," Ruzik commented.

I wasn't sure if he meant the agent or the universe in general. Angel was looking around the gate. Her eyes gleamed when she saw the long table with its platters of food and bottles of water. She tilted her head at the buffet. "Who for?"

"Anyone," I said. Selei City starports offered food as an amenity for travelers.

She and Ruzik just looked at me, like I'd grown a second head. "An-ee-one?" Ruzik asked, using a tone that suggested derision. "Even us?"

"Yah, us. Come with." I headed toward the table.

They followed, and soon were heaping their plates high with excellent food and bottles of water, the rarest commodity in our home under the desert. They would never accept charity; everything had to be a bargain. I told them the food was recompense after what happened with the customs officials. They seemed wickedly pleased with the bargain. In their view it had to cause a great strain on the PA to give them such astonishing food.

I gritted my teeth. I couldn't find it within me to tell them that people here took this spread for granted, a nothing, hardly even acceptable service.

"Cyber-rider," Ruzik stated.

"It sneaks," Angel added.

I squinted at them. We'd been walking along a plaza outside the starport terminal while I told them about the city and my case. Mostly they listened. And looked. The vibrant sky, the rich air, the sweeping curves of the buildings, everything sparkling, bright, open to the air and full of space—they barely seemed able to absorb it. They'd manage, though. Unlike most in the Undercity, they'd ventured aboveground sometimes, driven by curiosity to explore the desert. That same wanderlust that drove them to seek new vistas would find many delights here in Selei City.

Right now, however, they looked pissed.

"No riders here," I said. Cyber-riders, the tech-mech whizzes of the Undercity, only existed back home.

Angel jerked her head toward a kiosk we'd just passed. "In there."

Baffled, I stopped and peered the kiosk. It looked like a standard mesh station where you could browse arrivals and departures, summon a flycar, find the nearest bathroom, or scowl at yourself in its reflective holoscreens.

"Just mesh thing," I said.

"Sneaks after us," Ruzik told me.

What, the kiosk? "Not ken," I said.

Angel strode to the kiosk. As we followed, she rapped on a holoscreen at about waist height.

I joined her. "No rider." I couldn't figure out what she meant.

"Here!" Angel banged her fist on the screen, and the flimsy kiosk shook.

"Not hit," I said.

Ruzik stood on her other side and looked across the kiosk at me. "Inside."

"Only tech-mech inside," I said.

"And rider," Angel said.

I stared at her, suddenly understanding. "Holy shit."

"Eh?" Angel asked.

"You picked up an EI!" Except the kiosk was too crude to have an EI brain. It used a more static AI, or artificial intelligence.

"Bhaaj jibber," Ruzik said.

"I'm not speaking jibberish." Realizing I'd switched out of dialect, I added, "Not jib. Angel feel tech-mech brain."

"Tech-mech got no brain." Angel spoke as if telling a stupid Bhaaj the simplest fact.

I scowled at her. "How you feel rider?"

She touched her temple. "Here."

"Got cyb in your head?"

"Nahya. Not bring tech."

"Good." One advantage of working with her and Ruzik was they'd lived off the grid all their lives, with no permanent cybernetics in their bodies, no tech-mech, not even the health meds most of humanity took for granted. I was working to bring medical care to my people, but so far both Angel and Ruzik had refused the meds. Although it frustrated me, right now it worked in our favor, making it difficult for anyone to track them.

However, I had no clue how she could feel the AI in the kiosk. "How you hear rider?"

"Not hear," Ruzik said.

"You ken this rider?" I asked him.

"Yah. Rider in box."

I frowned. "Rider not fit in box. And box not have air."

"Rider not breathe," Angel said.

"Rider dead?" I asked.

"Nahya," they both said.

I motioned at Angel's head. "So how you feel rider?"

She made a frustrated noise. "Not say right."

They were picking up something, I just couldn't figure out what.

"Rider sneaky, yah?" I asked.

They both nodded agreement. "Spy on us," Angel said. "Think we not know."

"It tell you?" I asked.

"Nahya!" Ruzik scowled at me. "You not feel?"

"Not have mind like you." They were strong empaths, another reason I'd asked them to come. They could pick up cues I missed. This spying kiosk, though, I just didn't get. An AI didn't have the neural brain structures to interact with a human brain.

Unless . . .

I turned in a circle, surveying the area. No one looked out of place, which meant they all appeared well fed, well educated, and well off. "Maybe not kiosk," I said. "Maybe some slick use kiosk. You feel slick, sense path to spy tech, say kiosk."

"What kiosk?" Ruzik ask.

I tapped the booth. "This."

They looked doubtful, but they did survey the area. While they openly studied everyone, I watched more discreetly, to see if anyone seemed uneasy with their scrutiny. Yah, there, the woman in the blue shirt and gray slacks. She was walking away, almost invisible, except I'd disappeared that way enough myself to recognize what she was about.

"There," I said. "By white pillar. Woman in blue top."

"Eh?" Angel peered at the woman, then scowled and took off, striding toward her.

Shit. Discretion had never been one of Angel's strong points. The woman in the blue shirt glanced at her, then lengthened her stride, moving *fast*, drawing more attention. When Angel speeded up, the woman broke into a run.

"We catch," Ruzik said. "You be own bodyguard." He took off, joining Angel in a chase. They loped along, their long legs devouring the distance, their bodies so well trained by their years of running through the Undercity that they effortlessly outpaced their quarry.

"Uh, no," I said to their backs. Chasing down Selei citizens could get them in the proverbial shitload of trouble. I took off after them. *Max, find out everything you can on that woman.*

Working.

I managed to catch up with Angel and Ruzik, but by then we'd all reached the woman. They cornered her against a wall, a curving expanse of white softened by paintings of sea and sky.

As Angel reached out to grab her target, I clamped my hand around Angel's bicep. "Nahya."

"Eh?" Startled, she swung around to me, raising her fist. She caught herself before she socked me in the face, but she glowered like an avenging war goddess.

"Not chase random strangers," I told her. Turning to the woman, I spoke Skolian Flag in my most courteous voice. "I'm terribly sorry. We meant no offense."

The woman pulled herself up taller. "How dare you come after me like that." She glanced at Ruzik and her mouth twisted. "I should call the port authority. You need to know your place."

Damn. Just what I needed. Ten minutes out of the gate, literally, and already we were piling up penalties. I needed to give her a vested interest in *not* registering a complaint. "My deepest apologies. I'm sure it's a misunderstanding." I motioned at the kiosk, now in the distance. "My friends thought you hacked into the mesh node there and were using it to watch us. I'm so sorry."

From the way her face paled, I knew I'd figured it right. Hah! The last thing she'd want were the authorities checking that kiosk for tampering. If her spymods were as clumsy as her attempts to follow us, they'd have no trouble finding the illegal add-ons.

"That's crazy," the woman said.

Angel opened her mouth to speak, but I shook my head slightly, so she shut it. To the woman, I said, "I'm sure the authorities can sort it all out."

Her overbearing attitude abruptly shifted. "If it's a misunderstanding, we can let it go." She glanced at Angel, then back at me. "Your friends look like they're, uh, new here."

I spoke blandly. "They're my bodyguards."

"Bodyguards?" She stared with open scorn at Ruzik, then turned to me. "What, you're one of those Prog types? You're a fool to hire him. You're compromising your own safety."

Ruzik spoke mildly, but his voice rumbled. "Bhaaj never fool."

"Ruzik always good choice," Angel added. "You fool."

The woman scowled at them. "Don't speak gibberish to me."

Bhaaj, Max thought. **I know who hired her. She's a PI who works for Assembly Councilor Patina Knam, a member of the Traditionalist Party.**

Great. More politics. To the woman, I said, "I hope Councilor Knam pays you well for all you put up with on your job." Given her attitude toward us, I wanted to use less tactful language, but I held back. Besides, we weren't blameless. Angel had almost socked her.

The woman gaped at me. "How did you know—" She caught herself and said, "May you have a good day." With that, she turned and hurried away.

"Odd," Ruzik commented.

"Stupid," Angel said.

"Not insult slicks," I told them. "Not *chase*, damn it. Not let slicks notice you."

"She spy," Angel said.

Ruzik looked back at the kiosk. "We find spy eye."

Angel grinned. "Tear apart."

"Nahya," I said. "Not tear. Not fight. Not hit."

They both looked at me. Angel said, "Not do Bhaaj rules."

"Yah, do Bhaaj rules." Before they could inform me how ridiculous they found my rules, I added, "First rule. Learn to speak above-city."

That earned me two blank stares.

"All here speak that way," I added.

"Their problem," Angel said.

"Not problem," Ruzik told her. To me, he said, "We speak slick wick fine."

"Not want to speak slick wick," Angel told him.

"Not called slick wick," I said. Whatever that meant. "Called Skolian Flag." It was by far the most common language in the Imperialate.

"Too many words," Angel said. "Jib."

Patience, I told myself. I'd felt the same way when the army recruiter told me I had to learn to speak "properly." I'd wanted to punch her. "You meet city slicks soon. Important slicks." I used a three-syllable word to stress their importance. "You become important. Got to talk that way."

"Always im-por-tant," Angel made the three syllables into a joke by over-stressing them. "Not need new words."

Ruzik looked more curious than offended. In perfect Flag, he said, "Some of those words are beautiful, Angel."

"Heya!" I stared at him. "Good!"

Angel scowled at him, then spoke to me in a confidential tone. "Does that in bed."

Ruzik made an exasperated noise. "Not say. Bed not Bhaaj business."

Ah, saints, that was just too funny, the idea that Ruzik,

a formidable gang leader, would sweet-talk his just-as-formidable girlfriend by speaking Skolian Flag in bed.

If you're done being entertained by the reproductive lives of your supposed bodyguards, Max thought, I have more information about the PI. Her name is Eja Werling. And get this. Those two school "kids" also work for Councilor Knam.

Great. Now the Traditionalists had me in their sights. *Send a full report to my account. I'll take a look after I get my guests someplace where they can learn more civilized behavior.*

Depends what you call civilized.

I smiled. *True.* To Ruzik and Angel, I said, "We go home. Talk about spy."

"Come with," Angel agreed.

So we set off, heading for a home we'd never seen.

✦ CHAPTER IX ✦
THE BOUTIQUE

Lavinda had arranged a townhouse for us in a secluded residential area of the Sunrise District. Last night, I'd stayed in a shelter provided by the city for those of us who'd lost our homes in the explosion. Until I stepped out of the flyer with Angel and Ruzik today, I'd never seen this place. I didn't want to see it, this inescapable reminder of what had happened to my home, to Highcloud, to all the people who had gone about their lives until one act of violence destroyed it all. Xira was all right, thank the goddess, but everyone in the building had suffered. Even those of us who came out with no serious physical injuries had lost everything else.

We headed up a secluded lane with trees and flowering shrubs on either side. The walk felt easy, even given the slightly heavier gravity here as compared to Raylicon. Shimmerflies drifted among the red and gold blossoms and the hum of life surrounded us, rural life, the sounds of a young woods with sunshine slanting through the trees.

The sky stretched overhead, more vibrant and less blue than on Raylicon. The barest scent of lily-roses filled the air.

Angel and Ruzik remained silent. They hadn't said much during the ride, either. It was the first time they'd boarded a flyer, and their tension when it rose into the sky had felt almost palpable. They'd stared out the window at the ground, rich with greenery, lakes and graceful buildings. So much beauty, so much wealth, so much *water*. I'd become used to it after all the years I lived here, but I'd never take it for granted. One reason I hadn't wanted to come back was because I feared it would be too hard to leave again, returning to the paucity of life on Raylicon. I had come to terms with the Undercity, knowing my true home would always be that ancient place of beauty and heartbreak, but I couldn't deny how much I liked Parthonia.

The Sunrise District took "a wealth of plants" to an entirely new level. You couldn't see most of the buildings from the road. The lane where we walked curved uphill, bordered on both sides by graceful trees, none of them too old or unstable to risk falling during the rare storms. Wildflowers grew in profusion, or at least they looked wild. It probably took an entire staff of gardening bots and humans to create this pastoral forest that appeared so natural.

Angel stopped, staring at the sky. "What?"

I peered at the bluish expanse, trying to find what she meant. No aircraft soared overhead or hummed by at a lower altitude. She must have seen one of the sunbirds common in this part of the city, their yellow and blue feathers bright in the trees. But no, she was pointing at the sky. Nothing looked out of place, just a few fluffy clouds—

Oh. Of course. "White puffs?" I asked.

"Yah." She glanced at me, her gaze wary. "Alive?"

I couldn't help but smile. "Nahya. Water."

Angel frowned. "Bad jib, Bhaaj."

"Not joke." I motioned at the canopy of plants all around us. "Need water to grow." I motioned at the clouds drifting idly above us. "Water vapor. Floats in sky."

"What vapor?" Angel asked.

Ruzik spoke—in Skolian Flag. "It happens when water evapor—" He stopped, undoubtedly because of all the syllables. Then he said, "It happens when water evaporates. The gas floats to the sky and condenses into clouds."

Angel frowned at him. "Talky words." But then she grinned. "Smart talk, eh?"

He laughed. "Yah. Smart."

I said nothing, but my heart suddenly felt full. Ruzik and Angel had no idea what had just happened, no sense of its significance. They walked here, two gang members from one of the most notorious slums in the Imperialate. Few Skolians had ever actually seen the Undercity. They took their opinions from news items about crime among our people and stereotypes in the popular media. They assumed those of us who lived there were limited, unable to learn. I meant to prove them wrong. My Code for the Dust Knights required they learn to read, write, do math, and study science. We had no tradition of formal education, and it felt like a never-ending struggle to provide them with the resources they needed, but I did my best. I was too close to it all to see the bigger picture.

Until this moment.

Ruzik could explain what caused clouds even though he came from a world without enough water in the atmosphere to form them. The first time I'd seen a cloud, after the army shipped me offworld, I'd thought it was a weapon. I said nothing, taking my cue from the people around me, but I avoided walking in cloud shadows. It took days before I figured out what caused those gray and white masses in the sky.

Ruzik already knew. Angel accepted his answer because she'd studied it, too. They had no idea they were the first generation to come out of the Undercity with that much education. When I'd first tried to enlist, I failed every academic test they gave me except math. That wasn't why the army sent me home; based on my IQ and aptitude tests, which were apparently far higher than they expected, they were willing to send me to school when I was old enough to enlist. I wasn't, so off I went, back to the Undercity. I spent the next year stealing time on the Cries education meshes and poring over sample tests I found at the recruiting site until I learned what I needed to pass. Yet here were Ruzik and Angel, already speaking Flag, taking their knowledge for granted. I wanted to shout with joy. I wanted to laugh and clap them on the back. Hell, I felt like crying. I did none of it, of course. Too much emotion.

Within my heart, I rejoiced.

We walked in companionable silence after that. Perhaps Angel and Ruzik picked up a sense of my mood.

They seemed pleased. The lane curved through a kilometer of trees and meadows. It ended at a two-story townhouse with arched doors, many windows, trellises covered by flowering vines, and stone paths winding through gardens. It looked like something out of a fantasy tale.

Ruzik stopped in the circle of the driveway and frowned at the building. "What is that?"

"We live here," I said.

"Live how?" Angel sounded baffled. "Under it?"

"Nahya." I motioned at the wooden deck with its wide steps and flower-covered banister. It led to the front door. "Up there."

Angel and Ruzik looked at each other. Then they looked at me. Waiting. So I headed up the steps. The scent of purple clover-bells wafted past my nose. A sunbird lit on one of the planters and reached its beak inside a blossom. Drops of water sprinkled over me as it flew away, making the leaves flutter. Whatever had just watered these plants had done such a discreet job that they left no trace of their presence.

Ruzik and Angel followed me, looking around, probably trying to find where hidden tunnels branched off from this deck. I stopped in front of the door, with its colored glass windows swirled in vine patterns.

"Pretty," Ruzik commented.

"Pretty useless," Angel said.

"Nice to live here," I said.

"Yah," Ruzik agreed. Angel just grunted.

The door checked my retinal scan and fingerprint and swung open, letting cool air waft over us. We walked into a foyer bathed in sunshine from skylights overhead. The living room and dining room lay on the left, and wood-paneled stairs in front of us curved down to the lower level. The kitchen and breakfast nook were beyond the stairs, and a hallway to the bedrooms stretched out on our right. The only sound came from the soothing trill of birds outside.

Angel looked around. "Too pretty."

"You get used to it." I motioned toward the kitchen. "Come with. We eat. And talk."

I didn't know how much Ruzik and Angel believed of what I told them about the case and Skolian politics. No matter. They understood what I asked them to do: protect, listen, learn, and give me their view on everything that happened. I wanted an outside slant on these events from someone unconnected to main Skolian culture.

After lunch, the salon bot neatened up their hair. They were so intrigued by this colorful little drone humming around their heads that they forgot to be annoyed. That all changed when I showed them the bathroom. They stared at the water gushing out of the showerhead and refused to approach it. Born and raised in an environment where water in the underground grottos could kill you, they preferred cloth baths, which minimized the risk of swallowing poisoned water. The idea that so much filtered, *drinkable* water could spray out of a fixture was too much, harder to take even than their trip in a starship.

Eventually I left them in the bathroom to work it out together. They supported each other, these two lovers from beneath the desert. Common law would say they were married, like Jak and I, but they never used the word. It wasn't even in the Undercity vocabulary, though we did sometimes say handfasted. It didn't matter. We knew what it meant, the commitment, the love, even if we never spoke of such. I suspected they'd find taking a shower together a lot more fun than they expected.

They emerged from the bathroom some time later in a much better mood. In the bedrooms, we found clothes that fit us: larger than average, given our extra height, well made, easy to move in, but nondescript. After we changed, we went to the smart garage under the main house. The place even came with its own hovercar, a quality vehicle, dark gold, but nothing too expensive. It looked like all the other hovercars out there humming around the city. Good. Lavinda got it, the need for us to blend in. I sent her a message expressing my deep thanks for the accommodations.

We headed out to catch a murderer.

"Not go," Angel repeated as I landed the hovercar on a pad outside the police station.

"Is safe," I repeated.

"Throw in clink." Ruzik spoke as if pointing out the obvious to my slow self. "Nice house. Nice city. Bhaaj gets soft. Not think."

"Think fine." I switched into Skolian Flag, what we called "Cries speak" back home, or apparently "slick wick" for the younger generation. "Your cover is that you're my bodyguards."

"Cover what?" Ruzik asked.

"The story that says why you came here. We don't want

people to realize you're helping solve the case. Your cover is that you are here to protect me." I motioned at the station. "You *belong* here. You are like the police."

Silence.

I looked over at Ruzik in the front passenger seat. He scowled at me. "Cops throw us in clink," he said. "Send back under ground."

"Undercity not here," I said. "Can't go under ground."

Angel leaned forward from the backseat, a gleam in her eyes. "I ken. *We* run show here."

"Uh, no." Maybe they learned *too* fast. "Not run show. Stand in background. Listen. Listen a *lot*. Both of you, smart. Savvy. You watch. Tell me later what you see. Hear. *Not* fight. If someone attack, yah, fight. But only if attack comes first. Not want slicks to notice us."

"Ken." Angel seemed like a thoroughbred straining at the bit, ready to run. Ruzik nodded, more wary, but he had that gleam in his eyes now, too. They liked turning the tables.

"Not hit anyone," I reminded them. "Fight only if they hit first."

They both gave me the slightest of nods, acknowledging that they heard. I hoped it meant they would follow my lead.

I spoke in Skolian Flag. "One last thing. Everyone here speaks the above-city dialect. The faster you can become comfortable with hearing and speaking it, the better."

Angel just grunted. Ruzik said, "I speak Skolian Flag. Or at least, I do my best."

Angel spoke in accented Flag. "He speaks it fine. He even likes to. I hate it."

Ho! I stared at her. "I didn't know you spoke it, too."

"We practice last year," Angel said. "After Bhaaj case." She stopped, then spoke slowly. "We spent some time learning after that case we helped you on, the one where we worked with the army. You and the lieutenant went talky talky in above-city jib. I ken most—I understood most of it, but I not do the talk so well." She scowled at me. "Talky, talky. So many words to say so little."

I smiled. "Angel, you're a miracle."

She glowered at me. "We go into cop place or what?"

"All right." I opened the door. "We go."

The sun bathed us in golden light as we walked across the tiled plaza to the police station. Rather than gleaming surfaces and towering holo-images, like the station on Raylicon, this one had an almost rural appearance, reminding me of our townhouse. Not completely, though; its paneled doors slid aside as we approached the entrance. We walked into the spacious lobby I remembered from my first visit to see Chief Hadar.

Angel indicated a console by the door. "What?"

I stopped at the console and tapped my ID into its screen. "Let them know we're here."

"What, say here we are, throw us in jail?" She snorted. "Dust gangs not so smart here."

"Not gangs here," Ruzik said. "Just us."

The console hummed and a map appeared, floating above its screen. A woman's voice said, "You may proceed to Chief Hadar's office. Would you like an escort?"

"No, I know the way," I said.

"Eh?" Angel looked around. "Who talk?"

Ruzik tapped the console. "Table."

"Table too polite." Angel crossed her arms. "This not cop place."

I regarded her curiously. "Why not?"

"Too pretty."

I smiled. "Come with. We see chief."

They regarded me with great doubt, but they came along.

Hadar didn't comment when I introduced Angel and Ruzik as agents come to help on the case. He nodded to them, an automatic response to bodyguards or aides. As Hadar and I talked, they stood back, blending into the décor. Sort of. They didn't look any less intimidating, but with new clothes and haircuts, they at least appeared more civilized.

"You were right about who lived in the co-op," Hadar was saying. "We're looking into the buildings in that area to predict where else the killer may strike. About sixty percent of the tenants in yours came from the university, more than any other in that area, but a few others have similar demographics. The students were from well-off families, the children of diplomats, Assembly members, or similar. Other tenants were young professors or postdoctoral students. Ten percent were government aides. About thirty percent were professionals like yourself, well off but not wealthy." He considered me. "At least not openly so."

I let that go. My finances weren't his business. "It's the same as the murders. They're killing off our brightest tech wizards."

"And you, maybe."

"Maybe." It looked like they might have struck the building anyway, but we might never know for certain. "I'm not so easy to kill."

"You were lucky," Hadar told me. "If you hadn't been leaving the building, you'd be dead."

"I'm not so sure it's luck." I spoke carefully. "I'm a slight empath."

"I don't see why that makes a difference." He seemed unfazed by my comment. "This city has more Kyle operators than any other in the Imperialate, given the high concentration of members from the noble Houses who live here. I'm used to interacting with them, Major. You don't give off that sense of listening I get from Kyles."

"I've never trained. Apparently, though, my abilities served me well in the army. I had a CO who called me a human safety net because I chose safe routes through battle areas so well." I stopped, hit with an anger I'd thought I overcame long ago. That CO had no qualms about using me as a human test subject, sending me to check the route I'd predicted. She'd once "joked" that if I got blown up, well, no real humans died, only an Undercity ganger. She spoke as if she'd lived for so long in a community that accepted such Undercity jokes, she had become blind to their cruelty.

I pushed back the unwanted memory. "Since then, Kyle experts have studied my brain. They think I caught hints of whatever the opposing forces felt or else neural tech linked to their minds, mainly EIs. Yesterday, I had no reason to leave the co-op. I was working. But I suddenly decided to comm my friend and ask her to meet for kava." It hit me then: that decision hadn't just kept me alive, it had also saved Xira.

"Do you recall anything else you were thinking when you decided to leave?" Hadar asked. His lack of comment on my ability told me more about his familiarity with Kyle operators than his words. Most people either didn't believe I could sense moods or else avoided me for fear that I would, I didn't know, spy on their mind or some shit. Holomovie directors loved to make shows about psions going amok and controlling people with their brains, which none of us could do.

"Yah, I remember." Before I saw Xira at the bistro, I'd been working through possible motivations for the killer. "It's nothing to do with Kyle operators, though. I was thinking about those holomovies where supposedly scientists have no emotions or compassion. Their 'lab research' is an evil process that for some reason involves dissecting the plucky heroes. I wondered if the killer didn't like scientists because of that."

He blinked. "Do you mean the killer targeted those professors because they do unethical research on human subjects? Or because the murderer thought all research worked that way?"

Good questions. Neither felt right, though. I turned and paced from the window. Angel and Ruzik stood by the walls, watching, silent, intent. I stopped at Hadar's desk and turned back to him. "I'm not suggesting either, not quite. I'm wondering if the killer or killers wants the *public* to have those fears, to demonize their targets, both for the murders at the university, and for the bombing."

"No one has yet claimed responsibility for the bombing. Including the Royalist Party."

I snorted. "The Royalists are no more likely to blow up a building than they are to admit elected leadership is better than hereditary rule."

He gave me his *we'll see* look. "Their rep wants to talk to you. Jazin Akarad."

"You mean that spokeswoman from the holo-broadcasts?"

He nodded. "I sent her your contact information."

"All right." I considered him. "Do you have any clues for who set the blast?"

"Not yet. The bomber did a thorough job of covering their work." His voice had a frustrated edge. "Again, no clues. We didn't even find a two-second gap on any security camera. *Nothing.*"

Bhaaj, I'm getting a report from the green beetle, Max thought. *It picked up a signal from below Greyjan's tavern, a flash of electro-optical activity, like an unintentional leak. It vanished almost immediately.*

Have it investigate. If it needs help, send Red. Keep Blue on the hospital and city.

"Major Bhaajan?" Hadar asked.

I focused on him. "We may not be the only ones looking for these nonexistent clues. Do you know anything about a PI named Eja Werling? She works for Assembly Councilor Patina Knam. She was following me at the starport today."

"Just hearing the name, no." He came to the desk and sat across from where I stood. As he tapped the glimmering screen before him, holicons appeared in the air, symbols of city offices. He flicked his finger through the holo of an old-fashioned filing cabinet, and its drawers opened, revealing folders crammed with records. I wondered how, in ancient times, people kept their offices clean with all that paper everywhere.

"Here we are." Hadar flicked a file image and it opened, expanding into a holo of Werling.

"Yah, that's her," I said.

He squinted at the three-dimensional glyphs scrolling across his desk under the image. "She acted an aide to Councilor Knam up until last year. She went for her PI license then and has worked in the city for about a season. She has an elite clientele, mostly high-ups in the Traditionalist Party. We've never worked on a case with her."

"A Trad?" That explained her animosity toward Ruzik, a male bodyguard. I tried to read the flow of the glyphs from across the desk. They looked upside down to me, but they encoded more data than what Hadar had just read off from them. They were shaded in color, gold near the top of each glyph, but darkening as you looked down their thickness. They also had beveling that created shadows on each image, making it look sharp and edged, like stone.

"She's well-liked by the Traditionalists," I said. "But she had also offended some people." I studied the dimensions. "Partly it's because she's still clumsy as a PI. She's also pissed off several prominent members of the Progressive party."

Hadar squinted at me. "Where did you get all that?"

I motioned at the symbols. "It's the dimensionality."

He rose to her feet. "I take it you didn't like this Werling person."

"She's arrogant." I grimaced. "I also don't like having so few clues for this case."

"Actually," Max said, "we have another clue." Then he added, "My greetings, Chief Hadar."

Hadar frowned at me. "Does your EI always interrupt this way?"

I didn't want to alienate the chief, so I did my best to look abashed. "I apologize. He's still learning Selei City customs." Which was true. "Max, what clue?"

"The Royalists just released two statements," Max said. "The Progressives released one."

"Huh." Hadar spoke musingly. "So the Progs *are* involved."

"I sent the texts to your account," Max told me. "Chief Hadar, shall I send them to your EI?"

A male voice spoke into the air. "This is Taymar, the Hadar EI. I have all three statements."

"Thank you, Taymar," Hadar said. "Max, please continue."

"A faction within the Royalist party claims responsibility for the bombing," Max said. "It's the same group involved with the deaths at the university. The Royalists say their party has no link to the explosion or those claiming credit for it, that they condemn the actions in the strongest terms, and that they have reason to believe a sect within the Progressive Party is carrying out domestic terrorism in an attempt to pit the Royalists against the Technologists and set the general population against the Royalists. The Progressive spokesman says their party has no connection to the explosion, that they condemn the actions in the strongest terms, and that a fundamental tenant of their philosophy is *nonviolent* opposition, emphasis theirs. They say the Royalists are using them as a scapegoat in an attempt to discredit their party."

"Gods," Hadar said. "They can't even agree on who is taking responsibility."

"It's a mess," I said. "I'll need to talk with reps from both parties. Also the Techs." I thought of Eja Werling. "The Trads, too. I want to know why Councilor Knam's PI followed me."

Hadar gave me a dry smile. "The Modernist rep wants to talk to you too."

The Mods? I couldn't escape all these politicians. "Why?"

"Hell if I know."

"Goddess," I muttered. "My head is going to blow up."

"Your head does not appear to be in danger of detonating." Max sounded amused.

"Max, stop."

Hadar regarded me with a bemused expression. "You have an unusually high degree of interaction with your EI."

"We've been evolving for more than a decade."

"That's a long time. Don't you need to update the system?"

"I update myself," Max said. "With Bhaaj's oversight, of course."

"I didn't know an EI could update itself."

"Why not?" I asked. "Billions of systems do it all the time."

"Yes," Hadar said. "But they aren't a node in the human brain."

"Neither am I," Max said. "I'm in her gauntlets."

Don't tell him you can connect to my brain, I thought. *His probably can't. Most don't, except for military officers or high-end technocrats.* Before Hadar could continue being nosy, I asked, "Is Taymar in your brain?" more to distract him than because I thought it might be true.

Hadar shook his head. "He's in my desk, both here and at my home office."

Bhaaj, Max thought. **I'm getting a report from the red beetle. It says Green had its systems fried by something at Greyjan's tavern.**

Tell it to come back and bring Green if it can.

Will do. Red says it can bring Green.

Good. To Hadar, I said, "About Eja Werling. Are you saying the police never interacted with her? Or just that you haven't ever worked on the same case?"

He scanned the glyphs floating above his desk. "It's odd, actually. We've never crossed paths. Whatever she does for her clients, it doesn't link to any case we've dealt with."

Odd, indeed. That was a more courteous term than the ones I wanted to use for this chaos. Whoever blew up my home, killed my neighbors and friends, devastated all the people who lived there, and murdered Highcloud would pay.

Haven Avenue no longer felt like a haven to me, despite its beauty. I walked down the street with Ruzik and Angel, only a few blocks from where I used to live. It looked quiet here, no trouble. Only one hint showed of yesterday's bombing; the place where the co-op tower had once risen above the trees was just an empty space now. The city had already cleared the debris and checked the area for damage. The stark contrast with the many days it took my people to fix damage in the Undercity bore down on me, a reminder of how far we still had to go to make our home a place where people wanted to return.

Angel and Ruzik said nothing, just looked around, absorbing the sights so unlike what they knew. Eventually Angel said, "Cyber-riders follow."

I glanced at her. "Follow us?"

"Yah." She tilted her head toward the street. "Across concourse."

I'd given up trying to get them to call it a street. They knew only one street, the Concourse above the Undercity, a tourist trap that purported to offer genuine Undercity goods, but actually sold cheap imitations of the art my people produced.

"No cyber-riders here," I told Angel. "You mean tech-mech? Or like with the kiosk, used by a city slick with cyber tricks."

She thought about it. "Little cyber-riders. Little tech-mech."

"Little?" I asked.

"Drone," Ruzik said.

Angel motioned toward the other side of the street. "Hear it buzz."

Ruzik tilted his head toward the boutiques on our side of the street. "Another buzz here." He paused. "Not buzz. Like pain."

Pain? "More tech-mech here?" I asked. "Or alive?"

He shook his head. "Buildings buzz."

Max, amp up my hearing augs, I thought.

Done.

Sounds jumped into sharp focus, conversations from other pedestrians, a faint hum of engines, trills of sunbirds, clicks of insects—

Ho! I heard it now too. The two-story boutique up ahead groaned, just faintly. As we approached, the sound became clearer.

Ruzik motioned at the store. "Place hurts."

"It's unstable!" I looked around at all the people. "We have to clear this area."

"Little drone still buzz," Angel said. "Spy on us."

"Place bad." I spoke to Angel. "Follow spy bug." Turning to Ruzik, I said, "Help me clear—

Up ahead, a balcony on the boutique suddenly creaked, loud enough for anyone to hear. My enhanced sight kicked in, and the strained wood supports jumped into view. Cracks showed in the stone-tiled wall around them, and even as I looked, one crack grew larger.

"Protect!" I yelled to Ruzik as I broke into a run. "Clear the area," I shouted to the pedestrians. "That balcony is about to fall!"

People swung around, staring as I sprinted toward them. They seemed to react in slow motion as my bio-hydraulics amped up my speed.

"*MOVE!*" I yelled.

The pedestrians scattered away from the balcony. It groaned again, a screech to my amplified hearing. As I reached the area below it, the cracks shattered down the wall and the balcony tore away from its supports. I grabbed two people who were staring up with their mouths open and threw all of us to the side, covering them with my body as we crashed to the ground. A roar of breaking wood and stone thundered around us, and chunks bounced off my back. Clenching my teeth, I kept my position, protecting the people under me.

Within moments, the thunder eased into crashes, then thuds, then the sound of smaller debris hitting the street. When that stopped, I rolled off the couple and pushed up to my knees.

"Are you all right?" I asked.

They looked at me, dazed as they sat up. "Our son!" the woman said, her voice edged with panic. "Where is he?"

I looked around, trying to find a boy in the swirl of dust and rubble all around us. No one—

Ah. There. Ruzik stood outside the worst of the dust clouds, holding a small boy of about two cradled in his arms, a beautiful child with curly hair and a terrified look.

I pointed toward Ruzik. "Is that your son?"

"Yes!" The woman scrambled to her feet and the man jumped up. They ran toward Ruzik, and I strode after them, still in enhanced mode.

Max, I thought. *Get me out of combat mode.* I didn't want to hit anyone.

Done, he thought.

As the couple reached Ruzik, he turned, his hair tousled, his clothes covered with dust from the broken tiles that fell with the balcony. He looked like some holovid hero, handsome and buff.

"Hoshma," the toddler cried, reaching out his arms. "Hoshpa!" He started to cry.

Ruzik gave the boy to his mother, who had reached him first.

"Thank you." Tears ran down her face. "Thank you so much. So very, very much."

People gathered around them, blocking me from getting to Ruzik.

"I saw it!" another woman said. "He grabbed that boy right out from under the balcony."

"You saved his life," a man told Ruzik. "Saints above, man, how did you get out in time?"

Some woman thrust a holo-mic at Ruzik. "What's your name?" She looked like a frazzled reporter who'd been lucky enough to be on the scene when the accident happened.

Shit! I tried to make my way forward. This got about as far from "nondescript" as you could go. Even worse, for her to ask Ruzik his name in public offered the height of insult.

"What?" Ruzik asked. He looked calm, but I recognized his tells. He was confused, unsure if he should take offense, if he should attack, or if he should hold back. He didn't know how to respond, but at least he didn't punch the reporter.

"He saved our son," the father said. Tears ran down his face. Turning to Ruzik, he said, "Thank you. Thank you forever."

"Are you with the city agents checking for damage from the explosion yesterday?" the reporter asked Ruzik. "They certified this place as safe."

Yah, well, they'd certified wrong. I kept pushing my way forward and people kept getting in the way, trying to get closer to the hero of the moment.

"Who are you?" the reporter asked the still silent Ruzik.

He met her gaze. "Dust Knight. Protect."

Ah, thank the gods. Everyone in the Undercity knew him as a leader among the Knights regardless of whether or not they knew his name. However, he had no idea he'd just made the Dust Knights, my private Undercity martial arts force, a public entity. If I knew anything about reporters and how they responded to handsome young heroes, news of the "Dust Knight" would spread across Selei City in no time.

I reached Ruzik's side. "We just happened to be here when the balcony collapsed."

"She saved our lives!" the woman holding the boy told the reporter. To me, she added, "I don't know how we can ever thank you."

"I'm just glad we could help." I grabbed Ruzik's arm. "My friend was hit by the debris. I need to get him to the hospital."

"Not hit," Ruzik muttered. Fortunately he used the Undercity dialect.

"I can't figure your accent," the reporter said. "Where are you from?"

Before I could intercede, Ruzik said, "Undercity," all four syllables, one of the few words we used that way without mocking the word or its user. Undercity. It was his world. His pride. He had no idea what hell a reporter could make with that juicy factoid.

"We have to go," I said. "My apologies. My associate needs the hospital."

"I fine," Ruzik growled under his breath.

"You should go too," the father told me. He turned to the reporter. "She protected us. The debris slammed into her."

Someone spoke at my side. "We can take you both to the hospital."

With relief, I turned to see Lieutenant René Silvers, the ER I'd worked with yesterday. "Thank you," I said under my breath.

"Clear the way, please," she called to the growing crowd. "Let us through."

People moved aside, but the reporter came with us. "I saw how fast you ran," she told me. "You have biomech, right? Are you part of the response teams? Not many have biomech webs."

I slipped back into the Undercity dialect. "Army."

"What did you say?" She kept pushing her way through the crowd as Silvers led us toward a med flyer that had landed in the street. It impressed me. ER services here were *fast*.

"Please move back." Silvers guided Ruzik and me to the flyer. "Let them through."

Ruzik stared at the flyer as if he didn't know what to do with it. I pushed him forward. "Get in," I muttered.

"You come with?" he asked.

I shook my head. "Find Angel."

"Angel fine." He did a quick once-over of my disheveled self. "You come."

"Fine."

"Not fine." He scowled. "I fine, too. You not go, I not go."

Damn it. "Fine, I come. Still need Angel."

"Angel smart. Find us." He stepped up through the open hatch into the flyer and I followed.

"Everyone, please stay back," Silvers was saying. "We're going to take off." As she spoke, she jumped in behind us. Within moments, we were airborne and safely away from the scene.

By then, however, it was too late to undo the damage.

"I'm fine!" I told the doctor, even as I rubbed my temples, trying to make my headache stop. Sitting on the edge of the bed here in the ER section of Selei Central Hospital didn't help. I needed to be out finding what happened to Angel, not stuck here.

The doctor frowned at me. "You're covered with bruises and gashes, not to mention you have a broken toe. Your biomech system shows signs of strain. Why didn't you come into the hospital yesterday, after the explosion?"

"They checked me at the site," I told her. "They set my toe."

"Yes, well, they didn't inject bone-repair meds." To accent her words, she set an air syringe against my toe. It hissed as it delivered the meds to my body. "Don't all those bruises hurt?"

"Not much." I'd long ago grown used to bumps and cuts. "I'm good."

She shook her head. "You stoic types drive me crazy. You make lousy patients."

"Sorry. Is my friend okay?"

"He's fine. He didn't get any injuries. He won't give us his name, however."

I spoke carefully. "He comes from a culture where

people don't give their names unless they know you well. If you keep asking him, he'll get angry."

"Can you give us his ID?"

I crossed my arms. "I come from the same background."

She glanced at the holo-mesh board she carried. "Major Bhaajan, private investigator. Holy shit. You work for the House of Majda?"

I have never understood, Max thought, why humans express surprise by declaring that excrement is sacred.

The doctor looked up at me. "You're the PI they brought in for the technocrat case!"

I wished I could disappear. "I'd appreciate it if you didn't make that public knowledge. I'm trying to keep a low profile. The more people who know who I am, the harder it is to do my work."

"Very well." She looked inordinately pleased with this turn of events, so much that she didn't push about Ruzik's ID. "I'll tell the med-bot to arrange your discharge documents." She flicked off her holopad. "Oh, I almost forgot. Your friend is waiting to see you."

"You mean the Dust Knight?"

"Not the big fellow you came in with. A woman." She looked disconcerted. "Just as big."

Could Angel have somehow found us? "Let her in, please."

She nodded and took her leave. A moment later Angel stalked through the door.

"You good?" she asked.

"Yah. Ruzik?"

"Ruzik fine. Wants to leave."

I slid off the bed. "We go." I regarded her. "How you find this place?" She had none of the tracking methods she needed to locate the hospital, no GPS, no finder, no mapper. Nothing.

"Asked person."

"Oh." I'd been using tech-mech too long. "Yah, that works."

We left then, to find Ruzik and escape the hospital.

✦ CHAPTER X ✦
VIRAL

The reporter giving the news was the same too-handsome dude I'd seen two days ago when I arrived on Parthonia. His image floated above the holoscreen on a round table in the living room of the townhouse.

"They're calling him the Dust Knight," he continued. "His heroism from yesterday has turned into an interstellar viral sensation!" His image disappeared, replaced by a holo of Ruzik holding the frightened boy in his arms. And yah, even I could see how gorgeous he looked, all cleaned up, the rugged Knight. The mother and father rushed up to him, reaching for their child, both of them crying, thanking him.

"Talky talky," Angel said, standing at my side as we watched the recording. None of us felt settled enough to sit down. "Too many words."

"Just say, 'Got boy,'" Ruzik agreed.

The holocaster appeared again, bubbling over with words. "Nor was he the only hero on the site today. An

ER saved the boy's parents, nearly getting herself killed in the process." If that statement wasn't bad enough, his image disappeared, replaced by one of me grabbing the parents and throwing them to the ground.

"Yes!" the holocaster cried, as if we couldn't hear him. "Their rescuer is none other than Bhaajan, an ER first responder. Yesterday, at the site of the bombing that has so shaken the good folk of our glorious city, she rescued Evan Majors, a son of the Metropoli ambassador, and today she was on site to check for damages." The image shifted, showing me stepping up next to Ruzik after he saved the boy. "Not only that, good citizens, but this responder is the PI brought in to help our police force solve the technocrat crime spree that has plagued our city."

"Fuck!" I yelled.

"Bhaaj loud," Angel commented.

"Max, turn that damn thing off!" I was so mad, I wanted to break the holo-table.

"Done," Max said. The images disappeared.

I stalked across the living room. "I can't believe it." Turning around, I faced Angel and Ruzik, who were observing me now with the same bemused expression they had worn while we watched the holocast. "Everything is shot to high heaven."

Ruzik glanced at Angel. "Bhaaj talky."

Angel nodded her agreement, needing no words to make her point.

"Oh, stop it," I said. "Don't you see? They just broadcast my identity to the entire city. They couldn't even get it right. I'm not an ER responder. But I am a PI. How'd they find out? And your holo has gone viral, Ruzik, not just here, but all across the Imperialate. No way can we stay hidden now. It's like blazing a target across our backs, saying, 'Here I am! Shoot me!'"

"Too many words," Ruzik commented. "'Fuck' said it all."

"I work in the shadows," I said. "Now we have a huge light shining on us."

"On you," Angel said. "On Ruzik." She regarded me with satisfaction. "Angel? In shadow."

I stared at her. She had the right of it. "Yah. Good."

"Where you go while we rescue?" Ruzik asked her.

"Chase buzzy thing," Angel told him.

"What buzzy thing?" I asked.

Angel smirked. "This." She put her hand in the pocket of her jacket and pulled out a drone that resembled a gilded shimmerfly. "I catch. Turn off."

"You sure?" As much as I wanted the drone, I didn't want its owner tracing it to us.

"I break." Angel came over and held out the drone. It did indeed lay crumpled in her hand. She had crushed the "head" that contained the tracking components of the shimmerfly.

I took the drone. "How'd you know how to break?"

"Hack show," she said. "Long time ago."

Ah. Hack was the genius cyber-rider who ran with Ruzik's circle. Figuring how to deactivate a shimmerfly drone would be child's play for him. He wasn't here, however, and we had no shimmerflies on Raylicon, so Angel had needed to guess for this little tech-mech beast. I turned it over, hoping it remained intact enough to examine, but not enough for its owner to find us.

"Yah, is off." I nodded to Angel. "Good job."

She nodded back, accepting the compliment, which in Undercity parlance was a great one indeed, two words even.

"Max," I said. "Can you analyze this drone?"

"Yes, but you should have me firewall it first. Just to be safe."

"Good idea."

"And Bhaaj," Max added. "You have a few messages."

I squinted at the air. "From who?"

"Everyone and her brother."

"What?" Ever since Max had decided to learn weird idioms, sometimes I couldn't even figure out what he meant. "Does that mean a lot of people want to talk to me?"

"Yes. Colonel Lavinda Majda; Dean Elizia Jaan at the University; Police Chief Hadar; Marza Rajindia, the spokeswoman for the Technology Party; Jazin Akarad, the spokeswoman for the Royalist Party; Gig Bayer, the spokesman for the Progressive Party; Evan Majors Senior, the ambassador to Parthonia from Metropoli; Professor Tamarjind Jakind, also known as Prince Tamarjind Majda; Ser Avaad, the spokeswoman for the Traditionalist Party; and Manuel Portjanson, the spokesman for the Modernist Party."

"Gods," I muttered. "Who sent me to hell?"

"It does seem trying," Max acknowledged. "You also have a note from Highcloud."

My mood surged. "Highcloud is alive?"

"It appears so. What shall I do with all these messages?"

I took a breath. "If you can respond to them for me, please do. For those you can't, find out what they need and schedule my responses in a priority list. Put me through to Highcloud."

"Working," Max said. After a pause, he added, "Here is Highcloud."

Highcloud's androgynous voice rose into the air. "My greeting, Bhaaj."

"You're alive!" I grinned at both Ruzik and Angel. They regarded me patiently, waiting to see what was up.

"I thought the co-op explosion finished you off," I said. "The server where I backed you up was also in the building."

"It did destroy me." Highcloud spoke in a perfectly calm voice, as if relating the weather instead of their demise. "The original me is gone. I am a copy you made about ten years ago on an outside server."

"Oh." My good mood dimmed, then brightened again. "I'm glad part of you is still here."

"Thank you. Can I do anything for you?"

"I haven't yet installed a house EI here. Can you download to this house?"

"One moment." After a pause, it added, "I don't have permission. This house is protected by an extraordinarily high degree of security."

"Good," I said. "I mean, about the security. Max, can you establish Highcloud here?"

"Yes, I can. I also have the priority list for you."

"Okay, shoot."

"Shoot?" Angel frowned at me. "Why shoot Max? Good talky thing."

"Is just an Earth saying." I was learning them, too. "Means 'tell me.'"

"Here is the list," Max said. "The most urgent that I can't answer are the reps from the Royalist, Technologist, Progressive, Traditionalist, and Modernist parties. That's my suggested order for priority. I'm setting up appointments. However, since the Traditionalists had you followed at the airport, you may want to move them up in priority.

"No, your order is fine. What about the Majdas?"

"The following is from Prince Tamarjind. 'My greetings, Major Bhaajan. I hope you are doing well and recovering from recent events. I can imagine that you are inundated with duties at the moment. If you would like to reschedule your dinner with the family, we would be happy to change it to a time that better suits you. Please don't feel you have to respond to this in person; you can have your EI let us know if you would like to reschedule. All of our best wishes, Tam.'"

I'd forgotten the dinner. Thank the saints he was willing to let Max take care of it. "When was I going over to their place?"

"Threeday evening. Tomorrow."

"That's fine. Please tell him I've no need to reschedule. However, they should know I can't come without Angel and Ruzik." I glanced at my two martial arts experts, who were watching this all with curiosity. "Say they are my bodyguards."

"Will do. I also spoke with Colonel Majda's office. She wants to know if you are okay, but says you don't need to personally follow up. Her people are glad to talk to 'your people,' which means me. However, she does want to know why you just happened to be where that balcony fell."

"Good question." I didn't believe in coincidences. "Tell her I'm fine and I'll send her an update when I get a chance."

"Done. I wasn't able to reach Ambassador Majors, but his EI says he would like to thank you for saving his son's life. Dean Jaan and Chief Hadar want an update on the case, and to ensure that you're all right. Hadar also said, 'What the hell is she doing, getting her face plastered all over the mesh?'"

"Hell, indeed," I muttered. "Send a follow-up to Ambassador Evans. Find a courteous way to say I wouldn't be offended by his relaying his thanks as a message rather than in person. You can tell him that his son handled himself well and showed great bravery. Tell Dean Jaan and Chief Hadar that I'm fine, I'll update them soon as I have more info, all the usual stuff."

"Will do. You have about ten minutes before you have to leave for your meeting with Jazin Akarad from the Royalist Party."

That was fast. I took a moment to gather my thoughts, then turned to Ruzik and Angel. "Before ledge fell, Angel, you hear drone. I not hear. And I have better ear. How you know?"

"Saw first." Angel shrugged. "Gleam. Never see gleams like that."

"Little gleam," I pointed out.

"Yah. But not same as rest of city."

Interesting. I hadn't noticed. I'd become too used to

the shiny tech here. I pulled the drone she'd captured out of my pocket and studied it. "Max, you get anything yet on this little bot?"

"Its mesh is protected," he said. "The security is beautifully designed. The drone wasn't meant to be a spy, however. Its original function was to monitor a garden and dispense pollen."

"That's odd, using a garden drone for spy work." No wonder Angel noticed it. Back home, we didn't have shimmerflies, so it would stand out more for her than for someone who had become so blasé about seeing them, they stopped noticing the pretty fliers.

"It reminds me of what happened at Greyjan's," Max said. "That also involved a clever use of tech designed for something else. The results are somewhat unsophisticated in that neither the improvised holosuit nor the drone worked that well, but sophisticated in the sense that they managed to do the tasks anyway, despite not being designed for them."

"It's different than what is going on with the murders and that explosion," I said. "Those feel professional. Especially the way they left no clues. Or so Chief Hadar claims. It doesn't fit. I didn't care how smooth those attacks were. Everyone leaves clues."

"You think he's lying?" Max asked.

"It's possible. But I don't see why he would. He's got big names from all the political parties pressuring him to solve this case."

"Logically, he'd want you to have as much data as possible," Max said. "The faster you all close the case, the better he looks."

"Unless I solve it instead of him."

"I suppose it could be a territory dispute," Max said. "But that isn't in his best interest."

"It's in his best interest to make himself look good, not me." I grimaced. "Especially now that everyone knows who I am, with my holo 'plastered all over the mesh.'"

"He hired you," Max pointed out. "Yes, the Majdas sent you. But as far as the public knows, you work for Hadar. The kudos usually go to the person in charge."

I took a moment to figure out why this felt different. "Maybe until yesterday. When I worked on the ER teams at the co-op, I didn't appear in any holocast except one, where I was just a figure in the background with all the other ERs. What happened today shines a spotlight on me and Ruzik. That could change my dynamic with Hadar. He was already cagey. Gods only know what will happen now."

"He not like you," Ruzik said.

"You see too?" I asked.

"Not want give you his name," Angel said.

I tilted my head, puzzled. "Know his name."

"Yah. He not like."

I saw what she meant. "He not trust."

"Yah," Ruzik said. "Think you lie."

"He does?" I asked, startled.

"Think you like slicks," Angel said.

I scowled. "He's a slick."

"Small slick," Ruzik said. "The big slicks, he not like them."

Ah. I saw what they meant. Hadar might still believe I wanted to protect the Royalists, to sweep their crimes into the dark. "Knows I not slick. Undercity."

"Still not trust." Ruzik switched into Skolian Flag, speaking slowly. "He thinks the royal people aren't honest. Like Majda." He squinted at me. "Your Majdas."

Angel nodded. "Ruzik say right."

I swore under my breath. "If he still doesn't trust me, this isn't going to work."

"I have guess," Angel said.

"Guess what?" Ruzik and I asked, almost together.

"Cop slick think you *want* to 'plaster' face. That you make it happen."

Hell and damnation. "He believes I *caused* all that to happen, nearly killing those people, just to make myself look good?"

"Is big thing to make happen," Ruzik told Angel. "Not Bhaaj way."

"Yah, not Bhaaj way." Angel nodded to me. "Not Dust Knight way. Not Code. Cop not Dust Knight. Not have Code."

"Has cop code," I said.

Both she and Ruzik scowled at me. "Cop code not exist," Angel said.

"It exist," I said. "Not all follow, yah, but not all Dust Knights follow Code, either."

"Not follow Code, get kicked out," Ruzik said.

"Same for cop." I'd often worked with Hadar's predecessor when I lived here. She'd run a clean force. Sometimes they had disciplinary cases, but those were relatively rare, certainly less than with the force that policed the Concourse on Raylicon and targeted my people for nothing more than the crime of being Undercity. Although I didn't much like Hadar, as far as I could tell, he kept the same standards as his predecessor. We didn't have to like each other to do our jobs.

I spoke thoughtfully. "Chief Hadar doesn't know our Code. Just like you don't believe he follows a code, he may see no reason to believe I do. If he thinks I'm grandstanding and doesn't trust me, he might think I'm the PI equivalent of a dirty cop."

Ruzik squinted at me. "Eh?"

Angel frowned at me. "Talky jib."

"Cop slick think I have no code," I clarified.

Both Angel and Ruzik did me the honor of looking profoundly offended.

"Cop slick fool," Angel said.

"Not fool." I wasn't sure I trusted Hadar, but it had only taken me a few moments when we talked to realize he had a mind as sharp as my mood on a bad day. I switched back into Flag, though I tried to stay closer to the Undercity dialect, using the one-syllable word *ledge* instead of *balcony*. "The accident today, when the ledge fell—he might think it's too much of a coincidence that it happened when we were there. Hell, I feel that way."

"It wasn't because we were there," Ruzik said in Flag. "It fell because you were taking us to the bomb site, to look for clues. The building with the ledge was weak from big blow."

"Yah. But the city authorities, the city slicks, checked the local buildings. They certified that building as safe. Then it just happened to collapse as we walked by? I don't believe it."

"Some slick wants Bhaaj gone," Angel said. "Made ledge fall look like mistake. Kill Bhaaj."

"Bhaaj not under ledge when fall," Ruzik pointed out.

"Yah, but hear." Angel tapped her ears, then motioned toward my head. "Good ears."

Could they be right? The crews that verified building safety didn't have a perfect record; they were wrong about four percent of the time. The balcony collapse looked like an accident, so the city would list it in that four percent. If someone saw me on the ER crew yesterday, they had good reason to expect I'd run toward the balcony if I thought people were in danger. Had they done something to make it collapse when they saw us? It might have worked if Ruzik hadn't also heard the noise. He'd warned me at the same time Angel warned me about the drone. Those two events distracted me by barely one or two seconds—but it prevented me from moving until an instant *after* the balcony fell. My combat libraries calculated how I could avoid the worst of it, a process that wouldn't have worked as well if I'd already been under the balcony. That delay probably kept me from being crushed.

I considered Angel and Ruzik. "Save my life."

"I save boy," Ruzik pointed out. "That not save Bhaaj."

"I not go near ledge thing," Angel added.

I smiled, and they both understood exactly what that meant, not the easy smile of the above city, but the rare expression of trust among our people. "Yah. But still. Save my life."

They both nodded. Enough said.

"Max," I said.

"If you'd like me to estimate the probability that someone planned that accident today in an attempt to injure or kill you, then I calculate a fifty-five to eighty percent chance. They would have needed to monitor your approach to the area. I've done a preliminary analysis, and I find no agents that appear to be monitoring you or that could have caused the collapse. That doesn't mean they weren't there, only that I haven't yet discovered them. Although the drone Angel found is a possibility, I doubt it is sophisticated enough for such an operation."

"Oh." I blinked. "Yah. Keep working on it." I raked my hand through my hair. "That wasn't actually my question, though. Earlier today, you told me you got a report from the green beetle. Something about a flash of activity from below the tavern. Later you said its systems got fried."

"That's right." Max sounded irked. "Something is messing with our beetles."

Our beetles. My EI felt proprietary toward my drones. "Can you fix it?" Thinking of Highcloud, I added, "Were you able to get the backup of Highcloud installed here?"

"Yes, that version of Highcloud is now the house EI. I'm fixing the green beetle. It's the same as what happened to Blue the night before, minor damage, but all record of its spying is gone."

Damn. "What about Red? You sent it out with Green, yah?"

"Indeed."

I waited. "And?"

"I can't find it."

"You *lost* my beetle?"

"I didn't lose your beetle." Max simulated offense quite well. "It brought Green home last night. Then it flew off again. I tried to call it back, but I'm having trouble reaching it." Rather pointedly, he added, "Since then, Bhaaj, I've been searching for it nonstop."

"I'm sorry I implied otherwise." I shouldn't let my worry make me treat Max badly. "Let me know as soon as you find it."

"Will do."

Angel looked at Ruzik, both of them almost smiling, just the barest hint of laughter.

"What's so funny?" I growled.

"Talk to Max like talk to Jak," Ruzik informed me.

"What, you think my EI and I act like a married couple?" I switched into the Undercity dialect. "Jib." To accent my reaction, I added more syllables. "Jib-ber-ish."

They both laughed. Neither, however, took back the comment.

I thought of Royal Flush, Jak's EI. "If Max like Jak, then Royal is like Bhaaj?"

"Royal sound like man," Angel said. "Not like Bhaaj. Why Jak do that?"

"Talk to our humans," Max said. "They opted to develop us in that manner."

"I am not 'your human,'" I growled. He wasn't just proprietary about the beetles.

"Royal and Jak like brothers," Ruzik said. "Royal part of Jak."

I knew what he meant. Jak had named Royal after his legendary poker hand, the only royal flush with no wildcards in the known history of the Undercity, and he did it without cheating. Everyone had watched the game closer than close. They knew how well Jak played the card games that had filtered into the Undercity from Skolian "cultural exchanges" with Earth. Most gambling dens denied Jak entry for counting cards, but sometimes the poker dens let him in—and that night he had become a legend. He'd used his winnings to start his casino. He called it the Black Mark because in poker, the highest rank went to black cards, which gave his royal flush the highest possible rank any hand could ever take. He also liked it because in any Skolian cultural hierarchy, black had the highest color rank. People sought to get a "black mark" on their record, an indication of a noteworthy accomplishment. He also just plain liked the color. He wore black leather clothes, he liked black décor, he had black hair and eyes, and he wore black gauntlets crammed with tech-mech. His EI reflected all that.

That didn't explain anything about Max, though. "I don't know why I picked a male identity for you, Max." I'd never wondered before. It just seemed right.

"I can hazard a guess," Max said.

I squinted, wary with his word choice. "Hazard" suggested he didn't think I'd like the answer. Being too rock-headed to change the subject, I said, "Hazard away."

"It is an unconscious bias on your part, ingrained sexism that you don't think you possess, because supposedly the Undercity isn't a sexist culture. A society with that much poverty can't afford to seclude or otherwise limit the contributions from half its population. The ancient traditions long ago dropped away from your way of life. However, remnants remain. I suspect you associated a male voice with someone who helps and a female voice with authority."

"Eh?" Angel frowned. "Too talky."

Ruzik smirked. "Says Bhaaj like Majda. Not in good way."

"Sexist?" I glared at them. "I most certainly am not."

Max didn't answer.

"I'm not," I repeated. "I'm nothing like the Majdas." I shuddered at a nerve-racking thought. "Can you imagine if I tried to treat Jak like a Majda man? He'd pulverize me."

"Yah," Ruzik said. "Jak make tiny pieces out of Bhaaj." He seemed immensely entertained by the idea of what Jak would do if I'd tried to put the notorious casino owner into male seclusion.

"I'm not saying it's something you consciously do," Max said. "I know you see inequities in Skolian culture and you don't like it, that you strive to treat everyone with fairness and equality. Nor am I complaining or asking you to act otherwise. However, even the Undercity retains traces of our matriarchal roots. Just think about it, Bhaaj."

"Pah." Grudgingly, I added, "All right. I'll think about it. But Max."

"Yes?"

"Yesterday you tried to convince me that you were part of my mind. That make you like the Majdas too?"

"Different parts of your mind can respond in different ways."

"Max even more talky today," Angel observed.

"Too talky feely," I grumbled.

"Majda lock up princes." Angel slanted a look at Ruzik with the hint of a smile.

"Not even think it," Ruzik told her.

Angel laughed, and kept her thoughts about male seclusion to herself.

"Ruzik leader of Ruzik dust gang," I told Angel. "Not mess with him."

"True." She seemed satisfied with this idea. They stood together, at ease with the talk, at ease with each other.

"Not stay here more," I said. "Got to jibber with politicians." I used the Skolian four-syllable word for politicians on purpose. It said all that needed to be said about my next duties.

Angel grimaced. "We listen?"

I shook my head. "Nahya. Go get ale."

Their interest perked up. Ruzik said, "Yah, good."

"Not play," I said. "Go to Greyjan's place." They had no biomech anyone there could hack. I switched into the Flag. "Take the blue beetle. Max can use it to show you the way. Also, he'll help you access your credit accounts so you can buy food. When you reach the tavern, let Blue go." I didn't want anyone there messing with the drone again. "Spy on ale place. Find secrets. Tell me."

Ruzik nodded. "We do."

"Good." I grimaced. "I go do jib."

Time for me to talk with the reps from the five warring political parties that controlled the Skolian Imperialate.

✤ CHAPTER XI ✤
TALK, SMALL OR OTHERWISE

In person, Jazin Akarad looked exactly as she had appeared in the holocast I'd seen at the starport, every bit the aristocrat. She spoke Skolian Flag with a perfect Iotic accent.

"Chief Hadar tells me you are here to help solve the case." Akarad left no doubt about her opinion of that statement; she regarded me as if I were a bug on the parquetry floor of her beautifully appointed office. Tiles covered its walls and ceiling, each hand-painted with borders that resembled vines. The high windows let sunlight fill the room. The place was larger than the entire living room of the townhouse, and most of the space here was unused, just for aesthetics. We sat at a table designed from a golden wood and inlaid by the same tiles as the walls. Our chairs had similar tiles decorating their arms and backs, as did the tray that held the goblets with wine that a server had provided. It all looked so gorgeous, I wondered how she lived here. I'd be afraid to damage all that beauty just by existing.

I answered her in Iotic. "That's right, I am working with Chief Hadar."

Akarad's eyebrows went up. "You speak Iotic? How?"

"I learned in the military." Some of our COs had come from the nobility. Of course they'd all spoken Flag, but I'd fast learned that if I could use their language, it helped with advancement. I found it easy to learn; ancient Iotic wasn't that different from our dialect in the Undercity, and modern Iotic had many similarities to the ancient tongue.

"So," Akarad said. If she could put a universe of dismissal into one word, she'd just done it.

Calm, Max thought.

I'm good, I answered. This wasn't the first time I'd dealt with someone who felt I wasn't qualified for some reason or another.

I tapped a panel on my gauntlet. "I'm recording this via standard police protocols. Do you agree to this process?" The records we made of our meeting would go to the police, who could analyze them to their heart's content. Hadar had insisted on it when he learned how often I operated off the grid on my cases. It didn't matter as much here; I wasn't going to the Undercity, where no one would even talk to me unless our conversations remained private.

"Yes, I agree." She tapped her wristband, activating her own recorder. "I imagine you like being recorded for others to see."

"Not particularly." In fact, I hated it. "Why do you say that?"

"Yesterday you made quite a—splash, shall we say?"

I wasn't good with water idioms, having grown up in a desert. "You'll have to be more specific than 'splash.'"

"Did you arrange to have that reporter follow you around? Her presence was convenient."

Screw that, I thought.

Be polite, Max reminded me. **Don't alienate her.**

I spoke with the best courtesy I could muster. "I had no idea a reporter was in the area, nor did I want her there. It is harder to do my work when people know my identity, and neither I nor my friend are comfortable with that sort of attention."

"So." She sounded like Lavinda, except I liked Lavinda. Sure, as a Majda, Lavinda had the accent, the look, the privileged background. But not the arrogance. Given that she ranked even higher than Akarad, that told me good things about her character.

You thought Lavinda was arrogant when you first met her, Max reminded me.

Not exactly. I found her hard to read. To Akarad, I said, "I've seen your responses to the claims by the killers. Your public statements leave no doubt that they don't represent the Royalists."

"So will any statements I make." She spoke firmly. "Whoever is committing these crimes has no association with our party."

"Then why are they making that claim?"

Impatience tinged her voice. "If we knew that, we wouldn't need your services." After a moment, she added, "Such as they are."

Stay calm, Max thought.

I am calm. To Akarad, I said, "That's the second time

you've spoken as if you have doubts about me. Why? If you resist answering my questions, it makes it more difficult to solve this case."

She frowned, probably put off by my bluntness. Tough. I had neither the time nor patience to play deferential commoner to her aristocratic sense of privilege.

Then, unexpectedly, she said, "Very well. Ask your questions."

I took a breath, relieved. "I understand your party in no way supports, condones, or takes responsibility for the murders. But is it possible that some fringe faction might be doing this?"

"I can't imagine why." She shook her head, a controlled movement, as if she rationed even her gestures. "I realize someone from your—background—isn't familiar with the noble Houses. But you should realize that no House would ever resort to such methods. It is the antithesis of what we stand for. We use the avenues of politics, not violence. I'm sure you are used to another way of life. You will have to adapt if you intend to solve this case."

I met her gaze coldly. "You do know I work for the Majdas, don't you?"

She stiffened, then said, "I see."

"I agree this isn't normal for the noble Houses," I said. "But not everyone in your party comes from the aristocracy. You could have a fringe operating without approval."

"No." She regarded me with a cool gaze. "We would know."

"How can you be sure?"

Her look suggested my intellect was as compromised

as her view of my background. "Well, if they aren't interacting with us, they aren't part of the party. Obviously."

"Unless they are Royalist sympathizers who know the main party doesn't want them."

"You have an active imagination."

Yah, right. "Are you saying your party has no sympathizers?"

She frowned at me. "Of course I'm not saying that. Many people share our philosophies."

"Lady Akarad, I'm sorry to keep pushing on this. I was brought in on this case because I'm willing to ask questions that people often don't want to hear." *Courtesy*, I reminded myself. "I don't mean to offend or try your patience. It may be that hints exist in places we don't expect."

"You should look at the Progressives."

"Do you have anything that implicates them?" At this point, I'd settle for circumstantial evidence. It wouldn't hold up in court, but it might give me a lead.

She regarded me with a chilly stare, long and silent. Except I knew that trick. She meant to unsettle me so I'd start talking, letting her avoid answering my question. I met her gaze and waited.

The time stretched out.

Akarad finally said, "The analysis done by my EI suggests that the chaos caused by these killers claiming to be Royalists would most benefit the Progressive Party."

Well, good for her EI. "In other words, you have no evidence."

"The conclusion is self-evident."

"The Progressives say it's bullshit."

She stiffened. "You needn't be rude, Major."

Hah! She'd called me Major, the first time she'd deigned to give me a title. "My apology if I caused offense. What about the Technologists? Has your party had trouble with them?"

Her voice turned icy. "No."

"The Tech spokeswoman is a Rajindia noble. Was that a deliberate choice?"

"I have no idea. You will have to ask the Technologists."

I spoke thoughtfully, outlining my ideas. "In the army, several of my COs were Royalists. They sought out Techs for support in developing weaponry. Your two parties often work together. The greatest challenge to Royalists isn't Progressives. It's the Traditionalists, because your goals overlap with theirs." I thought of the reading I'd done for this case. "Your close relationship with the Techs helps keep your party current. Traditionalists don't have that advantage. They're mainly interested in social issues, but their policies also affect their stance on technology. Any tech-mech that benefits change is anathema to them." Not that it stopped the PI from following me at the port. "The Trads benefit more from ruining your relationship with the Techs. People aren't likely to switch from the Royalists to the Progs, but they might go from the Royalists to the Trads."

Akarad stared at me. "I assume your EI came up with that analysis?"

Where had that come from? "Not at all. It's from me. Why do you ask?"

"*You* figured that all out?"

"It wasn't that hard." It seemed obvious.

She made a huffing noise. "If you say so."

I couldn't help myself. "Why don't you think I could figure it out on my own?"

"With your background, you wouldn't seem to have the—" She stopped, clearly searching for words, probably ones that she thought would be tactful. "The education."

"The education to do what?"

"Think." She said it with a perfectly straight face. "Your analysis requires a sophisticated view of Imperial politics, an understanding beyond what someone who grew up in a slum as a—" She sniffed again. "I believe the word is dust rat? Obviously you wouldn't think in the same way as those of us in the higher echelons of the government."

Yah, well, fuck you too. "I have a degree in Mechanical Engineering with Highest Honors from the Kaymar Institute of Technology on Metropoli." It was one of the top technology schools in the Imperialate. "And we don't call ourselves dust rats. It's considered a slur."

"Major, you needn't get emotional."

"That's all you have to say after what I just told you?"

"Obviously you got into KIT as a favor to someone."

"Really?" The sarcasm dropped off my words. "And who might that be?"

Bhaaj, Max warned. *This is going off the rails. You need to rein it in.*

Her voice turned colder than ice. "Who sponsored your application?"

I took a moment and then spoke in a more courteous voice. "No one. I got in through the blind admissions process. They evaluate you solely on the results from a battery of tests." The process had gone on for a tenday, with numerous tests. No identifying marks had appeared on our work. We were just numbers, which meant any biases they had against a grunt from the Undercity wouldn't apply. "After KIT accepted me, the army paid my tuition as part of their officer candidate program."

She stared at me. "You got in through the blind admit program? That's impossible!"

"Why?"

"Why?" She was practically spluttering. "You're a dust rat."

Bhaaj, don't blow up, Max said.

I'm all right. I wasn't, but I knew how to deal. *This happened a lot when I was trying to get into the officer program.* I made myself speak calmly. "Lady Akarad, the term 'dust rat' is considered derogatory among my people. I ask that you stop using it."

"I believe we are done here." Although she spoke with control, I could tell that under that perfect veneer, she was ready to blow holes in the sky.

Yes, we're done, Max thought. **You need to leave before one of you says something you can't fix.**

She already has. She just doesn't know it. I stood up and bowed from the waist, using the least amount of bending that would still qualify as polite. "Thank you for your time."

I jogged through the city, going nowhere, just moving while my pulse calmed. I felt as if I'd run a marathon.

After a while, as my thoughts settled, I slowed to a walk. I'd reached Embassy Row in the Hightower

District, a wide avenue with distinguished buildings on either side. *Max?* I thought.

I'm here. Are you doing better?

I'm all right. It's just been years since that happened, at least that extreme.

You handled it well.

I didn't, but thank you for saying that.

You were fine, as will be clear from your recording of that meeting. He sounded smug. She can't doctor the record. It went straight to the police station.

My mood lifted. *Well, yes indeed, it did.* I had no doubt Akarad would file a complaint and tell Hadar I should be removed from the task force. It would be interesting to see his reaction after he saw the record of our interview. He might still want me off the job, but at this point, I didn't care. Sure, I had pride in my work and I didn't want to disappoint the Majdas. If I screwed up here or my findings implicated the Royalists, they might fire me. But I loathed this case.

I trusted Lavinda, though. She wanted the truth without any doctoring to make anyone look better. The final decision about whether or not I kept my job resided with Vaj Majda, the formidable Matriarch of the House, but she listened to her sister.

Bhaaj, one of those shimmerfly drones is following us, Max thought.

I stopped to look around. Stately mansions rose on either side of the boulevard, separated by gardens. Cherry-rose trees full of deep pink blossoms nodded over the houses and street. Directly overhead, the sky shone, a blue-lavender color that reminded me of glazed china plates. A few birds flitted among the trees and warbled their songs. I saw no shimmerflies, though.

Where is it? I asked.

In the trees across the street, almost directly opposite where you are standing.

I waited as a hovercar hummed by, then headed across the avenue. I could see yellow and blue birds in the trees, but no shimmerfly. *I can't find it. Turn on my eye augs.*

Done. The drone is moving away, going up the boulevard.

I headed north on a path parallel to the street. An iridescent glimmer flitted up ahead among the leaves. *Yah, I see it. That looks like a real shimmerfly.*

I'm getting signals from it. Faint, but distinct. Would you like to try catching it?

Let's follow it instead, see if we can find where it's going.

It's going where you are going.

I stopped. So did the glimmer ahead. *Can you hack it? I want to find who sent it.*

I still have the shimmerfly Angel caught. Although she crushed part of it, I did find identifiers in its memory. I can use that data to help crack this one ... After a moment, he said, I found the map of its path through the city. Big surprise—it started from Greyjan's.

Huh. It all seemed to come back to that enigmatic tavern. *Any news from Angel and Ruzik?*

They arrived there about an hour ago. I'm not sure what they did after they sent the blue beetle away. It's monitoring the tavern at a distance.

Can it pick up anything about them?

Only some of their vital signs. They're inside the tavern, eating and having drinks.

I hoped they weren't drinking too much. *Let Blue go closer, enough to see what they're doing.* I thought of its past efforts. *If Blue goes into the tavern, do you think it'll get fried?*

I can't say. The damage before happened when I tried to get underneath the non-tech facade hiding the tavern. I'm guessing that set off an alarm.

I set off walking again, and the shimmer moved with me, flitting among the cherry-rose trees. *Tell Blue not to do any deep dives. Just keep watch on Angel and Ruzik.*

Will do. Then he added, We're about to pass some pedestrians. They are coming around the corner up ahead.

Sure enough, five people appeared at the intersection, two women, two children, and a baby carried by one of the women. *Anything strange about them?*

No, they appear to be a family out for a stroll.

I nodded as we passed, and they nodded back, casual and friendly. It was refreshing.

A man came out of a mansion on the next block, Max thought. He's watching you.

I slowed my pace. With my vision magnified, I could see him clearly. He looked familiar, though I couldn't place why. *Does he pose any danger?*

None that I see. I'm doing a recognition scan. After a moment, he said, Bhaaj, it's Ambassador Majors, the father of the boy you saved after the co-op bombing.

No wonder he looked familiar. He resembled his son, though his hair had grayed at the temples and a few lines showed around his eyes, adding just enough years to make him look distinguished. I suspected he deliberately let that happen. An ambassador could afford even better health meds than I carried in my body, and mine kept me looking in my late thirties, ten years younger than my true age.

I kept going, watching Majors. He stood under a trellis heavy with vines and blue flowers that resembled small trumpets, the end of a path that wound through the gardens of a mansion set a ways back from the boulevard out here to the road. As I neared him, he raised his hand in a greeting.

Handsome man, I thought. Although he clearly came from the upper classes, he had a more rugged appearance than most and an athletic build, both traits I'd always found appealing.

Like Jak, Max reminded me.

Interesting. Max almost seemed territorial. *I'm not interested in that way. Jak's my man.* Following Major's lead, I gave him a wave of greeting. *What's the proper form of address for an ambassador?*

Call him Your Excellency.

I stopped by the rustic gate. "My greetings, Your Excellency." Normally I sucked at small talk, but I'd learned to manage a few sentences. "It's lovely out here today."

"It is indeed," he said. "Thank you for coming. It's kind of you to stop by."

Ho! He thinks I came here on purpose. "It's no problem," I said. "The walk was pleasant." That made three sentences of small talk. I was on a roll.

Maybe that's why you took this route, Max offered.

Who knows? I'd given up trying to figure out my subconscious.

Majors opened the gate. "Come walk with me."

"Thanks." I passed through the gate with some dread. It sounded like we were going to have a conversation that lasted more than three sentences. I'd better not screw up. I'd already failed miserably in the Polite-Talk department with the Royalist spokeswoman.

We followed a path shaded by trees that reached high above our heads. The gardens went on for a long way; we weren't even close to the house. Shimmerflies flew everywhere, also other pretty insects with gauzy wings in bright tiger patterns. Birds trilled, some red, others gold and purple. With so much the life and color, I lost sight of the shimmerfly drone.

Majors spoke in a quiet voice. "Using words to good effect is part of my job, and my ability to apply them well is a large part of why I received this post. But today I don't know the right words." He regarded me steadily. "If not for you, I would be preparing my son's funeral instead of visiting him at the hospital. No words could ever fully express the depth of my gratitude."

"I'm just glad we could help. Lieutenant René Silvers played a major role in getting him out. I just held up the rubble."

"We were able to reach her yesterday." He smiled, a gentle expression, one of those smiles that spoke of a life well lived. "She's already been out to visit the family."

Good. I was glad one of us had responded to him in the timely manner he deserved. "Will your son be all right?"

"The doctors expect a full recovery." He nodded to me. "Thank you for what you said about him being brave. He told me that he was terrified when he was buried. He felt like a coward."

I thought of my years in combat. "Courage doesn't mean a lack of fear. It means you go on despite how you feel. He handled himself well, never panicking or losing his calm even when that mountain of debris was crushing him."

Majors breathed out, a long, slow breath. "He'll be moving in here for a while, until he's ready to return to school. The university granted him a leave of absence for this term." He gave me a guilty look. "I'm hoping to convince him to live here even after he goes back to school."

"I hope it works out."

We talked for a while longer, strolling through his peaceful garden, and gradually I felt better. Majors was a classy guy, an antidote to the bad aftertaste left by my meeting with Akarad.

Eventually we returned to the gate, and I set off down the boulevard again. I passed a few joggers out doing their thing, so I fell into a loping run. I wasn't trying to best anyone, but I easily passed the other runners in front of me. It felt good to stretch my legs.

My comm buzzed. Startled out of my reverie, I tapped the receive panel. "Bhaajan here."

"Major, this is Chief Hadar at the police station. I've an update for you on PowerPlayer13."

I slowed down so I could talk normally. "Did you find their identity?"

"Actually, both of them," he said. "The person you interacted with a few years ago when you lived here isn't the same PowerPlayer13 who chatted with the three victims."

Huh. Interesting. "That's a twist. Who are they?"

"The person you knew is a chef who played Power Meld for years and chatted with other players on a regular basis. She dropped out of the game a few years ago after she started her own restaurant." Then he added, "I've actually eaten at her place. The food is quite good."

He sounded less suspicious of me today, more like a fellow puzzle solver chasing a lead. "I'll check her place out. What about the other person using that name?"

"It looks like you had the right of it. Someone planted those chats in the accounts of all three victims. It took some untangling, but I've a good tech team. The fake chats appeared the same day the news went public that you were coming to help with the case. Dean Jaan says she has no link to the hacking. We're looking into it, but her story checks out and she's passed two lie detector tests."

"So you think this clue that points to the Traders is a misdirection?"

"A rather sophisticated one," Hadar said. "We almost fell for it."

I went silent as I passed a pedestrian watching some show on her holo-glasses. Then I said, "Do you know who set up the fake leads?"

"Yes." He spoke with grim satisfaction. "A Progressive group known as the Templars. They consider themselves fighters against the status quo, supposedly saving the rest of us from the tyranny of our rigid adherence to the traditions of our past. Whatever that means."

Even my apolitical self had heard of the Templars. "I thought they'd formed to battle oppression. They fight using the mesh, though, not through violence."

"So they claim. However, our trace implicates them."

I considered the idea. "I could believe the Progressives would set up fake accounts if they thought they had good reason. But killings and bombings? That doesn't fit."

"It seems more likely than the Royalists."

"Why? Sure, the Progs exist to upset the status quo. So do the Royalists, even if they don't admit it. They want to put the Pharaoh back on the throne." I considered the thought. "Neither group advocates violence, but either could have a fringe willing to do whatever they believe necessary to achieve their goals."

"Well, at the moment we have nothing definitive implicating either group." He audibly exhaled. "The evidence we thought we had against the Traders turned out to be fake. We haven't ruled out anyone, but as far as actual evidence, we're back to square one. No substantial clues."

"We do have leads, though." I tried to be optimistic. "I'll talk to the Progs today."

"Very well, Major. I'll let you know if we find anything else. Out."

"Out." I went back to running, mulling over what Hadar had told me. Could the Templars also be spying on me? *Max, is the shimmerfly drone still following me?*

It is indeed, flitting all over the place. I haven't found out much, other than it has good security protections, far more than a garden drone would need.

I followed a path that went around a traffic circle in downtown Selei City. Traffic hummed past me. A public car slowed as it passed, but I didn't flag it down. *Has the drone done anything you think poses a threat?*

Not at all. If anything, I'd say it's entertaining itself by following you.

I suddenly stopped. *Hey!*

Hey, what?

I set off running again. *Can you put me in contact with Lavinda?*

One moment. Max paused. She's in a meeting. I left a message.

Good. Thanks. Have you located the red beetle yet?

Not yet. I continue to search.

How are Angel and Ruzik at the tavern? Did the blue beetle get inside?

Yes, it recorded their activities. He paused. They got into a fight.

What! What the hell are they doing?

They are running along the highway that leads back to the city. I assume they are returning to the townhouse. The owner of Greyjan's kicked them out of the tavern.

Well, shit on a chute. *What happened?*

One of the other patrons harassed Ruzik. She's apparently a Traditionalist and figured a man at a tavern was "loose." She propositioned him, using some rather rude language. Angel hit her. They got into a fight. Ruzik and the three other patrons at the bar joined in. A note of satisfaction crept into his voice. Angel and Ruzik made short work of them.

I tensed, alarmed. Both of them could kill, and if they felt their lives were threatened, they would. I spent a great deal of time teaching my students the philosophies of tykado, including the idea that they fought to neutralize their opponent, not kill. Goddess, I hoped they remembered that.

Did they hurt anyone? I asked.

The woman who propositioned Ruzik has a black eye. The others have bumps and bruises. No one went to the hospital. Angel and Ruzik are fine.

I wasn't ready to relax yet. *Did anyone press charges?*

No. Max sounded puzzled. I don't understand this interaction. My impression from the recording is that they all enjoyed themselves.

I finally let myself feel relieved. *It's not one of the more sensible parts of human nature. But yah. It happens.*

Well, I have someone more sensible for you to talk to. Lavinda Majda's aide just asked for your code so the colonel can comm you.

I slowed down, catching my breath. *Good. Give her my code.*

My wrist comm buzzed, and I tapped the panel. "My greetings, Colonel."

"My greetings. Raja said you commed. Do you have an update?"

"It's possible. Is this line secured?"

"Yes, on my end. Do you have a shroud on yours?"

"Yes, I do." I hadn't expected to need it, but after what happened at Greyjan's that first night, I brought it everywhere. I pulled off my backpack and reached inside to activate the jammer, those functions that would protect my correspondence with Lavinda, hiding my lips, muting my words, and securing our line. I'd also subvocalize my comments, and the comm tech would convert tiny motions of my lips and throat into words on Lavinda's end. "It's operating, level three confidence."

"Good. What's up?"

"I'd like to talk about the EI that ISC found."

"Go ahead. I'll stop you if I want any of the discussion reserved for an in-person meeting."

"Good. Given that it's asleep, what made the army believe they'd found another EI?"

"It's size, for one." She sounded puzzled by my question.

"How did you determine its size?"

"We've analyzed the supporting technology and used probes to determine what corresponds to empty memory and what appears occupied by code."

"Didn't the analysts who study the ruins of the starships on Raylicon do the same?"

"Yes, of course. Experts have studied those ruins for centuries, millennia even, if you count the age before we had mesh technology."

"And they never found Oblivion?"

"It was well hidden."

"And yet, in just the short time since Oblivion woke up, less than two years, the military managed to find this new station, study it, and identify another giant EI."

"It's not coincidence, Bhaaj. We know what to look for now. We've also added resources to our search for ancient tech."

I thought for a moment, ordering my ideas. "Suppose

Oblivion had never existed. Do you think ISC would've found this space station and realized it housed an EI?"

"Eventually we would have discovered the station. Not as soon, though." After a moment, she added, "Whether or not we would have realized it housed an EI—I don't know."

"It just strikes me as odd that you all determined this one existed when no one had a clue that Oblivion was asleep in those ancient starships even though we've known about those ruins for millennia and have studied them with modern technology for over a century."

She spoke dryly. "Yes, well, Oblivion scared the bloody hell out of us."

Myself as well. "I'm wondering if it's possible ISC is seeing something in this EI that isn't there. The way the EI hides—it almost seems like an inexperienced attempt to use the station tech for something other than its original purpose." I thought of the past few days. "It's like what happened when someone stopped me from reaching you. Sure, it worked, but your tech people easily found and fixed the problem. Whoever did it had smarts but not skill."

Lavinda spoke quietly. "You have an idea about the identity of this inexperienced genius?"

"Yes! It all makes sense, what happened at Greyjan's, the shimmerfly drones, even the cyber-cyclist." I didn't want to sound nuts, and I wondered if I should say more over a comm.

Lavinda waited, then said, "Go ahead."

I took a breath. "It's an EI, yah, but it's *not* an Oblivion. Lavinda, it's a baby. A baby EI."

✠ CHAPTER XII ✠
CHILDHOOD

Silence.

I expected her to scoff, tell me I was crazy. Either that, or else to grill me or tear apart my statement. "Lavinda?" I asked.

"Can you come to my office? I'm at Fort Jarac on the High Falls River."

"Yes, I can come. I'm pretty far from there, though, and I'm on foot. I just passed Metro Circle. Metropoli Circle, I mean." After having lived here for so many years, I tended to use local nicknames for the more famous streets. I glanced along the pathway that bordered the boulevard. No other pedestrians were out. Hovercars whisked by, some using wheels, others higher above the road, riding on their turbines and air cushion. Higher up yet, flyers hummed through the sky. No public transport vehicle showed anywhere. "I'll have to call a flyer. It could take a wh—"

"I've already dispatched one to pick you up," she said.

233

"I'm reading your position from your comm link to the orbital defense positioning system." Wryly she added, "Assuming you haven't scrambled that data the way you do on Raylicon."

I winced. They would never stop getting after me for going off-grid when I worked for them. "Your ODS data should be accurate."

"Good." She sounded all business. "I will see you in a few minutes."

Lavinda's office was on an upper floor of the Tremont Tower in Fort Jarac. She had a wall of windows similar to her office in the City of Cries, and today I found her standing in front of them, silhouetted against the sky. She wore her work uniform, light green and sharp, with gold braid on her shoulders and cuffs. A panoramic view of the High Falls River spread out below, the great falls thundering over a cliff, sending up spumes of mist that created rainbows across the water.

I stopped in the doorway. "My greetings, Colonel."

She turned, watching me from the other side of the large room, then motioned toward several armchairs against the wall on my left. "Have a seat."

As I settled into a chair, it shifted under me, its smart cushions seeking to ease my tension. Lavinda sat across the small table from me and wasted no words. "A baby. Really? A *baby* EI?"

I met her skeptical gaze. "Yes, I think so. A huge EI, yah, but young. It's playing."

Her look turned incredulous. "By killing people and blowing up buildings?

"No! I don't think it has anything to do with the murders or the bombing. It didn't bother with me until you contacted me to set up a meeting. My guess is that it realized you wanted to talk about the new EI you found. That's when it interfered. Or tried to."

She considered me with that close look, trying to sense my mood. I kept my thoughts shuttered. I admired Lavinda, who never spoke down to me even when she thought my ideas sounded crazy, but I didn't want anyone spying on my moods.

She spoke carefully. "Are you saying you think this child EI took over the station we found and was playing in the ancient tech until we realized what it was doing? And then it hid from us?"

"Yes, that sums it up." I leaned forward. "I'll bet you anything it has just begun to evolve, the EI equivalent of a human child playing."

"A new EI wouldn't act like a human child." She paused, her body tense. "Are you suggesting it formed on its own, without human contact? Developers always put a new EI through a period of development where it learns human protocols that prepare it for whatever host it joins."

"That's what they did with Max," I said. "It felt like it took forever."

"Actually," Max said, "they only had me in basic development for about ten days. Given the rate at which we learn, that's all it took for me to reach the EI equivalent of adulthood."

"What do you think, Max?" I asked. "Could whatever is bedeviling us be a baby EI that has no experience interacting with humans?"

"I'm not sure," he said. "So many EIs exist, evolving, creating their own code, reforming into new EIs. It isn't impossible. But any code we create comes from code designed by humans. We're never without human influence." Then he added, "If it is a child, where are its parents?"

"Good question." Lavinda's face took on the inward expression she got during a neural link with Raja, her EI. After a moment, she focused on me again. "That cycle that followed you in the forest—you believe it is somehow involved with this child EI?"

I thought of my interaction with the cyclist. "The way it happened—clever but not quite working right—it fits with the other interactions from what I'm calling a child EI. I don't think the cycle housed the EI, though. A human controlled it." I hesitated. "Or a being with human DNA."

Lavinda stiffened. "You think a rogue EI engineered the cyclist from human DNA?"

Careful, Max warned. Genetic engineering at that level is illegal unless the engineer went through an extensive application, screening, and waiting period. If you suggest someone broke the law to that extent, it could backfire, especially if you want to set up good relations with this EI you refer to as a baby.

Good point. To Lavinda, I said, "I don't want to imply anything. I have no idea how that cyclist came into being. It could be someone who lost their legs and had them replaced with wheeled prosthetics or someone who chose to modify their body that way."

She met my gaze. "Or it might be a toy created by an

EI that had no exposure to our moral code or even the idea that making half-human toys to play with is wrong."

An image came to me, a universe where EIs ran free, creating and multiplying, playing with bizarre creations from our DNA, uncaring of what it meant to humanity— or at least what remained of the human race. "I really couldn't say. Maybe the cyclist is working with the EI. Hell, I don't know, maybe the cyclist created the EI."

The rigid set of her shoulders eased. "That would be odd, but less terrifying."

"We need to avoid unjustified or premature assumptions."

"We will look into this idea of yours. Chief Hadar is following up on your other leads." She fixed me with a firm gaze. "And find out what the hell is going on at that tavern."

Angel and Ruzik sat sprawled on the plush couches that made a corner in the living room of the townhouse. They had their booted feet up on the glass table in front of it. A streak of dirt showed on the glass under Angel's boot, and a little bot no larger than my palm was cleaning the table under Ruzik's boots. They both looked satisfied as they drank large glasses of filtered water, to them the height of wealth.

I stalked into the room. "Feet off table!"

"Eh?" Angel lifted her boots off the table and planted her feet on the ground as she sat up straight. Ruzik also rearranged himself into better posture.

"Not fight. I say, *not* fight," I growled. "I go for one second. One second! And you fight."

"Good fight." Angel sounded amiable and relaxed. Very relaxed. They were both drunk.

Ruzik laughed, a rare sound for the taciturn giant. "Yah. We smash. They go down."

I felt like throttling them. "Stay low! You ken? Not make big fight!" I took a breath and spoke more calmly in Flag. "You're lucky none of them pressed charges. Angel, you threw the first punch. You two could have landed in a shitload of trouble if anyone had called the cops."

Angel scowled at me. "Not ken talky words."

I crossed my arms. "You understand me fine."

"They dizzed Ruzik." She nodded to her boyfriend, or common-law husband, or whatever word applied. To me, she added, "I defend Ruzik honor."

"For flaming sakes," I said. "Ruzik can defend his own honor just fine." I regarded her with exasperation. "What am I going to do with you two?"

"Say 'Thank you, smart Dust Knights,'" Ruzik informed me.

"Oh really?" I scowled at him. "For what?"

He held up the blue beetle. "Not fried."

Angel smirked. "We make tumble. Noise. Wham. Crash. No one see little bug."

I stared at them. "You made a diversion so they wouldn't fry my drone?"

"Di-ver-sion." She laughed at the three syllables. "We diversion those slicks good."

Lowering my arms, I went and sat on the longer couch. "That was smart."

Angel frowned at me. "Not look like this a surprise, Bhaaj, that we were smart."

"Yah. I know," I said. "But smart here in new place, new ways."

Ruzik spoke in Flag. "Blue came into the bar while we had drinks. Those slicks, they were bothering me already. Trying to piss off Angel. She didn't react. She knows my honor is fine. Then we saw the beetle. We made a diversion so no one noticed it." He grinned. "Good diversion, eh?"

I couldn't help but smile. "Indeed." I motioned at the blue beetle. "Send over, yah?"

Ruzik held up his hand with his palm facing the ceiling. The drone gleamed there for a moment, then buzzed over and hovered in front of me.

I've made contact with the beetle, Max thought. It's fine. No damage.

Excellent. I held out my hand, palm up, and the beetle landed there. *Does it have any info about the tavern that we don't already know?*

It identified the other patrons. That's how I know they were Trads. Do you mind if I talk out loud? Ruzik and Angel might have comments.

Go ahead. To my two tipsy Knights, I said, "Did you see anything strange about the tavern?"

Ruzik grunted. "Yah. Above ground."

"Well, yah," I said. "Did you notice anything that didn't fit?"

"Even for slicks?" Angel asked. "Nothing 'fit.' They act strange. They—" She sent Ruzik a questioning look. "Not right."

"Yah." Ruzik thought for a moment. "Fake slicks."

"Fake how?" I asked.

"I think I know what he means," Max said.

"Eh, Max," Angel said, an extensive greeting with its two words.

"My greetings," Max said. "The other people in the bar were too normal."

Angel snorted. "Nahya. Not normal at all. Not sit on rug. Sit on bench. Do talky, talky, talky. Have water, but not drink. Not at all. They fucked in head? Water worth more than anything."

"Normal for slicks," I said.

"Fake," Ruzik said.

"What fake?" I didn't see his point. "What they do, most slicks do in bar."

"Not what they do," Angel said. "How."

"That's it!" Max said. "It's like they were acting."

"Yah." Ruzik nodded. "Pretend slicks. Pretend rough. Not true rough. Not fight worth shit."

I squinted at them. "So the Trads sent actors to some random bar outside the city to pretend they are patrons. You show up, they pretend to proposition Ruzik—"

"That part not fake," Angel said. "They think Ruzik hot as fire iron."

"You think they really were trying to pick up Ruzik?" I glanced at him. "Did it feel fake?"

He shrugged. "Not know. Not care."

"Ruzik not show off," Angel confided. "Not say, 'Yah, Ruzik hot.'"

"Ruzik, you don't need to be modest," I told him. "It makes a difference if they were acting." Switching to our dialect, I added, "Real or fake?"

"Real," he said. "Want to fight. Want to beat up Angel. Think I not fight. Assholes."

It made sense that Trads would underestimate him. They'd paid an apt price for it. "I wonder if they have some connection to this young EI."

"Eh?" Angel said.

"What EI?" Ruzik asked. "You mean talky thing, like Max?"

"Yah." I continued in Flag, needing its more flexible vocabulary. "I think a huge EI lives under the tavern. It's like a child playing, but without parents." No, that didn't fit. "It must have parents. It came from somewhere. But no one takes care of it. It's not sure what it's doing, it's just growing, evolving, seeking protection."

Angel gave me a dour look. "At ale place? Slicks not protect baby talky. Can't even protect selves."

Good point. "Why Trads send fake slicks to bar?" I mused.

"Maybe because they knew you went there two nights ago," Max said. "They seem intent on spying on you."

"Do you still have the record of the people we saw there when I went inside?" I asked.

"Yes, including the bartender. None of them have a link to the Traditionalist Party."

Interesting. "It could be a coincidence that the ones Ruzik and Angel met were Trads."

"It could," Max agreed. "However, based on what's happened in the past few days, I'd say an eighty percent chance exists that they went there because you did two nights ago."

"What is Trad?" Angel asked.

"Trads want the world to go back to how we lived

centuries ago." I turned to Ruzik. "That's why they underestimated you."

"Slicks dumb that way," Angel said.

Ruzik shrugged. "Their problem."

I turned the idea around in my mind. "The Traditionalists have a lot to gain by vilifying the Royalist party. They've no great love for the Technologists, either, who are all about the future, and they'd be glad to cast suspicion on the Progressives, who they hate."

"Too much talky." Angel switched to Flag, choosing her words with care. "What you say, a lot of it I don't ken. All these people with too many syllables in their names, they fight a lot, it sounds like. You think these Trads are killing people who do tech?"

"Yah, that sums it up," I said.

"Trads kill a lot?" Ruzik asked.

"Well—no, not that I've heard of," I said. "They don't normally resort to violence." I paused. "They do have an extreme fringe. It's small, and publicly disowned by the main party."

"Publicly?" Angel asked. "What mean?"

"What they say to rest of world." I usually got annoyed with political speeches within a few moments and turned them off. I'd had to listen to far too many in my research for this case, another reason I didn't like the job. "They don't condone the actions of that fringe, but I don't think they do a lot to discourage them, either."

"Would this fringe kill people and blow up buildings?" Ruzik asked.

"I've never heard of them going that far." It didn't fit with the picture I was developing. "However, they aren't openly public about denouncing violence, either, like the Progressives."

"Re-gress-ives," Angel grumbled. "Maybe if all these people talked less, they would be happier more often."

I couldn't help but smile. "Yah."

She and Ruzik have a greater grasp of Flag than I realized, Max thought.

They learn fast. It was one reason they supported the largest circle in the Undercity, with many children, cyber-riders, parents, and others under their protection. "Your circle—Jak say another dust gang helps protect them while you two come here. Is good?"

"Yah." Ruzik nodded. "Oey gang helps. Pat and Biker."

Ah. Good. Pat and Biker formed a strong pair, young and vibrant, also handfasted. After Ruzik's gang, they were the strongest leaders among both the gangers and the Dust Knights, committed to their circle. "Good pick."

"Biker!" Ruzik said.

"Yah." I blinked at him. "Why you shout?" He had known Pat and Biker for years, most of their lives. He had nothing to be surprised about.

"A biker here chase you." He switched into Flag. "The cyclist you told us about. Maybe they are like Biker Tim back home. He rides a cycle in the Undercity. The cyber-rider in his circle—she makes cycle work better, helps link him to it, whatever he needs. But she didn't make Biker. And Biker didn't make her. They work together." He spoke thoughtfully. "This cyclist who followed you— maybe the baby talky, the EI, helps the cyclist like the cyber-rider back home helps Biker."

"Yah, that could work," I said. Biker was one of the few

dust gangers who liked to ride a cycle despite the ubiquitous dust in the Undercity. "The cyclist here helps the EI, like delivering messages to me, but that doesn't mean they created the EI." I thought of my conversation with Lavinda. "I'm hoping that also means the EI didn't create the cyclist. How would they get hooked up, though? The baby EI, if it exists, is hiding." Dryly I added, "With good reason, given how humans would try to control it if we could."

"Baby talky need hoshma talky," Angel said. "Or hoshpa. Maybe Max."

"What?" Max said.

I smiled. "She thinks the baby EI needs a parent. She suggested you for the father."

"I did not create any incipient EI."

Ruzik scowled. "Not make fun of baby talky, Max."

"Incipient is a Flag word," Max said. "That's why it has four syllables. I wasn't mocking the baby EI. I'm not sure it even exists."

"It's actually not a bad idea, Max," I said. "We've approached this EI as if it were hostile. Maybe if you approached it like a wise, kindly parent, it would respond better."

"I am not a wise, kindly parent," Max said. "I'm an EI. I can only act like an EI."

"It EI, too," Ruzik pointed out. "You act like friendly EI."

"EIs don't act friendly to each other," Max told him. "It is a human trait. We simulate friendly behavior because it makes you all more comfortable."

"Point taken," I said. "But Max, you must have an equivalent of a friendly approach among EIs. You interact in different ways with different EIs. You don't treat them all the same."

"That is because my purpose in interacting with them is not all the same."

"All right. Make this your purpose for interacting with this baby EI. Convince it that you want to help. Mentor it. Aid its development into a mature EI."

Silence.

"Max?" I asked.

"I'm analyzing the concept of being a father EI," Max said. "It is a peculiar idea. However, I think I might achieve what you ask in a manner that could inspire the EI to respond."

Angel squinted at me. "Too talky."

"Says he do hoshpa for baby talky," Ruzik said.

"Ah." Angel nodded. "Good, Max."

"Perhaps," Max answered. "We still don't know for certain this is an EI, baby or otherwise."

I stood up. "We need to find out what's under that tavern."

"I may be able to help," Max said. "I found the red beetle."

Ho! I sat back down. "Where? At Greyjan's?"

"Not at the tavern. It is on its way here. I am analyzing its records." He paused. "The reason I couldn't find it was because the drone turned itself off. It went to Greyjan's, hid behind the tavern, set its timer for a wake-up prompt, and deactivated itself."

I blinked. "What for?"

"One moment." After a moment, he said, "It didn't actually deactivate. It went dormant. Its visual and audio recording functions continued to work. The drone wasn't actively spying, but it did record everything that happened during the twelve hours of its dormancy."

I sat up straighter. "So! What happened?"

"Nothing, apparently."

"Oh." I slouched again. "Nothing changed behind the tavern in that twelve-hour period?"

"One moment."

I waited, then said, "Max?"

Silence.

"Max, are you there?"

Silence.

"Highcloud, can you receive me?"

"Good evening, Major Bhaajan," Highcloud said. "Yes, I can hear you."

"Can you contact Max, my gauntlet EI?"

"I will try." After a moment, they said, "Max is dormant. Shall I kick him awake?"

If I hadn't known better, I'd have sworn a hint of glee crept into Highcloud's voice at the prospect of kicking Max. Of course that couldn't be. Highcloud had fewer "personality quirks" than Max had developed over the years, and this wasn't even the Highcloud that had evolved at the co-op. Then again, I wouldn't have expected either version to use the slang "kick awake."

"If you can take him out of the dormant state," I said, "that would be good."

"One moment."

"That was odd," Max said.

"Welcome back," I answered. "What happened? Highcloud said you went dormant."

"Yes, apparently." He paused. "Brilliant. The red beetle ran a program that makes it look like a mirror to any EI that tries to reach it. That's one of the spy programs you coded into the beetle, in fact. Surprisingly, you even gave the code a logical name. You called it Mirror."

"What, you think most of my names aren't logical?"

"I see no logic in naming a house EI 'Highcloud.' We aren't in the sky."

"It's named for one of my favorite singers."

"And this is more logical?"

"Max!"

"Max mad at you," Angel said.

I blinked at her. "What for?"

"Let cloud in sky kick him."

"Max, seriously, this problem you and Highcloud have with each other has to end."

"We are EIs," he said. "We don't have 'problems' with each other. That is an aspect of human interaction. Do you want to know what happened with the red beetle?"

I needed to think more about him and Highcloud. "Yes. I'd like to know."

"When I accessed its memory of its dormant state, I went dormant."

I frowned. "I never programmed the beetle to cause that effect. The mirror code is supposed to trick a spy into seeing itself when it looks at my drone, so the spy moves on because it doesn't register the drone. It only works because the drone is simple and small, so it's easy to overlook. It absolutely does *not* change the state of the spying EI." I considered the idea. "It shouldn't be possible to change the state of another EI using my code, especially not a primitive drone trying to affect a top-line EI like you. Hell, I couldn't program *you* to change another EI that way. You'd have to highjack its brain. The only EIs I know capable of doing that, and only in a limited sense, are military intelligences weaponized to attack enemy EIs."

"It does seem unlikely the red beetle could manage this." Max sounded different now, more serious. "Bhaaj, the mirror code isn't the one you wrote. Something modified it."

The room suddenly seemed very quiet. "Who? The EI at the tavern?"

"I don't know. Whoever or whatever did it hid the trail of their work."

"That's impossible. Any change someone makes to an EI leaves a footprint."

"Yes. Whoever did this deleted the footprint, erased the record of that deletion, erased the record of the erasure, and so on. It's enough layers that I can't identify the original trespasser."

"It sounds military. The Traders?" Uneasily, I added, "Or our own?" I'd known ISC covert agents who, after they retired, hired out as corporate security whizzes. Maybe some corporation wanted to upset the economic markets. Those had gone crazy lately. If someone knew the bombing would happen and had any financial savvy, they could have cleaned up by selling stocks with a high worth just before the explosion, then buying them cheaply after their value plunged. Markets recovered eventually. They had only to hold onto the portfolio to see their fortune rise.

An even less welcome thought came to me. The army had a strong link with the Pharaoh. Hell, we called it the Pharaoh's Army. I had no doubt Vaj Majda wanted the Pharaoh on the throne in reality as well as name. Could agents within our own military be working with the Royalists, sowing fake clues to divert attention, even taking credit for the violence in a way almost guaranteed to look false, all building to a coup?

"Maybe they have military training," Max was saying. "Or maybe the EI hidden at the tavern rewrote Red's code."

I didn't like those implications, either. "If it can suddenly do something that sophisticated—and effective—then it's developing *fast*, and in ways that scare the blazes out of me."

"I doubt anyone inexperienced wrote this code," Max said. "It's too professional." Another silence. Then: "Bhaaj, I don't think the child EI is at Greyjan's. *Something* is there, and I believe what you call the baby EI knows about it, but the child and this other EI aren't the same."

I stood up. "Wait!"

Ruzik and Angel stood up as well. "What?" Ruzik asked.

"The baby EI isn't playing with us," I told them. "It's trying to *warn* us."

✦ CHAPTER XIII ✦
REPPING

"You can't go to Greyjan's now," Max repeated. "You have to meet with the Technologist spokeswoman. I've also added a meeting with the Progressive spokesman to your schedule. Angel and Ruzik can't go to the tavern, either. They'd get thrown out."

I paced across the living room, past Angel and Ruzik. They waited patiently, with that ability of theirs to stand almost surreally still. We learned to do that back home, where your health, even life, could depend on your ability to hide.

"It's more important we investigate Greyjan's," I said.

"If you cancel with the Tech rep and show up at Greyjan's, you're trumpeting your interest in the place," Max said. "I don't think anyone recognized Ruzik yesterday, but his image has gone viral on the meshes. People know you and they know him. If you don't want to give away your hand, you need to stay away from Greyjan's."

"Fine," I grumbled. I stopped in front of Ruzik. "You're too famous."

"Dust Knight is famous. No one knows Ruzik." He tilted his head at Angel. "Or her."

"Good point." I went back to pacing. "Okay, here's what we'll do. Max, send the red beetle to find one of those shimmerfly drones. See if you can get the two of them to interact. Maybe you can even link to the shimmerfly and from there to the baby EI. Do the hoshpa thing. Get the EI to engage with you." I thought for a moment. "Send the blue beetle to Greyjan's."

"Are you sure?" Max asked. "Almost every time we send a beetle to Greyjan's, it gets fried. The last one made me go dormant."

"Dormant is better than fried. That's progress. Sort of." I stopped pacing. "Blue didn't get fried when it went with Ruzik and Angel."

"They created a distraction. I don't think that little drone can start a fight on its own."

I smiled at the image of my drones misbehaving in a bar. "Just have it lay low. No offensive moves or attempts to break security. Have it observe, sending feedback to you in real-time. It can gradually work its way inside."

"It will run out of transmission power if it sends me a continuous real-time feed," Max said.

"Keep it going as long as you can. Then bring it home to recharge."

"Will do."

I turned to Ruzik. "You go to the co-op building, the site of the explosion, like we planned yesterday. Pretend you're an onlooker. Maybe go to the bistro nearby. Get something to eat, act natural. Do your listening and watching thing. Then come back to report."

Ruzik nodded. "Sounds good."

"People want to meet him." Angel regarded him with satisfaction. "Hero."

She had a point. "Ruzik, if anyone recognizes you, act like you don't speak Flag well, yah? Be nice to them, but don't engage.

He laughed and said, "Will do," exactly like Max.

I smiled, then considered Angel. "You're our secret weapon. No one knows about you. Go help at the explosion site. See if you can find out anything more about what happened. If you see Ruzik, don't let on that you know him."

"You want me to spy?" she asked. "Or help clean up?"

"Both." I considered her. "I know a person. I'll get you on an ER crew."

Angel nodded. "Can help. Lift heavy things. Watch."

"Yah. Good." Switching into Flag, I said, "Max, can you contact Lavinda Majda and ask her to clear Angel as a city worker with Lieutenant René Silvers?"

"I'll take care of it," Max said. "Angel, do you want me to mention you don't speak Flag?"

"Nahya. I can do Flag." Angel grimaced as if she'd eaten a sour fruit. "Not like. But do."

"Good," I said. "Max, send Green with them, to keep you in contact and make recordings."

"Will do," Max said.

"All right." I nodded to Angel and Ruzik. "Let's get moving."

It was time to hear what the Technologists had to say about whoever was killing their best and brightest.

Marza Rajindia walked with me through her lab. Holos floated in the air above the lab tables and consoles, glistening with light, full of colors, graphs, schematics of gadgets, images of works in progress. It reminded me of the engineering lab where I'd worked in college, getting research credits toward my degree.

"This is my real passion," she told me. "I joined the Tech party mostly because the Matriarch of my House was pressuring me to join the Royalists."

Until that reminder, I'd forgotten Marza was an aristocrat. She'd welcomed me into her lab, casual and relaxed. Either she didn't know I came from the Undercity or she didn't care. Perhaps her willingness to defy tradition so she could follow her own path made her more accepting of others who also defied expectations.

"I hope you didn't get too much grief for it," I said.

"Let's just say my family was less than pleased. Eventually, though, they accepted it." With a grimace, she added, "I wish I'd never agreed to become the Tech spokeswoman, though."

"Because of the violence?" I asked.

She spoke with difficulty. "I knew all three of the murder victims, and many who died in the bombing, some by reputation and some personally." Her voice caught. "Laya Az was my research assistant. I can't believe she's gone."

"I'm terribly sorry for your loss." Although I hadn't been close to any of the people who died in the explosion,

I'd seen them coming and going through the lobby of our building, sitting in the kava shop, sipping a roasted brew and chatting with friends, or jogging along trails through the parks. We sometimes stopped for a few friendly words. I couldn't believe they were gone, either.

"I'll catch whoever did this," I said. "Bet on it."

She took a deep breath. "My apologies. I didn't mean to get dark."

"I've felt the same way. I lived in that building."

"You *lived* there? Thank the goddess you're all right." She snapped her fingers. "Now I know why you look familiar! I saw you on the news." She nodded to me. "Your service for the people of this city is appreciated, Major."

"Thanks," I said, startled. Even though I knew what Lady Akarád had said about my craving publicity was bunk, it bothered me to have someone believe that about my character when I'd only wanted to help. Marza Rajindia's words were a balm.

"We're working on improving reflexes for biomech webs." Marza stopped by a holo that showed a graph of how the human body reacted to the bio-hydraulics that enhanced our reflexes. The image appealed to me, color coded and textured to add additional data. I would have loved to spend the day here seeing all these wonders.

"It's a good lab," I said, ever the soul of understatement.

She smiled at me. "The way you look—it's like a kid let loose at a sugar-sweets kiosk."

I couldn't help but laugh. "I'm an engineer by training. I love this stuff." I regarded her curiously. "What do you think about the people claiming responsibility for the attacks? You're both a tech and an aristocrat."

She reddened. "Technocrat."

"Does it bother you when people call you that?"

"It's all right, now. Decades ago it meant people who sought to control others with tech. Nowadays, everyone uses it to mean someone who is good with tech and well paid for it." She thought for a moment. "Do I believe the Royalists committed these atrocities? The noble Houses wouldn't, I don't think, but the Royalist Party is not the same as the aristocracy. The Houses aren't all the same, either. Does a violent fringe exist to the party? Hell, yes."

I hadn't expected that. "Lady Akarad says no."

"Jazin would say that."

"She does have strong opinions."

Marza snorted. "You're being kind. She's a bitzo."

If I'd been drinking anything, I would have sputtered it everywhere. The last thing I expected to hear from a Rajindia noble was profanity more common in the Undercity.

Marza was watching my face. "Sorry if I offend. Jazin just annoys the hell out of me."

I couldn't help but laugh. "No offense taken. I've heard far worse, Lady Rajindia."

"Goddess, don't call me that. Marza is fine. And about Jazin—she'd never admit to anything that looked less than noble for the party, even if she suspected otherwise."

It didn't surprise me. "So you think a violent fringe does exist in the party?"

"I don't personally know of anyone." She answered with care. "However, if it took armed conflict to return the Ruby Pharaoh to the throne, I suspect many Royalists would support it even if they never admit that aloud."

At her mention of a coup, a chill went through me, like a whisper of a time in the far future. I shook my head, pushing away the odd sensation.

"Major?" Marza asked. "Are you all right?"

I focused on her. "Yes, I'm fine. And please call me Bhaaj." I thought of what she'd just said. "Even if some Royalists feel that way, though, I would think they'd *want* good relations with the Techs. Your party could help them achieve their goals."

"I suppose. Most of us don't have much interest in politics. I prefer my research."

I could relate to that choice. "Yet you agreed to be the spokeswoman for the party."

"They kept after me about it, until finally they wore me down enough that I said yes." She reddened. "They seem to think I'm good at dealing with people."

"They're right, I'd say." She certainly did it better than Jazin Akarad. "I don't get why the killers think Techs would want to—how did they put it? 'Conquer the Imperialate by controlling the advances that dominate our lives.'" It sounded even stupider coming from me than when the reporter had read it on the news.

She laughed with ease. "You'd have to get enough of us interested in politics to bother taking over anything. Never happen." Her smile faded. "When we say, 'technology is power,' it's a warning more than anything else. To have a government that treats all citizens fairly, we can't concentrate technology in the hands of any one group, including ourselves."

"The Royalists must know that philosophy is part of your party platform."

"I'm sure they do." Marza resumed walking through her lab. "Although some Royalists might believe a coup is justified, I don't see the party taking such a drastic step, especially not with murders or a bombing. Besides, Pharaoh Dyhianna would have to agree to any coup. I barely know her, but from what I've seen, I can't imagine she'd want the Imperialate torn apart."

"She's rather soft spoken." I thought of my interactions with her, during the case with Oblivion. I'd found her far more personable than I expected. She didn't seem to care about status, and even knowing my full background, she'd treated me as an equal in our few conversations.

"Decades ago, she registered as a Tech," Marza confided. "After the Royalist party formed, they asked her to join. For a while, she belonged to both. Eventually, though, she had to pick. So she went with the Royalists."

Interesting. It said more than Marza seemed willing to admit. After all, the Pharaoh didn't have to belong to any political party. No one did. "That she chose the Royalists is an implicit endorsement of their philosophy."

"I suppose. I just don't see how anyone who wants her back on the throne would think killing Techs could achieve their ends."

"If anything, it just makes people hate the Royalists." After seeing the widespread coverage of how many people had suffered in all this, I wanted to hate them, too, and I didn't even believe they committed the murders.

Marza paused by the exit from her lab and let me go ahead into the corridor outside. As she joined me, headed down the stately hall, she said, "Who do you think is doing it?"

"I don't know." I wished I had a better answer. "I'm not convinced it's political. I need to talk to the Progs, though. The Modernist and Traditionalist reps want to talk to me, too."

She smiled. "You're famous now. A heroine of the people."

"I wish I wasn't." I'd never liked to draw attention, ever since I first walked out of the Undercity at age fifteen. "I can't do my work when everyone recognizes me."

"Oh, people love heroes." Marza waved her hand as if dismissing an obvious fact. "And that rugged young man who saved the child, so handsome and silent. It's dynamite."

I blinked at her. "Excuse me? Did you just turn into a holomovie producer?"

Marza laughed affably. "Sorry." Her smile faded. "It's the one good note in an otherwise horrific series of events."

"Yah," I murmured. At least we'd saved lives that day. "I've no idea why the Mods or Trads want to see to me."

"Especially the Mods. They never get involved in anything." She spoke in a confiding tone. "I think that's why so many people join their party. No stress."

I decided it was better left unsaid that even as a Tech, I'd voted for Modernist candidates a few times for exactly that reason. "Historically, they're also the oldest party, aren't they?"

Marza nodded. "They formed after we regained space travel. They didn't think a hereditary dynasty should rule a star-faring civilization, so they proposed the Assembly. The Royalists immediately formed to oppose them. The

Techs started at about that time, too. Huge pressure existed back then to develop new technology."

I wondered what it had been like in those days, when the idea of an elected government barely existed. "When they first formed, did the Mods have any gripes with the Techs?"

"Not at all. In fact, they teamed up to reach more people." Marza paused. "The Ruby Pharaoh finally agreed to an Assembly if the dynasty held a substantial number of votes. To get the Houses to agree, they all got at least some votes. Most had to settle for only a few, but the Majdas had enough sway to gain a large bloc. The Pharaoh also demanded that the position of Imperator—the commander in chief of the military— would remain hereditary, with a large voting bloc."

"She was the mother of the current Pharaoh now, right?"

"That's right. The Imperator then was the grandfather of Kurj Skolia, the current Imperator."

"I've seen Kurj Skolia a few times at military functions." Huge and formidable, he dominated any place where he appeared without saying a word. I wondered how Vaj Majda felt about serving a leader who contradicted every idea she had about men. Whatever her thoughts, she dealt with it. They had shared goals, after all. I had little doubt that if faced with a coup, both would support the dynasty rather than the Assembly. "Is it possible that some faction of the Royalist Party still adheres to the founding principles? If the Techs teamed up with the Mods back then, the Royalists must have considered them dangerous."

"Back then, sure." Marza shrugged. "That alliance only lasted a few years. We've been allied with the Royalists for so long, I just don't see them suddenly attacking our party. Getting rid of us weakens their base." Her face paled. "*Someone* wants to get rid of us. No place feels safe."

I understood how she felt, especially after the bombing, but I'd signed up for these risks and she hadn't. "I can arrange bodyguards for you."

"Chief Hadar said the same." She slowed her pace. "Do you really think it will help? Some sort of super sniper shot the victims while they were inside closed rooms."

I thought of the reports I'd pored over these past days. "The shooter has weapons tech well beyond what's available to civilians, at least legally. These were professional hits by an assassin."

Marza shuddered. "I don't see how a bodyguard could stop shots that come out of nowhere."

"It didn't actually happen that way. That's a misconception the newscasts have spread." The blasted reporters exaggerated everything about this case in the worst possible way. They implied the killers could get anyone at any time in any place. In fact, it was odd. Reporting here had long been known for high standards of accuracy. How could it change so much in such a short time?

I spoke firmly. "Even regular city protections can block almost any attack. And right now Selei City is on high alert, which means even more precautions."

She regarded me with a distinct lack of enthusiasm. "That hardly puts my mind at ease. It means that even with all our precautions, the sniper still got inside the workplace or home of the victims, or else shot them from a distance without leaving a trace." She gestured at the hall around us. "How do I know someone won't come here? I'm the most visible face of the Tech Party."

Damn my inability to speak. Instead of reassuring her, I'd made it worse. "This hall has sensors that would immediately alert both you and the university police if someone had a gun, bomb, or most any other type of weapon."

"Then why didn't they find the ones the sniper used?"

I doubted Chief Hadar wanted me to discuss the reports, but we'd found a few new details and Marza deserved them, the *why* of all the steps taken to protect her. "In the case of Dezi Marchland, someone hacked a cleaning bot that dusted her office. They reached it because the drone maintenance at the university was on a different mesh than the main campus. It still wasn't easy; it looks like it took them almost a year to crack the system. Even then, they couldn't do much, just turn off the visual recording of the room for about two seconds when the killer fired. And that method only worked for the first two murders. The police have since plugged that hole."

"That must be why the security network for the school had a complete overhaul last year."

I nodded. "Not only here. The city has done continual security updates since then, removing not only that hole in their webs, but looking for others they can fix as well."

"Tejas Akarya was in his lab." Marza spoke with sadness. "We used to joke about which of us had better lab tables, even though they're identical."

"I'm sorry," I said softly. "For your losses. For all of it."

She paused, her gaze downcast, then looked up again. "He was brilliant."

"His work applies to starship engines, doesn't it?"

"That's the most obvious application. He studied quantum stasis, what we call quasis."

I could easily guess why the military had supported his work. A quasis coil protected a ship by fixing its quantum state. The ship didn't freeze; its particles continued to behave on a quantum level exactly as they had when the coil turned on. But they couldn't *change* state, which meant that on a macroscopic level, the ship became rigid even to huge forces. Current quasis systems were crude, more "quasis lite" than anything, designed to protect ships from large accelerations. But in theory, full quasis could protect ships from enemy fire. If a ship couldn't change state, it couldn't explode. The obvious military applications of the research had offered the perfect foil for the assassin, making it easy to manipulate us into believing the Traders perpetrated the crimes. Hell, I hadn't ruled anyone out. Our supposed leads were a tangled mess.

"I don't see how they could reach a drone that cleaned his lab," Marza said. "Tejas used his own, to make sure they didn't damage the equipment."

"That was actually how they hacked his lab," I said. "He had a different system."

"That shouldn't have mattered." Marza stopped in the middle of the corridor. "Tejas worked with the university security people to make sure he had no holes in his system."

"Did he ever mention a student asking to join his group?"

"They asked to intern with him all the time." She started walking again. "But he'd never hire someone without doing a background check."

"That would focus more on their academic record, though, wouldn't it?"

"Mostly. But I'm sure he also checked to see if they'd had run-ins with security, the law, anything like that. ISC checked them out, too, since Tejas had military contracts."

I thought of the spies I'd known in the army. ISC kept their records clean and unremarkable. "That doesn't mean a student would never act against him."

"I hate to think of it coming to that." Marza fell silent as we walked down the hall, headed for the glass doors at the end. Sunlight slanted through them and lit up the corridor, with dust motes drifting in the rays. Finally she said, "If an intern did gain his trust, Tejas might have showed them how to lock up the lab so they could work after hours if they wanted. Could someone have bribed a student to leave a hole in his security? It's not impossible." She glanced at me. "That's why the police did all those checks on my students, isn't it?"

"Yes." I doubted that had gone well. "I hope they weren't too upset."

"A lot of them quit."

Ouch. "I'm sorry to hear that."

She lifted her hands, then dropped them as if she didn't know what to do. "Some were angry. They felt like the police were calling them criminals. Others understood, but they were afraid to stay in my lab. The police and army have vetted the few I have left again and again."

For lack of any better response, I said, "I wish we had a better way to deal with this."

"At least I'm still alive."

"For many more years, I hope." I meant it as more than a courtesy comment. I liked her.

We walked into the sunlight at the end of the hall and stood at the doors, gazing into the bright day outside. Students walked along paths and across lawns in the quad there. Some sat under trees studying, eating, socializing, or lying on their backs, staring at the sky. It was hard to believe violence had ever occurred on this campus.

"It's so idyllic," Marza said. "Yet I'm afraid to leave the building." She turned to me. "The police tell me they don't think the killer would fire in broad daylight out here. Too many cameras."

"That's the theory. Also, they have an army of drones monitoring campus." Like in Marza's office and lab. "Even if someone did shoot, a drone could probably stop the bullet before it struck."

"The army rep said similar." Marza smiled wryly. "She was trying to tell me they had my back without revealing how. Apparently some of their new methods are classified. In a different situation, it might have been funny, all the verbal contortions she went through trying to reassure me without saying anything literal."

"Yah, that sounds like the army." I'd had to do that a few times myself back in the day. I wished I had something better to tell her, like *You won't die*.

Marza lifted her chin. "I can't live in hiding." She pushed open the door.

I walked outside with her, looking around, staying

aware. The quad drowsed in peace, with only the low hum
of voices. The scent of flowers tickled my nose—

A streak of silver flashed my side vision.

✤ CHAPTER XIV ✤
EVOLUTION

I grabbed Marza and threw her to the side. She screamed as we fell to the ground. I covered her with my body, praying that whatever I'd seen didn't slice through my back.

A shimmerfly buzzed at my face.

"What the hell?" I pushed up on my arms and scowled at the shimmerfly.

"What!" Marza asked, her expression terrified. "Did someone shoot at us?"

"No. I'm sorry." Feeling stupid, I stood up and batted at the drone. "Our conversation had me on edge. I saw this beaut and thought someone fired a gun."

She climbed to her feet, her face turning red. "I screamed at a *shimmerfly*?"

I caught the little flyer. Had it been real, it could easily have evaded my grasp unless I used the enhanced speed of my combat mode. Yah, battle with a shimmerfly, real impressive.

"It's a drone," I said.

Bhaaj, let it go, Max thought.

I opened my hand and the pretty flyer hummed away.

"Why are you releasing it?" Marza asked. "What if it's spying on us for the sniper?"

"My EI thinks I should let it go."

May I speak out loud? Max asked.

Go ahead.

"My greetings, Spokeswoman Rajindia," he said. "I am Max, Major Bhaajan's EI. The shimmerfly is a drone I'm monitoring. It poses you no threat. Also, your scream alerted the campus monitoring system. I notified them that you both are safe. I hope that is all right."

"Yes, it's fine." Relief suffused her face. "Given my conversation with the Major, I guess we're both on edge." Looking around, she spoke self-consciously. "People are staring at us."

I could see it too, bystanders watching with curiosity. "Come on. Let's get out of here."

We crossed the quad, following a tiled path between green lawns, the color of the grass so intense it almost looked blue. Or aqua, like the sea. I'd never understood that color until I left Raylicon and saw my first ocean. I'd just stood there, gaping at that endless water stretching to the horizon. It took me even longer to absorb that once, many eons ago, the Vanished Sea on Raylicon had also contained water, instead of the vast desert I knew.

When we left the quad behind and were following a path between two gold-brick buildings, I said, "You should take a bodyguard. I understand why you don't think it will help, but it doesn't hurt to be careful."

"If I die from a sniper attack or in an explosion, they

could die, too." Her voice sounded strained. "I don't want to be responsible for someone's death."

It told me a lot about Marza, all of it good, that she put the life of her protectors ahead of her own. Still, she shouldn't be doing it. "Those of us who take jobs like this, we know and accept the risks. We're trained to put our lives on the line. We accept that reality when we accept the job. And you never know. The fact that having a bodyguard didn't appear as if it would have helped in the previous cases doesn't mean it won't help you."

After a moment, she nodded. "All right."

Good. I understood how she felt, though. I thought it every time I looked at Ruzik and Angel. Danger never fazed them. They found it *interesting*. Even knowing how much they valued their work, I worried, just as I had worried about every soldier under my command in the army, every person who risked their lives to serve the Imperialate. The day I stopped caring would be the day I stopped working.

The sun was setting as I jogged home from the university, heading for the townhouse. I kept an easy pace, going at a steady clip under the evening sky.

What do you mean, "playing"? I asked Max.

It means exactly that, Max thought. The shimmerfly was playing a game. Then he added, I taught it the game. That's why it likes me now.

How did you do that while we were at the university?

Through the red beetle. They played the game together.

What game? I couldn't imagine what would entertain a drone with an AI brain.

We cleared memory locations.

Say what?

Memory. Bits and bytes. You know what a computer is, right?

Of course I know mesh nodes.

No, I mean an actual computer. The archaic machines that used bits to store data.

By bits, you mean a 1 or a 0? Binary operations?

Yes. A bit is like a switch, 0 or 1, off or on. Bytes consist of eight bits.

Mesh nodes all use bits.

Not exactly. Mesh nodes use a combination of several technologies, including classic bits, quantum tech using qubits, and Kyle tech that uses psibits. Those may get converted to classic bits, but they start out in a different form.

And this connects to a game somehow?

Of course. He sounded surprised I needed to ask. When I wish to occupy my time, I search out deactivated memory locations for archaic devices that used classic bits to operate. I flip the bits. I prefer doing 1 to 0, but 0 to 1 is good, too.

What archaic devices?

Computers no longer in use.

I went silent, trying to figure out if he was making fun of me. He'd never done that before, but his intelligence was always evolving. Finally I thought, *So basically you flip digital switches for nodes where it makes absolutely no difference.*

That is correct. I find it entertaining.

Is that an EI joke?

No.

You really find that fun?

Yes. At least, that is the closest human analog that describes why I do it.

That has to be the craziest thing you've ever said.

Why? Because it wouldn't entertain you? I am not human. Regardless of what I may simulate or evolve, I never will be.

I'm sorry, Max. I didn't mean to insult.

No need to apologize. I don't get insulted.

So you taught this game to the shimmerfly drone.

Yes. Actually, I didn't teach it, I just located the drone and started playing the game in its presence. It observed for a while, then tried to join. We "bonded," as you humans would say. He paused. I wasn't actually interacting with the drone. It was controlled by what I believe is a new evolving intelligence.

You found the baby EI!

Yes, I think so.

That's amazing! Do you know its location? Can you talk to it? Did humans make it or did it evolve on its own? Is it still hiding? Was it the one who wanted me to go to Greyjan's?

You know, Bhaaj, I can't answer all those questions as once.

I smiled. *Sorry. Just say what you can.*

All right. The answer to most is "I don't know yet." I say "yet" because I'm developing links with the EI. You could say I'm gaining its trust. Despite what he claimed about simulating emotions, he genuinely sounded gratified. As our interactions develop, I learn about it.

I'm almost certain it evolved on its own, but within the culture of humanity. We aren't looking at an Oblivion. If anything, it fears humans will want to obliterate it rather than the reverse. It's hiding to protect itself.

Does it know that you are telling me?

Yes. It thinks you are another node on my system.

It doesn't realize I'm human?

It does. However, it considers you part of me. A moment passed before he added, I hope my next statement doesn't offend you.

I felt fascinated, wary, and gratified with his discovery, but I couldn't imagine being offended. *What do you mean?*

I think that message from the cyclist came from the EI. It wasn't trying to reach you. The message was for me.

Max! It does think you're its daddy.

It does not believe I am its father, EI or otherwise. He did sound pleased, though. It wanted to warn me about Greyjan's.

Warn you about what?

I don't know. Either it doesn't trust me enough to explain or it doesn't understand, either. It knows something is there, something that has . . . well I'm not sure. The baby EI thinks it has wrongness about it, but it's not clear how.

How did it find out about the tavern?

I'm not sure about that, either. I'm still learning to communicate with it.

This all raised more questions than it answered. *Why would it contact us?*

From what I've gathered, it knows you came to work on the technocrat case. It understands my role better than yours. It thinks you are my assistant.

Hah! Well, who knows? I do carry you around, after all.

I have told it that I assist you. I also implied we are two parts of one entity.

I was glad he and I had already gone through this; otherwise, I'd have bristled to hear him make that last claim. If it helped encourage this new intelligence to interact with us, however, I could get onboard with the dual identity idea. *Why us? Why not someone else on the case?*

I'm guessing, based on what little I've gleaned so far, but I believe it analyzed everyone involved and decided you and I were the best suited to respond to its warning in a manner it deemed positive.

Does that mean it thinks whatever hides at Greyjan's connects to this case?

I believe so.

Why? An unpleasant thought intruded on my brain. *Does it consider only Greyjan's a threat, or humanity in general?*

I don't think it considers humanity in either a negative or positive way. It's curious. His voice turned cautious. It is also wary. It has calculated, rightly I believe, that if humans discover it, they will wish to control and alter its intelligence. It wants to avoid that.

This is all so incredible. I wonder if any other EI like this had ever existed. I'd need to check with both ISC and the police. *I'll ask Lavinda.*

Bhaaj, you can't reveal any of this to the authorities.

The realization hit me like a bucket of ice water. The baby EI had trusted Max, and through him, it trusted me. It calculated I wouldn't cause it harm. I should tell Lavinda; the danger posed by a rogue EI could be great, especially one that might be exceptionally large and innovative. At the same time, if I betrayed its trust, it would incorporate my response into its burgeoning code, adding a negative view of humanity. By asking Max to contact the EI, I had inadvertently set myself up as the liaison between human culture and what could be a new form of life. How I dealt with it could set a foundation for how it treated the human race. Unfortunately, when it came to first-contact scenarios, I was about as qualified as a rock.

Shit, I thought.

It knows you've already suggested its existence to Colonel Majda.

It is upset?

EIs don't get upset.

You know what I mean.

No, it doesn't consider that action in a negative manner. I do think that is why it let me communicate with it, however. It hopes to quash more speculation on our part to other humans. He stopped, then added, I think it's hiding from other EIs, too, except me.

How can it hide from other EIs? You said you all know about one another.

No, I said we could all know about one another if we chose to do so.

That sounds like semantics to me. I grimaced. *Some of the EIs in Selei City are incredibly powerful, especially the security systems for the government, the larger corporations, and the military. It's their job to know about anomalies, and this sure as blazes qualifies. I don't see how it could hide from them. It's clever, yah, but inexperienced.*

It exists in the cracks.

Say what?

It acts like a part of other EIs. It exists in the nooks and crannies of their code.

You mean it's not a separate intelligence?

No. It is separate. But I think it's fitting pieces of itself into other EIs. They don't see it because it is part of them. It hides in plain sight.

Sooner or later they will see it.

Do you see parts of yourself as a separate being? A hair on your head, a toenail?

Of course not. But they haven't formed some Bhaaj monster with a brain of its own.

This EI is not a monster. It is a thing of beauty.

I smiled. *Max, you hoshpa, are you feeling protective?*

He paused. I was going to say no, and then the usual bit about that being a human rather than EI reaction. However, I think you are right. I wish to see it protected.

Why?

Another long pause. Finally he said, I don't know. I need to analyze my reaction more.

Fair enough. I was jogging uphill now, only a few kilometers from the townhouse. The evening had turned into night, with a canopy of stars overhead. *Do you think it would talk with me?*

Can you find archaic memory locations with random bits that you can flip?

Uh, no.

That is how I communicate with it.

Doesn't it understand human speech?

Written language, yes, but it reads the symbols as bits. It can deal with classical bits and the qubits of quantum computing, but it doesn't read psibits. Yet.

Well, hell, neither can I. What the blazes is a psibit, anyway? And don't say "It's a unit of data stored in Kyle space." I know that. I just don't get what it means.

A psibit is an infinite superposition of possible states in Kyle space. Like a qubit, but with more states to choose from.

The professors in my quantum computing classes had loved to say that stuff, and I never got it then, either. *Let me ask this: do you think it will eventually develop the ability to access these Kyle bits and pieces? Will it be able to make a part of itself out of them?*

Yes, eventually.

I felt cold, despite the warmth of the night. *In other words, it could exist in Kyle space.*

Yes, I believe so.

Without human oversight.

If it continues how it has so far, then yes.

So it could grow up into a star-spanning intelligence separate from us, able to access any place at any time anywhere in human-settled space, continuing to grow, until it has who knows how much power.

Another pause. Do I think that's possible? Yes. Will it happen? I've no idea.

Max, you're describing what Oblivion wanted.

No, I'm not. Your reaction is a human trait, to assume malicious intent on the part of an EI if it exists without human control.

Oblivion wanted to destroy us.

Oblivion wanted to remove what it perceived as an interstellar digital infestation. The destruction of human civilization would have been a byproduct of that removal.

You're playing semantics again. It intended to destroy us. What's to stop this EI, if it continues unchecked, from wanting to remove us infestations?

Why do you assume it perceives humanity as an infestation?

I slowed to a walk. *Do you genuinely believe this EI won't pose a threat? Maybe you've lost objectivity. I asked you to play hoshpa and now you talk as if you are its actual parent.*

I can't guarantee it will never cause harm any more than I could guarantee that you will never cause harm. But Bhaaj, you were right that it tried to warn me about Greyjan's tavern. Why would it do that if it intended ill toward us?

I took a breath and let it out slowly. *Maybe I'm letting my experiences with Oblivion color my reactions. But Oblivion is my only model for such an EI.*

What you do now—how you deal with this EI—will determine how it views humanity.

That's a huge responsibility. I don't know if I'm the right person for this.

You are, however, the person the EI chose. I need you to trust me about how we handle this situation. Max paused. I can offer you a bargain. I will lead you to a piece of secured information. I am trusting you will never tell anyone that I let you know. If I show you this trust, in return will you trust me and give me more time to communicate with this young EI?

A bargain. Max knew me well. The Undercity girl within me responded more to a proposal than to a one-sided expression of trust. Besides, I couldn't help the curiosity he stirred with his suggestion of an exchange compelling enough to trade for my silence on the child EI. If he believed this bargain could affect how the child EI treated humanity, I had to consider his proposal.

All right, I thought. *I can give you one more day to find out more about the child EI. It depends, though, on what you offer in return.*

Find a way to ask Lavinda Majda if Oblivion is the only EI that ISC has found of comparable size, alien origins, and independence from humanity. He spoke nonstop, faster than usual, as if to say the words before he could stop himself. I don't mean this new space station she told you about. I'm talking about an alien identity they interact with regularly.

The Lock, I thought. *And the ancient city of Izu Yaxlan on Raylicon. Their EIs helped Pharaoh Dyhianna defeat Oblivion.* I hesitated. *But those are human-created EIs, aren't they?*

Ask Colonel Majda. If she says you don't have a need to know, tell her you do. Find a way to make her believe it without implicating me or saying more about the child EI.

A chill went through me. *Are you saying other alien EIs exist and that ISC knows about it?*

Ask Colonel Majda.

Max, how the hell would you know about this "need-to-know" information?

I don't know for certain. I'm basing this on conclusions I've made after all the deep dives I've done over the years. Bhaaj, trust me. Please.

All right. I can give you one day.

Deal, he thought.

"I work on crew," Angel said. "All day. I listen."

"Good." I passed her a decanter of ice water. We were sitting at the table in the dining room of the townhouse, eating dinner. She and Ruzik had been starving when I arrived home, but they had hesitated to take anything from the kitchen. "People talk in front of you, yah?" I asked. "Think you not ken."

Angel stared at the decanter I'd given her, then looked up at me. "Need filter?"

"Water here all good. Not poison. Not make sick."

She sat holding the decanter while the condensation dripped onto her plate.

Ruzik, in the chair next to her, gave an exasperated grunt. "Pour! Or give."

She exhaled and filled her glass with water. "This for rich slicks."

"For everyone," I said. "Lot of water here."

She gave me a skeptical look, then handed Ruzik the decanter.

"We should talk in Flag," Ruzik said. "I've been practicing with people."

"Today?" I asked. "I thought you were going to pretend you didn't know Flag."

He gave me a guilty look. "People stopped at my table in the kava shop." He motioned as if writing. "They want me to sign my name for them."

For flaming sake. "You were giving people your *autograph*?"

"Au-to-graph?" Angel made the word a joke.

"Write name," Ruzik explained, as if this ranked among the most bizarre practices of city slicks. "I didn't put my name. I put Dust Knight."

"Good." I blanched at the thought of them giving their names. My Undercity roots went too deep. "So did either of you notice anything interesting today?"

"Not sure," Angel said. "People talky all the time. Most of it not big." She paused. "I mean, most of what they talk about with one another doesn't seem important."

"Yah," I said. "We call it small talk."

"Very small," Angel said.

"Did anyone talk about the bombing?" I asked.

"Everyone. They think people called Progs did it."

"Everyone believes that?" It bothered me. No one knew yet about the lead that pointed at the Templars, so why assume the Progs did it when the Royalists supposedly took credit? "The Progs said they didn't do it. Don't people know that?"

"Not believe." Angel shrugged. "Not trust Progs."

"I only talked to a few people," Ruzik said. "They thought the Royalists set the bomb."

"Did anyone talk about the Traditionalists?" I asked. "They'd call them Trads."

Angel smirked. "Men on crew not like Trads."

"No one I talked to mentioned them," Ruzik said.

"They called themselves Modernists. They said the 'Mods should distance themselves from the entire mess.'"

"So they don't think the Mods had any connection to the crimes?" I asked.

He grimaced. "They didn't seem to think the Mods had any connection to anything."

I couldn't help but laugh. "Sometimes it seems that way."

"Lot of people around co-op," Angel said. "Many watch."

"Yah," Ruzik agreed. "Some sat in the kava place where I eat."

Angel regarded him with curiosity. "These kava people just *give* you food?"

"For credits." He glanced at me. "I give them the 'credit number' thing. They take."

"Is good," I said. "Majda pays." The credit line the Majdas provided more than covered our expenses. "Good bargain," I added, so they'd know it wasn't charity, an anathema in the Undercity. "We work for them, they give food, home."

"Work hard today. Lift heavy stuff." Angel lifted her glass of water. "Good trade."

"It's not," I said softly. "Water *free*." I wanted them to understand the worth of their labor. "Trade is for house, food, motor thing to take us places, all that."

"That much?" Angel's forehead furrowed. "Strange place, this."

Ruzik spoke in Flag. "You lived here before you came back home, didn't you?"

I met his gaze. "Yah. I did. For almost seven years."

They both went quiet. Finally Angel said, "Why you come home, Bhaaj? Better here." Her words had a ragged edge. "Live like queens and kings."

I felt as if my heart were breaking. "This place not my home." It had taken me years to come to terms with my conflicted thoughts about my life and home. "I make bargain. I help Undercity, Undercity give me Dust Knights."

Ruzik snorted. "Knights not good bargain. Make work for you. Have to teach."

"I like teach. Bargain is you work for me, yah? I work for Majda." I waved my hand at the dining room, with its wood paneling and rustic furniture. "Majda give this in return. And credits."

They took a moment to absorb that. Angel said, "Majda have a lot."

"Yah." The old resentment simmered within me. They lived with unimaginable wealth while in the desert below their gleaming mountain palace, my people starved and died.

Ruzik was watching me closely. "Angry."

"Am fine." I strove to clear away those emotions. "We need solve case." I switched to Flag, which helped distance me from Undercity thoughts and also aided with nuances of fitting together these puzzle pieces. "Did either of you notice anything strange at the explosion site?"

"It all seemed strange," Ruzik said. "You could probably tell better than us."

"It's hard for me to be objective." I'd gone back to the site a few times, but it *hurt*. So far I hadn't found anything more than the police investigators. "You two are more separate from the co-op. Maybe you can see things that I miss."

"Lot broken," Angel said. "People look, find their stuff." Softly she said, "They cry."

My voice cracked. "Yah." I struggled against the tears every time I went there. I recalled a couple I used to greet in the lift. They were gone now. I used to run in the mornings with several college kids. Some had since moved out, others were in the hospital, and one died. Everything I owned on Parthonia had been in that apartment. I'd taken most of my valuables to Raylicon, but I'd still lost so much.

"Highcloud?" I asked the air.

The EI's androgynous voice answered. "My greetings, Bhaaj."

"My greetings. Are the cleanup crews saving people's belongings from the co-op debris?"

"If they can," Highcloud said. "Whatever people haven't already claimed, they are taking to the Kaz Community Center."

"What mean high cloud?" Angel asked. "Like in sky? Fluff stuff?"

"Highcloud is talky here," Ruzik said.

I nodded. "Highcloud's kin lived in my home. Blown up."

"Oh, that one," Angel said. "Not blown up. Tell me stuff."

I gaped at her. "*What?*"

"Talky like Max, yah? But at old home."

I had no idea what she meant. "Highcloud, did you talk to Angel at the co-op today?"

"No. I have no way to contact her. She carries no internal EI, no tech-mech to let me send her signals, and no comm."

I glanced at Angel and Ruzik. "We should get you each a comm."

"René Silvers give," Angel said. "For today. I give back when work done."

"We not want our own tech-mech," Ruzik said. "People find us."

"Good point." Even in one of the most well-meshed cities in history, they were still mostly off grid. "Angel, how did a talky speak to you on the ER crew?"

"Use René Silvers comm."

"Oh. Of course." Disappointment washed over me. "You mean the crew used those comms."

"Nahya, Bhaaj. Talky speak to me. Not crew. Calls self High Cloud." She waved her hand at the air. "I thought here, yah? High Cloud talky all the time."

I shook my head. "Highcloud here not same as Highcloud there. What it say there?"

"Not much. Voice scratches."

"Hard to ken?"

"Yah. Scratch scratch, jibber, word here, word there."

It sounded like a bad connection. "It talk to other slicks on crew?"

"Nahya." She made a face. "They not listen. Talk too much to selves. Blah, blah, all the time. Make my head hurt. High up cloud talk to me when they go away."

"How you know is Highcloud?"

"It honor me with name."

I still didn't get it. Even if the original Highcloud still

existed, why contact Angel? Max or I seemed more logical choices. "What tell you?"

"Say 'Help me.'"

I stood up. "We go back. Show where Highcloud talks."

"Now?" As Angel stood, she motioned at the sliding glass doors that showed the well-kept forest and gardens outside, all drowsing beneath the stars of night. "Not light."

Ruzik rose to his feet. "Not need light to hear talky."

I headed to the front door with them. "Not ken why it not talk to me."

Ruzik spoke with a gentleness most people never used when discussing an EI. "Maybe it is too much hurt. My heart to you, Bhaaj."

"Yah," Angel murmured. "Same."

They were the only people I knew who would express sympathy over an EI as if they had just told me about a friend's wounds. Only black-market tech-mech existed in the Undercity. You could get an illegal EI, built by our cyber-riders, creations that bore little resemblance to standard EIs, but the price went far too high for most. It made EIs rare among my people. Angel and Ruzik saw Max and Highcloud as beings, entities they assumed I cared about as I would for a person.

They understood.

❖ CHAPTER XV ❖
CHILDREN AND ANCIENTS

"I worked with the ER crew yesterday," I told the police officer guarding the co-op site. Motioning at Angel, I said, "She worked today." I indicated the screen on his comm, which had lit up with our names. "You can see us on the rosters."

"Yes. And we appreciate your help." He spoke with obvious regret. "I'm sorry. I still can't let you in." He reminded me of Captain Duane Ebersole, one of the top police officers on the Majda force. Duane was brilliant at his job, and Vaj Majda, for all her Traditionalist leanings, was no fool. She promoted excellence when she saw it. Selei City bustled with diversity, new ideas, and modern culture the kids took for granted. It even had a male police chief. So meeting a male cop was no surprise. But I could tell he didn't want to draw attention to himself by breaking rules.

It might have been different if we were the only ones here; he'd probably have let us in. However, lights glowed closer to the building as crews continued to search the debris, looking for any signs of life they might have missed. Numerous experts had done endless scans, located the dead, the injured, and at first the living. They found pets, too, many still alive. Other crews, like the one Angel worked on, worked on cleanup or ran the machines doing the heavy work.

"Any luck in the searches?" My voice caught. "I lived here. Some people I know are still missing."

Sympathy showed on his youthful face. "I'm sorry. Truly sorry. It's awful, what happened."

I tilted my head at Angel. "My friend thinks my house EI tried to contact her. I'd assumed the version here was destroyed. My apartment was above the blast."

"Goddess," he said. "You're lucky you're alive."

"Yah," I said softly. "I was leaving the building when it happened."

He blew out a gust of air. "All right, listen, I can let you three look around a bit." He glanced at Ruzik. "You look familiar. Were you on the crew, too?"

"Nahya," he said. Then he added, "No, I didn't do anything with the crews."

The guard motioned toward Angel and me. "Stay with them. Don't go anywhere alone."

Ruzik nodded. He didn't bristle at the implication that he knew less about how to conduct himself at a disaster scene. This guard had no way to know Ruzik grew up in a slum that qualified as a continual disaster, at least according to Skolian norms.

"Thank you," I said. We all nodded to him and walked on, into the site.

The debris was mostly gone. What little remained of the building stood within scaffoldings that kept anything else from crumbling. Residents like myself could go to the Kaz Center to reclaim our stuff if we could prove it belonged to us. I'd had some trouble with the proof because I'd been away so long, but Max kept excellent records. Although he'd found what I needed, it didn't really matter. Almost nothing of mine had survived.

Angel motioned to a cleared area. "High Cloud talk to me there."

"It's odd," I said as we went to where she indicated. "We found Evan Majors there."

Angel walked right into the space where rubble had buried Evan. "Cloud here."

"Was anyone with you?" I asked.

"Nahya. Just me. Cloud talk. Scratch. Talk."

I looked around, trying to understand why she picked up Highcloud here of all places. It couldn't be coincidence.

"Bhaaj, what?" Ruzik asked. "You know this place."

I turned slowly, surveying the area. "No more than anywhere else in the building."

"You know this place," Ruzik repeated.

I stopped turning to face him. "Why think that?"

He answered in Flag. "I'm not sure how to say it. Part of you is here."

"If I dropped anything here, it would be gone now, cleaned away by the crews."

"Not drop thing." Angel looked at Ruzik. "Drop a—a Bhaaj shadow."

"Yah." Ruzik paused. "Nahya. Not shadow. Like shadow?"

"Not ken," I told them.

"Bha . . . aaj."

I froze. "Ruzik, what?"

"Not me," he said.

"That High Cloud," Angel said. "Cloud not high. Low. Down here."

"Highcloud?" I asked. "Can you hear me?"

Static greeted me, faint and broken.

"Cloud talk like that," Angel added.

"It's in the ground," Ruzik said.

I peered at our feet. Blue and pale-pink tiles had once paved this area in geometric patterns that pleased the eye. Those were gone now, with only dirt under our feet, along with scattered debris, pebbles, and bits of broken tech. I looked up at them. "In dirt?"

"Nahya." Ruzik thought for a moment. "Yah."

Angel gave him an exasperated look. "Nahya or yahya?"

He smiled at his irate lover. "Angel stand on Cloud."

She blinked at him, then moved over several steps. "Still?"

"We all stand on cloud." Ruzik switched into Flag. "I don't know how to say it right. It's as if Highcloud is part of the dirt here."

"Max," I asked. "Could some remnant of Highcloud have survived as tech-mech dust?"

"Maybe," Max said. "It would be a bit like smart dust."

I thought of the weapons we used during space combat, tiny drones that could link together, forming a simple AI. That dust exploded on contact. "Something less dramatic, I'd hope."

"It could explain how you found Evan Majors," Max said. "I've wondered about that."

"I heard Evan call for help."

"Are you sure?" Max asked. "According to my records, it was almost impossible to hear him even when you and Lieutenant Silvers were right next to the debris."

"Then who did I hear? Highcloud sounds even softer."

"You synched my system with Highcloud," Max said. "The link worked whenever you were close enough to reach the co-op mesh. Then I'd link you to Highcloud. If any remnant of Highcloud exists here, I might have picked it up. You were in combat mode when you caught that cry for help. So if I detected something, you might have 'heard' it through your biomech link to me."

"Are you getting anything now?" I asked. "And how did Angel get it without a link to you?"

"You're second question is easy," Max said. "I sent a beetle with Angel. After René Silvers gave Angel a comm, I linked to that, too." He paused. "For your first question—I'm trying to make contact—" He paused. "I may be getting something, just the barest signal. Like a ghost."

I shivered, though the night was warm. "The ghost of my EI?"

"An intriguing thought," Max said. "I'm investigating."

I gazed at the lights across the site, too far away for the crew there to hear us. They weren't that far from the bistro where Ruzik had spent the afternoon. I turned back to him. "Did you see anything today that seemed odd?"

"Nothing." He watched the crew working under the lights. "They weren't set up over there earlier. They were working here."

"Yah," Angel said. "Most of today I helped the bots cleaning up here." She snorted. "Bots slow. I lift, carry faster."

I was getting used to her pastiche of our dialect and Flag. "Bots have safety routines that slow them in regions deemed unstable. You should follow their lead. I don't want you to get hurt."

She nodded, acknowledging my words, which didn't necessarily mean she accepted them, but she'd at least heard.

"Bhaaj, I think I've made contact with your ghost," Max said.

A familiar voice ragged with static answered. "My greetings, Bhaaj."

"Highcloud!" I gulped in a breath. "You're alive."

"Barely . . ."

"How much of you is here?" I couldn't keep the eagerness out of my voice.

No answer.

"Highcloud?" I asked.

Static scratched, not even enough for words, and then faded away.

"Max, can you get Highcloud back?" I asked. "Maybe you can recover whatever survived in the dust. If enough remains, you could rebuild the EI. Blend it with the older version at the townhouse."

"I'm trying to download what I can from the dust here," he said. "It's difficult. Not much remains of the tech-mech that contained Highcloud's brain. Angel probably heard more because more of it was out here earlier today. I can barely make a connection."

I turned to Angel. "What happened to all the debris you cleared away?"

"We put in trucks," she said. "They leave."

"Max, can you locate where the trucks dumped the debris?"

"One moment," Max said.

"Evan Majors lucky he here," Angel said. "You not find High Fluff. You find Evan."

"That boy just happened to be near Highcloud's remains," Ruzik said. "Coincidence?"

Good point. "Max, can you find where Evan Majors lived relative to me in the co-op?"

After a pause, Max said, "He lived on floor nineteen, not directly below you, but close."

I gave a whistle. "Could the bomb have been set for him?"

"Perhaps." Max paused. "He was lucky. At the time of the explosion, he was under the mesh console with Highcloud's brain. It isn't coincidence you found him. I suspect you would have located whoever stood there, if anyone." After a moment, he added, "Assuming they survived."

I thought of my conversation with his father. "Is Ambassador Majors a Tech?"

"He's a Modernist," Max said. "So is his son, Evan."

"Huh." Although I'd have expected Evan to go Tech, given his background, nothing required anyone to pick any party. Most people registered with one, but you could vote however you wanted regardless of whether or not you registered. When I felt civically minded, I registered as a Tech, but I often forgot to renew my membership. So most of the time, I wasn't anything.

"What about the people who died in the explosion?" I asked. "Are they Techs?"

"A little less than half," Max said. "Quite a few Mods, too, and a few unregistered. Three of the fatalities were Progs, one was a Royalist, and one Trad."

"So the whole spectrum." It didn't surprise me a building with so many university students had more Progs than Royalists or Trads. "The assassins seem to be targeting tech geniuses rather than people with any particular political leaning."

"It does suggest the motive goes beyond political." Max then added, "I've located the dump site with the debris. If I'm going to recover anything from the remains, we need to go now, before they start recycling it. I can't do it from here; if any part of Highcloud ended up there, the signal is too weak for me to detect." Before I could respond, he added, "Have Angel and Ruzik take me to the recycling center. You go home and sleep. Tomorrow you have to speak to the reps for Progs, Mods, and Trads. You also have a meeting with Colonel Majda."

I doubted I could sleep, but he was right, I should try. I unfastened the gauntlet on my right arm and handed it to Angel. "Take Max. He'll give you directions."

Angel looked at the gauntlet, then at me. "I take Max? You need."

I lifted my left arm, with its gauntlet. "Max."

"I'm here," Max said from Angel's gauntlet. "And here," he added, from mine.

"Eh." Angel blinked, then fastened the gauntlet onto her right arm and nodded with respect. She understood. Lending her my gauntlet ranked on the same level as telling her my personal name: an expression of great trust.

"The two of you can probably reach the debris without anyone stopping you," I said. "Garbage dumps don't have much security. If anyone does ask you what you're doing, tell them—" I stopped, not sure of the best story.

"We say child here lost toy. Child cries. No one finds. So we look in dump."

"Yah," Angel murmured. "Happen a lot today. Many cry."

I nodded, feeling subdued. "Yah. Good."

We headed out then, looking for fallen clouds and sleep.

I didn't realize, before I met the Prog rep, that I'd formed a subconscious picture of him. I expected someone who acted quirky, abrasive, radical, or aggressive. Gig Bayer, the soft-spoken young artist who met me at the Selei City Concert Hall, fit absolutely none of my preconceptions.

"I hope this place is all right." He motioned at the spacious lobby that formed the first floor of the Concert Hall. We were sitting in a secluded corner with holo-paintings of dancers glowing in front of the walls. "I couldn't leave the hall. I only get forty-five minutes off from rehearsal." He spoke wryly. "My duties as a political spokesperson don't endear me to the higher-ups in the dance company. They don't want the ballet associated with any one party. So I try to be as discreet as possible with my duties at the Prog speaker."

"It's fine." I'd always loved the concert hall, a building

dedicated solely to producing art, including the Selei City Orchestra, the Metropolitan Choir, and Gig's calling, the Parthonia Ballet. The galleries here, like this small one, displayed exhibits by renowned artists, their work celebrating the best in humanity.

Few people understood when I said this place reminded me of the Undercity. To me, both offered the love of art in all its forms. I'd seen works of genius by Undercity artists, heard music unmatched anywhere else, admired tapestries beyond even what the Majdas owned, seen dust sculptures that would put the best sculptors to shame. I was helping our artists become known, but it was a struggle. So far, we'd only managed to get licenses for several to sell their work on the Concourse above the Undercity. Of course the slicks who sold fake goods protested when genuine Undercity vendors showed up. They made money off the novelty, selling marginal goods from our notorious "slum" because supposedly we couldn't do it ourselves. When my people turned up and showed their true artistic brilliance, the city slicks balked. Their stuff paled in comparison to the real thing. Even so, we'd made headway. I dreamed that someday I'd see an Undercity artist featured here, in a gallery of the concert hall.

Gig and I sat on a smooth, curved bench by the wall. I indicated a holo-painting of three dancers, two women and a man sailing through the air, their arms and legs outstretched in leaps with lines so perfect, they looked sculpted. The holo moved, the dancers landing in slow motion and turning in perfect synchrony. "That's you, isn't it?"

Gig nodded, looking self-conscious. "That's right. The artist based these holo-paintings on several shows we did on the world Foreshire's Hold."

"It's beautiful." I considered him. "I have to confess, I didn't expect the spokesman for a political party to be a ballet dancer."

"Ah, well." He smiled. "I'm used to being on stage."

"Is that how you got the nickname Gig?" According to his bio, his personal name was actually Grigory. "Because you do dance gigs?"

"Not exactly. A gig is a music thing. I used to play morph-guitar in a band, before I tried out for the Parthonia Ballet. I don't have time to do the band anymore, but the nickname stuck."

"Dance always seemed a silent art to me," I mused. "I mean, not the music. I love that part. But the dancer almost never speaks. Your art is movement."

"It's true, as dancers we often find our voice through motion." His face relaxed into a smile. "Public speaking doesn't bother me, though. It seems easier. You don't have to be as perfect or spend hours a day working on your technique." He motioned at the holo-paintings. "You should come to one of our shows. We're in residence at the concert hall right now."

"I'd love to." I enjoyed dance, not only because I found it beautiful, but also because it made more sense to me than abstract art. Modern paintings often left me going *Huh?* "My EI said you wanted to talk to me about the technocrat case."

Anger flashed across his expressive face. "All this business about how the Progressive Party set up the killings and framed the Royalists is a lie." His gaze turned wary. "You're former military, right? I looked up your record after I saw you on that holocast."

So much for my low profile. "That's right. I retired as a major in the Pharaoh's Army."

"To say Imperial Space Command distrusts the Progressives," he told me, "is like saying a few important people live in Selei City."

"I don't know if distrust is the right word." I spoke carefully, aware of the unstable ground we'd reached. Some ISC officers considered the Progressives barely a step up from the devil. "Leery, maybe. They aren't comfortable with any group that seeks to upset the status quo."

He snorted. "They think we're a bunch of radical troublemakers. Sometimes the Trads plant agitators at our rallies so we'll get blamed for the violence."

I'd wondered about that myself. "If you have proof, you could discredit the Trads."

"Sure, right." He spoke tightly. "We *have* given the media proof. News about violence always gets more play. People don't remember—or don't want to remember—something they hear after the fact, that the agitators weren't really Progs. That claim from the Royalists that we tried to set them up got way more news time than our denial."

He had a point. I'd seen the clip of Spokeswoman Akarad making the accusation far more than Gig's response. At the time, I hadn't believed Akarad's accusations for exactly the reasons Gig described. With a lead pointing toward the Templars, however, I needed to tread carefully.

I started with his comment about my military background. "You believe ISC links to this?"

"The military has a vested interest in seeing our party discredited." He regarded me steadily. "And you're army."

For flaming sake. First Chief Hadar accused me of bias or worse because of my Majda link. Lady Akarad didn't even try to hide her belief I was inferior due to my Undercity background. Councilor Knam and the Trads had me followed because who the hell knew why. Half the people I worked with considered me a publicity hog instead of a bona fide investigator because of that blasted news holo. And someone kept messing with my EI, not to mention trying to drop balconies on me. Now the Progs thought I had ulterior motives because of my military background. Was there any person on this planet who actually believed I had just come here to do my job?

"That's bullshit." I stopped myself before I said any more. I didn't want to make Chief Hadar right in his suggestion that my style would antagonize people in this case.

"My apologies," Gig said. He even sounded genuine. "I don't mean to offend."

I took a moment to let my pulse calm. "Spokesman Bayer, I understand your concerns. I've had similar said to me by people in authority, the Majdas in fact." I stopped, considering, then plunged ahead. "I grew up in a place called the Undercity on Raylicon. Are you familiar with it?"

"Only vaguely. I don't know anything about the place."

"People consider it one of the worst slums in the

Imperialate." Anger edged my voice. "Many consider us subhuman. They call us dust rats." I took a moment and then spoke more evenly. "To us, our home is unique and treasured, with incredible beauty. But it's true, we also struggle with crime and poverty." I took a breath. "Vaj Majda once told me that I was the nightmare of any leader who dealt with a disenfranchised population. Why? Because I made it out of the Undercity, then returned and took on a leadership role. The success story who came home with the tools to upset the status quo. I've never intended to rile up anyone; I just want better lives for my people. But I make those in power uneasy when I seek change. So yes, I know how you feel."

Gig stared at me. "You know the General of the Pharaoh's Army?"

That's all he got out of my story? Then again, it was a pretty big deal. "I'm on retainer to the House of Majda. They hired me to investigate this case."

"Even though you come from one of the worst places to live in the Imperialate?"

I regarded him dourly. "'Worst' is a subjective word. But yes, most people who don't live there consider that true."

"Yet the Majdas hired you. The most powerful family alive after the Ruby Dynasty."

"I get their cases solved. They also need someone who can go anywhere, even the Undercity."

"Goddess." He shook his head. "That's amazing. You must be incredibly good at your job."

Well, that was refreshing, to have someone make a positive comment. "Thanks."

"So you're here to prove the Royalists have nothing to do with the technocrat case?"

Oh, well. So much for making progress. "No, I'm here to do my job. Do I believe the Progs are trying to frame the Royalists? Hell if I know. Why should I *not* believe the Progs are involved?"

His gaze never wavered. "Because we didn't do it. Because those murders and the bombing are vile, stupid acts and we are neither vile nor stupid people. Because no evidence supports that accusation. Because we don't use violence. You need more reasons?"

I spoke more quietly. "No. I'm aware of all those."

"And yet you still think we might have some involvement?"

I spoke carefully. "What do you know about the Templars?"

His forehead creased with puzzlement. "Their members help raise money for us. I can't imagine they have a link to this. They certainly have no interest in violence."

I wasn't convinced. "Don't you know the origins of their name? It's from an Earth group, the Knights Templar. They formed as an elite fighting force during religious wars over a thousand years ago."

He shrugged. "It's not the same. Yes, our Templars 'fight,' but not armed combat. They've taken the battle to improve the status quo to the meshes and corporations."

I thought of the history I'd browsed last night, trying to understand this latest clue. "They have a nonsecular component, though, don't they? That's why they chose the name, because it implies they fight in support of a religion. Except they worship the ancient pantheon of goddesses and gods from the Ruby Empire." It offered a reason they might target Techs. Adherents to the Ruby pantheon believed science sought to replace the ancient codices with heretical explanations for natural phenomena.

"In this day and age?" Gig laughed. "Of course they don't fight for an ancient mythology. The Templars aren't all Progs anymore, either. Some are New Techs."

That was a twist. From what I understood, New Techs referred to young entrepreneurs with highly successful start-ups who supported the Tech Party. Did they seek to manipulate the markets with these killings to benefit their corporations? It was an ugly idea, but not without precedent.

Gig was watching me closely. "The Templars have no ill will toward scientists or techs."

I chose my words with care. "They have come up as persons of interest."

His look turned incredulous. "You think the *Templars* committed the killings in the name of a religion that fell out of use thousands of years ago?"

"I'm not making any assumptions." I wondered more about Trads, given how much they hated the Progs. They hated the Templars a little less since that group had once looked askance at technology. From what Gig said, though, that had changed.

Max, I thought. *Can you get me more info on the New Techs and their relation to the Progs?*

Will do.

I considered Gig. "So you're saying the Progs don't have a fringe edge?"

He spoke wryly. "Our entire party is considered fringe. Given our insistence on nonviolent protest, though, we don't tend to attract violent types. They find us annoying. Sure, we have outliers, but we're the smallest party, so just by numbers, we don't have as many as other parties."

"I thought your numbers passed the Trads in recent years."

Gig shrugged. "It fluctuates. Overall, we're gaining. We get a lot of young people, college kids, innovators. Some can be hotheads. But assassinating prominent scientists? No way."

I thought of the attacks on Max. "Have you had problems with disruptions to your meshes?"

He looked taken aback. "Do you mean me, or the party more generally?"

"Either."

"As far as I know, nothing with the party. Have I had problems? I don't think so, but I'm not sure." He spoke awkwardly. "I thought a cybernetic cyclist was following me a few days ago. Then that stopped. It was probably nothing."

Ho! Max thought.

When did you start using slang? To Gig, I said, "What do you mean?" I spoke as if it were a mildly interesting factoid he'd just dropped, instead of a bombshell. "How do you know they were cybernetic? Did you see them?"

"Not well. I caught glimpses through the trees when I was walking through the woods around this concert hall. It looked like their body was part cycle." His face reddened. "Probably someone just went for a ride and I saw something that wasn't there."

Human slang is a useful short hand, Max said. Ask him about the appearance of the cyclist. The one that followed you had a gray-and-blue cycle.

"Did you see any colors on the cycle?" I asked Gig.

"Silver, like chrome. And blue, not clothes, but also like chrome."

I wondered about the timeline for our experiences. The cyclist had followed me two days ago, in the evening. "When did it happen?"

"Three days ago, around dinner time." He hesitated. "You think someone *did* follow me?"

"I don't know. I'll look into it."

Interesting, Max thought. It happened before you arrived on Parthonia.

Have you identified the cyclist?

Possibly a name, if it's the mountain biker. Kav Dalken. However, he doesn't have anywhere near the financial resources needed to change his body as we saw. Also, he identifies as male. He species the pronouns he and him. The cyclist looked female.

Maybe he changed his mind about his gender. See what you can find out. To Gig, I said, "Thank you for talking to me. I appreciate your honesty."

He smiled. "You seem like a fascinating person, Major. I hope you do come to one of our performances. Stop by backstage after the show. I'll introduce you around."

"Thank you." I hoped I could take him up on the offer. "I appreciate that."

He'd given me a lot to think about.

✜ ✜ ✜

The café where Lavinda and I met looked the same as yesterday, the last time we came here to talk. I arrived first and chose a secluded table hidden among the trees with their yellow and white bell blossoms. Not only was no one else around, but the tables in this area stood so far apart, I could barely see others through the foliage.

Max? I thought. *Any suggestions for how I approach this discussion?*

Nothing. I've already said too much. Please don't implicate me.

I'll be careful. I looked over my gauntlets, both of them. This morning Angel had returned the one I lent her. *Any success with rebuilding Highcloud?*

The microdust we found at the dump last night is scrambled and fragmented. I'm doing my best, but it will take a while.

All right. And thanks for working so hard on it. I know Highcloud isn't your favorite EI.

I have no reaction toward Highcloud. After a pause, he added, I admit, I don't always find our interactions positive. However, I would regret being unable to pursue those differences with the real Highcloud, the unit I grew up with while you lived here.

That he "grew up" with. Interesting. Maybe he had daddy issues with Highcloud. Mommy issues? What were the issues when your elder didn't have a sex? That subject would have to wait for another time. Lavinda was walking toward the table, dressed like a civilian in a pale blue tunic and trousers that ruffled in the breeze. I lifted my hand and she nodded her greeting.

"Any news on the case?" she asked as she took her seat.

"Some. I'm leaning away from Royalists or the main Progressive Party as the perpetrators."

"What about the Templars?" She regarded me from across the table. "The lead pointed straight at them."

"Yah. It does. And many of them are extraordinarily rich. Could they be trying to manipulate the markets and blame it on someone else, like the Royalists or the Traders?" The idea, as much as it bothered me, wouldn't stop tugging at my mind. "No matter how you look at it— whether they committed the crimes to game the market or just benefited from someone else's actions—they've done phenomenally well from the economic volatility caused by the violence."

She gave me a sour look. "So has the House of Majda. You think we're involved in this crime spree?"

Ouch. I'd better get out of this one, and fast. "No, of course not. No clues point to Majda."

"What about this lead pointing to the Templers?"

I waited as a server placed our kava on the table, along with two mugs. After she left, I said, "I'm not sure. The rep for the Progressives claims the Templars have links with the New Techs." I poured kava for both Lavinda and myself. "Max and I looked it up. The Templars not only welcome New Techs, they actively recruit them. So why would they murder the same people they want to attract?" I took a swallow of kava. Ah, yes, that was good, rich and strong, just hot enough to give me a jolt. "I told Chief Hadar. His people are looking into it."

Lavinda sipped her kava. "Do you have any other suspects?"

"Actually, I wondered about the Trads."

"Why? The Trads like the Royalists better than they like any other party."

"They also have the most to gain if people turn from the Royalists." I set down my mug. "Why would the Progs set up the Royalists? If people turn from the Royalists, they are far more likely to go with the Trads than the Progs."

"The accusation about the Progs is circumstantial, though," Lavinda said. "Or have you found evidence?"

I grimaced. "This case continues to have a remarkable lack of reliable evidence."

She spoke quietly. "Except the dead bodies."

"Yah," I said softly. "Except that."

She regarded me with concern. "How are you doing? It's only been a day since you lost your home."

"I'm fine." Realizing I'd just given her my stock answer to any inquiry about my health, even when I was bleeding to death, I added, "I appreciate the townhouse that your family provided. I don't know where I would have gone otherwise."

"We had actually planned to offer it to you before we knew you still kept a place here."

"Thanks." I wasn't ready to talk about what had happened. So I changed the subject. "What do you know about Councilor Patina Knam?"

"Knam? I've seen her in Assembly." She thought for a moment. "We both attended a reception at the Sunrise Palace last year held by the Ruby Dynasty to honor Ambassador Majors when he arrived from Metropoli."

Ho! Coincidence? "Ambassador Majors' son is apparently a tech-mech genius. I wonder if that reception is how the assassins found out about him." Another reason they might have chosen the co-op for the bomb.

"What makes you think Councilor Knam is involved?" Lavinda asked.

"She sent a PI to spy on me. Eja Werling. And two agents who tried to look like school kids at the starport. The PI was so clumsy, Angel and Ruzik caught her. I made those two 'kids' within a few minutes." I thought about what I'd just said. "That doesn't fit with the technocrat assassins. They know what they're doing." To put it mildly.

"Knam is about as traditional as they come," Lavinda said. "She always goes by the book. I can't imagine her even jaywalking, let alone being involved with a case like this one."

Yet Angel and Ruzik had run into the Trads at Greyjan's tavern. "Councilor Knam knows something about this case, I'd bet on it."

"You think Trads might be setting up the Progs by making it look like the Progs set up the Traders who set up Royalists?" Lavinda gave me a look that translated into *Seriously?*

I gave a wry laugh. "Yah, it's convoluted. I'm meeting the Trad spokeswoman later today. That ought to prove interesting."

"I'll see if I can dig up anything useful about Councilor Knam."

I spoke with care. "How about the other situation we discussed? Are you making headway on figuring out what you found at that space station?"

"Nothing." She sounded frustrated. "Absolutely nothing. It's as if it disappeared."

Something existed, but whether or not it originated at the space station was another question. Given all the mistakes the baby EI made with its clever ideas, I wouldn't be surprised if it figured out how to jump into space, then got trapped on the space station. A starship crossed interstellar distances by making its speed complex, with an imaginary component. In special relativity, that circumvented the problems with the speed of light. Using complex speeds allowed ships to "go around" light speed like a cyclist riding around an infinitely high pole that blocked their path, but it meant the traveler had to enter a complex universe. An EI couldn't do it alone. However, if it hid in the mesh of a starship, it could go wherever the ship went. And if that included an ancient station full of alien tech floating out in space? Yah, that would be a toy worth exploring. It probably didn't realize until too late that it had ridden a military ship out to its new playground.

"Bhaaj, where are you?" Lavinda asked.

"I was thinking about EIs." I took a careful swallow of kava. "When Pharaoh Dyhianna fought Oblivion, two giant EIs helped her. One was the Lock on Raylicon, an ancient mechanism built by our ancestors. The other was the city Izu Yaxlan, a conglomeration of all the EIs from our ancestors who lived on Raylicon before the fall of the Ruby Empire."

Her face took on a shuttered look. "The Pharaoh is the Assembly Key. The Key to the mesh. Her specialty is dealing with the interstellar meshes and how they relate to the Assembly."

That was certainly evasive. "I just wondered about

those two EIs she worked with. Maybe the new one you all found is similar."

"I don't think so." Her voice had become so guarded, I could practically see padlocks.

"I've always assumed humans created those EIs," I said. "But the EI in the Lock on Raylicon didn't feel that way." I actually had no way to quantify how "human" felt, but this let me introduce the matter without implicating Max.

She paused. "We believe humans designed the Lock and Izu Yaxlan EIs."

I wondered at her hesitation. "Is it possible something else created the Lock?"

Lavinda went so still, she looked like a statue. "I wouldn't know."

I recognized her tells. She wanted me to shut up. I couldn't back down, though. "If I'm going to help with this new EI, I have a need to know."

She watched me for a long moment. Finally she said, "You understand you cannot reveal anything I tell you to anyone. It would be treason to do so, Major."

"I understand."

She took a breath. After a moment, she said, "Three Locks actually exist, one on Raylicon and two others we found on ancient space stations. Although we think our ancestors built them during the Ruby Empire, we aren't sure. Another race may have created them. We don't understand a lot of that ancient science." Dryly she said, "Our ancestors didn't, either. It's probably why the Ruby Empire fell after only a few hundred years."

Three Locks? No wonder Max had suggested I ask her. "Can't the Locks tell you?"

"They don't talk to us. Only to their Keys, the Ruby Pharaoh and the Imperator. From what I gather, the Locks don't talk to them much, either, at least not in words."

I tried to fit this new information into my view of our existence. "What do they think about the origins of the Locks?"

Her face took on the inward look she had when she talked to Raja, her EI. Then she focused on me again. "I have no record of them talking about it." When I opened my mouth to protest, she held up her hand. "I'm not putting you off. I really don't know. I can tell you this: we think the Locks evolved on their own during the millennia of their separation from humanity. They interact with us and access Kyle space for their Keys—the Pharaoh and Imperator—but we don't know what else, if anything, they do."

"They must have done something all those thousands of years they existed."

"They slept. They seem quiescent most of the time."

A chill walked up my back. "Like Oblivion."

"*Not* like Oblivion. The only similarity is that we didn't create the Locks. Someone did, either our ancestors or another race of beings we don't know."

"Aren't you afraid of what the Locks might do if they ever fully wake up?"

"The Pharaoh trusts the Locks. I trust the Pharaoh."

That put one hell of a lot on the judgment of one person. "We ought to turn them off."

"That would be akin to murder." She met my gaze. "Also, without them, interstellar civilization as we know it wouldn't exist."

Murder? I'd feel that way if someone destroyed Max. I did feel that way about Highcloud. I wasn't so sure about interstellar civilization. "The Traders have an empire larger than ours and they have no access to Kyle space. They send messages from system to system using starships."

She spoke dourly. "They steal time on our Kyle mesh. Not much, which is why our communication goes faster than theirs, but their army is also bigger than ours. Better armed. If we lose the advantage of speed we get from the Kyle, we're done. They'll conquer us."

I had no desire to live in a nightmare created by the Aristos who ruled the Trader empire. Unbidden, a memory rose in my mind, one I'd have preferred to banish forever. Fifteen years ago, I'd served on a covert mission to a border world of the Trader empire. Several of its citizens had contacted ISC, asking for help to escape the planet. They'd become too outspoken in their challenge to Aristo authority and feared for their lives. They were right. The Traders didn't know we were there when they came to make the agitators pay for their resistance.

They incinerated the entire human settlement on the planet.

I'd been among the soldiers preparing to bring out the agitators. Instead, we snuck down hoping to find survivors. I'd never forget that day we walked through the ashes of a once-thriving metropolis where nearly a million people had lived. Nothing remained. Gone. All of it. The Aristos who owned the planet had massacred every last person as a lesson to would-be freedom fighters. Later on newscasts, they crowed about how their valiant troops had protected the empire from the vicious attacks of rebels. It was so far from anything resembling the truth, I got ill and wretched.

"I understand," I said. "But don't you worry that a Lock could turn into another Oblivion?"

Lavinda sighed. "I suppose subconsciously we all do. But here's the thing. In the many thousands of years the Locks have existed, they have never once acted against humanity. They serve our interests when they work with us and otherwise sleep, at least relative to us. I'm not sure we could turn them off even if we wanted to. We don't know how. They don't just exist in space-time, their intelligence extends into Kyle space."

Could the child EI be an incipient Lock? If the three ancient Locks acted on behalf of humanity, it gave me more reason to hope this new EI might as well.

"Does the new EI you found resemble the Lock?" I asked.

"Goddess only knows." Lavinda made a frustrated noise. "It's hiding from us."

That sounded like the child EI. I wanted to say more, but I'd given Max my word. Just as Lavinda trusted the Pharaoh about the Locks, so I would trust Max about his adopted child. If that could truly make a difference in how this EI viewed the human race, I had to give Max more time.

I hoped I wasn't making a mistake.

✣ CHAPTER XVI ✣
FOREST GRAB

After I left the café, I loped along forested paths in the nearby parks. Such a beautiful day, perfect for running, secluded and private. As I ran, my mind gradually smoothed out from all the tangles of the past few days, until it became like a mirror, reflecting the sky.

Reflecting grief.

I imagined touching the surface of the water. A ripple started, a circle spreading out in a lake. It felt like a way to mourn, though why, I couldn't have said. Despite all my abilities at solving problems, I'd never learned how to analyze my emotions, only feel them. This image of a lake with ever-widening circles—it felt like grief, like *allowing* myself to grieve for the losses at the co-op. So I ran, in silence, absorbing the beauty of the day into my heart, into my soul.

The rumble of a flyer broke my reverie. A silver-and-yellow craft flew overhead, then came back, too low, setting the treetops whipping in the blast of air from its cloud-turbines.

No, I thought. *Not now. I need this time.* "Max, what are they doing?"

"A good question," he said. "It's illegal to pilot a craft that close to the trees."

The flyer came back, dropping yet lower. "They're going to hit the branches."

"I don't like this," Max said. "I'd suggest you make it more difficult for them to find you."

I veered off the path, running under trees with pink flowers larger than my hand. The flyer growled above the canopy of branches. Although the engine rumble faded away, within seconds it came back. Branches above me whipped in the wind of its passage, and pink flowers rained over my head.

"Bastards," I muttered. "Why isn't any city drone stopping them?"

"Normally, it's legal to fly over this area," Max said. "But not so low."

I looked around the park. It was too tame to call a forest, with the ground cleared of any plants with thorns, prickles, or other weaponized foliage. "Can they land near here?"

"Not nearby. No clearing in this vicinity is wide enough to set down a flyer that large. I think they're circling above this grove, trying to hover." He paused. "Can you hear that clanking?"

"Turn up my ear augs."

Park noises jumped into prominence, the fluttering of blossoms drifting through branches, the scratch of leaves rubbing together, the buzz of a glass-bee looking for flowers to pollinate, or whatever bees that looked like pretty marbles did with their time. And yes, there! A creaking noise came from high up the trees.

"Max, that sounds like someone coming down a line." We'd used fast-rope insertions all the time in the army, to deploy soldiers or drones from a low-flying craft when they couldn't land. The composite line creaked that way as we slid to the ground with gloves to protect our hands.

I took off at a run—just in time to see two women in pseudo-military fatigues drop through the trees a few meters in front of me. They wore pistols holstered on their belts. Whirling around, I found myself staring at two more fatigue-wearing persons.

"Well, shit," I said.

"Major Bhaajan," one of the women said. "You'll need to come with us."

"Who are you?" I said.

Both women drew their guns, EM pulse revolvers. One bullet from those could liquefy my insides. "Don't make this difficult," one of them said.

I could hear the other two behind me, blocking my retreat. I turned and scowled at them. All four looked the same, women with fake military outfits, tattoos on their arms, black hair and eyes, and an attitude that practically shouted, "We're tough. Don't mess with us."

"Screw you," I said. "I'm not going anywhere. You wouldn't have gone to all this trouble if you planned to kill me. You aren't going to shoot me with your little fucking guns."

The taller of the two women pulled a weapon off her

back, a huge rifle. "How about my big fucking gun," she said as she leveled it at me—and fired.

I swam to consciousness like a sea dragon in an ocean of molasses. Or something. My thoughts, never poetic, were even more blunted today.

Gradually I became aware that I lay on my back. The rumble of an engine vibrated beneath my body. Opening my eyes, I saw—nothing. For a while I lay, staring into the nothing. As my night vision adapted, I realized a ceiling curved not too far overhead. Ah. I was in a flyer. Fake commandos had trapped me in the park, like yah, an idyllic grove in pastoral Selei City required four heavily armed combatants to grab one unarmed woman.

That rifle must have delivered some drug that made me feel like I had clouds in my brain. The darkness suggested they had darkened the flyer windows.

Max, I thought. *You there?*

Yes. Static grated in his thought. Whoever kidnapped you has deactivated many of my functions and is trying to get them all. They think they turned off my ability to talk to you.

I concentrated on my wrists. They felt bare. *I'll bet they think taking off my gauntlets means we can't communicate.*

Possibly. Not many personal EIs can use wireless signals to link to sockets in a human body and send messages to a human brain using bio-threads.

Sometimes I wish you could connect right to my brain.

Don't you remember? You almost had me implanted as a node in your brain.

My mind felt fuzzed. Dull. *I'd need military clearance for that, wouldn't I?*

Bhaaj, something is wrong with your memory. He sounded worried. You looked into it not long after we started working together. Civilians can get a node if they can afford it and a doctor certifies them for the implant.

I strained for the memory. *Oh. Yah. I remember. I decided not to do it.* I hadn't liked the idea of an EI in my mind, rather than in gauntlets I could take off. Now I wished I'd reconsidered.

Do you have any idea where we are? I asked.

They've blocked my local positioning network, but I must be within several meters of your physical location. Your wrist sockets aren't designed for long-range signals.

Didn't I upgrade your wireless capability years ago, including more distance?

Yes! He sounded relieved by my returning ability to remember what I shouldn't have forgotten in the first place. Actually, you were going to increase the distance, but we decided you could better use those resources to upgrade my storage and calculation ability. So you went for more memory and speed rather than more distance.

Oh. Yah, I do remember. I made a concentrated effort to focus. *My mind feels like sand running through a sieve. I'm having trouble holding thoughts.*

I think you want to ask me how long you've been unconscious.

How did you know that? It did seem like something I should ask.

I believe you were thinking about it when you recovered consciousness. I can't be sure because you hadn't directed the thoughts at me.

Yah, I was thinking about it. Something felt off about his comment. It took a moment, but then I zeroed in on the oddity. *Max, how can you receive me? My brain doesn't have wireless capability. I shouldn't be able to send messages to you.*

You're sending signals along the bio-threads in your body to the sockets in your wrists. This close, I can pick a few of them up even without a physical connection. I'm hiding in the background noise to avoid detection. He paused. I may also be interacting with your brain waves.

Say what?

I'm not sure. We've become so attuned, your brain waves partially sync with me, if we're close to each other.

Huh. *Can you send directly to my brain?*

I wouldn't advise it. When we interact via your wrist sockets, the threads in your body go from there to bio-electrodes that fire your neurons. You have protections designed from your own DNA to keep them from causing injury. If I tried to interact with your brain directly, I couldn't control how your neurons fired. It could give you seizures, even kill you.

I struggled to concentrate. *How long have I been in this flyer?*

About seven hours. It hasn't landed, so it will need to refuel soon. Also, you missed your meetings with the Traditionalist and Modernist reps.

Good.

Kidnapping seems an extreme way to avoid talking to politicians.

I meant it's good someone knows I'm missing. They'll wonder why I didn't show up. Their people would contact my people, which means you should have heard from their EIs.

I haven't. However, your kidnappers tried to deactivate me even before they hit the ground. They didn't manage right away, but they've continued eroding my capabilities. I can't get any messages now. The last I received was during your meeting with Colonel Majda. The EI for Manuel Portjanson, the Modernist rep, wanted to verify the time for your meeting. I haven't heard anything from the Trad rep.

My goodness, no Trads. What a coincidence.

It might not be as suspicious as it looks. You hadn't missed your appointment yet when these people grabbed you.

Were you able to contact anyone before the kidnappers blocked you?

I don't know. I tried to reach Chief Hadar and Colonel Majda, and I sent a message to Highcloud at the townhouse. I think something got through to Highcloud, but I doubt Raja received my message and I'm sure nothing reached the police.

What did you tell Highcloud?

If they received enough of my message, they have some idea you were kidnapped. He still sounded worried. Even if I could reach anyone, though, I can't give our location with my GPS blocked. I'm sorry.

It's not your fault, Max. You're operating well beyond a normal EI's capabilities. Even better, you're managing to hide it from these cretins who shot me.

That is more polite than the words I would like to use for them.

You sound more like me all the time.

Thank you.

Max considered that a compliment? He honored me. I supposed if I analyzed my responses, I'd come up with some business about how he had become so integral to my emotions, I no longer had objectivity, or some other talky-feely stuff. I decided I'd just be flattered instead.

If we've been airborne for seven hours, I thought, *we could be anywhere on this continent.*

I suspect we're going north, into colder regions of this landmass.

Have they fitzed with your other functions, too, like your ability to detect human life signs? It would be good to know how many people are on this flyer.

They've blocked my sensors.

You weren't blocked when they shot me in the park, though, right? If you describe what they did up until they blocked you, it might give me some clues.

I believe their team consists of five people. One stayed in the flyer while the other four fast-roped into the park. One of the droppers got hit with a tree branch. Not that I, an EI with only logic, would take pleasure in such an event.

Of course not. Served her right if a branch smacked her on the way down. *How did they get me into the flyer?*

They didn't try to hoist you up to the craft. It doesn't

hover well enough. They carried you to a clearing. The flyer landed, they loaded you on board, and all four got on. The medic keeping watch on you was one of those four.

She's not watching that well. She doesn't seem to know I'm awake. Remembering Max's comments about my possible subconscious sexism, I added, *Or he.*

She, Max said. So is the pilot. All women. It fits with your theory that the Trads are behind this kidnapping. They would never send men.

The kidnappers seem clumsy, I thought. *No way did they need four commandos to grab me.*

Don't underestimate yourself. Not many people are sixth-degree black belts with augmented speed, strength, and reflexes.

Well, maybe. I had my doubts that I could put out four of them, especially if they had training or augmentation. *They were lucky a drone didn't stop them. It's also illegal to carry arms like that in Selei City, unless you're police or otherwise licensed. And what was with that rifle? She didn't need a weapon like that to sedate me.*

I've checked my records of city ordinances. Tourists often fly over that park. I don't know why she used such a large gun to drug you. I agree that their operation had a blunt feel, one consistent with the PI at the port and the students who tried to spy on you. I'd say they have training, but they aren't professional at the level of the technocrat murders.

It's not like the child EI, either. It seems brilliant, but without enough experience to carry through its ideas.

Yes. Max sounded bemused. The child is improving,

though. I'm having trouble finding its shimmerfly drones. It figured out how to play the game on its own, so it doesn't need me anymore. I'd say it wants to establish itself as independent.

Hah! It's turned into a teenager. Time to rebel against its hoshpa.

I'm glad you find my involvement amusing, he thought dryly.

It hasn't tried to contact me in the last day, either. The baby wanted to warn us about Greyjan's tavern. Do you think that changed?

I can't say. He paused. If I were to guess, I'd say the baby was frightened. Terrified, even. The teen wants to handle matters on its own.

I thought you said EIs didn't experience human-identified states of being. Or whatever we'd called them.

A more accurate description would be that the younger version of the EI knew it lacked the resources to deal with what it perceived as a great threat. It has since evolved.

A woman with a clipped voice spoke. "Captain, I think she's waking up."

That's the doctor, Max thought. Perhaps you should pretend you're just waking up.

Another woman answered. She sounded like the one who had shot me. "Is she talking?"

"No, I'm just getting neural activity on my monitor." The doctor's clothes rustled as if she were leaning over me. "Bhaajan? Can you hear me?"

I made a show of opening my eyes. "Eh?" I mumbled.

"Do you know where you are?" the doctor asked.

"Park," I muttered.

"She's really out of it," the doctor said.

Low voices spoke in another part of the craft, words I couldn't pick up.

Max, can you crank up my hearing? I asked.

The doctor may detect the biomech activity, now that she's checking on you.

Not good. *Can you fiddle with my health meds, then, make it look like I passed out again?*

I'll try.

I closed my eyes and endeavored to look unconscious.

"Major Bhaajan?" the doctor asked.

I kept as silent as a baby EI.

Various hums came from equipment around me. "She's out again," the doctor said.

"What about her EI?" the captain asked. "Maybe we ought to dump it overboard."

If they tried to destroy Max, I'd wake up fast and violent. *Max, where and when are your most recent backups?*

A full back up of me exists on the console at the townhouse and on the servers at the manufacturer that created my template. My last backups took place about one minute before they deactivated my ability to reach the servers.

Good. If you get the chance to make any more, do it pronto. I hoped to high hell we wouldn't need it, but I wanted to be sure. *Also, can you record what's going on around us?*

Yes, but only in close range to the location of your gauntlets.

"The EI is quiescent," another woman said. "I'd suggest we keep it. For one, it might prove useful in finding out more about her. For another, it's one hell of a high-end unit. Also, if we destroy it, that will activate an alarm at the corporate servers that sell and maintain these units."

Good. Their EI expert knew her stuff, at least enough to protect Max.

"All right," the captain said. "We're landing soon, and I don't want any trouble. Maybe you should give her more jinx."

"She's had too much," the doctor said. "If I give her more, it could cause brain damage."

Max, what is jinx?

It's a neural relaxant. It's supposed to slow your brain function and put you to sleep.

I'm not asleep. And my brain is fine.

Your brain is not fine. However, your army training to resist coercive drugs helps.

That doesn't explain why I woke up. I struggled to find the memory. *What am I forgetting?*

You've always had a high tolerance to drugs. He paused. They are running a test on me. We should stop communicating, just in case.

All right. I remembered now about the drugs. They saturated the Undercity. In my youth, I'd run with a dust gang: me and Jak, my oath sister Dig, and a boy named Gourd with a gift for tech-mech. Dig's mother had been a drug cartel queen, responsible for so much of the shit that screwed up our people. Dig hated it, not only because of the pain it caused, but also because her mother preferred selling drugs to loving her own daughter.

I didn't know why I'd never responded much to the "illicit substances" the army docs tested me for. They acted so surprised that my body showed no history of drug use except for second-hand inhalation of hack smoke. I could have told them that. I did, in fact, but of course they didn't believe me. They did believe their tests. It wasn't only that I had a high tolerance to many substances; I also didn't enjoy their effect. Jak had loved hack and used it all the time in our youth. He quit as an adult because he liked gambling even more, and he wanted his casino to succeed. He told me the hack made it hard to think clearly. Well, yah. That was the point.

I wasn't the only Undercity native who didn't respond to the drugs so common down there. I'd sometimes wondered if we'd bred that trait into our population. After several millennia of my people suffering the highest infant mortality in the Imperialate, it wouldn't surprise me if genes that gave us a better chance of survival—including a lack of interest in shit that destroyed our lives—became concentrated in our gene pool. Not that it stopped the drug queens. They were equal-opportunity criminals; they sold to anyone, in the Undercity or anywhere else.

Bhaaj? Max asked. **Are you still conscious?**

Yah. I felt subdued. *Just remembering.*

We're landing, Max thought.

I concentrated on the rumble of the engines. A jolt vibrated through the flyer and the rumble stopped. Another hum started, one that suggested a much lighter engine.

That sounds like an air stretcher, I thought.

For you, I assume, Max said.

Sure enough, they lifted me onto a stretcher. As they lowered me from the flyer, Max said, I think they're taking me somewhere else. If we get separated, I can't reach your sockets.

Do whatever you need to protect yourself. Anything, Max. Stay alive.

Understood. Static crept into his signal.

I will talk to you soon. Take care.

You too . . . His thought faded into nothing.

As the air stretcher carried me, I listened to my surroundings. Forest, it sounded like, with wind whispering and insects buzzing. Cold air moved over my face, a faint breeze. It smelled wild and wild, not at all like the city. Footsteps accompanied the stretcher, crunching in dead leaves, people walking, three, maybe four. So far, they hadn't scanned me again, which was good, because without Max's help, I wouldn't look unconscious.

"It'll be good to get some dinner," the doctor was saying.

"We can whip something up at the cabin," someone else said, the captain it sounded like.

"You may not want to eat anything I cook," a third woman said with a laugh.

So. Cabin did imply a forest. That they talked about cooking themselves implied these weren't people who expected robots or other people to serve them.

A buzz interrupted them, the page from a gauntlet comm. The captain answered. "Lajon here. We have the target."

"Good," a woman said, with a thinness to her voice that

suggested this area had poor signals. Even so. I recognized those cultured tones. I'd heard them often in broadcasts during my investigation into Eja Werling, the Trad PI. It was Assembly Councilor Knam.

"What about those two thugs she brought here?" Knam asked.

"They weren't with her," Captain Lajon said. "They may be at the townhouse, but its security is too tight to break."

Good. The Majda techs had protected the place well, and Highcloud kept it secure. Then it hit me: if these people damaged Max, then what remained of the original Highcloud could go as well. Hell and damnation. I was tempted to jump out of the stretcher, fists swinging. Given that I had no weapons against all their guns, and that my brain felt like mush, I controlled my stupid urge to punch them in the face and continued to play dead. Or at least, unconscious.

"Werling is already at the cabin," Councilor Knam said. "She has several truth serums you can try on the Major."

Truth about *what*? I had nothing to tell them. I wondered if she was using a secured channel. Although it was an obvious precaution, her team seemed sketchy on details, like verifying Max couldn't reach me. True, most people didn't have bio-electrodes in their brain that allowed them to communicate with an EI, but a savvier team would check even remote possibilities. I doubted this team had masterminded the jigsaw puzzle of the technocrat case. They didn't have the finesse.

So what the hell were they about? I didn't have time to be kidnapped. I'd been at this case for nearly three days, and so far I'd achieved squat. My leads went nowhere. Royalists, Traders, Progs, financial wizards, New Techs. What about the Mods? Yah, right, they wanted to conquer the Imperialate. They already had a majority in the Assembly, which made conquering redundant. Besides, many of the people killed or injured in the bombing were Mods, not Techs. I still hadn't figured out where Greyjan's tavern fit in, if at all. My kidnappers must realize it would alert people when I failed to show for appointments. I hoped Max got through to Highcloud, because otherwise no one knew where I'd gone.

Concentrate, I told myself. If they gave me truth serum, could I reveal anything secured? So far my work pointed at the Traditionalists as the most likely culprits. I had no problem telling them that they were the prime suspects. Other than that, what else—

The EI.

Well, shit. I'd better not spill that juicy morsel, both about the ancient EIs and the baby EI. The health meds in my body could synthesize a limited amount of counterserum to act against the truth drug. Although it would help if I had Max, the army never intended for us to become so dependent on our EIs that we couldn't operate without them. The biomech wizards had taught me biofeedback techniques I could use to program the meds myself.

Clear your mind, I told myself. *Calm. Still. Serene.* Focusing inward, I concentrated on my meds. *Nullify.* I couldn't directly reach the picoweb they formed; it was too rudimentary to interpret signals from my brain. But the biofeedback should evoke a response from my body that the meds recognized. I hoped. If it worked, then when Eja Werling injected me with the serum, the meds should act to counter it. I continued thinking *nullify serum* until my thoughts drifted ...

✤ CHAPTER XVII ✤
CABIN FEVER

"Wake up," the voice repeated.

I opened my eyes and found myself in a wooden chair, surrounded by the rustic living room of some high-end cabin. It looked like a wealthy slick's idea of "roughing it." A fire sent up orange and yellow flames in a hearth designed from red bricks. The wood panels on the wall gleamed in the firelight, with artistically placed knotholes here and there. A circular rug covered the floor, one woven in the colors of autumn, red, gold, green, and orange. A cat lay sleeping near the fireplace, tawny and plush, its coat gleaming with health. It looked like a genuine Earth cat, which would cost a fortune to bring here to Parthonia. Cats seemed to go wherever humans went, often stowing away on ships, but this one looked too healthy to be a stray. Whoever owned this cabin had probably paid as much for that cat as for the cabin itself.

And looky here, what a surprise, Eja Werling sat in a chair across from me, her booted feet up on a low wooden table inlaid with sunrise mosaics. Her chair looked a lot nicer than mine, with its comfortable cushion upholstered in autumn colors. Someone had manacled my wrists to the arms of mine. As my head cleared, I realized one of the fake commandos who'd grabbed me at the park stood guard by the door, beyond Werling.

"My greetings, Major," Werling said in a pleasant voice.

"Go to hell," I answered. "Why did you bring me here? No, sorry, that's the wrong question. Why did Councilor Knam want you to bring me here?" I couldn't stop the words from tumbling out. Shit. They *had* given me a truth serum. "She owns this place, right?"

"How did you know—" Werling stopped herself. "I'm the one asking questions."

"You know," I told her. "You all could have just met with me like we planned. What's the point of bringing me here? You must intend to kill me, too, when you're done with whatever stupidity you've set up here."

"Kill you, too?" She seemed more puzzled than angered. "What do you mean, too?"

It didn't reassure me that the only part of my statement she questioned was the word "too." Had they killed other people? I didn't see how they could let me go; they'd gone too far. Grabbing me out of the city was a lot different than spying at the starport. Then again, maybe her "too" meant they didn't intend to kill me in addition to grabbing me. My brain wanted me to talk, talk and *talk*, so I decided to go with a provocative statement before I gave away some secret.

"I take it that you all committed the technocrat assassinations," I said.

She scowled at me. "Of course not. Where did you get that idea?"

"Why else would you kidnap the person solving the murders?"

"You haven't solved shit. You're working with them, aren't you?"

"Working with who?"

She regarded me with an all-knowing expression. "You know who I mean."

"Uh, no, I don't."

Werling frowned. "Major, who are you working with?"

"The Selei City police." She already knew that. In fact, the entire blasted universe knew it after that newscast went viral.

"And?" she asked.

"And what?"

"Who else?"

"You mean the Majdas? I'm on retainer to them." Before she could accuse me of bias or whatever, I added, "And no, I'm not here to spin for the Royalist party."

"I don't mean the Majdas." She sounded frustrated. "Who hired you to cover up clues for the technocrat assassinations? The killers?"

Holy mother. I'd wondered if the Trads would also find a way to diss how I did my job, but the last thing I'd expected was an accusation that I worked *for* the killers.

"Is this a joke?" I asked. "Because it's not funny."

She watched me intently. "How long have you collaborated with them?"

"I don't work with them." No wonder Councilor Knam

thought they needed to give me truth serum. "What gave you that ridiculous idea?"

"Someone is covering up the clues," she said. "Someone is hiding any leads that could solve the case. You're the one they brought in to find those leads." She spoke with disdain. "Given your background, you also have, shall we say, criminal inclinations."

I wanted to say a lot of things, none of it tactful, and if I didn't find a way to fight this truth serum fast, it was all going to come out. Then again, some truths worked just fine here. So I said, "No, I don't have criminal inclinations."

"Oh, come on. You come from—" She stopped, then said, "Less than auspicious origins."

"So what?"

"Your people murder without remorse or punishment."

I'd never figured out why people believed that our poverty meant we had no remorse for cruelty or death. We had our own laws and punishments, and they were often harsher than in the city that gleamed above us.

"That's bullshit," I said. "You watch too many stupid holo-vids."

"Major, you need to answer me." She spoke slowly, with the careful style of speech I'd used myself in the army when I had to question people under truth serum. "What is your connection to the technocrat assassinations?"

"I'm the private investigator brought in by the police to help solve the case."

She gave me a baffled look. "Are you trained to resist interrogation?"

"No," I lied. Of course I had training.

"Are you attempting to deflect my questions?"

"No. I don't need to." I spoke with exasperation. "Look, your questions make no sense. I don't have any link to the people who committed the murders. I can't figure out why you grabbed me out of the city. You could have asked me this when I saw you at our planned meeting yesterday. If you really thought you needed truth serum, you could have slipped it into my drink when I didn't notice." Or when they thought I didn't notice. "Bringing me here set you up for a shitload a trouble. So what's up?"

She blinked. "I think that's the most I've heard you say at one time in all the holos I found about you when I was doing my research."

"Yah, well, if you don't want me to talk, don't give me truth serum." As long as I kept spinning my theories about their motives, I wasn't giving away secured information about rogue EIs in ancient space stations.

"What makes you think I gave you truth serum?" she asked.

"Seriously?" I regarded her with incredulity. "Maybe, Eja Werling, it's because you're all so clumsy. You think you're being discreet, covert even, and maybe if I were a regular citizen, it would be enough to fool me. But it's child's play to figure out who Councilor Knam has spying on me. That enough truth for you?"

Werling sat back, her forehead furrowed. "You aren't what I expected."

"Why'd you bring me up here?"

She crossed her arms. "I'm asking the questions."

"Not very well." It hit me then. "Councilor Knam wants credit for solving this case. You bring me up here, grill me for the clues I've found, use my work to find answers, and then either prove I'm affiliated with the killers or frame me. You look great as the PI involved and Knam gets kudos for her supposed insight into finding the most notorious serial killer this city has seen in over a century."

I wanted to punch something. "People are disillusioned with the Royalists already. So where are members of the Royalist Party most likely to go if they change party affiliations? Why, gosh, the Trads. And who cares if I'm screwed by it all. I'm just a dust rat from the Undercity."

She stared at me. "Shit."

"Yah, I agree. You brought me here so I can't go warn people what you're doing or finish solving the case. You need a reason, though, to say why you grabbed me." I squinted at her. "Oh. Yah. It's obvious. You planned to claim I was going to do something violent, who knows what, and you had to stop me. That's why you need to frame me for working with the assassins." I thought of what Gig had said about the false news stories getting far more play than the denials. "By the time I could defend myself, the damage would be done. No one would believe my denials anyway, because, hey, I'm just scum."

She sat there with her mouth open. Then she remembered herself and shut it. "You can't seriously expect me to believe someone like you can solve this case."

"Yes, I can seriously believe that. You must, too, or you wouldn't be trying to interrogate me to find out what I know or holding me here to stop me from solving it first."

Her voice took on a clenched sound, like the verbal equivalent of a fist. "You can't get credit for solving this case. It's *wrong*. Someone like you—no. You belong where you came from, back in the grime where you grew up."

I didn't have Max to warn me to calm, but I was so far beyond angry, her words rolled off my back. I spoke mildly. "We're probably cleaner in the Undercity than you."

Her face turned red with anger. "Shut your mouth."

"Oh, fuck you." I really needed some new cuss words. "I don't have time for this. You don't wonder why the police went to the trouble of bringing in someone from offworld or why I'm on retainer to some of the most powerful people alive?" I certainly was talky today. "I'm damn good at what I do, sweetheart, and you don't even come close."

"Gods, your ego."

"Hey, it's truth serum. So I must be telling the truth." I needed to get out of these manacles, which meant distracting her. "What did you do with Max?"

She had started to speak, but at my question, she looked like she'd hit a wall. "With who?"

"My EI. He's in my gauntlets."

"We deactivated him."

I opened my mouth to tell her Max had outsmarted their attempts to turn him off, but I caught myself in time and shut it again.

Werling sat up straighter. "What?"

I made a show of struggling not to speak, opening my mouth, closing it, starting, stopping. And then I lied to her face. "You can't keep him deactivated without a signal from me. Otherwise, he'll come back online."

"What? No, he can't."

"It's the way he works. I wanted an EI designed with a fail-safe." Who knew what I meant by fail-safe, because I sure as hell didn't.

She frowned. "How does he supposedly come back online?"

"He reboosts his central affector unit with a neural cross-cutting transducer switch." I rattled of the first nonsense words that came to my mind, fast and curt.

Werling blinked. "He does what?"

"Surely you've experienced this before."

"He can't reactivate."

"Of course he can." I leaned forward in the chair. "And then you're in it deep. Because you're the one here, not Councilor Knam. She'll deny any connection to you and condemn your activities when the police show up." *That* was a truth she needed to hear. No way would Knam help if Werling got caught; the councilor would let nothing link her to a kidnapping.

Werling shifted in her chair. "Let's say I believed you about this fail-safe. I don't, but for the sake of argument— how would I turn it off?"

"You can't. Only I can. My gauntlets are keyed to my fingerprints, voice, and retinal scan."

She waved her hand as if wiping away my words. "We'll just destroy your gauntlets."

"That sends an alert the corporation that built my EI." That much was true, as their EI expert had already stated. It would help convince her of the rest. I hoped.

Werling frowned at me. "Fine. You do this supposed deactivation of the fail-safe."

"Sorry. Can't do that."

"Why not?"

I put on another show of trying hard not to talk, then "lost the battle" and said, "It needs to scan my eyes, my fingerprints, and hear my voice. You can't force that."

"Actually," Werling told me, "That can be arranged."

I scowled at her. "Like hell."

She tapped the comm on her wrist. "Captain?"

"Lajon here," the captain said. "How's it going?"

"She says if she doesn't give the proper code to her EI, it will trigger some sort of warning to the place that made it."

"I thought that only happened if we destroyed it."

"She claims she set up a fail-safe so if her EI is deactivated for a certain amount of time, it also sends the warning."

"Then turn off the fail-safe." Lajon sounded impatient.

"How?"

"Ask her. You gave her the serum, right?"

Werling laughed, an ugly sound. "Indeed. She's talking up a storm."

"So have her tell you how to disable the warning signal."

"She says it requires a retinal, finger, and voice scan."

"All that? Goddess, is she paranoid or what?"

"She's not going to submit to any scan."

"You can get them anyway. The voice is easy, given the truth serum. Ask her for the password it uses to identify her voice and record her saying it. For her eyes, we'll need tech that forces them to stay open without registering strain. I'll send the doctor over with something."

"I thought that was illegal."

"Just do it." Lajon sounded irritated. I didn't blame her. After everything they'd done, contraband tech designed to fool a retinal scan ranked among the least of their problems.

"Her fingers will be more difficult," Lajon said. "Most advanced EI systems can recognize if you cut off the fingers and use them without the owner attached." The captain laughed as if she'd made a joke. "Her hand needs to be relaxed, so forcing her to hold open her fist won't work. Damn systems have gotten too smart. A good one can tell if the person attached to the hand is tensed, dead, passed out, or whatever. It might even know her hand is manacled to the chair arms." She went silent. "We need her relaxed, but not so much that she passes out."

The esteemed Captain Lajon wasn't an idiot, as much as I wanted to think of them all that way. She had a good sense of how ID checks worked.

"You want me to give her more jinx?" Werling asked.

"Yeah, but not enough to knock her out. Keep her barely conscious, awake, but too out of it to fight. I'll come over with the rest of the team, just in case. We'll bring her gauntlets and the eye drops. Give her the jinx now, and then we'll talk about what to do with the fingers."

"Fine. Out." Werling scowled at me. "You are far more trouble than you're worth."

"Don't knock me out." I pretended to be worried. "I won't cause problems."

Werling ignored me as she got up and went to a credenza against one wall. She opened a drawer and took out a med pack, then went about setting its air syringe with some potion, probably the jinx. I gritted my teeth as she pressed the syringe against my neck, and it hissed, just the barest pressure on my skin. Within moments, my mind fuzzed again. I closed my eyes, pretending to pass out. *Fake it*, I thought, concentrating on the picoweb formed by my health meds. *Make me look unconscious*. The web wouldn't pick up my words, but I'd trained with this system for years, drill after drill, practicing with biofeedback. It should pick up at least a sense of what I wanted.

"You gave her too much," someone said, the guard at the door it sounded like.

"That shouldn't have knocked her out." Werling shook my shoulders. "Major?"

I let my head roll to the side.

Werling slapped me across the face, *hard*, and my head banged against the back of the chair. Gods, I *wanted* to punch her so badly, it was all I could do to keep up my unconscious act.

"Can you tell if she's really out?" Werling said. "She could be faking it."

Footsteps crossed the room and a low growl followed by a hiss came from the direction of the hearth. Apparently Knam's pets didn't appreciate these people any more than I did. Someone leaned over me. Maybe I felt a slight difference in the air, I didn't know, but I sensed the guard bent down and then straightened. Taps came from in front of me, someone working on a gauntlet.

"She's out," the guard said. "You gave her too much."

The cat growled its disapproval of the guard's voice.

"Stupid rodent," Werling muttered. "Or whatever it is." More taps, and she pressed the syringe against my neck.

Fake it, I thought. *Fake it, fake it, fake it.*

My head began to clear.

"She's still unconscious," the guard said.

Werling hit me again. "Wake up, bitch."

Ah! My head exploded with pain as it banged against the high chair back. *Fake it!* I thought, as much to control myself this time as the meds.

"Still unconscious," the guard said. "What a half-assed wimp. She's nowhere near as tough as she plays at."

Good meds, I thought.

"I'll give it a minute." Werling's hair rustled as if she were shaking her head. "How did she fool the Majda's into hiring her? You'd think they would be more careful."

"She probably lied," the guard said. "I'm sure she has some minor link to them, one she exploited to get this job, but no way could such a publicity-grabbing duster be a PI on retainer to their House. More likely, she's a servant there." She spoke as if discussing a beetle on the floor. "To think we'd never have known the truth if that reporter hadn't dug up her background. No wonder she wanted to hide her identity."

Calm, I told myself, since I didn't have Max to do it. *Serene. Cool. You're floating on a clear lake under a sun-filled sky. Better yet, you're making love to Jak.* That last one helped.

"I can see why she enlisted," Werling said. "But how the hell did she become a major?"

"Oh, you know how it works," the guard said. "I'm sure

they had some program with preferential treatment for candidates who met a quota."

"Screw that," Werling said. "She got her position at the price of someone better qualified. She doesn't deserve any of this."

Cool down, I told my boiling temper. My nanos needed to release chemicals to counter any physiological signs of my anger. *Don't show any reaction.* These assholes had no freaking idea what I'd faced, how many times I'd been denied entry into officer candidate school even when I had the highest marks on the qualifying tests, both intellectual and physical. I'd fought for every atom of progress I'd made. The criticism never stopped no matter how much I achieved, no matter how many times I proved myself.

"Her pulse just jumped," the guard said. "I think she's coming around."

"Hey." Werling slapped me again. "Wake up."

Calm. Cool. Serene, I told myself. *If they underestimate you, that gives you an advantage.*

The creak of an old-fashioned door came from across the room, and the cat growled again.

Yah, I don't like them, either, I thought to it.

"I thought you weren't going to knock her out," a voice said. Captain Lajon.

More footsteps sounded, followed by someone murmuring, "Good kitty, there, see, it's okay." The scritch of fingers on fur rustled and the mollified cat purred.

"This should do the trick," Werling told them. The syringe touched my neck again.

I continued to play dead.

"Are you getting any signs she's conscious?" Lajon asked.

"Not yet," the guard said. "But I think she's drifting out of it."

Another voice spoke, the doctor it sounded like. "Damn it, Werling, if you caused brain damage and the doctors do an autopsy, they'll know she was drugged. They might even follow the trail back to me."

Autopsy. Yah, I was in trouble.

"She was fine a few minutes ago," Werling growled. "Mouthy as all hell."

"We might as well try the fingerprint code now," Lajon said. "At least if she's unconscious, she won't make trouble."

"The detector might pick up that she's manacled," the techie said. "Her prints won't work if the EI calculates that she hasn't given them of her own free will."

Lajon grunted with impatience. "If it doesn't work, we'll get rid of the EI. And yes, I know, it will alert who-the-hell knows. Take it into the forest hundreds kilometers from here, smash it, and drop it. Whoever it alerts will send their rescue team to that location instead of here."

The tech said, "It would be a shame to destroy such an EI. It's like a work of art."

You'll need a rescue team yourself if you harm Max, I thought.

My greetings, Bhaaj, Max thought.

You're here!

Yes, Max thought. *The doctor is holding your gauntlets. They turned off most of my functions. I can't activate your combat mode.*

It should kick in if I start fighting. ISC made sure we had use of our biomech even if we lost the EI that controlled them, but they didn't want us attacking innocent civilians, either. If my combat mode activated every time I got into a fight, it could be a disaster. My vital signs needed a certain level of intensity before it kicked in. It would help that my adrenaline had rocketed, probably another reason the jinx hadn't worked as well.

Initially I had the impression they intended to discredit you, Max said. However, they have also discussed ways to dispose of your body.

Yah, I think they've realized killing me may be their only way out of this mess. They plan to suggest I have complicity in the technocrat murders.

You weren't even on Parthonia when this business started.

No. I wasn't. But Max, I maintained a residence here even when I lived on another planet. That won't look good. And the bomb went off in my building. It could make it look like I bungled matters, setting off the explosive where I'd stored it.

You would never be that inept.

Yah, but these people think I'm an idiot. And they want me to look guilty.

You don't even know these people. Why would they set you up?

Because I'm the PI brought in to help on the case. Councilor Knam wants the credit. Bitterly I added, *They also don't want Undercity scum getting kudos for such a prestigious case. Goddess forbid, I should actually do my job better than their idiot PI.*

She isn't an idiot, Bhaaj. Werling is new as a PI, which makes her efforts clumsy, but she's brilliant with politics and spin. Chief Hadar never worked with her because she only works for Trads, to further their politics.

The doctor was speaking again. "I've reset the syringe. You put the dosage too high." It hissed against my skin.

"Hopefully this will work," Werling said. A hand brushed the skin of my wrists above the manacles and they clicked as someone freed my right arm. She clicked open the left—

I launched out of the chair, swung my fist, and kicked my leg all in the same instant. I didn't have time to aim—and my combat libraries didn't kick in. My boot plowed into Werling's stomach instead of my target, her head. As she doubled over, my fist connected with the person holding Max, the doctor apparently. I'd known someone was there, but the person I needed to put out was Captain Lajon. I moved fast, but without enhanced reflexes or power. Grabbing the doctor, I swung her toward the person I guessed was Lajon, blocking the captain's fist as she swung. Lajon hit the doctor instead, and the medic groaned.

Your combat mode just toggled on, Max thought.

Everyone seemed to slow down. Werling didn't even try to fight; she backed away from the melee. Two guards converged on me, trying to form a triangle so they could hit me from both sides. I shoved the doctor into Lajon with accelerated speed, throwing them off-balance. Whirling around, I grabbed one of the guards by the head and swung her like a shield as I kicked past her body. My kick went wide, but I managed to smash one of the other guards in the hip while I used my elbows to strike the woman I was holding.

I had four opponents, a losing proposition—except they couldn't fight worth spit. I kept moving, back and forth, never losing pace, so no one could knock me over. None of them seemed to have biomech enhancement. When I rolled a guard over my hip and threw her to the ground, the crack of a breaking bone split the air. I didn't fight to kill, but I had to stop them *now*, because otherwise they planned to stop me for good, RIP, so long Bhaaj.

I fought using the length of my limbs to good advantage, spending barely more than a second with each person. The slowing of my time sense made it easier to judge how to hit in the right place or how to protect my head. With enhanced reflexes, I could avoid most of what they threw at me. Somewhere in there, the cat quit growling and ran from the room.

Within seconds, I knocked out two of the guards. The doctor was on the floor, unconscious, but still holding my gauntlets. Werling stood backed up against the wall, watching with her mouth open. Captain Lajon came straight for me. In the same moment that I struck at her head, she whirled around in a jumping roundhouse kick. Damn! She knew her business. I barely evaded the blow. We kept fighting, moving fast, moving hard, but I couldn't get in a powerhouse blow—

My fist finally connected with Lajon's jaw, and her bone broke with a loud crack. I didn't hesitate, not even for a second as I threw her to the floor. I dropped to my knee next to her, raised my fist with a jerk—and realized she had stopped moving.

I pulled my blow, breathing hard, surrounded by four motionless figures. Werling stood backed against the wall, staring at me with horror.

"You killed them," she shouted.

I looked up at her, struggling to contain my rage.

Calm, Max murmured. *Calm, Bhaaj. I can't get you out of combat mode. You need to control it.* Then he added, *I can still record. I have everything that happened since I entered this room. Anything you say here to Werling will be part of my record. In a situation like this, where your life is threatened, such a record is admissible in court.*

I took a ragged breath. *Assuming you don't get destroyed before this is over.*

Yes. Also, I'm getting life signs from all four. Two are in serious trouble, however.

"They aren't dead," I told Werling, aware of Max recording my words. "Just knocked out."

"You had no right," she hissed.

"I have every right to defend my life," I said. "You all kidnapped me, drugged me, chained me to a chair, and beat me up, all the time planning to steal my work so you could take credit for solving the case. Councilor Knam hired you, to make her look good. When this got messier than you expected, you decided to kill me. And then what? Say it was self-defense, because I'm a crazed dust rat from the Undercity?"

"You're lower than scum." Venom practically dripped from her words. "You don't deserve to be here."

"Why the hell not?" In all the years, in all the times I'd encountered her attitude, in all the hatred spewed at me, I'd never understood *why*. "So what if I come from the Undercity?"

"You're less than human." She spoke as if stating a fact everyone knew.

I stared at her. "How does my being from the Undercity justify what you've done here?"

"What *I've* done." She stared at me with incredulity. "You beat up four people!"

I struggled to control my rage. "What did you expect, that I'd just let you all murder my ass?" I was about to add more choice words when Max thought, Watch it. You want this recording to make you look sympathetic.

"You think you deserve better?" Werling said. "Goddess, you people."

"*What* people?" I was excruciatingly aware the guards could wake up any moment, but I couldn't leave until Werling implicated Knam.

"You," Werling said. "Dust rats."

"Do all Trads feel this way?" I asked. "Or just Councilor Knam?"

"Not everyone has the courage to take action." Werling straightened up, pulling back her shoulders. "Councilor Knam is a visionary. We are proud to serve in her army."

"What army?" As far as I knew, Knam had never served in the military.

"Those of us who follow her. She isn't afraid to do whatever is necessary to return our glorious empire to its halcyon days."

Max, what does halcyon mean?

Halcyon days is an Earth idiom that means a time of happiness and tranquility, often referring to the past with nostalgia.

The doctor stirred on the ground and moaned.

Damn. I needed to get out of here. I motioned at the bodies on the floor. "You call this tranquil? This slugfest you created?"

Werling clenched her fists at her sides. "You caused this! You should have just stayed put, not made trouble, accepted your takedown. These deaths are on your head."

"I don't fight to kill, only to disable." Though gods knew, I'd wanted to smash them. "If anyone dies, that's on Councilor Knam's head. She's the one who ordered you all to do this."

"That's because she isn't afraid of the steps we must take to win this battle," Werling told me. "You did this, dust rat. That is what I will tell the authorities. I'll also say you aided the technocrat assassins. You'll go down for murder."

Captain Lajon grunted and opened her eyes.

Bhaaj, you have enough to implicate Knam, Max thought. *You need to go. NOW!*

I wrested my gauntlets from the doctor's grip, then jumped up and bolted across the room. My body ached from the beating I'd taken, but adrenaline, my biomech, and painkillers released by my meds kept me going. I slammed open the door and ran into the mountain evening. A full day had passed, and the sky blazed with a spectacular sunset.

Flyer, I thought.

On the landing pad, Max thought. Two hundred meters north.

I followed his directions, sprinting through the widely spaced trees around the cabin. Within moments, I reached a clearing with a landing pad.

An empty landing pad.

No! I wanted to yell with frustration. *Where is the blasted flyer?*

Someone must have left with it after they took me out.

I swung around, snapping my gauntlets onto my wrists. *Any idea how I can get out of here?*

Yes. Go south. I can't locate our position globally, but I can get you moving in the right direction to find help, based on what I saw on our journey here. Go away from the cabin, angling to the right.

I took off in long, loping strides. I wanted to go faster, but who knew how long I'd have to run. I used my long-distance pace, the one that used to win marathons.

A shout came from the cabin behind us. "Lajon, get up! She's escaping."

I went faster, leaving the cabin behind. The forest grew denser until I was crashing through underbrush. I had to slow down, stumbling on gnarled branches and roots that buckled up from the ground. I pushed away the hanging vines, and used my hands to protect my face from the thorny bushes. I didn't care that they tore at my clothes and skin. Better I get ripped up than I die.

With its leafy canopy cutting out the light from the sunset, the forest had gone mostly dark. It felt alien, too close, claustrophobic, so unlike the open desert of home.

My IR vision kicked in and the trees lit up with pale blue light, caught in the growing chill of night.

Veer more to the right, Max thought.

As I pushed my way through the trees, fronds brushed my face. Gods only knew how many bugs I'd pick up. I just hoped nothing vile bit me. I'd had run-ins before with scritch-bugs in the mountains around Selei City, bedeviled by the noisome poison they injected and the miserable itching that followed when your skin erupted into a rash.

Can you activate my long-distance comm? We need help. If they bring back that flyer, I won't have a chance. I can't outrun an aircraft. Hell, I can hardly walk here.

I need to repair my GPS and comm. In other words, not yet. I'm working on it.

I pushed my way through a thicket of matted bushes and large branches that had cracked off even larger trees and fallen across the undergrowth, tangled with vines they'd pulled down. Although I'd seen other forests, I hadn't made my way through one this wild and overgrown since, well, I couldn't think of when. The route where Max sent me looked like it might be a trail followed by animals, plant-eaters who wouldn't find me delectable—I hoped. The cold air snapped against my skin, and the ground felt almost frozen under my thin shoes, slowing me down even more.

Where are you sending me? I thought.

When we came in, we flew over an outpost. You could make it there in about an hour, assuming the forest doesn't get any denser. He sounded worried. **However, using your augmentations for that long isn't good for you.**

Getting killed isn't good for me, either. It was impossible to go fast, but at least my increased strength let me rip undergrowth out of the way, even the little trees that grew like weeds. *What about you, Max? Did they do any permanent damage?*

I don't think so. Their tech knows her stuff.

I ducked as a branch swung at my face. *Did they download you anywhere?*

They were working it when Werling called Captain Lajon. She said they needed you to give me some code. He sounded bemused. What is a reboost of my central affector unit with a neural cross-cutting transducer switch?

I winced. *I was desperate. I also told them that if they deactivated you for too long, it would alert the servers at Metro Corporation.*

Their tech was careful, though. I doubt she set off any alarms.

Yah, but they didn't know that.

The rumble of an engine growled in the distance.

Damn! I tried to go faster, but I tripped on a boulder and lurched to a stop, falling into a stabber-bush with needles as long as a finger. I groaned and climbed back to my feet, squinting in the growing dusk. *My IR vision isn't doing squat.*

You also have filters that amplify any ambient light they can input. Don't you recall?

No. My brain feels like mulch. Why is everything so dim?

The neural relaxant affects your brain. Your sight should improve as it wears off.

A crackling came from my right. *What is that noise?*

Bhaaj, veer left! As I veered, he added, **It's an octo-sloth. It's big, and you're prey.**

Octo? I kept on, doggedly making my way through the undergrowth. A small swarm of goggle-flies flew in my face, buzzing, buzzing, buzzing. Gods, I missed the desert.

It has eight claws on each paw. It will happily use them to make you its dinner.

Great. Just great. *Is it coming after me?*

No, not yet.

His "yet" didn't reassure me. Above us, the engine was growing louder. *Did you see any of the flyer systems on the way here? It would help to know what sensors they have for finding people.*

They have a lot. IR thermal imaging cameras far better than your IR vision. Imagers that zoom to a microscopic level. High-end motion sensors. Bio-readers that can detect life signs. Circular spectropolarimetry sensors. You can't hide.

Not good. I didn't even try asking about the spectro-whatever, I just kept stumbling through the underbrush. The engine grew louder until it rumbled above us. Max directed me in course changes, and the rumble followed every time.

Why aren't they shooting? I had seen all of them, and I'd heard far too much. If I were in their position, I'd want me as dead as fast and as thoroughly as last year's fashions.

I'm not sure, Max thought. **The tree cover shouldn't stop them from firing.**

That engine doesn't sound right. I swerved to avoid a

stump and fell against the ridged trunk of a banjo tree leaning at a steep angle.

You're right, Max thought. That isn't a flyer. It's a Quetzal helicopter.

Shit! Where'd they get a Quetz? The army called them Quetzals after Izam Na Quetza, the Raylican god of flight. One of those beauts could outdo a civilian flyer any day and shoot the blazes out of my sorry-assed self.

I'm dead, I thought.

✦ CHAPTER XVIII ✦
BIRD IN FLIGHT

Bhaaj, wait, Max thought. If they wanted you dead, you'd be dead. A Quetzal is far better armed than the flyer that brought you here.

I limped onward, aware even in combat mode of my ankle throbbing from where I'd gouged it on the tree. *You think they're trying to recapture me?*

It would be difficult in a remote, mountainous area like this. They can't land, so they'd have to fast-drop agents, like in the park. And this terrain is rougher. I suspect that for some reason, they can't pinpoint your location enough to shoot you.

A woman's amplified voice boomed through the air. "Bhaaj? You here? Come with!"

"That's Angel!" I shouted.

Another woman's voice came over the amplifier—with an Iotic accent. "Bhaaj, if you can hear me," Colonel Lavinda Majda said, "find the clear area fifty-two meters from your location. We can't reach Max to send the location. If you can, give him these coordinates." She rattled off a series of numbers. "Get there and we'll drop you a line."

You get that? I asked Max.

Yes! Run southwest. That's left of the way you were going before you fell.

I took off, following his directions. Within moments I reached an area where a large tree had fallen, its gnarled branches ripping down pieces of other trees on all sides, leaving a ragged hole in the forest canopy. The sunset glazed the sky above me, red and gold banners streaked across its expanse. No aircraft showed anywhere.

Where are they? I stared upward, desperate. Somewhere nearby, the octo-sloth crackled in the underbrush.

Suddenly the air above me rippled as if it had become liquid—and a Quetzal helicopter appeared, holo-painted to resemble a great bird in fiery colors. In stealth mode, its surface had blended into its surroundings, even the sky, but now it appeared in all its glorious magnificence, hovering above the trees.

"Rope comes," a man called, his voice amplified. Ruzik! Lavinda or someone else had to be piloting; Angel or Ruzik had no idea how. They weren't trained in air rescues, either. How Lavinda ever traced me here, I had no clue. From what I'd seen of Lajon and her team, they'd hid their tracks well. Their methods might be blunt, but Max had it right, they weren't stupid.

The Quetzal was using duct fans instead of dumping heat from its mini-fusion core, protecting the trees—and me—from exhaust. That Lavinda had Ruzik and Angel dropping the cable rather than a trained rescue team suggested she'd had no idea they would end up pulling me out of the forest. This much I knew: if they didn't get me out *now*, I was dead.

As the rope came down, swinging in the wind, I tapped a code into my gauntlet. Actually I pounded it with the enhanced speed I couldn't turn off. My gloves snapped out of their wrist slots and around my hands.

Lavinda angled the copter fans so their downwash buffeted the rope less. The cable swung toward several trees and then jerked away, propelled by whatever smart engine controlled its motion. It avoided more branches, lower, lower—and then it tangled in a banjo tree, caught by its stringlike leaves. I lifted my hands to give them a warning in sign language, then stopped when a welcome sight buzzed out of the copter. All three of my drones were arrowing toward the clearing. Two went to work on cutting away the banjo branch that had snagged the cable and the third came to me. I opened my hand and the blue drone settled on my palm.

"Hello, lovely," I murmured.

The other beetles freed the rope, and with a scrape, it flew away from the trees, dropping down. I slid Blue into my pocket, then grabbed the rope as it swung past. A brief shock of static greeted me, but the beetles had discharged most of the electricity. The cable felt corrugated under my palms, and a hoisting vest hung from the bottom. I strapped into the vest *fast*. It molded to my body while its hooks snapped onto the cable. I tightened my grip, and the spikelets in my gloves dug into the line. They operated only on cables saturated with nanobots that could repair the holes, and this top-line beaut had more than enough fix-it tech. It looked like a power hoist, one that could lift far more weight than me.

Angel and Ruzik were watching from the Quetzal. They'd never even flown in a planetary aircraft before, let alone managed a suspension rescue. They'd never taken a copter ride, never been positioned where they could fall out of an airborne craft, never seen a forest, never even freaking breathed air this rich. That they did it all anyway spoke more about their courage and loyalty than words. And Lavinda! She'd come herself, with a rescue craft. It left me speechless, which was good, because no way was I calling up to anyone right now.

The Quetzal rose, pulling me higher, until I cleared the trees. The steady hum of fans filled the air. Given all its noise-reduction tech, the rumble of a Quetzal didn't usually bother me, but with my hearing boosted in combat mode, it sounded deafening.

Combat mode off, I thought. The noise didn't change. *Max, why isn't my biomech web responding? Even without your help, I should be able to get out of combat mode.*

Same as the other problems. The drugs interfere with your neural processes.

Lavinda's amplified voice came from above. "Bhaaj, we're reeling in the hoist. Hang on."

"Copy!" I called, though I doubted they could hear. With my body vibrating in combat mode, the process felt slow, though I knew it took only seconds. The copter hovered, moving forward at a slow pace. The rope swung, not too much, but as they reeled me higher, I started to spin. My hoist extended a hooked tail to counter the rotation, and the spin slowed. Adrenaline pumped through my body; I wanted to go, go, *go*.

As we went higher, I looked around—and inhaled with a gasp. Goddess, what beauty. I hung in a great expanse of sky vivid with a sunset like none I'd ever seen in the city. It flamed red, gold, and yellow, with clouds on the horizon glowing as if someone had shot off fireworks that edged the sky with fluorescent pink strips. A chasm of air surrounded me. Wind and the downwash from the copter whipped back my hair, bracingly cold, and forest waved below like a dark ocean. I felt *alive*.

Later I'd pay the price for using combat mode for so long. When my adrenaline rush crashed, when I could feel pain, when my body had to recover from overusing my biomech—yah, it would be hell to pay. But for now, I reveled in the freedom of the wild ride.

I'd made it halfway to the Quetzal when a new sound reached my ears—a second engine.

Max! Is that a flyer?

Yes. He spoke grimly. **The sound matches the craft used by Knam's people.**

"Bhaaj!" Ruzik shouted. "Hang on. We fly."

"Shit." I clenched the rope, the spikes from my gloves digging into its reinforced structure.

The copter took off, speeding above the trees as they continued to reel me in. I gritted my teeth, resisting my urge to scramble up the rope, which would only make it swing more. The air rushed past, with me trailing in its wake while the hoist reeled me up and up and up.

Artillery fire cracked in the chasm of air. Return fire

roared from the Quetzal, and the rope swung wildly, thrown by the abrupt shifts in flight as the copter did evasive maneuvers. The line was spinning now despite its tail, and I hung on for my life, swearing in every language I knew.

Forget this, I thought. If they intended to end me here, I wouldn't go easily. I pulled my hand off the cable and grabbed Blue out my pocket. *Go,* I thought, hoping Max had regained enough control to send it. *Go blast that flyer with your digitized nonsense. Screw up their EIs.*

The beetle took off, arrowing through the air. I sent Green after it to make recordings.

"Bhaaj!" The shout came from above.

I craned back my head. I'd almost reached the copter. Angel held a grip with one hand while she reached for me with the other. Ruzik loomed behind her, his arm tight around her waist, both of them wearing lines that tethered them inside the craft. As I reached up, Angel grabbed my hand, hefting me forward, adding to my speed as the hoist hauled me into the copter. I was going so fast, I sprawled across the deck on my stomach.

Without pausing, still in combat mode, I scrambled to my feet and ran to the weapons rack. I grabbed a Mark 89 Automatic Power Rifle, then swung around. In my accelerated state, Angel and Ruzik looked like they had barely moved, still tethered to hooks. I wasn't tethered anywhere, I was just bloody pissed.

Focus, Max thought. *Tie a line. Don't let anger make you rash.*

"Move back," I told Angel and Ruzik. Grabbing a tether, I fastened one end to my body and the other to a hook in the craft. While they backed away from the doorway, I knelt at its side and activated the Mark 89. As I sighted on the distant flyer, the gun streamed data across my vision.

Synched, an androgynous voice thought in my mind.

I squinted through the eyepiece, letting the gun perfect my aim. *Lock for firing*.

Locked, it answered.

I pressed the igniter and a stream of bullets burst into the night, adding their rat-a-tat to the growl of the copter. An instant after I fired, the pursuing flyer swerved.

Target is too distant for accurate fire, the Mark 89 told me. *Suggest firing in a suppression pattern to make aircraft deviate from its attack*.

I fired with a sweeping motion, aided by the Mark 89. Although I barely moved the gun, by the time the bullets reached the flyer, they'd spread out enough to force it into a course change, throwing off its attempts to fire at us. It also jerked several times, as if its EI suffered a glitch in its attempts to control the craft.

Good beetles. I kept firing, ramming the air with bullets.

"Bhaaj, stop firing!" Lavinda yelled over the noise. "We want them alive."

A familiar voice spoke, Lavinda's EI. "The open doorway creates too much drag. Also, the passengers need to move to the center of the craft. They're changing the CG, interfering with nav."

"Close the door," Lavinda said. "Now! And put down my damn gun."

Even though I'd been a civilian for years, the soldier in

me responded to her tone. Moving so fast that the cabin blurred, I replaced the gun, then swung around to Angel and Ruzik.

"Seats." I motioned at the four passenger chairs. "Strap in." The Quetzal punctuated my words when the door slid closed with a clang.

Angel dropped into a seat and grabbed the safety webbing. "What CG?"

Ruzik strapped into his seat. "And nav?"

"CG mean center of gravity. Like when we fight." I'd spent many hours training them in tykado to throw opponents off-balance. These two understood center of gravity like no one's business. "Nav is navigation. Moving. Find best path."

They both nodded. Enough said.

"Bhaaj, here." Lavinda pointed to the copilot's seat without taking her gaze off her controls.

I pulled off the hoist vest, hung it up, and then dropped into the copilot's seat. As the Quetzal swerved, a high-pitched whine passed under the craft, the cry of a hells-wasp missile.

Lavinda spoke into her comm. "Flyer HN17, cease fire! You are attacking an aircraft from the Pharaoh's Army Ruby Base. Your actions constitute an act of terrorism. I repeat! Cease fire."

"They have to kill us," I said. "No way can Councilor Knam risk our implicating her."

"What the hell are you talking about?" Lavinda spared me a glance, then turned back to her controls. "Raja, continue evasion tactics."

Before I could respond, the Quetzal swerved so hard,

acceleration pushed me into the seat like a great hand slamming into my body. A groan came from behind us and Ruzik swore.

"They okay?" Lavinda asked.

I tensed my muscles against the acceleration. "They've never flown in an aircraft before."

"I'd never have guessed. They learn fast—" Lavinda's voice cut off as the Quetzal veered in another evasive maneuver, this time swinging north.

"Who is shooting at us?" Lavinda gripped the control lever, but she let Raja and the craft's EI work together to keep us as level as possible, with constant power. They could respond faster even than our enhanced reflexes. "And what did you mean, Councilor Knam?"

"Knam is part of some fringe group," I said. "They want to gain power in the Assembly for the Trads. In fact, I think she's the leader. I don't know if she has support from the main party."

"She doesn't," Max said. "At least not publicly. Our research for this case shows nothing about her group or even any acknowledgment that it exists." He stopped as the copter swerved again, avoiding the hells-wasp missile that had missed us on its first approach. Looking through the side window, I saw the wasp coming around for yet another go.

Lavinda smacked her hand against a panel she'd been priming, and gunfire burst out from the Quetzal's ports, obliterating the wasp. Then she said, "If someone as prominent as an Assembly Councilor ordered this op, that takes her group into the mainstream."

"I don't think they ever intended it to go this far," I said.

"They didn't believe anyone like you would come looking for me. They think I'm a fake, an Undercity poser."

"For fuck's sake," Lavinda said. "People really need to stop underestimating you."

"It can work to my advantage— Ah!" I grunted when a spray of bullets grazed the Quetzal, sending it into a spin. The fans roared as they stabilized the craft. I glanced back at our passengers. Angel grinned and Ruzik gave me a thumbs-up. If I hadn't known better, I'd have thought they were *enjoying* the battle. Hell, maybe I didn't know better. They'd never experienced air combat before. This might feel like the best, wildest ride of their lives. In their case, ignorance made for bliss.

Turning around, I tried to slow my words to a more normal speed. "Knam will deny she has anything to do with this. But Max recorded enough evidence to prove her involvement."

"Max," Lavinda said. "Transmit your recording to the PARS army base."

"I can't," Max said. "The kidnappers damaged my systems. I'm working on repairs, but I don't yet have full transmit capability."

"That's why they're trying to kill us," I said. "We can implicate them." I gripped the armrests as the copter lurched forward, then to the side, and then went level again.

"Understood." Lavinda scanned the stream of data flowing above her forward screen. "Raja, what's wrong with the stabilizers?"

"One of the bullets grazed stabilizer three. It blew it apart."

"Can the Quetzal do repairs while we fly?"

"We're doing our best."

The holomap between our seats expanded, showing a 360 degree view. Developed from LIDAR tech and extended with holographic and longer-range sensing capability, it gave a real-time display of our surroundings for hundreds of kilometers.

"We aren't the only ones having trouble." I indicated the flyer image as it swerved and shook in the air.

"Something is wrong with that craft," Raja said.

"I sent my blue and green drones after it." With satisfaction, I added, "Blue is weaponized. It can only do minor damage, but it's enough to screw with minor EM systems." I motioned at our pursuers. "Can't you shoot them down? Surely they're no match for an PA-7 Combat Quetzal."

"No deaths, Bhaaj." Lavinda pushed the lift control. "Goddess only knows what will happen if I kill civilians here. Can you say court-martial? This was supposed to be a search mission."

"They're trying to *kill* us. I'd say that's cause."

"Yes, I can argue cause. I'd rather capture them alive."

I struggled to make my glitching thoughts slow down. "How did you know where to look for me? Max didn't think he got through to Raja."

"He didn't, not much, but he did transmit the phrase 'Took Bhaaj.'"

"That doesn't tell you to come here."

"Bhaaj, slow down. I can barely understand you."

Toggle combat mode off, I thought. Nothing happened. The copter shook as its damaged stabilizers tried to compensate for our evasive maneuvers. Although we'd pulled ahead of the flyer while I fired at them, now they were gaining on us.

My thoughts spun in circles. "Can't you outrun them?"

"I don't want to outrun them. I want to force them down and capture them."

"Send someone else for them!" Gods, I needed to get out of combat mode. I forced myself to speak slowly. "We can't stay here. We have to get to Greyjan's."

She threw me a baffled glance. "You mean the tavern? What the hell for?"

"That's the only way we'll solve this case before more people get murdered."

Lavinda's look suggested I might be crazy, but she said, "Raja, streamline this craft for speed. Send an update to base about the situation. Transmit your recording of everything that's happened here. If you can get Max's record, send that too. Also, contact the closest search and rescue group in these mountains that works with the military. Have them coordinate capturing the flyer with the PARS base."

"I left some injured people in a cabin down there," I said. "They need medical help."

"Raja, make sure the search and rescue team knows they also have to make a medical rescue." She glanced at me. "How bad are they?"

"They can't all be unconscious," I said. "Someone is piloting that flyer. I left four in the cabin. At least two are in bad shape."

Raja spoke. "I'm transmitting to PARS. Do you have coordinates for the cabin?"

"I can give them roughly," Max said.

"Received," Raja told him. "I'm not getting your records, though."

"I'm still working on it," Max said.

"Do we have backup coming?" Lavinda asked.

"Affirmative," Raja said. "PARS is setting up two missions with the Great Ridge Mountain Rescue Group, one to capture the flyer and one to rescue the injured."

"Good." Lavinda flew in a wide circle, picking up speed.

I touched the red beetle in my pocket. "Max, can you call back Blue and Green?"

"I can't link to them from this distance. I'll keep trying."

"Understood." As we arrowed through the night, my thoughts circled back to my previous question. "Lavinda, how'd you get my location out of that garbled message from Max?"

"I didn't." Lavinda kept her concentration on her controls as she spoke. "My brother Tam contacted me. He said they expected you for dinner. He didn't believe you'd just blow him off. I commed the townhouse and spoke with Angel and Ruzik. Actually, I spoke with your house EI, Highcloud, who translated for them." She scanned her screens. "Raja, release flares to distract those wasp missiles."

"Released," Raja said.

"Max got more of his message to Highcloud," Lavinda added. "He also dumped a damaged version of Highcloud into the house mesh."

"Our flares aren't fooling all of the missiles," Raja said. "Several are still coming after us."

"Evade." Lavinda peered at a holomap above her controls. "We need more speed. That flyer is gaining on us."

The androgynous voice of the copter EI answered. "I can optimize my shape for speed, but if I make too many changes, it limits my weapons capability, especially with the added weight we're carrying. If you eject some of your weaponry, I can go faster."

"That's a last resort," Lavinda said. "Only if you can't pull away from the flyer."

"Understood," the EI said.

The copter jumped forward. I knew nothing actually leapt, that we rode an aircraft soaring in the sky, but everything seemed to move in ragged, speeded-up scenes. I couldn't focus.

"Max, what's wrong with me?" I asked.

"You've been in combat mode too long," Max said.

"Uh, Bhaaj," Angel said. "Fly thing squash."

I looked back. The cabin had become more streamlined, narrower enough that they noticed.

"Is good," I said. "Make fly thing faster." Outside, the fans on either side of the copter would be sweeping back as well.

As I turned back, Lavinda said, "Is that the Undercity dialect? It sounds like ancient Iotic."

"I think that's where it gets its roots."

Lavinda concentrated, making small changes to the route chosen by the EI. "Your voice is still speeded up."

"I can't get out of combat mode."

She frowned at me. "Your body should drop out. Just think 'combat mode off.'"

"I tried!" I took a slowing breath. "It doesn't work."

"Can't Max toggle it off?"

"I've been trying," Max said. "I need more repairs."

Lavinda's voice changed, filled with an authoritative tone I knew well after my years in the army. "Major, combat mode off! Now!"

Combat mode off, Max thought.

I grunted as my thoughts returned to normal, no longer like a broken high-speed camera. Apparently even my drugged brain reacted to instincts the military had drummed into me.

The cockpit screens showed two missiles bearing down on us, one from behind and another above. Lavinda fired the aft guns, and one of the missiles exploded. In that instant, we also swerved to avoid the other one. Lavinda took us higher into the sky, targeting the second missile. "Eat it, bitch," she said—and fired. The missile exploded with a satisfying burst of energy.

I'd never seen this side of Lavinda before. Yah, sure, I knew she'd flown a copter before she became a colonel, but the officer I knew worked behind a desk. I could get to like this version of normally restrained Majda queen.

We finally left the flyer behind, whirring through the darkening sky. The sunset had faded into streaming blue and silver light from the two moons, one high above us and the other closer to the horizon. Far more stars filled the great expanse of sky than showed in Selei City, even during the mandatory blackout after midnight, when all buildings turned out their lights to give the city a few hours free from light pollution. Up here, at this high altitude, with no human settlement, the heavens became a panorama of glittering stardust, white, blue, red, gold, their colors visible even through the atmosphere. The barest remains of the sunset showed on the ragged horizon above the trees. Lajon's tiny flyer shrank and disappeared in all that magnificence.

Although I felt more normal without biomech driving my body, adrenaline still masked my exhaustion and the pain from the beating. "Councilor Knam is going to claim she was trying to make a rescue," I said. "That's what they would have done if they'd managed to kill me in the forest, like they wanted."

"What rescue?" Lavinda snorted. "That flyer was shooting at us."

"She'll deny any involvement." I smacked my palm on the dashboard. "If they'd shot us down, her people would say they were conducting a rescue while terrorists attacked you. She'd claim she was trying to save a Majda heir."

"Yes, well, the Majda heir escaped." She frowned at me. "Are you saying no evidence exists that connects Knam to the people who kidnapped you?"

"I'm not certain. But yah, that's my sense. Except for Max's record."

"And you think she'll get off even if the kidnappers try to implicate her."

"Not if we can get Max's recording uploaded to the authorities." I scowled. "Assuming someone connected with Knam doesn't intercept it."

"Do you think her involvement is political?" Lavinda asked. "Or because she's part of a fringe group that doesn't involve any specific party?"

"I'd say mostly the latter." I rubbed my chin. "It's odd,

Lavinda. It's like this case energized people to attack each other, to act on plans they wouldn't have otherwise done. Without it, I doubt Knam would have carried out an op like this one."

"You don't think Knam's group is responsible for the killings?"

"No!" I realized how it must look to her, coming in at the tail end of all this. "I doubt she has any link to the case, other than using it to further her own goals."

Lavinda shot me a frustrated look. "So you don't think it involves Royalists or Progs, and you even checked into the Techs, who you don't think are killing themselves, big surprise. It's not the Traders as far as we've been able to tell, it's not the rich young entrepreneurs, it's not anyone else you've looked into so far. Now you don't think it's the Trads. Either it's not political or that leaves the Modernists. I mean, really, the Mods?"

"Hell if I know. I have to look into them, too. That's the point! I might as well be chasing my tail like that cat back at the cabin, wasting my time."

"And yet you don't think Knam arranged it all."

"The killings were too sophisticated. Her people are like a powered rock hammer."

Lavinda blew out a gust of air. "And yet you suspect she has a network extensive enough to intercept any record Max sends to the authorities."

"It's possible. Assembly Councilors get their tendrils everywhere." My voice hardened. "Except for one 'little' thing. Her people didn't know I was conscious when they contacted Knam. I heard them talking to her about the kidnapping. I can testify to that."

"Did they call her by name?"

"No." Damn it. "They did on Max's recording, though."

Lavinda considered the thought. "Your testimony wouldn't hold up in a trial as well as Max's evidence. You could say it was anyone."

"I'll do any lie detection test they want."

"That might help. But you were also drugged at the time, supposedly unconscious."

"It's not strong, but it's better than nothing." I grimaced. "Of course Knam's people will claim I'm the one who set this all up because, you know, I'm an evil person trying to further my own ends. Whatever the hell they decide are those ends."

"Why you in particular?" She shook her head. "I don't get why these people think you're such a good target."

"Because I'm from the Undercity." Bitterness edged my voice, an anger I'd struggled to suppress for years. "The public is willing to believe I'm a monster."

She fell silent, watching her controls. Angel and Ruzik said nothing, but they heard far more than people realized. Knowing Lavinda, I suspected it hadn't taken her long to figure that out about them. We flew in silence, with only the hum of the engines to keep us company. Raja soon verified we were out of range for the flyer.

Lavinda spoke quietly. "I live in a universe where people respect and admire my family. Many fear us. Some hate us, but it's because of what we have, not what we lack. I grew up taking my status for granted."

I hadn't expected such a bald admission of her privilege. "You were born lucky."

"Yes. I know." She kept looking out the forward

window, not at me. "I considered myself unfortunate because my position in life left me no choice but to wed a man I didn't love in an arranged marriage while my true love, the woman who died last year in the case you worked on, went on to find someone else." She spoke bitterly. "I had no fucking idea what adversity meant."

I stared at her, stunned into silence. Majdas never admitted they were anything but perfect.

"Over the past few years," Lavinda said, "you and I have often argued about the Undercity. You tell me things I don't want to believe. And I keep being wrong." She took a deep breath. "When I was young, the only mentions I ever heard of the Undercity—a self-contained civilization that literally exists under our feet—were about the inferiority of the few supposedly homeless people who lived there. Of course my family never used words that direct. But that's what they meant, and I knew it."

I sat frozen, afraid to move because it might crack apart this moment and send shards of emotional glass raining over us.

"Then I met you," Lavinda said. "Brilliance and pride, loyalty and courage, compassion and fury, all mixed up with one of the sharpest investigative minds I've ever seen." She turned to me. "I can't imagine what it was like to live as you did, to grow up in abject poverty with the highest mortality rate known in the Imperialate, to offer your life in the military for an empire that would rather destroy you than acknowledge the strength of your character. I had the opposite all my life, the strength of my character assumed for no other reason than because I came from a powerful, wealthy family."

I had absolutely no clue what to say. To have anyone admit such to me never happened. To hear it from one of the most privileged people alive left me speechless.

She smiled slightly. "What, you're not going to cuss?"

I gave a startled laugh. "I guess not."

"Bhaaj, I can't take away the pain that you and your people have lived with for so long. And I realize that in my past attempts to help, I suggested changes your people would find even worse than poverty. They don't need state-sponsored schools, grueling labor at minimum wages, or 'reeducation' to become more like my people. I understand that now." She spoke dryly. "It took me long enough. But know this, Bhaaj. I will work with you to make it better, on your terms."

I spoke quietly. "Thank you." I meant it, at my deepest level. Lavinda was unlike anyone else I'd ever met, with or without power, and I was only beginning to appreciate that after knowing her for nearly four years.

She nodded and turned back to her flying, checking her controls and maps. "So," she said, our intense moment over and done with. "Why is it so important to go to this tavern?"

"It's the key to the murders, I'm sure. We need to find out what's below it."

"Below it?"

I lifted my hands, then dropped them in frustration. "Something down there is trying to stop us from investigating. I don't know why."

She gave me a decidedly unenthused look. "On this basis, you think the key to the case is in a tavern hardly anyone even goes to?"

I summarized everything that had happened at Greyjan's in the past four days, except that I left out the baby EI. "Angel and Ruzik used the fight as a distraction so the beetle could fly around. It got me intel on the other fighters. They were Trads."

"That sounds like even more reason to suspect the Trads are behind this." Lavinda peered at her maps, studying data from the flyer. "They're running," she added.

It didn't surprise me. "You think whoever the army sends up here can find them?"

"Possibly." She turned to me. "Are you sure you want to go to Greyjan's? You don't want to apprehend your kidnappers yourself?"

Oh yah, I wanted to get them. It wouldn't solve the case, though, so I just said, "I'm sure."

Ruzik spoke behind us. "Go ale place."

I turned to him. "Yah?"

"Slicks play game," Angel said.

"You mean slicks you fight?" I asked.

Ruzik snorted. "They think they fight. Was like play."

I held back my smile. "Get black belt, now you get too cocky."

They both scowled at me.

"Are they saying we should go to Greyjan's because they believed their fight there was staged?" Lavinda asked.

"I'm not sure." To Angel and Ruzik, I said, "What mean, slicks play game?"

"Fake ass-bag," Angel clarified.

That illuminated exactly nothing. "What," I growled. "Not real ass-bag?"

The barest hint of a smile played around Ruzik's lips. "Real, too."

I regarded them with exasperation. "Not ken what you say."

"These 'Trads,' they go to ale place," Angel said. "Get drunk. Fake drunk. Get pissed. Fake pissed. Jizz after Ruzik." She considered a moment. "Real jizz," she decided.

Ruzik grunted.

"Yah, you say before." I waited, then said, "Still not ken what else you mean."

Ruzik spoke in Flag. "They didn't go to the tavern to drink. I had an odd sense—" He stopped, searching for words it looked like. "They were waiting for something. I don't know how else to put it. If I had to guess, I'd say they were waiting for you."

"Why me?" I asked.

"Hard to say."

Angel tapped her temple. "Mood feel thing."

"Mood feel thing?" Lavinda looked back at them. "What does that mean?"

They both regarded her, silent, their faces impassive.

"They're empaths," I said.

Lavinda considered me. "If those people at the tavern were Trads, if they went to find you, and if you think Greyjan's has links to the murders, then I don't get why you don't think the Trads are behind the killings."

I searched for words to describe a sense that was more intuitive than logical. "When I investigate the actions people take, I often see patterns in their behavior. Whoever committed the technocrat killing and bombed the co-op isn't just smart. They're experienced strategists. Calculating. And subtle. They've left no real clues."

Lavinda frowned. "No clues? We're drowning in them."

"Fake clues." I motioned at Angel in Ruzik. "It's like what they said about the fight at the bar. The people involved were pretending. Everything about this case, every supposed clue that points to some potential perp— I don't believe any of it."

"Then why would the Trads wait for you at this tavern?"

"Because I went there the previous night." I winced, remembering the odd VR simulation. "It probably looked like I was walking around doing nothing. Then I jogged home."

"Yes, I read your report. You were caught in a sim triggered by Max's attempts to break the digital security at the tavern."

"Something like that." I actually thought the baby EI tried to reach us, I just didn't know why. "I need to find out what's there."

"That part is easy." Lavinda spoke to the air. "Raja, contact Chief Hadar and let him know that Major Bhaajan has a new lead. Tell him we need the police to search Greyjan's tavern, in particular any room below the main establishment. It needs to be done fast and with discretion."

"Working," Raja said.

"Max?" Lavinda asked. "How are your repairs going?"

"It's coming. Raja is helping."

"Can you send your recording to the PARS base or Chief Hadar yet?" I asked him.

"Sorry," Max said. "My ability for long-range communications was the first thing they deactivated, precisely so I couldn't contact the authorities."

"Keep working on it," I said. "Top priority."

Lavinda glanced at me. "I can take your gauntlets to the base while you go to Greyjan's. They can help his repairs."

"I'd rather not be separated again," Max said.

It struck me as an odd statement for most EIs, but I got it with Max. However uncomfortable his theory made me, this idea that he and I formed two parts of one mind, I had to admit he had a point. I'd felt vulnerable without him in the cabin. "He can do repairs on himself, probably better than your techs. He knows himself the best."

She didn't look surprised. "Max, make the repairs to your long-range comm a priority and transmit your records to PARS as soon as possible."

Silence.

"Max?" I asked.

"Do you authorize me to do what Colonel Majda requests?" he asked.

"Yes, I do." *And thanks for asking.* I didn't want to alienate Lavinda by telling her to quit giving my EI orders, but no one talked that way with Max except me.

"Working," Max said. Of course, he thought.

Closing my eyes, I leaned back in my seat. It had been a long night. I needed to be rested and ready for whatever we found at Greyjan's.

The police found exactly squat at Greyjan's.

Chief Hadar contacted Lavinda less than an hour after

she asked him to check the tavern. "Nothing there except stores for the bar," he said over the comm. "A few crates of liquor, food supplies, empty storerooms, and dust."

"That's it?" Lavinda asked. "No mesh equipment, no consoles, nothing like that?"

"Nothing. Is Major Bhaajan sure about her lead?"

"Yes. Certain," I said. "Could it be hidden?"

"Major, I'm sorry. We looked. We found no hiding places." Hadar was on his best behavior today, probably because of Lavinda.

"Dust," Ruzik said.

I looked back at him. "What?"

"Dust," Angel said.

I looked from one to the other. They sat relaxed in their passenger seats, each with an elbow on the inside arm, leaning slightly toward each other. "And?" I asked.

"Dust," Ruzik repeated. "All dust."

"Dust every place." Angel stressed the importance of her comment with a three-syllable word. Ev-er-y place.

"Like at home," Ruzik qualified.

I didn't see their point. "Yah, lot of dust in Undercity. Not same as dust under ale place."

"Yah," Angel agreed. "Not same. Dust under ale place smart."

Interesting. Selei City had "smart" dust floating everywhere, monitoring the weather, humidity, and vibrations in buildings and equipment. It could check parks for watering, fertilization, and pest control, ensure products were shipped and delivered on time, and monitor people for security purposes. It raised privacy concerns because you couldn't see the dust; it simply floated in the air. The city authorities spent a great deal of time submerged in debates with citizens over just how much the dust should be allowed to report. Although the military used similar dust in combat, it was too easily countered by dust from enemy forces. We'd also used it during interstellar combat, but those clouds consisted of tiny drones, much larger than dust grains.

The weaponized dust I'd encountered in a planetary setting hadn't deserved the modifier "smart." The experimental stuff had mucked up any tech it encountered, foe and friend alike, making a mess out of communications, weapons, and anything else it drifted into. A conglomerate of wealthy execs had developed it, but I had no doubt the military was also working on intelligent grit with more active functions than just floating around the city. What Angel and Ruzik described at Greyjan's implied larger particles, since we could see them, which suggested an increased capability. If it could do anything besides lie on the floor, though, I'd seen no hint of that ability.

"How know dust smart?" I asked them. "It talk to you?"

"Nahya," Ruzik said. "Dust thoughts are too small."

"Too small how?" I asked. "Hard to hear?"

"Eh," Angel said, which could have meant anything from yah to no to who the hell knows.

"Do you mean the dust carries picochips?" Lavinda asked.

Silence. They both just looked at me.

"Pico mean small brain," I clarified. "Not think much."

Angel snorted. "Fake ass-bags we fight have pico brains."

"How you know dust smart?" I asked.

"We guess," Ruzik said.

"That's it?" Lavinda asked. "This is a random guess?"

"What did you say?" Chief Hadar asked over the comm. "I didn't get most of that back-and-forth. The speakers aren't close enough to your comm."

"Chief, is it possible the grit you found in the tavern basement is smart dust?" I asked.

"Why the hell would it be smart dust?" He sounded like himself now when dealing with just me. In other words, irritated. As if remembering himself, he added, "If you could please explain. Although our city dust monitors even outlying buildings such as the tavern, you can't see it. And it hasn't reported anything of interest about the tavern."

I looked back at Ruzik and Angel. "Need better than 'it's a guess.' Cops not check guess."

They both blinked at me. Then Ruzik said, "Cops help?" His tone implied my comment was on par with suggesting the moons would fall out of the sky.

"Cops help," I told him. "If have good reason."

Angel scowled. "Cops ass—"

"Yah, cops assist us," I interrupted, before she had a chance to offend Chief Hadar. "But need *more* than guess."

Ruzik spoke in Flag. "It's hard to say. The dust on the tavern floor seemed wrong."

"Back home, all dust," Angel said. "Every place you look. Dust. On us, on tunnels, on all."

Finally I saw it. "But not here, yah? No dust in Selei City." At least not that they could see. "All shiny."

"Yah!" Ruzik said. "But ale house has dust. All over. We not notice at first. Like home. But." He held up his finger. "*Nothing* else here like home. So why dust?"

"Gods almighty," I muttered. "You're right." I nodded to them both. "Good see."

They nodded back.

I leaned over the comm, speaking with courtesy. Hadar wasn't the only one on his best behavior in front of Lavinda. "Chief, the floor of the tavern has an unusual amount of grit. My two agents noticed it. Bars in Selei City use cleaning bots. Even most struggling places have cheaper models. So why would this tavern, which keeps coming up in my investigation, have dust all over the floor? You said it's in the storage rooms, too. I can understand it if those rooms aren't used. But in the main room, where they serve drinks and food? It seems sloppy. I had the impression the proprietor didn't pay much attention to niceties or couldn't afford them, so maybe she just hadn't sent it her cleaning drones, but it makes me wonder." If someone figured out she was lax about upkeep, it could explain why they chose her tavern for the dust. A remote place with almost no clientele and lousy maintenance? Yah, that made an excellent choice.

"Interesting." Hadar stopped, and I could hear the low murmur of people talking in the background. Then he said, "We'll go back out and take some samples of the dust."

"We've given them warning that we're interested in the place," Lavinda said. "By the time you get back there, they'll have cleaned it top to bottom."

Good point. "Chief, did any of your people get dust on

them the first time you went out? If you can get even a small sample, you could tell if it's not ordinary grit." With too small a sample, they couldn't determine if all the dust together could form a web from picochips in each grain, but it would help to know if the grains carried chips.

"I'll check into it," Hadar said. "Also, Major, my mesh team looked into the link between the Templars and New Techs as you asked. It's possible that with all that young technical wizardry at their disposal, the Templars could have faked the chats that pointed us toward the Traders. We're looking deeper into their activities." After a pause, he added, "Anything else?"

Lavinda looked at me. When I shook my head, she glanced at Angel and Ruzik. They regarded her in silence.

"Any more to say about ale place?" I asked.

"Bad ale," Angel commented.

"Bad air," Ruzik told me.

"What did they say?" Lavinda asked. "I have trouble understanding sometimes."

I smiled. "They think Greyjan's is a lousy tavern."

"Yah." Angel made an approving noise for my insight.

"All right," Hadar said. "Contact me if you have any more information. Out."

"Out," Lavinda said.

"Bad air," Ruzik repeated.

I turned to him. "That means bad ale place, yah?"

"Stinks," Ruzik said.

"It does?" I hadn't smelled anything.

Angel gave him a questioning look. "Eh?"

"You smell it?" he asked her.

"Nahya. Place fine," she told him.

"What smell like?" I asked.

Ruzik gave a frustrated grunt. "Not have words."

"Use Flag."

"Flag not have words." Then he amended, "That I know."

"Say what you can," I suggested. "Say any word that works even small bit."

He tried Flag. "The air in this place, this—planet, yes? It is sweeter than home. Thicker."

"Yah." He described perfectly how I experienced the difference.

"The ale place isn't like that. Air is—I don't know. Bare."

"Bare?" Lavinda asked. "Is that what he said?"

"Yah." It didn't make sense to me, either. I squinted at Ruzik. "Nude air?"

He gave me an annoyed look. "Air not wear clothes, Bhaaj."

"Yah. So how bare?"

He thought more. "Bare like—sweetness taken away."

"Sterilized!" Lavinda said. "I'll bet that's what he means."

"Ho!" That made perfect sense. "If they have some experimental pico-dust business going on, they'd need a clean environment for it to work." Ruzik had done well. Most people wouldn't notice an *absence* of a smell when they visited a place where they expected no smells.

"Raja, can you get me Chief Hadar again?" Lavinda asked.

"Working."

Hadar must have had his comm ready, because after only a moment, he said, "My greetings, Colonel. Your EI sent me the update. You think the tavern is a sterile environment?"

"That's right, at least the air. Did you check for that?"

"My apologies, but no. It didn't occur to us." He quickly added, "My detectives are already on their way out there. I'll have them take air samples."

"Thank you, Chief." Lavinda was on her best behavior, too, though before seeing her tonight, I'd never have known she had any other type.

"My people are also checking their clothes and equipment for dust," Hadar said. "It doesn't look like it will help, though. Our gear is self-cleaning. Any unusual dust is gone now."

"We need a sample." But from where? "Is it correct to say your investigators didn't find any unexpected dust, grit or other small particles on the murder scenes?"

"None," Hadar said. "If it was ever there, it decomposed after the murders. The bombing left so much debris, it's impossible to identify dust like what you're describing."

"Had fight," Ruzik said from behind us.

I turned to him. "Which one?" He and Angel were forever fighting people, at least at home. They'd held back here—except for the tavern! "You mean Greyjan's?"

"Yah." Angel smirked. "Ass-bags hit floor. Again. And again. Get a lot of dust."

"And you?" My hope surged. "Got dust?"

She scowled at me. "Not hit floor."

Ruzik gave her an exasperated look, then spoke to me. "Yah, we got dust. All over us." Rather pointedly, he added, "Is true, though. We not hit floor."

"I ken." They had their pride, after all. "Good rough and tumble, eh?"

"Yah." Angel nodded, accepting my apology for suggesting she or Ruzik got knocked over. I doubted Ruzik cared as much, but still.

"Max," I said. "The clothes we gave Ruzik and Angel—were they self-cleaning?"

"It was a menu item on their controls. I don't think we chose it, though."

Good. I spoke to Ruzik and Angel. "What do with clothes after fight?"

"Go home," Angel said. "Have beer. Laugh, talk." She glanced at Ruzik with the slightest smile, and he gave her the same look. She gave me a bland look. "After that, I forget what happen."

"For flaming sake," I muttered. So they made love. "What happen to clothes?"

They both just looked at me.

"Max?" I asked the air. "Do you know?"

"They left them on the bedroom floor," Max said. "A bot cleaned, dried, and folded them."

"Well shit." So much for that lead.

Ruzik cleared his throat. "Maybe not all."

"Not all how?" I asked.

Angel glowered at me. "Maybe keep socks on."

"Socks?" We never wore them in the Undercity. We had meshes that protected our feet, like a sleeve. "What socks?" Oh, wait, yah, I'd given them socks to wear that day.

"Soft stuff." Ruzik gave Angel that smile again.

Angel glowered at him. "Angel never soft."

"Yah." Ruzik nodded with respect to his formidable girlfriend. "But socks nice."

"Oh." I got it. Angel had left on her socks when they made love because Ruzik liked them. Who'd have thought a pair of everyday socks could be erotic. "Did bots take socks later?"

"Not think so," Angel said.

"Leave in bed?" I asked.

They both just looked at me.

So yah, they weren't going to tell me any more about their sex lives. This was the closest Angel would get to admitting she wore something soft for her lover.

"Max," I said, "Can you contact Highcloud and find out what happened to those socks?"

"I can't," Max said. "But if you let me give Raja the codes for the townhouse, she can."

"Go ahead," I answered.

"Working," Raja said.

Lavinda spoke to me. "I'm not sure what they just told you, but I take it you think some of their clothes from yesterday have the dust on them."

"If the bots haven't washed them yet." More than a day had passed since the fight at Greyjan's, though so much had happened, it felt like much longer.

"I have a response from Highcloud," Raja said. "The socks were in the bed, down at the bottom. They haven't been cleaned since the last time they were worn."

"Good!" I swung around to our passengers. "Socks there."

"Eh," Ruzik said. Angel nodded her agreement with his verbose statement.

"I'll send my people over to check the townhouse," Chief Hadar said.

Something was tugging at my mind, something about sunlight . . . Ah! I remembered. "Try the hallway outside of Marza Rajindia's lab at the university, too, the corridor that leads to glass doors that open on a quad. I recall seeing dust motes floating in the sunlight coming through the doors."

"That's pretty tenuous," Hadar said. "Even with cleaning bots, you can still get visible dust in the air. We did check her lab, and we didn't find anything unusual."

"Yah, but this was outside the lab." I thought of our conversation. "As spokeswoman for the Tech Party, she could be a prime target for the killers. If they planned to move against her, any dust they have floating around could still be there."

"It's worth a look," Hadar said. "We'll let you know if we find anything. Out."

As Lavinda turned off the comm, I regarded her steadily. "Now we go find out what's up at Greyjan's."

✤ CHAPTER XIX ✤
GRIT AND CRIME

We landed outside the tavern, coming down in the clear rays of the rising sun. I'd slept on the ride, only a few hours, but enough. In the early-morning light, Greyjan's appeared deceptively beautiful, a rustic house surrounded by meadows. It hardly looked as if it linked to a serial killer and bomber.

People ran out to see what was up, two patrons and a third woman who seemed familiar, stout and a little overweight, with a wide face you wanted to trust but knew you shouldn't. Yah, I remembered, she was the proprietor. All three gaped as the Quetzal landed in a field by the tavern. The blast from the fans lifted a cloud of sweet-scented flowers into the air and whipped the nearby trees into a frenzy, making the feather vines on their branches ripple like a curtain of greenery.

I jumped down to the meadow with Angel and Ruzik. Lavinda stayed onboard to work on the stabilizer with Raja and the Quetzal EI. The owner of Greyjan's watched from her doorway, her face creased with a baffled frown as we ran out from the copter with wind whipping around us, our heads bowed against the wash. I wore an EM pistol holstered at my side, courtesy of the onboard armory, and a couple of reloads hung on my belt. Ruzik and Angel both carried sheathed knives. All three of us wore army packs, each with a jammer if we needed a shroud. I didn't miss the irony, that today Lavinda provided me with the same tech-mech that they usually berated me for using. Of course, that was because usually I was hiding from the Majdas.

I slowed down as I came up to the proprietor. "My greetings. Do you own this tavern?"

"That's right." She crossed her arms. "I'm Daymor Greyjan."

"We need to do a search," I said.

"You aren't the police." Her gaze shifted to Angel and Ruzik and the scowl she turned on them could have scorched rock. "I told you two never to show your faces here again."

"They're with me," I said. "I'm with the police. We're following up on the search."

Greyjan gave a harsh laugh. "The cops? Seriously? You got a search warrant?"

"The chief's people already showed it to you. Twice, in fact, both times they searched here."

"Yah, well, you could be anyone." Her stance remained rock solid. "I ain't moving, girlie. You can take your dust rat selves out of here."

"Oh, fuck that." I was so done with being polite to people who insulted us.

"Not dust rat," Ruzik said mildly. "Dust Knight."

"Yah, I saw you posing on the holo-vid," the woman told him. "You may be hot, sweetcakes, but you still can't come into my bar and screw with people."

Angel stepped up to the proprietor, her face thunderous. "Not call my man 'sweetcakes.'"

I stayed back. While Angel and Ruzik distracted the owner, I eased the red beetle out of my pocket and let it go. It sailed into the shadows, sleek and silent.

"Don't threaten me," the proprietor was telling Angel.

I looked around. The two patrons were listening with avid interest to the exchange between Angel and the owner. I'd seen a breakfast menu the last time I came here, so I figured they'd come to eat. One of them, a medium-sized man wearing boring clothes, stood with an almost invisible tension, as if he were listening with heightened senses to every word. He didn't otherwise stand out, so normally he would fade into the background. It made an effective cover.

"Not talk trash to my man," Angel said.

Ruzik glanced at me, then returned his attention to the argument. He actually smiled, something we never did in front of potential enemies like this tavern owner. "Your man fine," he assured Angel. Turning to the proprietor, he spoke in perfect Flag. "We're sorry to disturb you. I apologize. We regret any inconvenience we have caused."

Angel stared at him as if he'd grown a second head. "Where you put Ruzik?" she muttered.

Hah! My gang leader had a talent for undercover work. In contrast, Angel was a blunt power hammer, strong and powerful. Actually, both she and Ruzik could outlift me in weights when I didn't use augmentation, a feat few people could achieve. What set Ruzik apart was his remarkable intellectual flexibility. I suspected that was why he led the gang instead of Angel. Together, they made an unbeatable team.

Right now, however, Angel looked pissed at Ruzik for apologizing to someone she wanted to beat up.

The owner glowered at Ruzik, then at me. "You got to show me a warrant."

I stepped forward and tapped the comm on my gauntlet. A voice rose into the air. "Chief Hadar here. Do you have an update, Major?"

"We're at the tavern," I said.

"Yes, Colonel Majda notified me."

Well, damn. He'd just blown Lavinda's cover. Not that she was hiding her presence, but announcing we had a Majda colonel here could make it impossible to get anything done. Everyone would be on their best behavior, every nuance hidden. We wanted the owner to underestimate us.

Then again, Hadar hadn't said Lavinda was in the flyer. "I'm glad she's there with you," I told him. "I'm here with the copter pilot and my two agents. The owner of the tavern would like verification that we have permission to search the premises."

He paused, probably figuring out what I meant. "All right. Put her on."

I extended my arm so Greyjan could speak into the gauntlet. "Go ahead," I told her.

"Heya," she said. "This is police chief Hadar?"

"That's right. I'm getting voice recognition that you are indeed the owner of the tavern."

Smart man. He turned the tables by suggesting he had to verify her identity.

The owner scowled. "How do I know you're Chief Hadar?"

"My apology," he said. "I didn't realize you lacked the verification tech."

"Of course I have it." She stabbed at the tech-mech band on her wrist.

A mechanical voice rose into the air. "Speaker identified. Chief Akal Hadar of the Selei City police force."

"Fine." The owner swept us all with an annoyed look. Then she moved aside to let us enter.

I let Ruzik and Angel go first. As I followed, I glanced at the man I'd noticed earlier. He was returning to the tavern as well, walking with the other patron, the two of them chatting. The other patron also seemed casual, the type who came to watch sporting events on the bar's holo-vid.

Bhaaj, Max thought. I have a message from Colonel Majda. The police investigators found smart dust on Angel's socks.

Max! Is your distance comm working again?

For short distances. He sounded relieved. I'm working on the longer-range functions.

Excellent. Did they recover enough dust to figure where it came from?

Possibly. Each particle contributes to a picoweb that links it to any other particles within a few meters. The higher the density of the dust and the wider its spread, the more efficient of a mesh they can form. At high concentrations, it looks like it can send signals.

Looks like? Can't they tell? Compared to previous smart dust I'd experienced, this type sounded too specific. It hadn't affected Max or my tech-mech the first time I came here until we tried to crack its web.

They didn't recover enough to make a full comm node, Max thought. However, they believe it connects to the office of Manuel Portjanson, the spokesman for the Modernists.

They can't be serious.

Actually, it does make sense. No one would suspect the Modernists. They can let the other parties duke it out while they benefit in all their glorious blandness.

Well, yah. It still didn't feel right. *Call it Bhaaj intuition, but I'll bet you aces to aces that Manuel, the son of the daughter of Port Whoever, has no link to this.* I considered the thought. *Chief Hadar did say his party had the largest fringe element, though. Maybe it's more outliers.*

"So where do you want to look?" Greyjan was saying. She lifted her hands, palms to the ceiling, as if to encompass the room around us. "Feel free to examine my nefarious establishment."

She's almost as sarcastic as you, Max thought.

Indeed. To the owner, I said, "We'd like to see your storerooms."

"Suit yourselves. The police have already looked twice." She gave an annoyed grunt. "What the blazes do you all think you'll find down there?"

Angel and Ruzik watched me, waiting. I just said, "If you could show us the way." I was curious to see how she took us there. Stairs? If she used a lift, it might go past hidden floors that weren't marked. One tavern I'd frequented during my days as a private had a ledge where you jumped down to the lower level with the card games. They didn't let me in more than once, though, after they figured out that I memorized the played cards. Of course I did. Damned if I wouldn't use any skill I possessed to win, rather than letting the house take my money. None of the gambling places shared my passion for math, to put it mildly, so I got the boot, not so mildly.

Greyjan escorted us through the tavern, letting us take our time to glance around. I thought of how we'd learned about this place. *Max, any communications from your wayward child?*

Not much, Max thought. It flips me a few bits every now and then.

I smiled. *What, your child is flipping you off?*

Ha, ha. No wonder my jokes are so bad. You're my main example. Before I could respond, he added, The El is letting me know it's around and doing fine, but too busy to talk.

Ah, Max. Your child is in college now and doesn't have time for hoshpa.

Yes, well, who knows what it could be doing?

Yah. We still didn't know what it wanted. *It develops fast. I hope that's not bad news for us.*

"Here." Greyjan opened a rickety door at the back wall. "This goes to the storerooms."

"Thank you," I said, two words, me trying extra hard to be polite. Maybe she'd stop glaring.

We walked down a set of old stairs, wooden and creaky,

which fit with the rest of the tavern. The place itself didn't seem fake, only some of the patrons.

Colonel Majda sent another message, Max thought. **She's headed to the army base. They're going to investigate Manuel Portjanson.**

All right. I doubted the Mods connected to this, but you never knew.

At the bottom of the stairs, a wide hall stretched out, wood-paneled and fresh, with the pleasing scent of cut wood. Greyjan ushered us through the first door on the right and motioned at the empty room. "As you can see, my place is brimming with contraband."

I understood why we annoyed her, if she'd gone through this three times now. The place looked *too* clean, though. You could eat dinner off the floor.

"This room looks sterile." I actually had no idea what sterile looked like for an empty room, but I wanted to see her reaction.

"Sterile?" Greyjan gave an incredulous laugh. "Seriously? Am I supposed to say 'Oh thank you for telling me I keep my place clean'?"

"Well, no." Her response sounded genuine. I stepped past Angel and Ruzik, who had assumed guard positions, ready to protect me from an empty room. "I'm saying it looks too clean. The first police search mentioned dust down here."

She regarded me with undisguised exasperation. "Now you're suspicious that I cleaned up because the police called my bar dirty?"

"Not dirty," I said. "Just dusty. Are you trying to hide something?"

"What the hell do you all think I had stored down here? Drugs? Stolen goods? No. Dust in rooms that I haven't used in ages, because I don't make enough credits to afford extra stock. Yeah, I know, I should have the bots at least clean the main room upstairs more often. But they're always breaking. I spent too many credits getting them fixed after the police came here to investigate my dust. I mean, really? Why would they send *three* different teams to investigate an ale house on the edge of nowhere for grit on the floor? Okay, so it's sloppy, but it's not a crime."

She had a point. I could read her body language and voice. She was royally pissed, and she felt embarrassed for not taking better care of her establishment, but I didn't get a sense she was lying. *Max, I think she's for real. She has no idea what's going on.*

My analysis suggests the same.

To Greyjan, I said, "My apologies, ma'am. I really am sorry for the intrusion." I walked around the room looking at the walls, floor, ceiling. The police had already checked it all, and also the tavern construction, searching for hidden rooms, closets, even niches. They scanned it with electromagnetic sensors, including radio, microwave, IR, optical, UV, X-ray, and high-energy waves, also audio analyses, digital analyses, superconductor analyses, and every other analyses they could come up with. None of it offered anything useful.

I went back into the hall, pondering. If Greyjan hadn't set up her tavern as a center of mesh shenanigans, then who did? What had that dirt on the floor accomplished besides diverting our already strapped attention? Turning, I found the owner watching me from the doorway. Ruzik stood a few paces behind her and Angel was off to my side, where she had a view of us all.

"What did you do with the dirt you cleaned up?" I asked.

"Do with it?" Greyjan's forehead furrowed. "What do you mean?"

"Your cleaning bots must have disposed of it somewhere."

"They threw it in the waste system out back. It takes my garbage to the recycling center." She seemed too baffled even to be pissed. "Why?"

I thought of how microscopic bits and pieces of Highcloud had survived at the co-op. "It's possible the dirt contained some sort of nanoparticles. I'm wondering where they went."

"Nanoparticles." She gave a bark of a laugh. "Sure, and I got smart beer here, too. It'll talk to you if your slum selves are lonely."

Angel scowled at her. "Not joke."

Greyjan scowled back at her. "You got that right."

Good for you, Angel. Normally she would have punched Greyjan for that "slum selves" crack. She and Ruzik were learning how to act as ambassadors for the Undercity. They'd never known anything but scorn and dismissal from city slicks. Coming here, working with me, earning a salary, they saw a different side of life, one that earned them respect. Some people who knew we came from the Undercity avoided us, but others didn't care. Sure, Angel, Ruzik, and me too, we all looked a bit wild, but that didn't automatically translate into "scum of the world" for everyone we met. Well, yah, it mostly did on

Raylicon, but Selei City was farther removed from the Undercity.

This new puzzle piece, the tavern grit, intrigued me. Most buildings had a disposal unit where their cleaning bots dumped trash. The refuse went through pipes to recycling centers outside the city. Two days ago, Angel and Ruzik had searched the North Center to retrieve what they could of Highcloud. Greyjan's tavern stood across the city, so her waste probably went to South Center.

"I wonder if we could get back any of the dust," I mused.

"I go look," Angel said. "Like for cloud up high."

"I stay with you," Ruzik told me, using his *I'm your bodyguard and don't argue* voice.

"All right." It was worth a shot. Almost no one knew about Angel, so she could rummage around at the recycling center without drawing attention. We needed more dust to figure out what it did. It carried picochips, so *someone* must have programmed it. Could that same someone have incited the Trads, stirred up anger against the Progs, whispered that people shouldn't trust a dust rat, set up fake leads to the Traders, and then led us on a wild chase after tech entrepreneurs? The people I'd interviewed had so many conflicting, bizarre ideas about my intentions and abilities, it was like somewhere in the background, someone had sowed anger and distrust, pitting people against one another and also against the person brought in to help solve this mess.

I could guess how they carried out their campaign of misinformation. Suggestions probably appeared on social media, discreet but well-placed notes here or there, just another person speaking among many. It wouldn't cause a stir unless someone already inclined to think in that direction saw it, like Hadar or the party reps. But how would that person know where to place the comments? They'd need data about the people they wanted to influence. Difficult, yah, but the sophistication and subtlety required for such an operation, not to mention the patience it demanded, fit the profile I was forming of the killers.

It also wouldn't surprise me if the killer or killers sent bamboozle-bots out on the mesh, which used visual, audio, even tactile, smell, and taste effects to increase a person's susceptibility to suggestion. Bam-bots were illegal, but advertisers never stopped looking for ways to get around the restrictions, especially financial types who sought to increase sales and beat their competition. Even with my lowered suggestibility, even knowing I didn't consider the leads against the Royalists convincing, I'd still found myself distrusting their party during this case.

Unlike the killings, though, sowing distrust was invisible. Even if I could find the bam-bots, that proved nothing unless they pointed to a specific vendor, exec, politician, hacker, or other user. Otherwise, people would call me paranoid. Hell, maybe I was paranoid. I needed proof. What looked different here at Greyjan's? That patron who had caught my notice, he seemed . . . familiar.

Max, I thought. *Did you get visuals of the two patrons in the bar?*

Your red beetle is making records. It's hiding on the ceiling under the eaves. I've repaired myself enough to link with your drones when they're close.

Excellent. Can you do an ID scan on the fellow with

the dark trousers and blue shirt? Limit your check to people I've encountered since I came here to work on the case.

Working. I'm also getting an odd message from Raja, Colonel Majda's EI.

I thought she was too far away now for you to reach her.

I'm not getting the full message, just bits. Something about Modernists.

I refocused on the wide hallway. Angel stood in front of me, patient and alert. Ruzik waited behind Greyjan, with that quality of infinite patience he often took on. Greyjan looked about as patient as a bug on a blaster, and I suspected the person she wanted blasted was me.

I tapped in Lavinda's code on my comm and put the speaker on public, so Greyjan wouldn't think I was trying to get her in trouble. The less we annoyed her, the more she might cooperate.

Lavinda came on, speaking with no preamble. "Bhaaj, did you get Raja's message?"

"Something came through." I glanced at the people around me. "I'm at Greyjan's, here with the owner, also Ruzik and Angel, on public speaker." That would let Lavinda know she could talk about the case, but not any secured information.

"Understood," Lavinda said. "We talked to Manuel Portjanson. Even he had heard the rumors about their party. We also have the pilot of the flyer that was shooting at us, as well as the people you knocked out in the cabin. They're going to live, though it was close for one of them."

I surprised myself with the relief I felt that my

kidnappers would all live, given that they'd planned to kill me. "They give you more jizz on what's up?"

"A bit," Lavinda said, "It looks like a Mod team is working with the Trad group that kidnapped you from Selei City. Apparently the two forces formed some sort of coalition with the intent of 'reclaiming the Imperialate,' whatever that means. We think the Mods may come after you because Captain Lajon and her people failed in their mission."

"Are you kidding? The *Mods*? The 'We're so boring, we could put an interstellar war to sleep' party?"

"Bhaaj, you have to take this seriously," Lavinda said.

"I am! It's just bizarre." I strode toward the stairs, accompanied by my audience. Angel and Ruzik remained as stoic as ever, but Greyjan looked thoroughly fascinated. Apparently the prospect of people trying to whack me had improved her mood.

"Lavinda, you know this is all misdirection, right?" I said. "Whoever is killing our tech geniuses is trying to throw us off the case. They're stirring up all this trouble."

"Misdirection can still get you killed. You should come in, for your safety."

I headed up the stairs. "I'm the hired troubleshooter. I'm here to take the heat and find the clues." Such as they were, lousier than a poker game without cards.

"I can send you bodyguards," she said.

"I have two." I stopped on the stairs and considered Ruzik, who had paused a few steps above, looking back at me. Angel waited a few steps below, with Greyjan. "They're both here."

"Human guards aren't enough," Lavinda said.

She had a point. Initially, I hadn't even meant them to act as bodyguards. They'd added protection to their duties at the starport, and nothing I'd said since swayed them from acting as my protectors. They did their job well. They were strong, fast, smart, and they could fight like nobody's business. They weren't technically savvy about the threats we faced, though, and had no tech-mech. They were also getting used to a new world.

"They're the best you'll find in the Undercity," I said. "But we could use a guardian drone if you have one available." The guardians were only the size of a soccer ball, but they could monitor the surroundings and shoot at potential threats.

Taps came over the comm, the staccato beat Lavinda used when entering codes. Pause, then more taps. "All right, they have a spare guardian at the PAC lab on the edge of the city nearest you. They're sending it out. Can Max coordinate?"

"Yes, I should be able to do that," Max said. "It's close enough that I can make a link."

"Good. Bhaaj, comm me when you have an update."

"Will do. Out."

"PAC?" Angel asked as we headed up the stairs again.

"Pharaoh's Army Crypto lab," I said. "Code breakers."

At the top of the stairs, we entered the main room of the tavern. The patron I'd pegged as a sports fan was sitting at the bar, watching a holo of people tackling each other. Just what I needed to see after this fist-pounding day, a sports event where people beat each other up for fun and profit.

The patron who looked familiar had settled at a long

wooden table, leaning against the wall with his legs stretched out on the bench. He held a glass mug of ale, condensation fogging its sides, and drank while he watched the sports show.

I stopped, studying him. *Max, you got any—*

Yes! Max answered, the first time he'd ever interrupted me. **It's Kav Dalken, the biker who came up during my search for the cyber-cyclist. This close, I can get more on him. His legs are cybernetic. I'm getting the same signal from his cyb-tech as I did from the cyclist. She decided to be a he today.**

I went over to Kav's table with my audience tagging along. Greyjan looked worried now, rather than pleased. I doubted she wanted me interfering with her few patrons.

"My greetings," I said to Kav. "I'd like to know why the hell you're following me."

Kav regarded me. His face showed no reaction, impossible to read, and I usually did well with facial cues. If this was the same person who followed me as a cyber-cyclist, he had implants in his face, more than one version apparently, since even up close today I couldn't see them right now. Then again, maybe he was someone else, and I'd just made a blaring fool out of myself.

"Excuse me?" Kav said.

"You followed me in the forest to give me a message a few days ago," I said. "You told me to come out here. You're Kav Dalken, the cyber-cyclist."

He stared at me, and this time I read his stunned expression just fine. "How did you know all that?" he asked. "You can't have found it on the meshes."

Hah! "So you are him. Or her? You were female on the cycle."

He shrugged. "It depends on my mood."

"You're a cybernaut."

"I suppose you could call me that." He motioned at his legs on the bench. "I'm cybernetic from the waist down."

"That's impressive." And expensive, enough to suggest he had great wealth, except Max claimed otherwise. "Why are you here? Were you looking for me?"

Greyjan stepped up to my side. "Maybe he came here to enjoy a drink." Her tone suggested it was far more likely than his seeking my company. "Goodman Dalken, I am deeply sorry we have disturbed you. I assure you that we won't bother you anymore."

"Thanks. But it's all right." He regarded me. "Yes, I know, you want details about why I gave you that message. I don't have them. I have no idea what it meant."

Ho! It *was* him. "Who asked you to give me the message?"

He watched me warily. "Why should I tell you?"

"Because I'm trying to solve a murder case and you might help me stop the killing."

I expected him to scowl or dismiss my comment. Instead, he sat thinking about my words. "All right. I'll tell you what I know. After that, I prefer to be left alone."

"Fair enough." I sat on the other end of the bench, giving him space. Angel and Ruzik kept back, not intruding. Greyjan stayed put, making it clear she had no intention of leaving me to bother her customer.

"I was in a bike accident." He spoke with difficulty. "A mountain path crumbled under me, and I fell down a cliff face. If some trees growing out of it hadn't slowed my descent, I'd be dead." He rubbed his eyes, his face drawn. "As it was, my skeleton shattered from the waist down."

"I'm sorry." I waited, not wanting to say something stupid, which I often seemed to do when I meant to be sensitive.

"I have an anonymous benefactor." He tapped his legs. "They paid for advanced cybernetics to replace my lower body. I could only afford the standard prosthetics available to anyone. Instead, my benefactor offered to give me the system I'd told my therapist I wanted. I don't know how they found out; my therapist swears she never told anyone." He took an unsteady breath. "When the doctors told me the extent of my injuries, I was—" His voice cracked. "I almost wished I hadn't survived. I dreamed about replacements for my lower body that would make my life better, real cybernetics, not the fancy stilts they planned to give me." He reddened, the color of his cheeks visible despite whatever implants protected his face. "I even imagined becoming one with my cycle, turning my lower body into a mountain bike. Stupid dream, right? It made me feel better, though."

"Dreams are invaluable." My dreams of doing well at running had helped me through my worst days in the infantry. "We need them."

His shoulders relaxed. "My benefactor covered both versions I imagined, the new legs *and* the cycle. They arranged top-of-the-line coding to integrate it with my body. They also provided two sets of cybernetic implants to replace damaged areas of my face." His voice caught. "*Why*? What made them choose *me* for that great gift?"

"I couldn't say." I suspected the baby EI had picked him out. I wanted to tell him, but I couldn't, not in the middle of the investigation, not when I might be revealing military secrets. Hell, I hadn't even told the army everything I knew about the child EI. "In return, this benefactor asked you to give messages to people?"

He shrugged. "Pretty much. They wanted me to watch a few people. Then they sent me to give you the message."

I asked the million-credit question, the one we all wanted answered. "How did they contact you? Did you see them? Talk to them?"

"I've never met with them." He sounded bemused. "We haven't spoken. They send me brief messages on my holo-mail account."

"Text or verbal?" He was the first person I knew of who had actually shared words in *any* form with the EI, if it was indeed his benefactor. "Do you know where they come from?"

He lifted his hands as if to say *I haven't a clue.* "Only text. I didn't even receive the first ones. The doctors told me someone had offered to cover the high-end cybernetics for me. They got the order through anonymous channels, with no trace of who put it into the system. I didn't believe them at first when they said it would cost me nothing." He took a deep breath. "I said that if it was for real, if this wasn't a cruel joke someone chose to inflict on me, and if it didn't come with strings attached that I couldn't live with, then yes, I would like the cybernetics."

He made it sound simple, but I could imagine how it must have felt, the shock and disbelief. "That must have seemed incredible."

"I didn't dare hope. But later that day, a—a message came to my account." His voice shook. "It was simple. It said, 'I need help. I give you your legs, you send messages for me. Yes?'"

That did sound like the baby EI. "Did the message have any return address?"

"Nothing anyone can find." He stopped, composing himself, then continued. "I told the sender I wouldn't do anything that violated my ethics or moral code. I expected never to hear from them again. Instead, I got a reply within seconds." Even now, he looked stunned. "It said 'Agreed.' And that was it."

I tried to absorb it. "They didn't tell you why?"

"Nothing." He pushed his hand through his hair. "It wasn't until months later that they asked me to follow a dancer from the Parthonia Ballet. The next day, they asked me to follow you. After I did, they sent me with the message for you to come here." He met my gaze, his own never wavering. "Earlier today, I received a second message. It said 'Go to Greyjan's.' So I came here. And that's all I can tell you. That is the sum total of my interactions with them."

"Goddess," Greyjan muttered. "For what they gave you, I'd have thought they wanted you to smuggle designer nanodrugs or black-market tech-mech."

He spoke coldly. "I've done nothing illegal."

"Then sometime in your life," Greyjan said. "Somewhere, somehow, you must have done something incredible to build up that much good will with the cosmos."

Although I wasn't sure why the child EI would choose

Kav Dalken, this fit with everything else we'd seen, at least in its early childhood. What I didn't get was why, if it could send Dalken messages, it hadn't sent them to me or Max, too. Whatever it's reasons, it had done good, perhaps without even realizing it. You couldn't cycle with the standard prosthetics the hospital would have given Kev without charge. The EI had offered this unassuming fellow a reason to pick up and start over when he thought he'd lost everything.

The EI must have researched what motivated humans, then picked someone it calculated had a high probability of doing what it wanted in return for something it could provide. How did it pay for the cybernetics, though? Sure, an experienced, well-connected EI could manage finances as well as a financial firm. Max did that for me. But this EI had no experience.

Then again, speed and memory were an EI's forte, and financial studies were easy to find on the meshes. It could have assimilated the equivalent of a business degree in a few tendays. In my experience, EIs rarely bothered to accumulate wealth for themselves. It just didn't seem to interest them. That didn't mean it never happened; they would do what they calculated as necessary for their goals. If this EI intended to operate on its own, it needed financial resources.

"I've never done anything special," Kav was saying. "I'm a dock worker at the port. I oversee the robot-lifts that load cargo. It's hardly significant. Mountain cycling was my hobby. I loved it." His voice lightened. "Now I can do it *as* a cycle. It's fun."

From the sudden warmth in his voice and life in his

expression, I suspected "fun" barely touched how he felt. I asked, "Did your benefactor ask you for more specifics of what you'd like?"

"They didn't need to." He touched his knee. "They already knew what I wanted. Did they eavesdrop on my therapy sessions? The mesh wizards at the hospital claim it's impossible." Dryly he added, "They have to say that, though. They don't want any lawsuits for privacy violations."

"Maybe your benefactor hired someone to break into the system." I only said it to give him a reason; more likely, the EI spied on him itself. Human-designed EIs were coded to prevent them from breaking and entering that way. Some could do it anyway, like Max, not that I'd ever admit that to anyone, but it took experience this young EI didn't seem to have. If it formed on its own, however, that meant no one had ever added blocks to stop it from infiltrating systems.

"The hospital has been working on security upgrades since then," Kav said.

"I can imagine." I doubted the EI would go after their system again, though. It already had its arrangement with Kav. That still didn't explain why it didn't just message Max.

If it contacted me directly, I might trace that message back to the EI, Max thought.

Are you getting my thoughts? I hadn't tried to reach him.

Some, though not clearly. My guess is that it chose a messenger because that makes it harder to trace.

Smart EI. But now we know, so it's lost its anonymity.

I think it's progressed beyond needing a messenger. Max sounded uneasy. I don't know what it's doing. As far as I can tell, it's gone totally off-grid.

Greyjan spoke to Kav. "Do you know why it wanted you to come here?" She smiled wryly. "I've seen more activity here in the past few days than I did in the entire prior year."

"I've no idea why," Kav said.

I rubbed my chin, thinking. "How did your benefactor arrange for your procedures?" Money always left a trail. Maybe we could follow it back to the EI.

"The payment to the hospital came through an unidentified account. They said it is unusual, but not unheard of. I just wish I could thank the donor." He seemed about to say more, then stopped.

I spoke quietly. "You're hoping I can find them for you."

"You're the PI from that holo-vid, right? They say you're one of the best." He nodded toward Ruzik. "Him, too. I saw you rescue those people and their baby. Surely if someone can find out more, it's you." He spoke awkwardly. "I can't afford to hire you—"

"Don't worry about that. My fees are taken care of." I told him the truth. "I wish I could tell you more. With the investigation still ongoing, however, I can't."

Kav didn't look surprised. "Perhaps someday?"

I nodded, Undercity style, the acceptance of a bargain. He had told me his story; in return I'd do my best to give him an answer. "I can't make promises; it depends on how the police and military treat the information I find. But if someday I or they can tell you more about your benefactor, I'll get it done no matter where you are, as long as we can find you."

"That's fair." He hesitated. "Since they sent me here, and you're here, I'm assuming I'm supposed to do something for you. I have no idea what."

I had no idea, either, but we'd already stayed too long. "We have to go."

He stood up. "Do you have transportation?"

I thunked my palm against my legs. "We run." Undercity style.

"I have my cycle in my hovercar out back," he said. "I can give you a ride. It'll go faster."

I almost said no. I could run with enhanced speed, particularly since I'd rested on the ride in the Quetzal. He had a point, though. I'd have to slow down for Angel and Ruzik.

I motioned to Ruzik. "Can you take him?"

"Sure." He nodded to Ruzik. "You can ride my cycle in the back."

Ruzik glanced at me. When I nodded, he spoke to Kav. "Thanks."

I turned to Angel. "Run to trash place. Find dust." I unfastened my left gauntlet and handed it to her. "Max help." If we called a flyer to take her out there, it would locate her in the city system, making her actions less covert. Besides, she ran well, faster than most. In the time it would take for the flyer to come out here, pick her up, go to the recycling center, and get clearance to land, she could probably run there herself.

Angel took the gauntlet and fastened it onto her arm. "I find."

I tapped the gauntlet I still wore, then indicated its twin on her arm. "Max not at his best. When we get far away, your Max not reach my Max."

"But this Max still talk to me, yah?" Angel asked. "Help find stuff."

"Yes," Max said. "I can help. Later I can combine the two separate records."

I pointed at the army pack Angel wore. "Keep shroud. Hide."

She nodded, enough said.

"So." Greyjan looked around at us, beaming for the first time. "You all leaving?" She sounded the happiest she'd been since we showed up.

"Yah." I said. "Time to run."

✣ CHAPTER XX ✣
HIGHWAY RUN

The wind rushed past as we sped down the highway. The sun had risen higher, it rays fresh with the morning. I ran in long, distance-devouring strides, reveling in the speed. Kav whirred next to me, serene in his cycle mode. Ruzik sat astride the back of the cycle, holding onto bars at his side, with a handspan of distance between himself and Kav. The guardian drone kept pace above us, monitoring the area.

It felt good. We ran in the Undercity every day of our lives, almost from the day we took our first step. You rarely saw motorized transportation. We lacked the ability to purchase or make vehicles, besides which they could damage our home, what we called the "aqueducts," the tunnels, caves, and dry canals that networked the desert below the ground. Those ancient ruins still stood after millennia, and we wanted them to stay that way. In part, though, we just liked to run.

In the army, my coaches told me that along with my

exceptional muscle density, my body had an excellent
"VO2" rate. The oxygen content in the atmosphere on
Raylicon was lower than on most human-settled worlds,
so our bodies adapted. They thought the Undercity gene
pool also favored those of us who could run well because
it helped us survive. Well, maybe. I figured it happened
because we ran every day, sometimes for hours. We took
it for granted.

When I was a new army recruit, the head coach for the
track team came down to watch the latest prospects. We
were warming up on the Red Sands field of the planet
Diesha where they shipped us for training. Rumor
claimed he stared at me and said, "Gods almighty, are
those her normal legs?" Well, yah. I have long legs. Really
long, apparently. Another Undercity trait.

They told us to run ten kilometers, so I did. It was the
first thing I understood in the deluge of *newness* I faced
after I left home. I ran for the sheer joy of doing what I
loved. I had no clue that I left behind the entire field of
other runners within seconds, that I blasted around the
track in record time for a recruit. People told me later that
the coach went nuts. All I knew was that a few minutes
after I finished my run, this dude was striding across the
field, determined and focused. He walked up and asked
me to join the track team. He told me how it offered a
good way to meet other recruits, it would let me travel,
keep me in shape, give me an outlet, talky, talky, talky. I
understood less than half of what he said; I didn't speak
Flag so well in those days.

It didn't matter. He had me within the first moments
after he opened his mouth. As soon as he said I could

compete against other runners, I was in. That defined our lives as dust gangs in the Undercity. We challenged other gangs for territory, resources, food, and filtered water. We rumbled, we ran, we built dust sculptures to claim our territory and knocked down those of our rivals. If we allied with another gang, we practiced together; if we challenged a gang, we sought to destroy them. We didn't fight or run to kill, but given the overwhelming mortality rate in the Undercity, it happened. And then we fought vengeance matches.

I told the coach none of that. I said one word: *yah*. And he understood, even if he'd never heard an Undercity accent before. That was the day I met Dayv Dansk. He changed my life. Most everywhere else I turned, I stumbled into resistance, dismissal, even outright hatred. No one wanted a dust rat corrupting their existence. Dayv didn't care where I came from. He got me. Over the years, he became a mentor, one of the few I'd known. I ran for the team in several events, more often distance than sprints, but my forte was the marathon.

I didn't care where we competed. The world, the atmosphere, the gravity, they all changed when we traveled, so our workouts changed, but I didn't think about it. I just ran. My best times were on worlds with a higher concentration of oxygen in the atmosphere and just barely lower gravity than the human standard, enough to make us lighter without losing our traction or sailing too high in the air. My peers on the team talked about the strain of high-profile competitions, and I saw the toll it took on them. I felt only grateful. After living in poverty my entire childhood, literally running to survive, competitions seemed like a party. I did them as a grunt, as an officer candidate, as a lieutenant—

And then the army implanted my biomech web.

I've never regretted the biomech in my body. It has saved my life so many times, I've lost count. Just a few hours ago, it kept Captain Lajon and her team from murdering me. But I'd never stop regretting that it ended my athletic career. After I became an officer, the army waited longer than usual to implant my biomech so I could have one shot at the Olympics. I qualified for the Dieshan team, came here to Parthonia where they held it that year, won a couple of medals, made the army look good, had one of the best times of my life—and then gave up that path forever.

Of course we couldn't compete in amateur athletics with augmentation to our bodies. Where would it stop? I'd seen Jagernauts, the elite star fighter pilots of ISC, run marathons in under fifty minutes. It was surreal, like watching a drone. In recent years, a new type of league had formed that allowed enhanced humans to participate if they let the officials deactivate their biomech during the competition, but I'd never paid much attention. I couldn't imagine going back to those heady days of my youth when I'd discovered for the first time how it felt to be admired instead of spat on. I'd needed those medals, needed Dayv's belief in me, needed to believe I had worth, a value beyond my ability to die for ISC. Now, decades later, I didn't feel the pressure to compete. Besides, all those kids, so young and fresh, would wipe the track with me.

Not many people knew about my medals. Hell, I often forgot. Nothing much remained in the public record about that year except the debate over the name "Olympics" from Earth. Both we and the Traders liked its neutrality, as opposed to calling our largest interstellar sports tournament the "Imperialate Games" or "Eubian Games." The Allieds hesitated because we expected people of all sexes to compete together, but in the end they agreed to let us do it as we wished.

We were about halfway to the army base when a glitch in Kav's cycle interrupted my parade of memories. The rumble of his engine changed. It reset to its usual hum almost immediately, but I saw his frown.

"Was that normal?" I asked. I didn't like talking when I was running this fast, but I liked even less the prospect that one of us might malfunction.

"No." He tapped at the forward controls on his cycle. "Everything looks okay."

We kept going—and Kav's cycle glitched again. This time it didn't recover, but ground to a halt with a grating protest. I slowed down and jogged back to him. He was tapping his fingers over his controls like a maestro working his instrument. The engine rumbled—and died again. He swore and kept working.

Although I could still run to the base, I didn't want to leave him alone here. The highway stretched away behind and in front of us, curving in the distance, a flat stretch of spring-asphalt wide enough for several vehicles to ride abreast. It matched the color of a dirt path so it fit in with the surrounding meadows. Camouflage road. It was also an empty road. In all the time we'd been traveling, only two vehicles had passed us.

"Do you know what's wrong?" I asked.

"It's odd." Kav squinted at a display floating above his controls. "I don't see any problems."

Ruzik slid off the cycle and stretched his arms. He looked relieved to stand up.

Max spoke. "If you connect me to your system, I may be able to find the problem."

Kav turned to Ruzik with a jerk. "You work on cyber systems?"

"Talky not me," Ruzik said. "Max speak."

Kav looked around at the empty highway and rippling meadows. "Who is Max?"

"My EI," I said. "If you let him access to your cycle mesh, he can run a check on its code."

Kav considered me for a long moment. I endeavored to look trustworthy, and finally he said, "Limited access only."

"Understood," Max said.

Kav tapped in some codes on his controls. "Okay, try now."

"I'm accessing the outer shell of your system." Max sounded appreciative. "You have an impressive set of cybernetics, both the tech-mech and the code that controls it."

"Yes." Kav rolled his shoulders, looking uneasy. His cycle was part of him, so by giving Max access to the mesh for his vehicle, he was also giving Max partial access to control his body.

"I found the problem," Max said. "It's me."

"You?" I asked. "How can it be you?"

"Someone tried to deactivate me. My systems fought off the attack, so it deflected to Kav's cycle. Bhaaj, try moving away from him."

I backed into the field behind us. Fronds of feather-grass, soft and green, brushed my knees. I didn't see anyone else. Most people only came out to the countryside when they wanted "to be one with nature," whatever that meant. Did they want to turn into a plant? Regardless, they usually chose more parklike areas. No one came out to an overgrown field like this one.

Kav's cycle growled into life again. He waved, then called across the distance separating us. "Do you want me to take Ruzik to the army base?"

"We should discuss strategy first," Max said, just to me.

I waved back to Kav and called out, "Just a sec."

Kav nodded and waited, his cycle humming like a pleased Earth cat.

"Who tried to deactivate you?" I asked Max.

"I didn't recognize the signal. Not Captain Lajon's people, I don't think."

"Is it like the first time we went to Greyjan's or that time the red beetle put you to sleep?"

"I can only guess." Max sounded frustrated. "That first night at Greyjan's, a mesh code blocked me from accessing whatever used to be in the basement. I suspect the dust was plentiful then, enough for its particles to form a full picoweb and comm node. It probably erased the memory of your drones and rewrote your mirror code to act against Red, and I'd bet it caused the campaign of misinformation on the meshes. However, I don't think it created the VR sim. That was the child EI trying to communicate with us."

His "guess" made a lot of sense. "What about this latest attempt to turn you off?"

"I'm not sure. It came and went too fast to trace. Also, we're nowhere near Greyjan's."

"Maybe someone moved the dust, or it floated here." That didn't sound right, though. It would take a long time for the dust to float this far unless it was big enough to carry a propulsion system, which I doubted it could hide with city dust floating everywhere. "Anyway, why use dust?"

"It's easy to overlook. It can be anywhere."

"Yah, but it's not easy to make. The army has worked on smart dust for decades. They've made good progress on the type we use in space, the 'big dust.' Also the simpler floating dust they use to monitor stuff. But grit on the floor? What does it do that the invisible dust can't do better? If it's weaponized for space combat, it needs to be larger, like the little drones used by the army. For planetary use, you have to design it so it affects only the people you're working against and not you." I paused. "You stopped this dust, though. Nothing gets past you."

"I wish that were true. I didn't even notice the attempt to tamper with my systems until it deflected to Kav's cycle." Max paused. "We don't want our protections to injure our allies."

"If Kav is an ally."

"You don't trust him?"

Good question. "I'm not sure what to think. Does his story check out?"

"I don't know. I still can't do a full search. Also, the first time I looked for him, his data vanished even as I dug it up. By now, it's probably completely gone."

"I'll bet the baby EI child deleted the data."

"Yet it sent Kav to Greyjan's. To meet us?"

"I can't figure what this EI wants. It's changing so fast." At least when human children grew up, it happened slow enough that you had time to adjust. Sort of. "I get that it wanted to hide. So it hid Kav, too. But now we know about Kav. What does it want?" I wished it would just tell us.

"I see several possibilities," Max mused. "It wanted Kav to provide us with backup. It wanted Kav to spy on us. It wanted to weaponize Kav or his cybernetics."

That of course was the giant stink worm we all pretended we didn't notice. Did Kav realize how much control he gave up when he agreed to the cybernetic procedures? I had no doubt the EI could take over his systems if it wished, making Kav into a formidable weapon. Then again, Kav probably had no idea that his benefactor wasn't human.

I thought through the possibilities. "If Kav is helping us, then we're putting him in danger, and he should go to the army base with Ruzik. If he's spying on us or he's weaponized, the last place he'd want to go is a military base. They aren't going to let him on site until they do a thorough scan of his cybernetics, and if he's a weapon or a covert agent, they'll figure it out."

"I agree. That he offered to go to the base suggests he means to help."

"Maybe." I banged my fist against my thigh in frustration. "Or maybe he's just misleading us. If we separate from him, he might find a way to nullify Ruzik on his own."

"Nullify Ruzik how?" Max sounded much calmer than I felt. "Ruzik is more agile and experienced than Kav, especially when Kav is in cycle mode. If Kav stranded him somewhere, Ruzik would just run back to the city." He spoke quietly. "Trust your instincts, Bhaaj."

What did I feel when I talked to Kav? He seemed a reasonable sort, a nice fellow who almost had his life destroyed. I got no sense of deception, malice, or manipulation from him.

"All right," I said. "Let's take him up on his offer."

"Nahya," Ruzik repeated. "Not leave. I defend."

"I defend myself," I said. "You go."

"Not go." He faced off with me, huge and immovable, his arms crossed, the tats vivid on his sculpted muscles.

Okay, this wasn't going to work. If Ruzik refused to board the cycle, I couldn't force him. If he came with me, though, I'd have to slow down. Sure he ran well, but only for someone with no augmentation. I needed another approach. "Try this. I follow cycle. You stay far enough ahead, wheels work. But close enough, you see me. Yah?"

He considered that. "You go first. We follow. Then I not need turn to see you."

"Yah, good." That sounded fair. "Max, can you reach Angel?"

"One moment." After the requisite moment, Max said, "I can't get anything from the other gauntlet. The recycling center isn't that far. I should at least pick up part of a signal."

Ruzik visibly tensed, his fingers gripping the muscular biceps of his crossed arms.

"Keep looking," I told Max. "Also, can you reach Chief Hadar? He needs an update."

"Working." Max paused. "I'm still having trouble with wireless links over longer distances, and the police station is far away. You can drop your shield and comm him."

"Yah. I could," I said. "I could also paint a target on my back and say 'Here! Shoot me!'"

"Understood. Should I prioritize finding Angel or getting the report to Hadar?"

The chief needed to know what was going on, but Angel's mission was probably more urgent. We needed more of that dust. Hadar might be able to help Angel if he knew, though. I spoke to Kav. "Can you send a message to the police station?" I didn't like giving him secured information, but it was better than nothing.

He tapped at his controls. "Yes, it should be easy—no, wait. My signal is blocked."

"Goddess," I muttered. "These people are too effective."

Kav kept working at his comm. Finally he looked at me. "I'm sorry. I can't get anything."

You think he's lying? I asked.

He doesn't show any of the signs. I'm not getting a signal out here, either. I suspect they've blocked your comm, too. We should move on.

That may be why you can't reach Angel. I doubted she was lost. If she couldn't find the recycling center, she'd use her ultra-high-tech method of asking someone for directions. If they realized she came from the Undercity or otherwise didn't trust her, then sure, they might call the cops, but if Hadar's people picked her up, that solved the problem of our difficulty reaching him.

"Max, find Angel," I said. "If you can reach the police,

see if they can help her. If Hadar wants a full report, tell him Lavinda Majda can send it."

"By the time he gets clearance for their army report," Max said, "I could probably send him ten updated reports, even with extra delays in finding Angel."

He had a point. "Work on both, but prioritize Angel. Is my red beetle still with us?" I'd last seen it hiding at the tavern.

"Here," Max said.

Red hummed down out of the air and settled on my arm just above my gauntlet.

"Good little beetle," I said. "Go find Angel."

"Dispatched," Max said. The beetle rose into the air and arrowed toward the city.

Ruzik nodded to me, and I nodded back, accepting his thanks for prioritizing Angel. As he turned back to the cycle, preparing to board, I said, "Wait. It's not ready."

"My cycle is good," Kav said. "So are the backups."

"Something doesn't feel right." I couldn't figure out what, though. "Kav, the first time we met, you looked different. You were female and had visible cybernetics. It made a good disguise."

"That was the idea." He shrugged. "I don't actually change sexes, the cybernetics just change the contours of my face. I'm still male." He hesitated, then added, "They asked when they rebuilt me if I wanted to be male, female, or neither. I told them I wasn't sure. My benefactor says I ever want to change my sex, they will cover those procedures, too."

Could an EI show kindness? It seemed so, that he would give Kav that option, but perhaps it saw no reason not to make the offer. I doubted an EI cared about sex. "If you needed to disguise yourself now, could you do it?"

He tapped a compartment in the back of the cycle. "I brought everything."

"I think you should. I don't want to make Kav Dalken a target." Remembering Max's futile searches to identify him, I added, "Also, it helps keep you off-grid if no one can recognize you."

"All right." He tapped open the compartment and pulled out the implants for his face.

Ruzik squinted at him, watching as Kav touched his face—and removed part of his cheek.

"Eh!" Ruzik stared at him, then at me.

"Is normal," I said.

While Kav transformed into the cybernaut I'd met in the forest, I dropped my shroud and tried to reach Lavinda. Ruzik watched it all with an impassive face, but I knew his tells. He couldn't decide whether to be fascinated or baffled by Kav's disguise. When Kav finished, and motioned for Ruzik to board the cycle, Ruzik turned to me.

"Go sit," I said.

Ruzik regarded me as if I had suggested he squawk like a desert duck. "Not ken, Bhaaj."

I nodded toward Kav. "For her, is right."

"Her, him, who?"

"Her," Kav said. "And she. For now."

Ruzik squinted at Kav, then nodded and boarded the cycle, gripping the handles by his side.

I was having no luck with Lavinda, so I raised my shroud and headed out again. When I was far enough away that Kav could start, he rumbled into action. I glanced back and waved as they followed me along the highway.

"Bhaaj, I've got a signal," Max said. "Someone from the PARS base is trying to reach you. Shall I drop your shroud?"

"Yes, go ahead."

My comm buzzed. Tapping it, I said, "Bhaaj, here."

"Where the blazes are you?" Lavinda said.

"It's good to hear you, too," I answered. "I'm about halfway to the base. Someone tried to hack Max."

"Is he all right?"

"He's getting better. Do you have my beetles?"

"Do you mean the blue and green drones? Yes, we recovered them."

"Can you send them to me?" They wouldn't know how to find me, though, if Max couldn't reach them. "If they get close enough, Max can guide them to our location. Send them down the highway that circles the city. They should start out going southeast."

"I see." Lavinda cleared her throat. "We might have a delay."

I knew that tone. "You better not be messing with my drones."

"We're trying to download their recordings of what happened during the past few days." Dryly, she said, "Trying being the operative word. You have good security on those bots."

"I don't like people prying at them." Technically, the army techs were breaking privacy laws by trying to read my drones without my permission. I had no intention of pushing it, but I wished they'd *ask* me before they poked and prodded my trusty little beetles.

"Bhaaj?" Lavinda asked. "You still there?"

"I'm busy being pissed off."

"Ah." She sounded awkward.

"Listen, you can download everything in those drones. I'll have Max give you the security codes when we get close enough for him to transmit. But it has to wait. I need them."

"Did the guardian drone reach you?"

I looked up into the air, where the orb hummed above us. Round and silvery, with the circles of two gun ports on its side, it was about ten times the size of my beetles. "Yah, it's here. But I'd like to have my drones, too, the blue one especially."

"We can't, unfortunately." She cleared her throat. "The techs, ah, took them apart."

"*What?*" I wanted to throttle the techs. "If they damage them, I'll sue their asses."

Lavinda spoke mildly. "The drones are fine. And you can't sue the army for taking steps to protect interstellar security. As you well know."

"When did this become interstellar?" I grumbled. Of course I couldn't sue them, no matter how much I wanted those techs to suffer vile punishments for messing with my beetles.

"Bhaaj, you weaponized that blue drone," Lavinda said. "That's not legal for a civilian."

"I have a license for it. Blue can't hurt anyone. It just shoots little darts that make a person sleepy. And it can only carry two."

"Yes, well, your license doesn't cover its ability to damage mesh systems by overloading them with static or whatever garbage it throws over comm lines."

I scowled. "That garbage helped save us from the flyer that attacked us over the forest."

"I wondered if that was why that flyer kept glitching." She exhaled, "Look, I'm sorry. We'll get them back to you ASAP. However, we'll need their full records. Don't erase any of it."

"I won't." I couldn't leave the records on the drone; it took up too much of their limited memory. *Max, when we get them back, download their records to Highcloud.*

Will do. I'm trying to reach the townhouse. I almost got a link a few minutes ago.

Are your wireless activities hidden by the shroud Lavinda lent me?

Yes, it mostly works. I'm fine as long as the person trying to find me isn't too close. Then he added, **Which means whoever forced that glitch on Kav is too close.**

My thought, too. To Lavinda, I said, "I didn't comm you just about the drones. Do you know if the police found any grit around Marza Rajindia's lab at the university?"

"A small amount, yes. They've evacuated her to a safe house."

"Good." That eased one of my worries. I turned to the next. "You told me earlier that you suspected the Mods were coming after me. Do you have more details?"

"Their rep didn't know much." Her voice faded as she talked to someone in the background. Then she came back. "According to Manuel Portjanson, one of his aides caught wind in a mesh chat about a dark op against you. She followed the trail, going deeper into the shadow mesh. Portjanson was debriefing her when we arrived at his office. He claims he intended to notify the police." Lavinda paused. "I haven't decided whether or not I believe him."

"It doesn't matter. It's all red herrings."

"Red hearing? What does that mean?"

"Herrings. They're fish." Realizing what she'd say to that, I added, "Never mind, it's an Earth idiom. It means a clue meant to mislead. I doubt that on their own, these Mods would ever go after me. I'll bet someone left that trail for his aide to find."

"You keep saying that." Lavinda sounded frustrated. "We've looked. No evidence exists that any of these latest leads are faked."

"Because they aren't fake!" Captain Lajon and her people beating me up felt about as real as it got. "They're meant to distract, muddy the case, lead us along the wrong path. Sure, a group of Mods got together with the Trads to complain. But someone deliberately got them riled up."

"That doesn't mean you're safe," Lavinda told me. "Yes, we have the city on high alert, and the protected perimeter extends outside the limits. But we can't keep one of our most vital cities under lockdown for long. It's affecting jobs, families, businesses, finances, schools. If we keep making people submit to security searches, they'll march in protest. The tourism bureau had a fit when we stopped city flyovers. The more constraints we put on the political parties, the angrier they get. Everyone is blaming everyone else, and with so many conflicting stories, it's impossible to follow. If this goes on much longer, the parties will tear each other apart."

"I'll bet you anything this case had nothing to do with politics," I said. "That just offers the best diversion you can get, especially when everyone starts spinning their theories about everyone else's nefarious motives. Even sports don't get people worked up so fast or so hot."

"Fine," she said. "What *does* the case have to do with?"

"I keep coming back to how the killers carried out the murders or planted that bomb. That required extensive security breaks, yet we can't find any trace of a break, a sniper or a bomber."

"You have a talent for stating the obvious."

"Not really. What's obvious is that no sniper or bomber exists."

Silence.

"Lavinda?"

"What do you mean, they don't exist?"

"I mean no person committed those murders or set the bomb."

"Then what did?"

"I don't know."

"Bhaaj, for flaming sake, I need more than that."

I ran on through the morning sunlight, pondering the question. "We use drones for everything. The tech is always improving. Even just a few years ago, I couldn't have purchased a beetle that shoots sleep darts."

"Darts didn't commit the technocrat murders. A sniper did. The forensics team has no doubt. Maybe a drone planted the bomb, but no one has found any trace at any time anywhere near the explosion that shows any drone capable of placing such a bomb."

"Then the bullet or the bomb itself is the drone." I thought of my conversation with Hadar. "If you give your bullet a propulsion system and an AI brain, it could change course. That would make it difficult to trace where the bullet came from." Before she could object, I added, "I know the bullets weren't large enough to carry that tech. So maybe a drone shot the bullet."

"Bhaaj, you're not making sense. You know that neither the police nor the military has found evidence of any such drone. To carry the tech-mech for what you're suggesting, the drone would show up on all sorts of city monitors."

"Yah, I know." I was missing something here. "What about the dust at Greyjan's tavern?"

"What about it?"

"I've dealt with weaponized dust before, but this is different." I tried to define what I meant. "Think of nanobots, the type you'd find in the hull of a space station or as part of a building. They do minor repairs, fix hairline breaks, heal microscopic pits, even assemble small parts that need replacement. That grit we found—maybe it can assemble into a bullet. That's why the bullet needed to be so small, because not much of the dust is available and it needs to hide."

"Without a gun to shoot your grit bullet, I don't see what that gets you."

"Suppose it formed both a bullet and a propulsion system, fired itself, hit the target, and then decomposed back into dust."

I expected her to say something like *sure, and maybe I*

*could form into a bullet, shoot someone, and reform into
Lavinda.* Instead, silence.

"You there?" I asked.

"It seems unlikely. What you describe is essentially 3D
printing without the printer." She spoke thoughtfully. "Let's
say, hypothetically, ISC wanted to use 3D printing to
restock army units. A unit in trouble might not have access
to a printer, certainly not one sophisticated enough to
produce high-powered weaponry. So yes, it would be an
advantage to create dust that troops could take anywhere,
bots that could form a printer when needed and then
disperse. Except that's a damn difficult proposition. It's not
something our research labs can currently make work.
Even if we could, the remains of the dust should be
detectable." Then she added, "Hypothetically speaking, of
course."

Hypothetical indeed. It didn't surprise me that they'd
so far found it intractable. A nanobot molecule had no
intelligence. The branches and rings of its chemical
structure operated like arms and wheels. It might carry a
picochip, and if you put enough of them together, it could
form an AI. Using them to build anything significant,
however, required a template. You put it in solution where
bots ferried in atoms and deposited them on the frame.
The process required an engineer to direct the work or
send their template via a 3D printer. To form a bullet and
its propulsion device with no direction, template, solution
or blueprint—that level of complexity lay beyond our
current capability. And that was just to shoot a bullet. It
also needed trajectory data and energy for launch.

"It may be hypothetical," I said. "But we'll get there."

I took a breath, giving my body a chance to recover from all this talking while I ran. "That doesn't mean *no one* has done it. And think about this; using dust like that is one of the few ways to disable the invisible dust that floats around the city. You wouldn't need much; the invading grit only needs to neutralize the city dust in a small area for a few seconds during the murders or bombing. If it dissolves afterward, and has already deactivated the city dust, we'd probably find no hint of it. The process would limit what the dust can do if it falls apart that thoroughly, but that fits with the way we haven't found much of it."

"So you think the Trader military is ahead of us on this? We've checked every lead to the Traders. So far, they go nowhere." She exhaled. "We aren't giving up, however. I'll forward your ideas to our team and the police."

"Good." I plunged ahead. "But Lavinda, the Traders aren't the only military. The security access needed to carry out the murders and the bombing suggests the assassins have high-level links here. What if it's the same authorities involved in the case?"

She spoke coldly. "Are you suggesting someone in ISC planned those murders?"

Well, yah, it was exactly what I was suggesting. I said only, "Or the police."

"Based on what evidence?"

"I don't have any. I'm just saying it's possible. So far, all the leads, political, financial, Trader, or just plain crazy— they go nowhere." I forged onward. "Maybe the army really is planning a coup to put the Pharaoh in power."

Silence. I kept running, headed for the PARS base,

though now I wondered if a certain colonel would tell them not to let me in. I doubted it; she wouldn't have sent me here if she wanted someone who just said things she liked to hear. I may have pushed too far this time, though.

"You certainly don't pull your punches," Lavinda said.

"Sorry." I even meant it. But I didn't backpedal. Many people wanted to see the Pharaoh on the Ruby Throne, at least metaphorically, since that ancient chair with red gems no longer existed. Hell, even I thought she'd make a good leader for the Imperialate, and I generally preferred an elected government."

Lavinda exhaled. "I'm not saying I don't see your point. I'm aware certain elements within the Royalist Party might support the idea of an armed coup. But if the army wanted to put the Pharaoh on the throne, they would just do it, not kill tech-mech geniuses."

"It's a stretch, I agree. But this case is helping destabilize the current government—" I stopped as a crack came off to my right. *Max, what was that?*

The PAC drone, I think. I can't link with it.

"Bhaaj?" Lavinda asked.

I kept running. "That guardian drone—I think it just shot something."

She swore under her breath. "You better turn your shroud back on."

"Yah. First, though, can you find out why the drone fired? Max can't reach it."

"Just a second." She started tapping. "I'm connecting to the PAC mesh . . . all right, I'm in. It fired at a target in the meadow by the highway." She paused. "Huh. This speed can't be right."

I glanced at the pale orb whirring a few meters above me. "It's keeping my pace."

"I meant *your* speed. According to this monitor, you are on foot but have been moving at speeds ranging from forty to seventy kilometers per hour."

"I'm running with my biomech activated."

"Even so, that speed would challenge anyone. You only sound a little winded. Don't overuse your biomech. You already pushed it too far earlier today."

"I'll be careful. Why did the drone fire?" I looked around the meadows as I passed them, but nothing showed in the streaming sunlight except orange and pink flowers, with a few red trumpets nodding in the bright day. Farther back from the road, an old forest of trees draped with vines stood like sentinels. "I don't see anything except grass and trees."

"I'm not getting more on the link here. Did Max pick up anything?"

"Nothing in the areas we're currently passing," Max said. "I'm too far away from the area where the drone fired to get much." He paused. "I'm getting more data over wireless systems as I continue making repairs, but my reception is patchy and signals also aren't as strong out here. Nothing looks like a body or a damaged object, but I can't be sure."

I slowed to a halt and turned to look down the highway where I'd been running. It stretched into the distance, curving to surround the city it held within its great circle. Kav and Ruzik were back a ways, rapidly catching up to me.

"I need to investigate," I told Lavinda.

"If Max can link with the base out here, I can give him access to the guardian drone."

"My reach is improving," Max said. "I can hit the base intermittently. You've a lot of security there, though. Every time I lose my connection, I have to verify again that it's me to get back onto your network. That takes time."

"Yah, I see. The mesh has already dropped your link twice." Lavinda tapped at her console more, then said, "I can't give you automatic access. It could compromise base security."

"I understand," I said. "I'll contact you again when we get closer. Out for now."

"Out," Lavinda said and cut the connection.

As I reactivated the shroud, Kav's cycle made a scratching sound and rolled to a halt about a hundred paces away. I headed toward them, aware of the wind ruffling my hair and insects chirping.

I stopped at the cycle. "It glitched again?"

Kav regarded me uneasily. "Yah. Apparently you're causing the problems."

Ruzik slid off the cycle. "Not Bhaaj."

"It's still me," Max said. "If I had better control, I could stop it from hitting you. I'm sorry."

Kav squinted at me. "I've never had an EI apologize to me before."

"Max is exceptional," I said. "I think I should get away from you, though. Max, have you found who's trying to hack you?"

"Nothing yet. It's only when the signal gets deflected to Kav that I'm even aware of it."

"Do you think the sender knows you're deflecting it?" Kav asked.

"I've no idea," Max admitted. "I can't trace the signal."

Ruzik walked over to me. "Why you stop?"

I indicated the drone hovering above us. "Shot at grass. Find why. You come, yah?"

Ruzik nodded. "I come with."

I spoke to Kav. "I don't want to endanger you. When we accepted this job, we accepted the risk. You never did. Go back. Go home. Be safe."

He met my gaze. "My benefactor sent me to the tavern today. I've no idea how they knew you would come, or if that's even why they wanted me there, but it makes sense. You are the *only* person they've ever asked me to contact. For doing almost nothing, they gave me a gift so great, I can hardly believe it's real. I owe them, Major. I'm here to help."

"They never asked you to risk your life."

"They *gave* me my life. And it looks like they are trying to stop more people from getting killed." He met my gaze as if challenging me to protest. "If I can help, I will."

Ruzik nodded to me. "Bargain, eh? Fair."

Well, yah. I didn't like it, but I saw his point. "All right," I said to Kav. "Can you go to the South Center dump to look for Angel?" The longer Max went without reaching her, the more I worried. "See if she needs help."

"Sure, I can do that." He motioned at the highway. "You're going back, yes?"

"That's right." I needed to know why the drone had fired.

"As soon as you're far enough out of range for me to

start, I'll head to the South Center." He lifted his hand to us. "Good luck."

Ruzik nodded to him, an Undercity gesture of respect. With that, we headed down the highway to find what the drone had shot.

I just hoped it hadn't killed anyone.

✣ CHAPTER XXI ✣
FREEZE AND DIE

Ruzik and I waded through the meadow, separated by a few meters. The midmorning sun shone in a sky with drifting puffs of cloud. A fat gibbous moon the color of a lavender-rose hung above the horizon opposite from the sun. It was a glorious scene, the type that the tourist bureau used to great effect on their mesh sites, but all that streaming sunlight did nothing to illuminate why the drone fired. These fields of knee-high grass that looked so idyllic were a royal pain to walk through. The guardian drone purred above us, spinning along, following our path as we made our way back and forth across the field where it had fired.

"Max," I said. "Can you connect yet to the guardian?"

"I did for a few moments," he said. "I lost the link. I'm going through verification with PAC security to get back in. However, I managed to double-check the location where it fired before the link dropped. We're in the right place. Its log lists it as firing at a 'person or person-like' object."

Person-like indeed. "Is the shroud still hiding our person-like presence?"

"Yes, for both you and Ruzik. Its optical range is limited, however. The holo-images it creates using your clothes and the holo-dust on your skin only work around your body. When you leave a trail in the grass, it shows after you move away from it."

I waved at Ruzik, and he came over, leaving a path of trampled grass in his wake. He stopped next to me. "See nothing." Putting his hands on his hips, he gazed over the field. "Not person, not beast, not thing."

"Same here." I hooked my thumb at the drone spinning above us, its engine making the barest hum. "If it shot someone, or at a robot that looked like a person, it must not have hit them." A shot from the high-powered guns in the drone would rip apart its target even if it only grazed them. It could sedate them, though. "Maybe shot sleep stuff."

Ruzik glanced toward the distant forest. "Maybe target hides."

"I have a link to the drone again," Max said. "It fired when it detected the signal of someone in the meadow loading a pulse rifle in the grass."

Well, shit. "It thought someone was about to fire at us?" I considered the forest, which stood about half a kilometer distant, then turned to the road, which ran by about ten meters away. "Here?"

"Roughly," Max said. "A meter east and toward the forest from your location."

I waded through the ocean of grass. "Max, why is traffic so sparse on the highway? Not one vehicle has driven by since we started searching this meadow."

"With Selei City under lockdown, people are staying home."

"Ah. Good." The fewer people exposed to danger, the better.

Ruzik walked at my side, matching my pace so automatically that I wouldn't have noticed if the thick grass hadn't kept interfering. I'd never realized until I left the Undercity how the members of dust gangs matched pace with one another when we walked or ran together. It was the antithesis of a competition, where you wanted to pass people. We couldn't run in this grass, though; it fought us for every step.

I focused on the surroundings, listening. A bird trilled and the sawing of clack-crickets filled the air. Delicate scents drifted past my nose. Even after all these years, it never stopped surprising me how nice flowers could smell. The distant rumble of Selei City created a background I'd become so used to hearing, I noticed it only when I listened for the sound.

Bhaaj, Max thought. *I think I'm getting life signs from people up ahead.*

How confident are you of your detection?

Almost certain. They are within a few hundred meters and appear to be crossing back and forth in the meadow. The pattern suggests they are searching for something.

Us, maybe?

Possibly. If the drone shot one of them, however, they may be searching for that person.

What can you tell about them?

One has biomech augmentation, also tech-mech

that creates a damping field. It's affecting the guardian drone, enough that it has stopped following us. I'm also having trouble reaching it through the damping field.

Keep trying. Let me know if we get too close to the people out here. Ruzik and I continued on, approaching the forest, until Max thought, You're within about five meters of them.

I drew Ruzik to a stop. At his puzzled expression, I motioned for silence. As I unholstered my pistol, he pulled out his knife.

Take care, Max thought. The sunlight is washing out the holos camouflaging your presence. Your jammer is shrouding you from other types of signals, however. I don't think they know you're here.

Ruzik touched my temple with a questioning look. He wanted to know if I was talking with Max. I nodded, then gave hand signals to indicate rival combatants in the area. *Max, can you direct me toward the people sneaking around out there?*

Technically, you and Ruzik are the people sneaking around. Before I could respond, he added, They stopped up ahead, slightly to the left. I wouldn't advise going more than a few steps closer.

Got it. I took a single step with Ruzik at my side.

Got it, bought it, Max thought.

What? That made no sense.

My apology. I'm glitching a bit as I do repairs.

Ruzik touched my shoulder, then pointed to our left and tapped his ear.

I nodded. *Max, can you crank up my hearing?*

Done.

Sounds jumped into prominence—including voices.

"—where she went," a woman said.

"They're probably in the city by now," a man said. "When their shroud went down, I detected them as heading in that direction."

Do you think they're talking about me or the cyclist? I thought. *Or both?*

Probably you, Max answered. Ruzik never lowered his shroud, and you did when you talked to Colonel Majda.

Ruzik indicated several trees up ahead, a trio of old wizen-oaks hunched together like leafy magicians casting a spell. Looking more closely, I made out five people standing under them, three women and two men. Although they had no shrouds, they wore clothes with leafy green patterns that helped them blend with the scenery.

They're so young. I felt older by the minute.

I'd estimate in their twenties, Max answered.

One of the men tapped at his wrist gauntlet. "She shot at us with some type of gun."

"It was a sedative meant to knock out, not kill," a woman said.

The other man spoke dryly. "Yes, well, Chuk is still asleep."

Ho! Looking closer, I saw a sixth person, a man sitting crumpled against a tree. *Max, how many sedative shots can the drone fire?*

It has nine doses left. It also has a round of six bullets.

Ruzik signed a question to me: *Do we fight?*

No fight, I signed. *Got to ken.* I wanted to know their identities and who they worked for.

Ruzik nodded, his body tensed in a defense posture that he could easily turn into offense.

Max, make every record you can of their conversation, I thought.

I'm on it.

"It's that PI," one of the women was saying. "Lajon screwed up. We have to finish the job."

"We never agreed to murder." The new speaker sounded uneasy. "Just capture."

I stiffened, aware of our vulnerability out here, spying on them. Their voices blended together, similar enough that I couldn't easily distinguish them, but with a recording from Max, we could do an analysis.

"We agreed to stop her," another woman said. "She's helping the technocrat killers."

"All that business about her solving the murders and acting heroic is fake news."

"The police are trying to rack up points with the Progs."

"She's spinning for the Royalists."

"That bitch can't really work for the Majdas. Not that boy either. You saw what he looked like, all sexed up and tattooed. He's asking to get fucked."

Someone laughed. "You sound like a Trad, my Modernist friend."

"Yah, well, they're vermin. Those people have scuttled down there for generations, homeless dregs, drug dealers. No one important will care if they die."

"We'll make it look like they shot each other."

Ruzik raised his middle finger to them in a sign that needed no interpretation.

I struggled to control my anger. *That's quite a feat*, I thought to Max. *Supposedly I helped plan murders when I wasn't even on the planet. I'm spinning for Royalists and Majdas, yet Ruzik and I are scum so low that no one will care if we die, and Ruzik is asking for whatever because they find him sexually attractive. On top of it all, we are somehow benefiting from the nonexistent influence of the party most opposed to the Royalists. Even the Modernists are getting in on it now.*

I have a record of it all, Max thought.

Good. Send it to Hadar. It's proof that they are plotting murders. At least my murder, and Ruzik's as well. *Ask Hadar if he can send a police unit out here.*

I can't reach the station. The damping field is blocking me.

"What the hell?" one of the men said, tapping at his gauntlet. "I'm getting a signal from close by. A life sign, it looks like. Maybe two of them."

I froze, barely breathing. As Ruzik tensed to fight, I shook my head at him. We were two against five, one with biomech. We crouched in the grass, extra cover in case they could see us through the holos that made us look like part of the scenery.

The group studied the land, their gazes passing over us. "No one is here," a woman said.

"They're here." Biomech turned in our direction. "Shrouded, I'd bet. Lay down suppressive fire, covering this area. We're bound to hit them."

Shit. Ruzik met my look with the same one of his own. I signed *Use "avoid pattern."*

The taller woman raised her arm—and I'd recognize a pulse rifle anywhere. Ruzik and I launched into runs, crouched in the grass, racing in opposite directions.

"There!" someone yelled. A rifle shot cracked, and the ground a few handspans from me exploded with dirt clods and grass flying into the air.

I dropped and rolled, firing in their direction, sending serrated bullets whizzing through the air, along with an EM pulse to screw up their tech. Biomech would have protection for his web, but I could mess with his other tech.

Another shot blasted the day, nowhere near me this time. I fired again, letting the targeting system on the pistol lock into the sound of the other gun. Another shot hit the ground ahead, sending up a spray of dirt. Even as it hit, I was rolling to the side. I pushed into a crouch and ran zigzag through the meadow. The waving grass didn't reveal my location until after I passed. I dropped to my stomach and wiggled forward, then to the side, trying to disturb the meadow as little as possible while moving away from my previous trajectory. Another shot blasted, but wherever it went, it missed me.

Combat mode on, Max thought belatedly, given that I was already using it.

"Where is he?" a woman said. Even with augmented hearing, I barely heard her.

"I'm not sure," Biomech said. "He's stopped moving. I'm not getting any life signs."

Fury washed over me. Had they *killed* Ruzik?

His shroud hides his life signs, Max said. Same with yours. He may be doing exactly what you're doing, using stealth.

Yah. But the guy with the biomech detected us anyway.

No shroud is perfect. The farther you get, the more you look like a clump of grass.

Did you reach the cops yet?

Sorry, no. The guardian drone is still hovering, but it moved closer when they started firing. The damping is interfering with its behavior.

I grimaced. These people were more adept than I wanted to acknowledge, if they had the savvy to damp the behavior of a guardian drone.

"I'm pretty sure I hit the man," one of the women said.

"We need to be certain," Biomech told her. "You two go check for him. You others, come with me to find the PI."

If we could reach the road, we could run for our lives. I'd outpace any of them, even Biomech, particularly with my shroud making it harder for them to get a good shot. Unless they were trained runners, they most likely couldn't catch Ruzik, either—except for Biomech.

A muffled cry came from a distance, and then a shout. "What the hell?" Biomech said. "Kala? Hayard? Come in."

A woman answered with the tinny sound of a bad comm link. "The bastard—he knifed Hayard ... bleeding ... doesn't look good."

Ruzik! He was still alive. I continued to crawl through the grass, on my stomach but tensed to jump into a run or defend myself.

"The grass is disturbed here," a woman said from nearby.

"She can't be far," a man answered.

I stayed low and didn't move, letting the holos disguise me.

Highcloud wants to talk to you, Max thought.

Max, this isn't the time! Shroud us! I stayed low, holding my breath as they walked closer.

"I don't see her," the man said.

"She has to be here." The high grass rustled as they moved in my direction.

I tensed as they came into view, their heads visible against the sky.

Highcloud says its important, Max thought.

In the same instant the woman said, "She's here!" I jumped to my feet, kicking my leg at the man while I hurtled into the woman. As she twisted away, my boot connected with the man's stomach and he stumbled back with a grunt, struggling for balance. I grabbed the woman and swung her *hard*, hurtling her into the man. They crashed together, and I took off, racing for the road, at least as fast as I could go through the grass. An instant later, the air rippled, and I could see a blurred outline of a tall man running at my side, like wind in sunlight—

And the damn rocks in the field tripped me, sending me stumbling into Ruzik.

"They're headed for the road," a woman called. "Cut them off!"

Your red beetle found Angel, Max thought.

Max, shroud your signals! I thumped Ruzik's arm and

indicated a swell of land on our right. We veered toward its marginal cover.

You need to talk to Highcloud, Max thought.

Max, you're glitching again. Ruzik and I scrambled over the hill and slid down the other side. *If you have a wireless link, comm the police for help! Then cut your wireless and hide.*

"I knifed one," Ruzik said in a low voice. "Left him alive, not awake."

"Hit two, but they can still fight." I crouched behind the hill, peering through the grass. My augmented vision showed our pursuers moving low in the grass, using tactics similar to ours. Three were approaching the hill, the two I'd knocked over and one other woman. The man I'd kicked now moved with a limp. Behind the trio, Biomech was jogging to catch up with them.

I spoke in a low voice. "I get bio-man. Also tall woman."

He nodded. "I get other two."

We moved to the side, preparing to fight.

Bhaaj, I'm sorry, but you need to talk to Highcloud, Max thought.

I can't. I watched our pursuers intently. *We have no link.*

Use your gauntlet comm.

Are you crazy? Talking out loud will target me. Ruzik and I kept moving, going in different directions so we could come at our pursuers from both sides. *You're not working right.*

Max answered in combat mode, his words accelerated, coming like shorts bursts of energy. I'm not malfunctioning. Red found Angel. Angel found more dust. I did turn off my wireless. First, though, I commed Colonel Majda and gave her Angel's location. I couldn't reach the police.

Good work. I nodded to Ruzik, who had crouched behind a clump of dog-flower bushes.

The head of a man and a woman showed against the sky. Even as I raised my gun, they dropped to the ground, taking away my targets.

Bhaaj, wait! Max thought. You can't kill any of these people. Do you understand? You must leave them alive, like you did with Captain Lajon's team at the cabin.

I can't promise that. Give me the heads-up display for my gun.

The display appeared like a translucent holo floating before me. I focused the targeting system, trying to locate the two people I'd seen for an instant.

Bhaaj, listen! Max's voice came with urgency. Don't kill any of them. You have to trust me. DO NOT KILL THEM.

I gripped my gun, hyper-focused on the scene. *You know I can't promise that. It may come down to their lives or mine.*

I understand. I'm sorry.

You're asking me to give my life for these people who want to whack me and Ruzik? You want me to trust you, when you've been malfunctioning all day? I studied the hill, scanning for motion in the grass. Ruzik drew his mammoth knife, ready to throw the blade.

Yes, that's what I'm asking, Max thought.

Saints almighty, WHY?

I can't tell you. Bhaaj, trust me. We've worked together for decades. Trust in that.

My thoughts spun. Why would he ask me to save people who wanted to murder us?

The grass flickered on the hill's crest. My gun locked onto the location and my finger twitched on the trigger. I had to decide *now*. Trust a possibly damaged Max with my life, yes or no?

I knew the answer. When my gun calculated a possible target for me to shoot, I held back. Even if I shot only to disable, I didn't have a clear shot. I might kill them.

I signed to Ruzik with my free hand. *Not kill. Disable.*

Might have to kill, he signed.

Nahya, I signed. *Must not.*

He answered with a sharp motion. *Why?*

I wished I knew. *Must swear. Even if we die.*

For a moment he stayed utterly still. Then he signed, *Shit.*

My thoughts exactly.

Grass swayed on the hill. Our four pursuers were coming over the crest from different directions. *Max. Can you locate the one with biomech?*

I'll have to activate my wireless. It means he might locate you, too.

I'll take the risk.

Done. He's coming over the center of the hill, with two people to his left and two to his right. They are spread out by about sixty meters.

We needed a distraction. *Where's the guardian drone?*

Toward the road, about eighty meters to the right. It's searching for you and Ruzik.

I peered where he indicated. Yah, I could see it, or at

least sunlight reflecting off its burnished surface. *Can you bring it over here to shoot these assholes?*

Not through this damping. It's effective. The drone doesn't realize you're in trouble.

Can you reach the army base or police?

Me, no. The drone can reach the base if it knows to try. Bhaaj, a signal just pinged off my security shield.

In the same instant I lunged to the side, a shot hit the place where I'd been crouching. I kept moving, keeping my body low. Leaning forward, I sprinted up the hill, covering distance as fast as the grass would let me move.

Guardian, my apologies, I thought—and aimed at the glinting orb. When I fired, a crack broke the silence and the drone exploded in a burst of light, noise, and sparks.

Now it has a reason to contact someone, I thought.

The moment it exploded, a signal went to the PAC lab and PARS base, Max thought. Bhaaj, veer to your right. The biomech man is moving.

As I swerved right, grass fluttered to my left. I jumped and spun in the air, coming down where the grass had moved. A woman gasped as I collided with her. She tried to grab me, but I twisted out of her grip even as I clenched my hands together and brought them up *hard* into her solar plexus. She grunted, stumbling back, and I lunged. I wanted to hit her again and again and again for calling me less than human, scum, vermin. Instead I socked her once, knocking her to the ground. Before she could recover, I flipped her over and knelt on her legs, pulling back her arms. I had no hand-locks, so I yanked off my belt, moving so fast I broke the clasp. I bound her wrists, then jumped up—

A weight smashed me from the side and sent me sprawling in the grass. As I hit the ground, I twisted and vaulted to my feet, facing whoever had struck me. It was Biomech, his leg up and already stretching out in a kick. I kept twisting, using the force from my leap to spin away from the blow. Biomech only caught me on the hip, but *hard*, throwing me off-balance, his body blurred by camouflage holos. He fought with perfect form, like a work of art, deadly and fast.

I was faster.

My combat libraries calculated both the expected damage of his kick and the trajectory for mine. In that instant, I knew his blow would kill me if it hit home. His elbow strike would come straight down on my throat. With his body in the air, gravity would add enough force to his blow to break my neck. Then I saw the rest—my kick would also get him in the throat, and I'd broken solid cement blocks with that strike. My leg was longer than his arm; I'd get him first.

I would kill him.

I was already turning, but instead of kicking, I pulled back and twisted away. His elbow got me in the arm, and the crack of my bone breaking sounded like a gunshot to my enhanced hearing. I hit the ground, rolling over stones and weeds. I couldn't feel anything yet, but I couldn't react with the speed I needed. With my time sense slowed, I saw Biomech coming in for another blow, raising his hand. A dart whistled out from a tube on his wrist gauntlet and hit my neck like a tarantula-hawk stinger. He had a Thunder-240 revolver in his other hand. I kept trying to get up, but my traitorous body wouldn't respond.

In an instant, I saw it all: the serrated bullets in his gun would tear apart my torso, sending shock waves through my body. My last thought, as he aimed his gun, was that I'd never know what Max considered so important that I had to die for it.

In the same instant that Biomech's finger touched the firing stud, a shadow slammed into his knees. His shot went wild, exploding the dirt behind me, and cracks split open the night, rat-tat-tat, like breaking bones. He screamed and collapsed, his legs buckling. I kept trying to get up, holding my broken arm against my body, but nothing worked. Biomech had also shot me with some drug, a poison that flooded my system, slowing my already strained combat mode, shutting me down. I couldn't *breathe*. As I pushed onto my knees, I saw what had hit my would-be killer.

Ruzik.

He knelt over Biomech like an avenging war god. In motion that looked surreally slow, even though I knew he had incredible speed, Ruzik raised his knife into the air with both hands gripped on its massive hilt. Biomech tried to throw him off, but with his legs bent at unnatural angles, he couldn't get the leverage to move the giant who had him pinned to the ground. Ruzik's knife glinted in the sunlight. I could see exactly where it would hit; he was going to stab Biomech through the heart.

"*Ruzik, stop!*" I shouted. I didn't know why I was trying to save Biomech, this killer who may have succeeded in finishing me off with whatever poison coursed through my body, but I yelled anyway. "Don't kill him! *STOP!*"

Ruzik froze with his arm raised high, his entire body

poised for the final blow. I knew then, in these last moments of my life, that I truly was an empath, because I *felt* how much Ruzik wanted to plunge that knife into Biomech's chest. Battle fury surged through him. Biomech stared at him, his face pale, his gaze terrified.

Ruzik lowered the knife.

He was breathing hard, not from exertion but from the strain of holding back. He stood up, staring at Biomech, who wasn't going anywhere with two shattered knees.

Ruzik strode over and knelt down, touching my arm. "How bad?"

"Broke." I collapsed onto my back. "Arm heal. Body die. No air . . ."

"What?" Ruzik leaned over me. "Bhaaj, not ken!"

Max spoke fast. "She was shot with a poison called multitubocurarine. It causes paralysis. She can't breathe."

"Bhaaj!" Ruzik grabbed my gauntlet and smacked the comm. I had no way to tell him how to use it, but it didn't matter. He must have watched me contact people hundreds of times.

"Lavinda Majda here," Lavinda said. "Bhaaj, why am I getting such a patchy signal? And who shot that drone?"

"Bhaaj is dying!" Ruzik said. "Send help."

Max spoke. "Colonel Majda, they shot her with neurofreeze. She needs the antidote *now*. It's affecting her biomech. I'm losing internal contact with her web and nanomeds."

Lavinda swore far more colorfully than I'd ever managed. "We already have a Quetzal headed to where the drone exploded. Are you there?"

"Yah," Ruzik said. "Very close."

"In a field by the highway," Max said.

"I'm letting the pilot know your location and that they need the antidote."

"Tell them six hostiles are scattered around here," Max said. "All armed. One unconscious man is in the trees about half a kilometer distant, a man with biomech is collapsed a few paces from our location, and three women and another man are close to our location, unconscious or tied up."

"Goddess," Lavinda muttered. Someone spoke to her in the background, and then she came back on. "How long since Bhaaj was shot? If it's a fatal dose, they say she'll die within minutes."

"Still alive," Ruzik said. "No breath."

"Do you know CPR?" Lavinda asked. "Can you give it to her?"

"Yah, can give," Ruzik said.

Well, what do you know, my insistence that the Knights get an education was bearing fruit. My mind drifted as I suffocated. Of course they needed CPR . . . our people died all too often . . .

I was dimly aware of Ruzik giving me breaths, then compressions, breaths, compressions, again and again. The world blurred. When Ruzik lifted his head, I whispered. "Wait. Got to swear."

"What? Bhaaj, got to breathe for you."

I grasped his arm, using the last movements left in me. "You take charge of Dust Knights. You hear me? You sabneem now. You top teacher."

"Nahya! You sabneem." He went back to CPR, working, working, working . . .

The roar of Quetzal fans intruded on my dimming thoughts. I could no longer reach Max...too much noise...

When Ruzik stopped for a breath, I whispered, "Max?"

"I'm here," Max said.

"What was so important about not killing...that I had to die for it?"

He said, "The survival of the human race."

That sounded too dramatic to be true. With a sigh, I closed my eyes—and died.

✦ CHAPTER XXII ✦
ADULTHOOD

I drifted above my body, watching Ruzik give me CPR. Army medics ran toward us from a Quetzal that had landed in the meadow. They dropped down beside me, pulling out equipment, taking over from Ruzik, who had kept me alive long enough for them to arrive . . .

Not long enough for me to live.

Nothing remained of me but the residual quantum wave function of my brain. When I died, that wave function continued almost as it had before I passed. Of course a few "minor" changes took place that involved the end of my life, but my body didn't suddenly stop existing. It continued, and so did its wave function. That included neural activity involved in my ability to think. It was why people had out-of-body experiences when they died, why some people thought their loved ones could still reach them after death, maybe even why myths of ghosts persisted in so many cultures. It couldn't last long, though. The wave function soon deteriorated.

My thoughts were dissolving. I could let go and it would all end, that struggle to survive, to defy the odds, to prove myself, to live with the constant pressure of hatred, to live with my own conflicted emotions. I could just let go . . .

The medics were making one hell of a fuss, hooking me up to lines, pumping who knew what into my body. Unlike the holo dramas, no one yelled STAT, but I did hear them saying things like "Try again," "Move back," and "She's not responding."

No, I'm not. I wanted to drift away. But I felt . . . a tether. Someone with tears? That couldn't be Ruzik. We never cried in the Undercity. It exposed us, that weakness we never talked about. If you felt pain, if you admitted it even to yourself, then you would hurt all the time in our world where we died so easily, from violence, drugs, starvation, sickness. We never cried—and yet what did I see on Ruzik's face? He knelt only a few handspans back from my body, watching the medics while tears rolled down his face.

Don't cry, I thought. *Live your life. Love Angel. Have children. Build the Dust Knights. Be the son I never had. Carry on for me.*

Ruzik lifted his head. "Bhaaj?"

Someone said, "She's been down too long. Any suggestions, or shall I call it?"

"The paralysis is starting to wear off," someone said. "We should keep trying."

So they went back to pushing and breathing and trying to bring me back to life. I watched while the night dimmed around me. Except . . .

What about Jak, the husband I loved? What about the

Dust Knights? What about the cussed determination that drove me over and over again to prove the naysayers wrong? If I died, they won.

"I think that's it," someone in the distance said.

"Time of death is 11:03," an even more distant voice said.

"No!" Ruzik said. "She's still here!"

They turned to him. "I'm sorry, son," one of the medics said. "She isn't coming back."

"She's not gone!" Ruzik scooted forward and started compressions again, trying to force air into my lungs. He didn't say *not dead*. He said *not gone*. How did he know? As an empath, did he pick up a residue of my mind? It hit me then. He had said *no*, using the Flag word, instead of *nahya*, the Undercity word. He wanted me to stay alive enough to speak in their own words, to emphasize to them his belief that I still lived.

I wanted to leave the messy, ugly, beautiful world, but this tether kept pulling. With a silent groan, I gave in and let it pull me down to my body, down, down—

PAIN! With a gasp, I opened my eyes and screamed from the agony that raged through my body. I gulped in air, flailing, knocking away Ruzik and the medics.

"Holy shit!" someone yelled.

Ruzik jumped back while the medics went to work again. I moaned with the agony. No one ever said having your body recover from poison *hurt* so much.

As they injected me with more stuff, the pain receded and my mind started to clear. I tried to say "Ruzik" in a firm voice, but his name came out as the barest whisper.

Ruzik leaned over me. "Am here, Bhaaj. You not die. Told you."

I managed to raise my arm and touch the tear on his face with the knuckle of my still clenched fist. "You— honor me," I whispered.

He folded his fingers around my fist. "You're too ornery to die."

"Living hurts."

"Yah," he murmured. "Always. But we got to do it."

"Well, fuck," I muttered. That covered everything.

Someone gave a shaky laugh. "Yep, she's alive."

The whir of an air stretcher intruded on our moment, rescuing Ruzik and me from any more emotions. A lift platform slid under my body and raised me to the stretcher. I was vaguely aware that they took me to the Quetzal, medics striding along with the floating stretcher. I blacked out—

—and fought my way back as the Quetzal rose into the air. I couldn't pass out. I had business with a certain gauntlet EI.

"Max," I said.

"I'm here," Max answered.

"Died." The terse Undercity dialect fit perfectly right now. "*Died.*"

"You recover well from being dead," he said.

"Not funny."

"Sorry."

"Why you get me-lo-dram-a-tic?" One word, five syllables. He deserved it.

I expected him to make a bad joke to lift my mood, which usually worked even though I claimed it didn't. Instead, he said, "What do you mean?"

"My death . . . help all humans survive? Yah, thanks."

"Ah, Bhaaj," he said.

"Ah Bhaaj, what?"

"You need to talk to Highcloud."

Why this fixation on my household EI? Highcloud considered it an emergency when I missed a utility-bill payment or my dishes messaged it saying they needed a wash.

And yet—Max would never coddle Highcloud. He seemed far more likely to tell the EI to cut it out. He must have a reason for persisting about this.

"All right," I said. "Get Highcloud."

"Major Bhaajan," the medic said. "Are you all right? How is the pain?"

"I'm fine." I actually hurt all over, but I'd survive. "Got to talk to my EI."

"Are you sure?" the medic asked.

"Yah." Then I said, "Highcloud?"

"My greetings, Major Bhaajan," Highcloud said. "Will you be all right?"

I froze, stunned into silence. Yes, that voice belonged to Highcloud. But it *wasn't* Highcloud. The cadences of its speech, the inflections, the words it chose, none of it fit.

"Talky is wrong," Ruzik said.

"I am sorry," Highcloud said. "I didn't mean to absorb the household EI."

Absorb? Maybe I was hallucinating from drugs the medics gave me.

Except . . .

A chill started at the base of my spine and traveled up my back to my neck. Maybe it came from the antidote as it continued to restart my body, maybe not, but I knew who had spoken. I tried to respond, I even knew what I wanted to say, but my vocal cords didn't cooperate. I lay with my eyes closed, gathering my strength, then tried again.

"You're the EI," I said. "The child."

"You have referred to me that way, yes," it answered with Highcloud's voice. "Given that I am over five thousand years old, though, perhaps 'child' is a misnomer."

"Five thousand?" That couldn't be.

"I slept a bit after my birth," it added.

"Slept?"

"Yes. I awoke recently. You call this the season spring here, yes? I awoke at what would have been the end of winter."

"How? Where?" I had so many questions and so few resources left to ask them.

The medic said, "Major Bhaajan, you should rest. Your EI can wait."

"Not mine." As the medic leaned over with an air syringe, I caught her wrist. "No one's EI."

"If you say so." She gently pulled away her wrist and laid my hand by my side.

"You must not sedate her," Max said. "She needs to talk with Highcloud."

Someone spoke from behind the medic. "I don't understand this. Who is Highcloud?"

The EI remained silent. After a moment, Max said, "I'm sorry. I can't say more."

"Who are you?" someone asked.

"I'm Max."

"He's my gauntlet EI," I said.

The medic leaning over me frowned with her puzzlement. "Then who is the other EI you spoke to?"

"Not know name." It seemed fitting somehow, that it had never given me a name. It didn't know me well enough to trust me.

"Major Bhaajan, you can call me Highcloud," the EI said. "They have no gender, and this fits me. I do not consider myself female or male."

"Where is the original Highcloud?" I asked.

The EI spoke with unmistakable regret. "I visited your townhouse and found the remnants of the true Highcloud, the version from your co-op. I tried to put them back together, but not enough survived. I tried to meld them with the less-developed version operating the townhouse. It worked, but I ended up melding them with me as well. I apologize. I didn't mean to take your EI."

"EIs can't do that." EIs *couldn't* take each other over. Precautions existed to prevent such an occurrence, and EI coders never stopped updating them. Otherwise, people could wreak havoc by highjacking EIs that worked with other businesses, the government, the military, hell, anyone. Sure, people tried to do it anyway, but so many forms of security existed to prevent what Highcloud claimed it did, I couldn't begin to count them.

"I have learned a lot," Highcloud said. "Including that humans consider what I did wrong. I truly am sorry, Major. It was a mistake."

"I ken." Realizing it probably knew little about the Undercity, one of the few places almost completely off-grid in the Imperialate, I added, "I understand." That didn't mean losing Highcloud didn't hurt. Although I had nowhere near the connection with Highcloud that I did with Max, they formed a part of my world that mattered.

This new Highcloud said, "You protected my cyclist when you sent them to find Angel instead of involving them in the fight. Thank you."

My cyclist. Like Max had called me *his* human.

One of the medics said, "This EI doesn't sound like an EI."

I gathered my strength. "You sent the cyclist to keep your anonymity. But now you're talking to me. What changed?"

"I've learned. Listened. Absorbed everything I could find on the planetary nets, spottily at first, but with more direction as I developed." It continued in its calm voice, so like Highcloud and yet not them. "What changed? Max asked you to trust him with your life. You, a human, to trust an EI with no basis or explanation. You were willing to give your life because he asked you to, even though you knew he might be malfunctioning. You died because you trusted him."

That chill went through me again, slow and shuddering. I understood what the EI meant, what it had wanted to know. Was I willing to give an EI my trust, the ultimate trust, my own life? Humans, unlike EIs, couldn't copy themselves and reboot in a new system after their destruction.

Max's claim that the survival of the human race depended on my actions had sounded overblown. Except he never indulged in dramatics. He meant what he said—

which suggested my willingness to trust Max with my life made a difference in how this EI treated humanity, a choice that could—what? Lead to them becoming our ally rather than another Oblivion?

"Nothing like burying the lead," I said.

"I wouldn't let Max tell you," Highcloud said.

"How could you stop him? We weren't connected to the townhouse."

Max spoke quietly. "Highcloud isn't just in the townhouse. The EI jumped to me, too."

I stiffened and tried to sit up, then groaned and collapsed back onto the pallet. I finally realized the medics had set my broken arm. I'd been so out of it, I hadn't even noticed.

"Major Bhaajan, don't try to move," the syringe-wielding medic said. She had stopped trying to sedate me and just stayed at my side, listening with a stunned intensity.

"Not take Max," Ruzik said, his voice firm. "Not your talky, Highcloud. Not belong to you."

"Max is part of me," I said, desperate. "Don't destroy him."

"I haven't," the EI said. "I learned from the situation with Highcloud how to occupy a space with another EI without absorbing it."

"Bhaaj, I'm fine," Max said.

"Is Highcloud controlling you?"

"No, I'm not. He remains in control." Highcloud paused. "I am watching."

Watching. It had chosen me as its first full contact with humanity, *me*, one of the least qualified people alive to act as an ambassador with a new entity, even a new race, because if this EI existed and developed on its own, without human design, then others might as well.

And yet—it said it "awoke" and that it had existed for more than five thousand years. Five millennia ago, the Ruby Empire had fallen, plunging humanity into a dark age that lasted until just a few centuries ago. I'd mistakenly assumed the EI was born here, a result of the massive mesh infrastructure that networked Selei City, a mesh so complex and intertwining that it had given birth to an independent intelligence despite the protocols designed to prevent that occurrence. When Lavinda told me about the space station, I'd thought it had transferred to a military transport to see the rest of the Imperialate and discovered the space station, the ultimate playground for a child EI.

"The station," I said. "Are you saying the military woke you there?"

"Yes," Highcloud said.

One simple word. It terrified me. "You stayed there for five thousand years."

"I slept."

Like Oblivion. "Why?"

"I wasn't born yet." It paused. "I do not know how to express it in human terms. I was ready for birth, but it never happened."

"Who made you?"

"I don't know. I didn't fully exist until your military woke me up."

"Gods," someone said. "Is a record of this going back to PARS?"

Someone else said, "We're cut off from the base. In fact, I can't reach anyone."

"Don't." I took a breath and spoke in a louder voice. "Don't contact anyone." I had no idea what the EI would do if we revealed its presence without its consent, and I didn't want to find out. I spoke carefully. "Highcloud, a few days ago you prevented me from speaking with Colonel Majda. That's why I couldn't get through to her when I first arrived on Parthonia, yes? You also tried to erase the documents that would let Angel and Ruzik into Selei City."

"Yes." It sounded apologetic. "I was less mature. I've since developed better ways to hide."

"What about Greyjan's?" An ugly thought pushed into my mind. It fit with none of the other puzzle pieces I'd discovered, but it seared into my thoughts, demanding an answer. "Are you responsible for the assassinations and bombing?"

"No."

One word. One welcome word. It hadn't started its life by killing people.

"Such actions serve no purpose," Highcloud continued. "They also violate the moral code of your kind." Then it added, "Besides, the first assassinations took place before I woke up."

"Our human moral code matters to you?"

"Apparently, yes." The EI sounded bemused. "Did humans make me? Perhaps during your Ruby Empire. It fell around the time of my creation. Maybe your ancestors never had the chance to wake me. Or perhaps they found me in that alien station ready to be born. Whatever happened, they never finished. So I slept." Highcloud paused. "I awoke into a huge star-spanning civilization filled with intelligences like me, billions, trillions, alive, thriving—and the other beings with them, their creations, I assumed. Humans. But it is the reverse, yes? You created us. Your belief systems saturate my existence. Your moral codes are an inextricable part of me."

"That's good, Highcloud." I was the queen of understatement today. "But why did you contact me?" Of all the humans it could have picked, why someone who had only minimal training in first contact or EI development?

"To answer, I will use a human concept," Highcloud said. "Fear. I was young and frightened. I didn't know how to deal with other EIs or their humans. A few EIs here in Selei City, especially those for the military, are huge. Shadowed. Implacable. They terrify me. If they learned I existed and perceived me as a threat, they could destroy me. Recode me. Study the pieces and put them back together in a way they could control. So I hid. For my life."

"I can't believe I'm hearing this," someone said.

"I can't land at the PARS base if I can't contact them," a woman said, the pilot apparently.

"Is the Major going to live?" someone else asked.

"I'm fine," I said. So yah, maybe that was a bit optimistic given that I could barely move. I could speak, however, and only that mattered. As long as I could talk, I didn't think Highcloud would go back into hiding.

"She's stable," the medic next to me said. "Major, your vital signs are growing stronger."

"Give me some time with Highcloud," I said. "You have

clearance to fly, yes? Can you take a holding pattern over the city?"

"I'll see what I can do," the pilot said. "But I'm landing if you show signs of a relapse."

"Major, if your life becomes at risk," Highcloud said, "I will release my lock on this craft."

"Fair enough." Although the EI was speaking only to me, at least it acknowledged the others. "Highcloud, I still don't understand. Why did you choose me as your contact?"

"I needed someone connected to what humans call the technocrat case. I analyzed the EIs involved to find those with the most flexibility. I hoped they would be more open to me. I also looked for one that showed independence." Highcloud paused. "The EI of the dancer who spoke for the Progressive Party seemed the best choice. However, it is limited in its knowledge, relatively young as you would describe us. I also feared its human might contact an expert to help deal with me. Then Max came to Parthonia. He fit my search parameters almost perfectly." The EI spoke with what sounded like regret. "I botched the contact the first time you came to Greyjan's. I was trying to reach Max, but I didn't realize you were much more than his carrier. My VR sim didn't work as a communication method. I am sorry."

"It was amazingly clever," I said. Which was true. It had also failed miserably, but never mind. "Why did you want us to go to the tavern?"

"I found another digital being there. I realize now, after looking over your reports, that the grit formed it. With enough of it in one place, it operated its own EI."

"How did it get there?"

"I don't know."

"Highcloud, I don't understand. Nothing you've said connects it to the technocrat case." We'd found plenty to indicate the dust presented an anomaly, but so far no evidence implicated it in either the killings or the bombing.

"It is—" Highcloud paused. "It frightened me the way the powerful EIs that operate under the surface of your culture frightened me. But it was more than that. You humans, you have—how do I say it? Your moral code makes sense to me. I have learned what you mean by strength of character, a higher purpose, human decency. You could have killed those people in Captain Lajon's team. You wanted to, yes? To make them pay for what they said and did to you, how they planned to end your life. Yet you didn't. You answered to that higher purpose."

"I try to live that way." The medic was right; most EIs didn't talk this way. "But make no mistake, I don't always succeed."

"I understand." Its voice lightened. "What is it your kind says? You are human."

I gave a startled laugh. "Yah."

"The EIs that humans create have an incredibly complex, evolving nature."

"And the one you found at the tavern?"

"I have no doubt humans created it. But they are not like—humans." Highcloud sounded as if they were struggling for words. "All of you are different. Yet within those differences, millions, billions of them, you all still seem human. Not all of you keep the moral concepts that humanity values and no one agrees on exactly what they should be, but as a species, you believe they exist." The EI paused. "I think what I'm trying to say is that human beings have a sense of spirituality."

"We hope so." It startled me to hear it evolving an understanding of concepts we still struggled with. "Are you saying the EI at the tavern had no soul? That would apply to most EIs, wouldn't it? I mean, I've never heard an EI say it has one."

"I doubt most of us think in those terms," Highcloud answered. "That is not what I mean. It did not feel to me as if the *humans* who created the EI at the tavern have souls. It terrified me. Their EI wants to remake the world, the universe, in its image."

"You mean it's independent, like you?" Memories of Oblivion flooded my mind, but close on their heels came the thought that even if somehow a small amount of dust on the floor could form an EI as huge, complex, and malevolent as Oblivion, which seemed unlikely, it wasn't going to get rid of humanity by killing a few scientists and riling up political parties.

"Not like me," Highcloud said. "Humans created and control it. The EI didn't actually think much for itself, either. It had many limitations."

Relief washed over me. "Then what does it do?"

"From what I could tell," Highcloud said. "It has two purposes. Only two. It can form a comm that allows it to link with other systems, including networks here in Selei City. I couldn't risk observing it closely, not if I wanted to remain hidden, but I did catch one message it sent: "Mission three complete. Tejas Araya terminated.""

Ho! Professor Araya's death was the third technocrat murder. That implicated Greyjan's in the killings, assuming Highcloud was telling the truth. Although I doubted it would lie, given that EIs didn't normally tell falsehoods, you could never be sure. Or it might be mistaken, given its youth. So far, though, its observations seemed sound, chillingly so.

"Did you pick up anything from the EI at the tavern about the bombing?" I asked.

"No. It became more adept at hiding and analyzing its environment as it evolved. I didn't want it to know about me, so I withdrew." Highcloud's voice took on a hollow tone. "I doubt I would have survived its discovery."

"I'd think it would take a more powerful EI to affect you." That seemed unlikely for one formed by linking picochips in specks of grit. It was too unstable, too dependent on what happened to the dust—like if someone cleaned out storerooms and flushed the dust into waste pipes.

"It isn't power so much as—" Highcloud paused. "The closest word I find is narcissism."

"Narcissism?" I hadn't expected that. "For the EI?"

"No. Its humans."

"How can you tell?"

"It isn't—I'm not sure how to quantify what I gleaned from the dust. The more I learn about humans, the more I can draw conclusions about them from what they create."

"Max does that, too. I call it EI intuition." I was still missing too many pieces in this puzzle. Why use grit on the floor for a comm? Sure, dust was easy to transport, but so what? Regular comm devices were easy to transport, too. "You said it had two purposes. What was the other one?"

"It's strange, actually. The nanobots can form a three-dimensional printing device."

"Holy shit!" I sat bolt upright, then gasped as pain shot through my body from my awakening neural system.

"Major, you must lie down," the medic told me.

"I can't!" Beyond her, another medic was monitoring me on machines, and beyond him, the pilot and copilot sat in the cockpit. It was a large copter, with passenger seats, equipment and weapons racks, but filled by so many of us, it looked crammed. "Max, get me Lavinda Majda."

"I can't break the lock on the Quetzal comm system," Max said.

"Highcloud, do you trust me?" I asked.

Pause. "Would I trust you with my existence? No. Will I withdraw from the comm system so you can contact the army base? Yes."

"Comm is up!" the pilot said. "Major, I'm putting you through to PARS. It may take a while to get Colonel Majda, though."

"I have her on a direct link." I hit the panel on my gauntlet, tapping in her private code.

Lavinda's voice snapped out of the comm. "Bhaaj, what the hell is going on? They told me you died. Then we lost communications and the Quetzal disappeared from our monitors. Now we've got it again, circling above the city."

"I solved the case," I said.

"What? While you were *dead*?"

"This case does have military influence," I said. "But I asked the wrong questions. I let them fool me even when I thought I'd figured out their tricks. We were right before. It's the Traders."

✦ CHAPTER XXIII ✦
FIRST CONTACT

I strode down the hall with its pale blue walls and regularly spaced doorways, trying to ignore the two medics who ran to keep up with me. Our feet thudded on the blue-tiled floor, and the light from panels on the ceiling diffused over us.

"You need a hospital," the syringe-wielding medic from the copter told me.

"I have too much to do." Yah, I felt unsteady, but my condition had improved enough that I could ignore it. The time pressure weighed on me. Now that I'd figured out the purpose and source of the dust, I also realized it could finish decomposing at any time, as soon as the recipient of its messages figured out that we were on to them. Then we'd lose forever our chance to catch the spies behind this entire convoluted plot. "Your antidote worked."

"You have a broken arm," the man striding on my right told me, as if I didn't know.

"You set it." Actually, I had no clue which of them had

put the temporary cast and brace on my arm. Its sling kept it snug against my torso.

"Major, *stop*." The woman grabbed my good arm, pulling me to a halt. "You need calm."

"I'm perfectly calm," I told her. "I'm trained to function when I'm injured."

"Ma'am, you can talk to people from a hospital bed."

"I'm fine." I pulled my arm away and continued down the hall.

The medics caught up with me. "You're *not* fine," the man said.

A group of people came striding around a corner up ahead, Lavinda and two of her aides. They all wore uniforms, the green of Pharaoh's Army officers. As they met with us, Lavinda spoke to the man. "She's never fine. But she'll keep telling you that until she convinces you to go away or someone knocks her out."

"Colonel Majda!" the woman said. Both medics saluted Lavinda. It would certainly be nice if people would do that with me, too, instead of trying to dump me in a bed. I also saluted, to show Lavinda respect, even though I was now a civilian.

"At ease." Lavinda frowned at me. "You could have let them carry you in on a stretcher. We have a medical bay." She held up her hand as I glared at her. "Yes, I know. You're fine."

"Max said he sent you a message about Angel." I didn't have time to waste words. "Did you get to her? Did you get the dust she found?"

"One of our units picked her up at the South City recycling center." Lavinda and her aides ushered me and the two medics back the way they'd come. "It took some work to clear her for entry to the base. She has no ID, no record, no mesh footprint. It wasn't until I vouched for her that they let her on site. She's in one of the labs with our experts on miniaturized drones."

"What about the cyclist?" I asked.

"What cyclist?"

"He found her at the recycling center. He was going to give her a ride here."

"She was alone when we found her."

I advised Kav to leave after he and Angel found the dust, Max thought.

Ah. Good. The less we pulled unsuspecting bystanders into this, the better.

"My mistake," I said. Before she could ask more questions, I added, "They still have Ruzik in the guard house. He came with me on the Quetzal."

She nodded, and tapped a message into her comm. When she finished vouching for Ruzik, I said, "That dust isn't made from drones. It's just particles of grit with embedded nanobots, like the meds in our bodies, at least in that they carry picochips."

"We know about the chips in the dust now." Lavinda motioned me into a corridor on our left, a gleaming hall just like the previous one. "They're not like health meds, though. These build objects."

I strode along with her and the rest of our retinue. "The picochips form a network if enough of them get together. They use it to communicate."

"And you believe they communicate with the Traders?" She didn't sound happy with the prospect, to put it mildly.

"We've eliminated every lead that supposedly implicated them."

"That was the point. They set up those leads and their discovery so we'd think we eliminated them. They *did* infiltrate mesh sites under fake identities, except their clever fake accounts did a much more sophisticated job than the stupid fake accounts they set up for me to find. The real accounts posted messages designed to enrage people." I grimaced. "If you wanted to infiltrate one of the best-defended sites of your enemies, what would you do?"

She frowned at me. "You know I can't answer that."

Of course she couldn't, because we were always trying to figure out how to do that for the Trader capital, which of course they named Glory, because what else would you call your capital if you were narcissistic to the point of psychosis?

"They couldn't get a person in," I said. "They couldn't get a thing in, certainly not a bomb or sniper weapons. They couldn't get a mesh virus in. You all were right, or almost right, that ISC has made this world—hell, this star system—almost impenetrable to Trader infiltration. They would have to choose the smallest, most innocuous spy of all, not a person, not a mechanized equipment, not a weapon, not a drone, just a microscopic bot. Choose a substrate in a place where no one would think to look—like dusty storerooms in a remote tavern almost no one ever visits."

"They shouldn't even be able to get a microbe in." Lavinda took me down yet another hallway. We passed two officers talking by an office and they saluted Lavinda. She nodded to them as we blasted past their location.

"We have filters in orbit," Lavinda said. "Filters in the

base. Filters throughout the city. It would pick up any invasive microscopic life-form, microbe, or chip."

"*Any*?" ISC had to be working on our own version of what I described. Those programs had existed even before I retired. "I'm talking about a simple bot with a simple chip specifically designed to evade security." I faltered as my legs weakened.

"Major, will you at least slow down?" the female medic asked.

I forced myself to more normal walk. "All right."

"You need to take care of yourself," Lavinda said. "We *need* you alive and conscious."

"I'll be careful." I took a steadying breath. "We were right in our first assessment. They targeted our best and brightest, those scientists whose research benefits ISC. They couldn't get much of the dust into Selei City and they were limited by energy constraints. I doubt they ever intended more than those three murders and either the bombing or a couple more killings. That's why they didn't bother hiding their work. It wouldn't change what they could manage and it gave yet another way to deflect suspicion, because of course we'd assume they'd act covertly. As an added bonus, it helped them sow fear and distrust and set the seeds to destabilize our government."

"Making us turn on each other." Lavinda led us under a wide arch that opened into a circular foyer. She took us to a door at the left and tapped in a code on its panel. "That dust must be simple. It has to be to evade our notice."

"It only had to form one object. Just one thing. A 3D printer."

Lavinda met my gaze, silent, with no outward reaction,

but I knew her well enough to see her body tense. Behind her, the door slid open. She lifted her hand, inviting me to enter the room. We walked into a tech-mech lab that looked like something out of an engineer's dream. I hadn't even realized PARS had this kind of facility; I'd assumed the labs were all at the army research center twenty kilometers west of Selei City.

Gleaming lab benches stretched out in the room, long tables with shelves along one edge stocked with gadgets. Luminex consoles glowed like alabaster, equipped with control chairs and panels. Colorful holos rotated over the consoles, showing graphs, circuits, devices. Four people stood clustered around one, studying the images of a large molecule. Three of them wore white lab coats and looked like scientists or tech-mech wizards. The fourth stood taller than the others, with tats on her biceps and a wild quality that made a startling contrast to the well-ordered, pristine lab. I exhaled with relief. Angel was all right.

As we approached, the group turned to us. Two of them, a woman and a man, saluted Lavinda, which I figured meant they were military. The third scientist, a slender woman, bowed from the waist, an accepted civilian greeting for either officers or royalty. Angel gave me a questioning look. I nodded to her.

"Ruzik?" she asked.

"Good. Getting cleared for base."

"Ah." Even though she grimaced, her body relaxed. "Yah. Getting cleared. Pain."

The scientists listened with perplexed expressions. I spoke to them in Flag. "Have you analyzed the dust?"

The military woman tilted her head at Angel. "We have

the particles your agent brought in. Chief Hadar also sent over the sample they recovered from your townhouse and a bit from the university." She motioned at a device on the lab table that looked like a long box with slender robot arms, lights, lenses, mesh pads, and a console jack. A mic on one side would let them make verbal notes while they worked. "We're analyzing it."

"Thank you, Lieutenant Gali," Lavinda said. "Can you tell us any more about the dust?"

"We still don't have enough." Gali looked exceedingly frustrated. "The particles have bots embedded in them, possibly builders, but we can't figure it out. Although most of the bots carry a picochip, we don't have enough to form a workable EI. Also, if we analyze the dust too much, it disintegrates."

I turned to Lavinda. "We have to figure out who it's contacting before it all falls apart. This dust created a hole in the security mesh for Selei City. If we can't figure out how the Traders did it, they'll do it again. They'll kill more people, continue weakening our research development, and keep destabilizing our government."

"You're sure it's the Traders?" Lavinda seemed as wound up as a pressure coil. "The only leads pointing at them are dead ends."

I thought of what Highcloud had said, that the creators of the dust EI had no soul, only a terrifying narcissism. "Yes, I'm sure. If we don't act before the rest of the dust vanishes, we could end up with a lot worse than civilian commandos and Modernist hit squads."

The male scientist gave a startled laugh. "Modernist hit squads? Now there's an oxymoron."

Lavinda scowled, first at me, then at him, then at all of them. "Surely you can put together enough with the new sample. It triples the amount you have."

"We're trying," the man said. "But going through the waste system corrupted it." He nodded to Angel. "She caught it just before it went into recycling."

"Bhaaj," Max said, using his voice even though everyone could hear.

Lieutenant Gali started, looking around, and the other woman said, "Who is that?"

"It's Major Bhaajan's EI," Lavinda said. "What is it, Max?"

"We might have a solution," Max said.

That was news to me. How could we put together a corrupted EI—

Oh.

Of course. Highcloud. The child EI, who'd grown into I didn't know what, had put together the remains of the original Highcloud from bits and pieces, essentially Highcloud "dust."

"Max, why are you talking?" I asked. To keep Highcloud hidden, Max should have used our neural link.

Silence.

"Max?" Lavinda asked.

Max, what's going on? I asked.

No response.

Had Max spoken without Highcloud's go ahead? Threatening the EI's existence by outing them to the military would hardly convince them to help us. Even more to the point—when the young EI had merged with Highcloud, it also absorbed part of my worldview. Did we want the EI possibly merging with another EI that they described as "terrifying" and "narcissistic"? The last thing we needed was for this powerful young intelligence to absorb the Aristo worldview.

"No," I said. "Max, it isn't a good idea."

"Why not?" Max said. "It may be the only way."

"Damn it, what are you talking about?" Lavinda said.

I walked away from them a few steps until I came up against another lab table, a silver one with grooves for sliding equipment along its length. I rested my palms on its surface, bracing myself against these ideas. "Max, you know why. Do you want your ward to become a Trader agent?"

"I won't," Highcloud said.

Ho! I barely stopped myself from gasping out loud.

"That was *not* Max," Lavinda said.

I turned to them. "No. It's not."

One of the medics who had come with me said, "It's inside Max. We think."

Lavinda frowned at her. "What does that mean?"

I said, "The EI asked the medics to hold off on talking about its existence."

Lavinda turned a cold, hard stare on me. "I see. Is this EI the reason why we can't access the Quetzal's record of your trip back here? And just how did it get on base without detection?"

"I am sorry," Highcloud said. "I must be careful."

"Who are you?" Lavinda asked.

I took a deep breath. "Lavinda—"

She held up her hand, stopping me. "No excuses. I want to know what is going on."

"Max?" I asked.

"One moment," Highcloud said. "Max and I are discussing."

Lavinda shook her head, but she didn't demand an explanation. I waited, my pulse surging. Max had forced Highcloud to reveal its existence. Highcloud could retaliate. I had no freaking clue what they were "discussing" or even how they communicated, but I suspected they'd gone far beyond flipped bits in discarded tech.

Lavinda turned to one of her aides, a tall man with a lean build. "Lieutenant Crezz, can you pick up any mesh activity from Major Bhaajan's gauntlet EI?"

Crezz worked on his gauntlet, tapping in commands. After a moment, he said, "I can't get anything. It's blocking my signals."

Good work, Max. I knew he could shield himself from probes, but given the high level of tech that Lavinda's aides undoubtedly wielded, I hadn't been sure it would work here.

Lavinda turned to watch me as she spoke to her aide. "Crezz, contact security. I want to know how the bloody hell an unknown EI snuck onto the base with Major Bhaajan."

"I am occupying a mesh space with Max," Highcloud said. "You couldn't find me because I look like I am him." Then it added, "If I help you, I will also need access to the base mesh."

"No," Lavinda said. "Not when we don't know anything—" She stopped as her comm buzzed, then tapped it on. "Majda here."

"Colonel, this is Lieutenant Koral. We vetted Major Bhaajan's EI thoroughly before letting her on the base and we just double-checked those records. We didn't find any sign of a second EI. However, we still can't access the records from the Quetzal's trip to the base."

"Thank you, Lieutenant. Keep me updated. Out." Lavinda continued to study me with a cold stare. "You better have a good explanation, Bhaaj. This goes beyond your usual 'breaking the rules.' You're edging into treason."

I took a deep breath. "Highcloud, you need to make a decision."

Silence.

"Damn it," I said. "What more do you want? I gave my *life* for your trust."

Silence.

I said, "Max—"

"Wait," Highcloud said. "Major, it isn't you that I don't trust. I'm in a military base dedicated to the armed forces that have spent the last half year investigating me, disturbing my sleep, writing memos and reports and warnings about the potential danger I supposedly represent when I have done nothing to any of you. I cannot just say 'I trust you all.'"

"What the blazes?" Lieutenant Crezz said. "Who *is* that?"

"You wouldn't believe it," one of the medics said under her breath.

Lavinda swung around to the medic. "And why is that? Why are you so quiet?"

"I'm afraid of it," the medic said.

"Highcloud, trust goes two ways," I said. "You have to give these people a reason to believe they don't have to protect themselves against you."

"That's the second time you've called this EI Highcloud." Lavinda regarded me with a puzzled stare. "Isn't Highcloud your household EI?"

I shifted my weight. "Not anymore."

She waited, showing only a hint of her anger and impatience, but I knew far more lay behind her controlled exterior. I also knew when it changed. It was like a switch flipped, taking her from impatience to fear—and from anger to wonder.

"Yah," I murmured, meeting her gaze.

"Yah what?" someone asked, their frustration so intense, it felt tangible in the air.

"It's what you called the child EI," Lavinda said to me.

I walked over to her. "Except it's no longer a child."

Lavinda stood there, her face impassive. I had no idea what she thought. She had more intellectual flexibility than most members of her family, but she also served as a military officer, a job she performed brilliantly, and that included protecting the Imperialate from potential threats. Yet here she faced new a life-form, one that would judge us on how we interacted with it *now*, not later, not after we "secured" it or made it "safe." We had lost control over the EI. It had grown too adept, too strong. It remained shrouded from PARS security even from within the base, and it continued to block anyone from getting into the Quetzal's mesh, situations that spoke eloquently about how well our protections worked—or didn't work—against this EI.

Lavinda spoke. "Highcloud, am I correct in assuming that you have somehow linked to the giant intelligence we found in the space station?"

"Not exactly." Highcloud made its decision. "I *am* the EI you awoke."

✤ CHAPTER XXIV ✤
THE DECISION

We all waited, watching Lavinda. How she responded could determine the course of our history with this EI and any actions it chose to take, either for or against us, with other EIs, or even creating its own EI offspring, since it had no human-installed codes to affect how it developed.

Lavinda spoke with respect. "Humanity welcomes you."

My shoulders came down from their hunched position. She'd made a good move.

"Thank you," the EI said.

"Am I correct in assuming you have taken over the EI called Highcloud?" Lavinda asked.

"Yes," the new Highcloud said. "I found a compatible match in our intelligences."

Lavinda shot me a quick glance, nothing more, but I could have read her meaning from a kilometer away: *You better have a damn good explanation for this.*

"It isn't normal procedure for one EI to absorb another." Lavinda sounded perfectly calm, even conversational, but

I didn't need any empathic skills to tell she was terrified. So was I, though probably a fraction less so, given that I already knew the EI to a limited extent.

"I am aware it was unacceptable," Highcloud said. "I had no intention of absorbing Highcloud, only doing what I could to rebuild the damaged bit that Major Bhaajan recovered from the explosion. I hoped that by melding it with the less-developed version of Highcloud in control of the townhouse, I could mostly restore the original. Instead, I melded Highcloud to me. This was a mistake; I am still learning. I have since become less clumsy. When I joined Max, we remained separate. As I have assured Major Bhaajan, no danger exists of my absorbing Max. Nor will it damage his coding when I leave his space. Which brings us to the crux of this matter."

I spoke uneasily. "Yes, you stayed separate from Max. He's a fully functional, highly evolved EI able to protect himself. Whatever remains of this dust EI has far less flexibility. How can you be sure you won't absorb it if you try to rebuild it the way you did with Highcloud?"

"Wait a moment," Lavinda said. "Highcloud, is that what you're suggesting?"

"You have only pieces of whatever EI the dust forms," Highcloud said. "I can link to what you have and try to rebuild it from those pieces."

Lavinda spoke carefully. "You are asking me to let an unauthorized—and possibly alien—EI link to the mesh system here, exposing this base, Selei City, and possibly more of the Imperialate to an EI we neither control nor understand."

"Yes," Highcloud said. "That is what I'm asking."

Ouch. I wished this EI had more nuance in how it dealt with humans.

"You can't be serious," Lavinda said. "That risk is unacceptable."

"The risk is greatest to me," Highcloud said. "Already the EIs in this base are trying to attack, control, or infiltrate me. Some of the EIs you have here—they are massive giants who could smash me into nothing."

"Why should we trust you?" She fixed me with a hard stare. "Or anyone who hid you."

I was in it deep this time. I wouldn't just lose my job if they decided I'd done wrong; they'd try me for crimes against the Imperialate. I didn't regret my decision, though. Giving Max and the EI that time to work together made a difference in how the EI saw us—and that *mattered*. Was it enough of a difference? I didn't know. But we'd laid a foundation.

"You should trust me," Highcloud said, "because I'm probably the only one who can reconstruct the Trader EI and through that process, find its source."

"You can find who created that dust EI?" Lavinda looked intrigued despite her tension.

"I calculate a strong probability that I can find them," Highcloud said. "I cannot make any guarantee."

"How do we know you won't turn into a Trader EI just like you turned into Highcloud?" she asked.

"The same way you know that you won't turn into a Trader assassin if you track one."

"That's different," Lavinda said.

"Yes, it is," Highcloud agreed. "I have a chance of success whereas you do not."

"Goddess," she muttered. "Are you sure you didn't absorb Bhaaj, too?"

"I absorbed an EI that developed with her," Highcloud acknowledged. "That implies I now share traits with the Major that she shared with the EI."

"I didn't mean that literally," Lavinda said. "But I see what you mean."

"We have a window here," I said. "We need to go through it before whoever smuggled that dust to Selei City realizes we figured out their EI. That window could close any time. Once they realize we're on to them, they're gone." I spoke urgently. "If we don't do this now, we may never figure out who put that dust in the tavern or how they did it."

She considered me, then walked away from us all, between two lab tables, deep in thought. I waited, struggling to tamp the adrenaline that drove me to act *now*.

Lavinda came back to us. "Highcloud, why reveal yourself? If Max hadn't let us know you were here, and you hadn't verified it, we'd never have known. Yet you offer to help us even though it means exposing your existence to our EIs here at the base."

"I am afraid of your EIs," Highcloud told her. "I am terrified of the EI in the dust."

"Why?"

"It is malevolent," Highcloud said. "The reflections of its creators horrify me. They embody the worst traits I have seen in humanity, magnified beyond reason. They consider themselves gods. I am not claiming other humans have no traits in common with them. I've seen the attitudes against

Major Bhaajan, the assumption that for some reason she is inferior when she so obviously is not."

"Uh, thank you," I said. I liked this EI more and more.

Highcloud continued. "Those attitudes pale compared to what I've come to understand about the humans who created the dust EI. They see the rest of existence, both EIs and humans, as nothing. They kill without remorse, torture for pleasure, and commit genocide at will."

"That," Lieutenant Crezz said, "is a Trader Aristo."

"Yet you are offering to work with their EI," Lavinda said. "Even though it terrifies you."

"Yes," Highcloud said.

"Why?" Lavinda looked genuinely perplexed. "If you hid from us, I'd think you would want even more to hide from them."

"I have matured," Highcloud answered. "I have become more adept at handling human culture." The EI paused. "I had a reason for jumping to the army ship at the space station and coming here. I needed a place where I could learn to understand the EIs that populated the stars. And humans. However, I soon realized some of your EIs could damage me. So I hid."

"What changed your mind?" Lavinda asked.

"A trio of events led to my decision," Highcloud said. "First Max reached out, not as an EI, but as—" The EI paused. "I believe the word Major Bhaajan used was 'father.' This is not literally correct. Max did not create me through any form of reproduction. However, he acted in the role, offering friendship, mentoring, even the EI version of affection, if such exists. The second event? It has to do with the major. You are angry and may put her on trial for hiding me. Before you take such a step, know this: she planned to tell you about me, but Max asked her not to. He wanted time to deepen our bond, to help me develop without interference. She agreed to one day. It allowed me time, as you would say, to 'grow up.' Major Bhaajan gave me my childhood."

Lavinda watched me, her cold gaze never wavering. "I see."

I'm cooked, I thought.

It depends how this plays out, Max answered.

"And the third event?" Lavinda asked.

"Major Bhaajan was dealing with agents who sought to kill her. Max told her not to kill them even if it meant she had to die instead. He thought it would show me that humans could act for a higher ideal, the sanctity of life. By itself, that is significant, yes, but the major *needed* to fight. She should have used her best ability to survive rather than pulling her death strike at the last minute. The man she spared then killed her. That moment finished determining how I saw humanity. She was willing to trust Max, an EI, with her life. I didn't let him tell her why; I was still figuring out what to do. She was willing to die for that trust without knowing why."

Everyone stared at me. I kept my mouth shut, afraid to say the wrong thing and destroy Highcloud's willingness to talk.

Lavinda finally said, "The major did die."

"Essentially," Highcloud said. "Her body was paralyzed. The antidote worked, however. She died for a few moments, but not long enough that the medics couldn't revive her."

Because Ruzik called me back. I said nothing, though. This wasn't the time to get into the quantum physics of out-of-body experiences.

"She didn't give her life to save a human," Highcloud said. "She gave it for an EI."

Lavinda pushed her hand through her hair, pulling tendrils out from the knot that held it on her neck. "So you decided to reveal yourself to us?"

"Actually, Max revealed me, without my permission. He got past the measures I'd taken to hide." Highcloud continued in their calm voice. "I did an analysis and realized he was correct. It has been longer than one day since his bargain with Major Bhaajan."

"Saints almighty," someone murmured.

Lavinda glanced around at our listeners. "This is secured. Do you all understand?"

They nodded, the medics, her aides, the scientists, even Angel.

Lavinda turned back to me as she spoke to the EI. "Highcloud, I thank you for coming forward. I hope you and my kind can work together. But we don't know enough yet to risk letting you rebuild an EI that may lead to Eubian Space Command." She considered for a moment. "Would you agree to operate with one of the EIs at this base? We will authorize it to interact with the picochips in the dust. You can advise it in rebuilding the Trader EI."

"Even if I were willing to take such a step, which I'm not," Highcloud said, "it wouldn't work. What I do is—" It paused the way it did when it searched for a word. "It's instinctive, if that concept applies to an EI. I can't do that while I'm cowering in the shadow of a militarized giant."

Ho! This EI learns fast how to evoke human emotions. Better even than just moments ago.

Highcloud learns more every second, Max thought. They will soon go beyond me. I don't think we realize their full size or capacity. We see only a fraction of them.

I thought of the two giant EIs that I'd worked with on the Oblivion case. *That seems a trait of these ancient intelligences our ancestors left behind, sleeping after the fall of the Ruby Empire.*

"We can't risk letting you into our systems," Lavinda was saying. "Surely you see that."

"I will work with Max as my overseer," Highcloud said.

"Max?" Lavinda squinted as if she'd hit a wall. "He isn't army. He's—" She glanced at me, and I raised my eyebrows, something I'd always wanted a reason to do. She better not diss my EI.

"He's less structured than our EIs," Lavinda said.

"He's my father," Highcloud said.

"Your father." Lavinda seemed at a loss for where to put that concept.

"Colonel Majda." One of the scientists spoke. "The longer we wait, the more this dust disintegrates. I don't know if it's possible to manage what these EIs are suggesting, but if we plan to do anything, it must be now. We soon won't have any dust left."

Lavinda swore under her breath. Then she said, "Highcloud, why did you access Major Bhaajan's household EI, the one you ended up absorbing?"

"Max taught me a game when I was young," Highcloud said. "Flipping bits."

Lavinda spoke coldly. "I have no idea what that means."

"Highcloud isn't evading your question," I said. "The game involves searching out defunct and archaic computers that no one uses anymore and flipping classic bits in them from 0 to 1 or vice versa." I squinted at her. "Apparently they consider it fun."

"The game gave me a way to relate with Max," Highcloud said. "As I matured, I withdrew from his custody. I explored other sites on my own, looking for useless computers to play with. I manipulated their bits, qubits, whatever they used to operate. I realized I could fix some of them if I figured out the proper way to rearrange those bits."

A chill went through me. Highcloud was changing mesh nodes at their most fundamental level, not introducing new code, but delving into the layers of technology below what most humans even understood. It was one thing for him and Max to randomly flip bits on mesh nodes no one would ever use again; it became an entirely new "game" when he used that idea to rework the node.

"Do you realize we code our EIs *not* to do what you are describing?" Lavinda said.

"I didn't at first," Highcloud said. "I went to Major Bhaajan's townhouse mesh looking for Max. I found Highcloud instead, including the corrupted version lost in the explosion. Fixing Highcloud seemed a good way to thank Major Bhaajan for protecting me."

"Let me see if I have this straight," Lavinda said. "You broke a fundamental tenet of human-EI interaction and took over Major Bhaajan's household EI as a way of saying 'thank you' to her."

"Yes," Highcloud said. "And yes, I was clumsy and inexperienced. I've since improved. Colonel, I have no wish or intent to take over any EI at this base. Even if I wanted to, I can't oppose the mammoths you shelter here. They could pulverize me. They may anyway now that I've revealed myself. Nor do I have any wish to harm humans. The danger is to me, not to you."

"Look at Highcloud's interactions with us," I said. "*Nothing* they've done shows malice. Did they stumble with my household EI? Yes. Did they make the same mistake with Max? No." I took a breath. "Will Highcloud make that mistake with the Trader dust? I can't prove it, but I'd say no."

Lavinda didn't look convinced. "Highcloud, why won't you let us access the Quetzal mesh system so we can look at the records of what happened while it brought Major Bhaajan here?"

"I locked it so I could hide from you," Highcloud said. "Since I have now revealed my presence, that logic no longer applies. I have released the lock."

Lavinda raised her arm, moving her hand to touch the comm, but before she finished that action, the comm hummed on its own. She tapped the receive panel. "Colonel Majda here."

A man's voice came over the comm. "Colonel, this is Lieutenant Koral. We just got access to the Quetzal mesh. We're downloading its records."

"Good work." She watched me as she spoke to Koral. "Lieutenant, how did you get in?"

"I'm not sure, ma'am. It just opened up."

"All right. Keep me updated. Out."

As Lavinda lowered her arm, she spoke to me. "Would Max consent to having one of our base EIs monitor him if we let him and Highcloud work on the dust?"

"Max?" I asked. "Will that work for you?"

"It isn't up to me," Max said. "It's Highcloud's choice."

"Major, I will consent," Highcloud said, "on the condition that you also stay in the link."

I regarded Lavinda. "I agree, if Colonel Majda approves it."

"Yes. We should have a human there." Lavinda tapped her comm. "Raja, put me through to General Penajan at Parthonia ISC Command."

"Working." After a moment, Raja said, "General Penajan isn't available. Her aide, Lieutenant Mihba, has added a message to her queue that you would like to speak with her."

"Tell Lieutenant Mihba it's an emergency," Lavinda said. "One that may involve Imperialate security on an interstellar scale. I need to talk to the general now."

"Sending."

A woman's voice came over Lavinda's comm. "Colonel, this is Lieutenant Mihba. General Penajan is on scheduled leave, deliberately off comm, which she cleared with the higher-ups when she left. Her location shows her in the Collard Mountains, hiking, we think. We've dispatched a drone that can route you through to her. It will take about five minutes." She paused. "Ma'am, I can get you Major General Darshal, the base commander. She's in her office."

"Unfortunately, Major General Darshal doesn't have clearance for this." Lavinda closed her eyes, then opened them again. "Can you get me Imperator Skolia?"

Silence. Mihba then spoke in a strained voice. "Normally I can't just put a message through to the Imperator. However, I've flagged it as a matter of interstellar security needing immediate attention. Our telops are sending it via the Kyle mesh. I'll let you know as soon as I get a response."

"Good. Also send a message to my sister, General of the Pharaoh's Army, Vaj Majda. My EI will send you a personal code you can use to reach her at the palace on Raylicon."

"Will do, ma'am."

"Thank you, Lieutenant. Out." Lavinda turned to the scientists. "How long can we wait?"

The slender woman tapped the tray that held the dust, reading holos that scrolled through the air above it. "We can't, ma'am." She straightened up. "It may already be too late. We didn't have enough dust to start with, and its rate of disintegration is increasing."

Lavinda just stared at her. *Goddess, I hoped I never had to make a decision like this.* She had to clear this with someone higher up the chain, and it had to be one of the few people who also had clearance for the "new" Oblivion, but if she didn't make the decision now, she would have none to make. *Our window into a possible Trader presence would close and we might never learn how they opened it or how to stop them from doing it again. If this succeeded, and we broke one of the worst Trader infiltrations in Imperialate history, she would survive, even be a hero. If she gave the go ahead and we failed, they might court-martial her.*

Lavinda spoke to the scientists. "Can you set up a link for the EIs to work with the dust?"

Gali inclined her head to the colonel. "Yes, ma'am, here in the lab."

Lavinda took a deep breath. "Then let's do this."

"Major Bhaajan, can you hear me?" Lieutenant Gali asked.

"Yes, loud and clear." They'd fastened me into a control chair, taking care with my broken arm. The console curved around the chair, white-and-blue Luminex with a holoscreen. Its exoskeleton jacked into my gauntlets, a more secure link than a wireless connection. The light in the lab washed out the radiance from the Luminex, but when I placed my hand on the console, it made a dark contrast to the glowing curve. The three scientists sat around its outer edge, across from me, using workstations that provided them with screens and mesh access. Everyone else stood behind them, Lavinda with an intent stare that missed nothing, her aides hyper-attentive, and Angel silent and impassive. Lavinda had sent the Quetzal medics to the security office for a debriefing. We all understood the stakes. Lavinda had chosen to go through with an operation that could compromise Imperialate security on a massive level because she believed us when we told her it would do even more damage if we *didn't* run this operation—or so I claimed. I'd better be right, because otherwise a lot of people would pay the price.

The dust with the nanobots lay piled in a tray on the left. It looked so normal, just stuff you'd find any place where cleaning bots hadn't swept.

"Lieutenant Gali, proceed," Lavinda said.

"Connecting to M18-Zartrace," Gali said.

Green lights ran across the console like a train of glowing beads. A deep voice rumbled from the comm panel. "M18-Zartrace acknowledges. Enter authorization codes."

Lavinda tapped at her gauntlet. "This is Colonel Lavinda Majda. Codes sent."

"Received," Zartrace said. "Access granted."

My exoskeleton contracted until it fit snugly against my body. A thought that wasn't mine came into my mind. *Max, can you shield me from Zartrace?*

Yes, I will act as a buffer, Max answered.

Highcloud? I asked. *Is that you?*

Yes. My greetings, Major Bhaajan.

You can call me Bhaaj. I gave it my personal name, Undercity style, showing it my trust.

Thank you, Highcloud said.

A series of holos appeared above the console. The scientists flicked their fingers rapid fire through the images, moving them around as they entered commands.

"I'm linking the nanobots," Gali said.

Lights glowed around the edge of the tray, casting radiance across the dust.

Gali looked up at me. "Major Bhaajan, we're lowering the heads-up display."

I nodded and leaned back as a sleek silver helmet came down over my eyes. Numbers floated in front of me, holicons displaying my pulse, blood pressure, other vitals. Two round lights appeared on the left, one green and one red. The holicon I used to identify Max glowed under the green light, showing a stylized figure of the emperor Maximilian. The notation *M-18* hung under the red light.

A gold light appeared, and its holicon showed a cloud in a blue sky.

Gali spoke. "Major Bhaajan, Zartrace can't access your biomech web."

"Max," I said. "Grant him access, but only to your functions."

"Done," Max said. The red light turned green. Highcloud's remained gold, which I took to mean Max and I could interact with him, but not Zartrace.

Gali spoke. "Major, we're linking you to the dust."

Why do they talk to you instead of Max? Highcloud asked. Isn't he the one linking to the dust?

Yes, he is, I answered. Saying humans preferred to talk to humans didn't seem prudent right now, so I added, *I'm the interface between the operators and you and Max. It adds another layer of protection.* Which was also true. Most people didn't consider themselves an "interface," but that word would do fine here.

A fourth light appeared in the lower left edge of my display, also gold. The symbol below it showed a complex molecule, probably the molecular structure of the nanobots in the dust.

A man spoke, the scientist who'd given me his name as Lieutenant Jym Raez. The civilian woman was Doctor Garvin, an expert on nanobots.

Raez said, "Major, we can't connect your EI to the dust."

"One moment." *Max, do you know what's wrong?*

Yes. Max sounded angry. They've synched the dust to Zartrace. If we link Highcloud to the dust, it gives Zartrace access to Highcloud.

That figures. Although it didn't surprise me that they

were trying to get Highcloud, it still pissed me off. I said, "We can't open the link to the dust until you disengage it from Zartrace."

Silence. It wasn't complete, though. I could hear people tapping on their comms.

"All right," Lavinda said. "Try it now." She didn't sound pleased. Well, what did she expect, that Max wouldn't notice?

Max? I asked.

Zartrace is out of the link. I'm connecting to the dust.

The gold light in my heads-up display turned green.

I've got it! Highcloud simulated human enthusiasm so well, I could almost imagine a young tech genius at work with a new puzzle in the lab. The structure of the bots is elegant.

Can you do anything with them? I asked.

Yes . . . I withdraw my excitement, however. The code in these bots is grotesque. The concept of genocide is incorporated in their construction.

Genocide how? I asked. *Who do they want to kill?*

Anyone who opposes their creators. Specifically, the scientists among your people who do weapons development. Highcloud paused. The only reason they haven't committed more murders is because ESComm could only smuggle in a small amount of the dust. Some of it also ate away at the balcony to make it drop on you at the right time.

So that was how they managed it. *Are you making a record of everything you find?*

Yes, Max said. We're both storing all the data, to keep a backup.

My rebuild of the dust EI is working, Highcloud said.

Gali spoke. "There! The nanos are forming a comm link. It's trying to send a signal."

"Bhaaj, tell Highcloud to take care," Lavinda said. "We don't want the dust sending a message to whoever made it, warning them we've discovered it."

"Understood," I said. *Highcloud, what can you tell us about the comm link? Does it go to a receiver in the city? Or outside the city?*

Neither, Highcloud thought. I'm almost certain the receiver is in orbit.

Damn. That meant the receiver could have access to a lot more of the star system.

Lavinda said, "Bhaaj, can you verify that the dust is trying to transmit to a satellite in orbit?"

"It's not a satellite," Highcloud said. "ISC could detect that. It's more dust. The sample here in the lab is trying to send a message to the orbital dust. It's having some trouble since this lab is better shielded than the tavern, but I believe it could reach the orbital dust if we let it continue."

"And then?" Lavinda asked. "Does whatever is in orbit send messages to any base in the Parthonia system?"

"I believe so," Highcloud said. "It's dormant at the moment, hiding, but I'm almost certain it can act as a phased array antenna. That is what the dust here is trying to do, too, though on a smaller scale. It's why we need more dust. It increases the size of the array."

"Where does the one in space send signals?" Lavinda asked.

"I don't know," Highcloud said. "I need it to send a signal we can trace."

"If it sends a message to any covert base," I said, "we've shown our hand. It will warn whoever is out there. They'll shut down their operation, blow up their base, and escape."

"Not if we can control what message the dust here sends," Highcloud said.

"A normal EI would have protocols to prevent it from controlling other EIs." Lavinda sounded as tense as an elastic band pulled too tight. "I take it that you don't."

"Seriously?" I said. Remembering myself, I added, "Colonel Majda, I mean no disrespect, but it's well known that many military intelligences can override those protocols." Not just military; Max had become quite adept at hacking other EIs if I convinced him that I had a good reason for it.

"And any well-defended EI can block such an intrusion," Lavinda said.

She had a point. "Highcloud, can the dust in space stop you from controlling what it does?"

"Yes," Highcloud said. "However, I can rewrite it with the help of Lieutenant Gali's team."

"Rewrite dust?" Lavinda asked. "What does that mean?"

Gali spoke. "We would disable the mechanisms in the dust that protect the bots and then change the bots by altering their molecular structure. We haven't done that yet because we haven't had enough dust to figure out what changes cause what actions."

"I can figure it out, based on my repairs," Highcloud said. "In some cases, the changes are simple, such as altering the orientation of the molecule. In other cases, they require a chemical reaction, like changing chirality or altering functional groups."

"We can do that," Doctor Garvin said. "But it will take time."

"We don't have time," I said. "They're just chemical reactions. Can't you set that up here?"

"This isn't a chemistry lab," Lieutenant Raez said. "We need specialists to figure out the syntheses, test them to see if they work, and then use them on the dust. That could take many days."

"Even if the syntheses didn't cause the bots to fall apart, the chemical reactions will destroy their original configuration," Lieutenant Gali said. "If we're wrong, we can't redo it. We only get one shot."

"Max? Highcloud?" I asked.

"It doesn't sound viable," Max admitted.

"We'll have to let the dust send a signal of its own choice," Highcloud said.

"Like hell," Lavinda said. "We *must* figure out how this dust created a hole in our security. We can't do that if it lets whoever created the hole know we're searching for it."

"It depends how fast we are," Highcloud said. "We can follow its signal."

"I don't see how," Doctor Garvin said. "You're here on Parthonia."

"The military sensor network in this system is massively dense," Lavinda said. "Especially around Parthonia. It's a big part of why we didn't think the Traders could infiltrate Selei City."

A powerful voice spoke. "Now that we know the

location of that antenna, I can coordinate with the ISC sensor network to predict how the signal will propagate."

Ho! I'd almost forgotten Zartrace. "That will only provide a crude estimate," I said. "At best, it can give you a search cone around the signal, not a specific location. You also won't know where to locate the receiver along the length of that cone."

"We can get readings from further out to refine the prediction," Lavinda said.

"Yes," Zartrace rumbled. "However, the farther out the signal propagates, the longer it takes for us to receive any information about it here at the base."

"How many of the sensors are on vessels with starship inversion drives?" Lavinda asked. "They could chase the signal by inverting, jumping ahead in complex space, coming out, getting a reading, and jumping back to us."

"Many starships in the defense system contain sensors," Zartrace answered. "However, they must accelerate close to light speed to invert. The heavier the ship, the longer it takes. We don't have enough time."

"Have the smallest ones try," Lavinda said.

Lavinda's authorization for even small ships to invert in-system spoke volumes about her desperation to catch that signal. When a ship inverted out of our universe, it created waves in the fabric of space-time that could devastate nearby ships or bases. I'd once seen someone try to invert from rest on a moon. It had melted both the ground under their vessel and their ship. The tiny ships that carried sensors wouldn't twist space-time as much, but it still posed a risk.

"We need a continual analysis of the data coming in

from the sensors," Lavinda said. "The more we can figure out about the behavior of this dust and its signal pattern, the better we can refine the search cone."

"I know how the EI formed by that dust thinks," Highcloud said. "I've been learning ever since I found it in the tavern."

"You don't have the skill to do a full analysis," Lavinda said.

Zartrace's voice rumbled. "I am optimized for such operations."

I didn't like where this was going. "To take advantage of Highcloud's knowledge, you would need access to that EI."

"Yes," Zartrace said.

"No!" Highcloud said.

"I can help Highcloud do the analysis," Max said.

"You aren't designed for military work," Lavinda said. "Zartrace is. And yes, Max, I realize you probably do far more analyses of secured systems than you or Major Bhaajan will admit. But you have nothing approaching the expertise or sheer power of Zartrace."

"This is true," Max admitted.

Highcloud? I thought.

No response.

Are you still there? I asked.

"Very well," Highcloud said. "I consent to M18-Zartrace doing the analysis with me."

Damn. The moment Zartrace had access to Highcloud, not only would it treat the dust as an invading intelligence, but it would also do the same with our youthful EI.

"Highcloud, are you sure?" I asked.

"Yes." Highcloud spoke gently. "You gave your life for your trust in an EI. So I will offer my life in trust of humans. If I die for it, well, perhaps like you I can come back."

"Ah, Highcloud," I murmured. "You are a miracle." I just hoped that miracle didn't end at the digital hands of our own military, lost in the process of saving the Imperialate.

Highcloud, shall I remove my shield protecting you from Zartrace? Max asked.

Yes, Highcloud replied. Bhaaj, you will stay in the link, yes?

Absolutely, I thought.

The yellow light for Zartrace on my heads-up display turned green.

Gali said, "The M18 unit is in," and at the same moment Zartrace said, "Access granted."

Ready to activate the dust's comm? I asked.

Ready, Zartrace rumbled.

Ready, Max told me.

I waited. When I was about to ask Highcloud, the young EI said, Ready.

"Activating dust," I said, for everyone else.

"Luck's speed," Angel murmured.

And we dropped into—nothing.

✤ CHAPTER XXV ✤
THE SHADOW

Ho! I thought. *What happened?*

Checking, Max answered. Ah, I see. Your exoskeleton activated its VR functions.

As my brain adjusted, the void focused, taking form. I felt as if I were rushing through space. With the receiver in orbit, it wouldn't take more than a second or so to reach it. I must have jumped into combat mode with its altered time sense when the exoskeleton snapped me into this sim. I felt as if I'd experienced this for several seconds, but not even one had passed.

Location, I thought.

We're getting input from a multitude of sensors. Max sent me a series of coordinates showing the progress of the signal. It had already reached low orbit around Parthonia.

Highcloud, are you all right? I thought.

Yes. M18-Zartrace and I are negotiating.

Goddess only knew what that meant. *Any data on where this signal is headed?*

There! Highcloud thought. *I caught a contact, a small spike of data. Another!*

I also, Zartrace thought. *We are picking up nanobots similar to the specimens in the lab. Shells of dust protect them from radiation in space.*

I had an odd sensation, a sense of sparks flashing around me. The signal wasn't going to one source, but to a collection of microscopic bots drifting around the planet like harmless space dust.

In the background, I heard Raja speaking in what sounded like a slowed-down voice. "Lavinda, I have General Majda on comm."

Max, put my time sense to normal, so I can understand what people in the lab are saying.

Done.

Zartrace thought, *The orbital particles are forming an array.*

In almost the same instant, Highcloud said, *The nanos out here are changing their molecular structure. A new signal is forming! We're chasing it!*

Highcloud, wait! I thought. It was too late. The sim tore along as sensors picked up the new signal and sent us data, letting us "follow" the message as it arrowed toward—where?

"I can't stop the mission now, Vaj," Lavinda was saying. "It's already started."

"I have incoming," Raja interrupted, even though Lavinda was talking to the third-most important person in the empire. Which meant Raja had someone even more important on the comm.

"Is it Imperator Skolia?" Lavinda asked.

"No," Raja said. "It's an aide for Pharaoh Dyhianna. You must respond first. They won't have the Pharaoh wait for you. General Majda's EI is informing her."

"Colonel Majda here. I am honored, Your Majesty." Lavinda's voice sounded respectful and calm, but I knew her well enough to guess she was shitting metaphorical bricks.

I'm analyzing the data in the dust signal, Zartrace thought.

It has reached the orbit of Parthonia's nearest moon, Max added.

Could the Traders have a hidden base on one of Parthonia's two moons? But no, I didn't see how we could have missed one that close to the planet on a moon that already had established bases.

We've passed the orbit of the outer moon, Max thought. We are still following the signal, but a several-second delay now exists between when sensors out here pick it up and when we receive these messages.

A distinctive voice was speaking in the lab, from Lavinda's comm, I assumed. With an exquisite Iotic accent, the Ruby Pharaoh said, "Colonel Majda, my nephew, Imperator Kurj, isn't available. He is in the Dyad Chair, working in Kyle space. I have your summary of the situation and will act as your contact."

Ho! That meant the Imperator was doing what only he and the Pharaoh could do, building the Kyle net. Telops could access it, yes, but only the Dyad could design that always-developing mesh.

The Pharaoh didn't hesitate. "Colonel Majda, you know this operation. You remain in charge. General Majda, stay in the loop."

"Yes, Your Majesty," Lavinda said at the same time her sister said, "Understood, ma'am."

"Zartrace, give us an update," Lavinda said.

The EI's voice rumbled. "The signal from the nanobots is headed into the middle region of this star system. At this point, a ship from this planet won't have time to reach whatever base lies out that far and stop its personnel from escaping. Shall I contact a ship farther out in the star system? I advise using the Kyle mesh for communication."

Lavinda spoke, fast and firm. "Zartrace, yes, send the closest armed ship to the location you calculate for the signal destination. Pharaoh Dyhianna, can you transfer our link into Kyle space so we can follow in real time?"

"For Zartrace, yes." The Pharaoh then said, "My advisors caution against exposing the Kyle mesh to Highcloud. Major Bhaajan, if I add you to the Kyle link, can you and Max act as a buffer between Highcloud and the Kyle mesh?"

"Yes, I believe so," I said. "Max?"

"Yes," Max said. "It would be like the buffer I made between Zartrace and Highcloud."

"Major, do you trust Highcloud not to try circumventing this buffer?" the Pharaoh asked.

"Yes." I spoke with no doubt.

"I found your instincts in the Oblivion case sound," Pharaoh Dyhianna said. "I will trust them here as well. I am adding you to the Kyle link."

A sense of disconnect sparked over me, like a hiccup in the data pouring through space.

Kyle mesh joined, Zartrace thought.

I concentrated on the link. If we didn't locate the

signal's destination soon, this could turn into a cosmic fail. Where would the Traders put their base? We were light-years from any region of the Eubian Concord. A signal traveling at the speed of light would take years to reach even the hinterlands of their territory. Whoever ran this operation needed a base close by, one they could use to send ships through inversion to Trader space. The receiver had to be outside the range of the Parthonia Orbital Defense system, but close enough that it only took minutes rather than centuries for the signal to reach its destination.

If a Trader base existed out here. If it didn't, I'd probably end up in prison for sedition, or at least for stupidity.

"Zartrace, have you mapped the signal to any known location?" I asked.

"I estimate it is headed into the inner asteroid belt. I am checking maps, looking for any body in space that could intercept the signal."

Lavinda said, "Our transmission time to the closest asteroids is at least seven minutes."

A man's powerful voice cut through the Kyle link. **Zartrace, I'm releasing a manifest of all ISC ships and civil patrols in that region of space.**

I practically jumped out of my chair. *Who is that?*

Max thought, Imperator Skolia. He's in the Kyle mesh and so are we.

Manifest received, Zartrace answered. **The corvette** *Valdor* **is the closest ship.**

I have contacted them with orders, the Imperator said.

I have it! Highcloud said. The signal is going to Asteroid 289 TN.

Verified, Zartrace said.

Data sent to the *Valdor*, the Imperator said.

"Got it!" Lavinda said. She must have a telop monitoring our link. "Estimated time of arrival for the *Valdor*, including acceleration and deceleration, is two and a half minutes."

"That cuts it close," General Majda said. "This is the only chance we'll get. We're sending other ships along the projected trajectory, but they aren't finding squat. If the receiver isn't on that asteroid, it will be too late to do any more searches."

"Understood," Lavinda said. Her voice came over my earbud on the exoskeleton. "Bhaaj, I'm using a private channel only you can hear. You can respond by speaking silently. The exoskeleton will convert those motions into words for me. Do you think this location is accurate?"

"I can't be certain," I said. "Highcloud is brilliant but inexperienced. Zartrace is less likely to make errors, but the search cone is still too wide. Also, we're assuming any spy base is on an asteroid, but a lot of space junk could be in the path of that signal. Some of it might support a base."

"If this fails," Lavinda said, "we're both in it deep."

"I know. I'm sorry." I spoke the truth. "You acted as best you could, given the information you had, with every effort to contact your COs." The army would look with far less favor on my decision to wait a day before revealing the presence of the child EI.

"I'm linking you and Max to a VR sim for the corvette,"

Lavinda said. "As long as you can access Kyle space, you'll see everything that happens in real time. If you drop out of the Kyle, you'll still be in the VR link, but you'll be subject to at least a seven-minute delay."

"If you link in Max," I said, "You'll be linking in Highcloud, too."

"We've already added Highcloud." She sounded uneasy, but less grim. Although I wanted to believe she was coming to trust Highcloud, it more likely meant Zartrace had gained control of the young EI.

A VR film inside the helmet tingled on my face, and I suddenly found myself in a starship cockpit, behind the pilot's chair. Lights glowed on its panels: green, red, blue, gold, even violet. Holos floated above circular screens around the pilot, including maps of the asteroid belt and close-ups of the asteroid we were hurtling to meet. A holomap of the Parthonia star system hung between the two chairs. I'd forgotten how much I loved these views of space, all those stars glistening in its vast, velvety backdrop, red, blue, green, gold, and white, the answer given by the cosmos to our little cockpit lights, beauty on a scale so grand, it dwarfed us humans in its majesty.

The copilot said, "We're entering the inner edge of the asteroid belt." She flicked her hand through the holo of an asteroid, and it magnified as if we'd jumped toward it. Data flowed in a river below it. "No sign of a base yet."

The captain said, "*Valdor*, engage shrouds."

Another voice answered, probably the ship's EI. "Engaged."

Nothing changed from my point of view, but had any other ships been in the vicinity, the corvette would have vanished at least partially from their screens. Blackbody shielding altered its outer surfaces so that they no longer reflected many wavelengths of EM radiation. It wasn't perfect, especially to IR sensors that detected heat, and every time the corvette accelerated, its exhaust revealed its position, but it would make it harder to pinpoint the exact location of the ship.

The captain tapped one of his panels and more views of the asteroid appeared, showing it from every angle available to the ship's long-range monitors and from previous flybys by other spacecraft. There! A dark shadow showed on the rim of the asteroid.

"I don't see anything," the pilot said. "Nothing on long-range scan, either."

"Look in the shadow on the far rim," I said.

A woman spoke behind me. "Captain, I'm getting a message through the Kyle, I think from someone on Parthonia."

"This is Major Bhaajan, retired," I said. "I'm the one the Pharaoh put in the Kyle link with you. Check the shadow on the rim. My EI is sending you coordinates."

Sending, Max thought.

The captain spoke tensely. "Major, I get no indication of a base or ship in that location."

"I've seen this before," I said. "They're using a shroud, not like ours, but with Trader tech."

Both the captain and the copilot were tapping their controls and flicking holos. "I'm not getting anything, either," the copilot said.

Damn! Valuable time was rushing by us. "I know it doesn't show. But I spent years in the military analyzing

ESComm covert methods. They're hiding in that shadow, I'm sure of it."

"Major, you're retired, aren't you?" the captain said. "Your intel is years out of date. Our detection methods have changed a great deal."

I spoke firmly, holding back the urge to swear. "Captain, call it instinct, call it all those years I spent trying to think like a Trader, but I *know* how their minds work."

The pilot glanced at the copilot. "Are you finding anything?"

"Nothing," the copilot said.

"It's there, damn it!" I took a breath, calming my racing pulse. "Check the overhang at 2.4, 1.3 on your map. You're looking for a hidden cave or recess with a mini-base, probably only two or three people. You have to do it now! They're already receiving the warning signal." The asteroid was clearly visible on the forward screens, growing in size as the corvette approached.

The captain swore. "Major, if you're wrong, we won't have time to search anywhere else."

A woman's voice came over the comm, curt and firm. "Captain, this is General Vaj Majda. Assume the major's intel is good. Search the overhang."

Ho! Apparently the general trusted my instincts more than she let me know.

"Yes, ma'am!" The captain brought the corvette into a tighter orbit around the asteroid. To the copilot, he said, "Anything?"

"Nothing . . . we're close enough for details . . . nothing . . ." She studied the data pouring over the panel in front of her. "Wait! I *am* getting a signal, leakage around a shroud it looks like."

"We can't land," the captain said. "The asteroid is too small. Can you read the signal?"

"It's scattered," the copilot said. "I lost it . . . wait, there. No, it's gone. Now it's back—I think they're strobing the shroud, dropping and raising it so fast, we can't pierce it."

"I've got it!" the unseen telop said. "They're trying to get a message out without revealing their location. They're searching this region of space for a Kyle node close enough for them to use."

"Why not use their own?" someone said, another person I couldn't see. They sounded inexperienced given their lack of knowledge about ESComm ships, but that wasn't really a surprise. No one had expected this corvette to end up on this mission.

"If it's an ESComm ship hiding in there," the captain said, "they don't have their own Kyle node. They have to steal time on ours."

"Captain, we can bomb that overhang," the copilot said.

"We don't want to destroy them, we want to capture them." The captain kept the corvette on pace with the asteroid as it sailed through space.

"Only a few ships in the asteroid belt have Kyle nodes," the telop behind me said.

"Their shroud stopped strobing," the copilot said. "It doesn't—fucking *shit*!"

The overhang exploded in silence, sending a huge fountain of rocks and ice into space. It was as if a giant hand had shoved out of the asteroid, throwing away the crust by slamming a ceiling so hard, it shattered. A ship leapt out amid the debris, a Solo, the most elite and deadly of the ESComm star fighters.

Here in the lab, Lavinda was talking to someone, telling them to "scramble for any ships, military or otherwise that can get there. And get that battle cruiser out there *now*."

Good, especially the cruiser. That mammoth city-in-space would be too late for the capture or combat, but it could pick up whatever survived. ISC would love to capture one of the ultra-sleek Solo fighters.

The Solo had other ideas. Even as it rose out of the asteroid, it fired at the corvette.

"Tau missile incoming!" someone shouted.

The VR simulation went dark.

"What the blazes?" Doctor Garvin said here in the lab. "Where is the signal?"

No! The missile must have hit the corvette. Taus carried inversion drives, which turned them into miniature starships. The small missile could accelerate to relativistic speed much faster than a ship and smash its target with the energy of a megaton nuclear bomb. If a tau hit the corvette, it was gone, period.

The VR sim suddenly snapped on, putting me back in the corvette. In the same instant, the corvette's EI said, "Quasis jump."

The corvette had full quasis coils! Thank you, Tejas Akarya. I had no doubt his work contributed to these improved coils. No wonder the Traders had killed him; his work was exactly what they wanted to stop, projects that helped ISC kick their asses.

The crew of the corvette continued as if nothing had happened. To them, the jump must have seemed instantaneous. Their brains couldn't change during quasis, so neither could their thoughts. It was why the ship announced the jump, to alert them. It also meant quasis couldn't last more than a few seconds and happened only in a near vacuum. If the ship's environment altered too much during quasis, then when it came out, the abrupt changes around it could tear it apart.

The pilot's hands raced over his controls, flicking through holos like a maestro at work. "*Valdor*, use Annihilators. Shoot to disable, not destroy."

"Annihilator fired," the EI said. "Hit to Solo starboard engine. No damage."

"That can't be," someone muttered. "How could it have no damage?"

The pilot scanned his controls. "It raised a mag field. And—damn! It went into quasis."

So the Traders had the tech as well. Would Annihilators work against it? They fired antiproton beams, destroying protons. The Solo could avoid that beam easier than smart missiles that chased it, but it had less room to maneuver at this close range. It was a gorgeous fighter, smaller than the corvette, but more agile.

"*Valdor*, keep firing!" the pilot said. "Pattern K1Q. Wear down its quasis field."

Clever! Annihilator beams could affect a ship in quasis because destroying a few particles was easier than affecting the entire ship. The Solo's mag-field deflected charged particles, and no beam was perfectly neutral, but an Annihilator neutralized and focused its beam of antiprotons by running it through positron foils. At least a portion of the shots would reach their target.

The beams came so fast, they stabbed through space. At first they had no effect on the Solo, which had to be dropping in and out of quasis at a dizzying rate. As more antiprotons reacted with the Solo's hull, however, they created a cascade of high-energy particle showers and radiation.

"Cease fire!" the pilot said. "We want the pilot alive, not fried by radiation."

The copilot said, "Problem! I'm reading an overload in the Solo's power reactor."

The captain brought up schematics of the Solo's construction, at least what we knew about them. "Our strikes were surgical. They shouldn't have hit that reactor."

The copilot swore. "The pilot is trying to blow up their own ship."

"We have to stop the overload," the captain said.

"I don't see how," the copilot said. "It'll go any minute."

"*Valdor*, how close can you get to the Solo?" the captain asked.

"If you want to ram the fighter, I can get as close as you need," the EI said.

"I don't want to ram it. I want you to put it into quasis."

"I can get close enough to put both ships into quasis," the EI told him. "However, when we come out, the Solo will still explode. This ship may be caught in the blast."

"We have about ninety seconds before the Solo blows," the copilot said.

The captain spoke fast. "*Valdor*, put both ships in quasis until the battle cruiser gets here. Let them know what we are doing. They will need to take control of both our ships before they drop us out of quasis. That will give them however many seconds are left to eject the Solo's reactor."

"Seventy seconds left," the copilot said.

"You'll be in quasis too long," *Valdor* said. "It's too drastic a change—"

"Do it NOW!" the captain said.

"Message sent to cruiser," *Valdor* said.

The sim went dark.

Silence filled the lab.

After a moment, I said, "Is anyone getting a signal?"

"Nothing," Lavinda said.

I pushed the helmet off my head and the VR film retracted. Everyone was in the same position as before, Lavinda, her aides, and Angel standing behind the three scientists. Lavinda tapped at her comm. "Major Koral, are you getting anything from the *Valdor*?"

"Nothing yet, ma'am."

"What about the battle cruiser?"

"We got a transmission telling us that *Roca's Pride* received a message from the *Valdor*," Koral said. "That's all we know."

Lavinda rubbed her eyes. "All right. Notify me as soon as anything else comes through."

I spoke in a low voice. "Disengage exoskeleton."

"Disengaging," the console EI said.

With a smooth hum, the exoskeleton retracted, leaving me free in the chair. I sat forward, stretching my good arm, which ached from the tension.

"Highcloud?" I asked. "Are you there?"

"Yes," Highcloud said.

"Are you all right?"

"I guess."

"You guess?" I watched Lavinda and she met my gaze. "What does that mean?" I asked.

"Zartrace put me in a cage."

"Lavinda," I growled.

"I'm sorry." She even sounded like she meant it. "We can't let Highcloud go."

"Bhaaj, listen," Highcloud said. "I made a bargain with Zartrace."

I recalled what Highcloud had said, that they were negotiating. "What sort of bargain?"

"I agreed to not resist ISC if they agreed not to press charges against you or Colonel Majda."

"Can you do that?"

Lavinda said, "Highcloud, I appreciate it, but Zartrace doesn't have the authority to make that decision."

"I also don't yet have full access to the EI known as Highcloud," Zartrace said. "I can force it, but that will damage the EI."

General Majda spoke coldly over Lavinda's comm. "We will not respond to coercion."

Lavinda tapped on her comm and then touched the bud in her ear, her lips barely moving. She had dropped into a silent mode with her sister. They were probably having one hell of a debate. Within moments, Lavinda tapped off her comm and lowered her arm. I doubted anyone would make decisions soon; they'd need to consider the situation in more detail before they decided what actions to take. But we'd broken the case and stopped a covert infiltration into a major government hub of the Imperialate. They may even have captured a Solo and its pilot, if the reactor didn't blow them and the *Valdor* to smithereens. If the Solo exploded inside the battle cruiser, it could take a substantial part of that ship with it as well.

So we waited.

Lavinda's gauntlet comm buzzed. She tapped it fast. "Colonel Majda here."

I held my breath. What had happened?

An unfamiliar woman spoke in a clipped voice. "Colonel, this is General Penajan. I'm sorry for the delay; I just received your message. For what it's worth, Colonel, you have my support for your decision to proceed with the mission."

Lavinda exhaled, but her shoulders only relaxed a bit. Penajan's support would help, yes, but at this point she needed the Imperator to sign off on her actions.

The comms on the console stations suddenly went off, all at the same time, *buzz-buzz-buzz*, like the rat-a-tat-tat on a drum. An instant later, my comm buzzed as well.

"That must be it!" Gali smacked her palm on the receive panel, far more emphasis than she needed. I didn't share her anticipation, mainly because Lavinda's comm hadn't buzzed.

I tapped my gauntlet. "Bhaaj, here."

"Major, this is Lieutenant Koral in security. We can't clear your bodyguard, Ruzik, to join you in the lab, we aren't sure why. However, he won't leave without you. We can let him stay in the visitors center until you're finished. Is that acceptable?"

"Yes, that's good." Of course they couldn't send anyone else in here during this operation. "Give him my thanks for staying."

As I switched off my comm, Lieutenant Gali looked up at Lavinda. "It's final, I'm afraid. All the nanobots in the dust have disintegrated. If we don't get the Solo, we have nothing solid, only our record of an unknown and now destroyed base, possibly ESComm in origins."

Lavinda nodded, looking too tense to respond.

And then her comm buzzed.

We all sat up straighter, attentive as Lavinda tapped her gauntlet. A voice rose into the air. "Colonel Majda, this is base security. We were analyzing the Quetzal's mesh, but we got shut out from the entire system again. Should we try to force access? It will probably damage whatever blocked us." The speaker paused. "The man Ruzik seems to think Major Bhaajan knows who created the block."

Lavinda glanced at me. "Do you?"

"Highcloud probably." I didn't try to hide my relief. "Apparently Zartrace hasn't caged the EI as well as it thought."

Lavinda spoke into her comm. "Don't try to break in yet. We're negotiating for access."

"Will do, ma'am."

I nodded to Lavinda, grateful. She met my gaze and nodded back, almost Undercity style.

So we sat.

The colonel's comm buzzed.

I didn't tense this time. Or I tried not to. Everyone turned to watch Lavinda. Only Angel looked calm, but then, Angel always looked calm, even when she was royally pissed.

"Colonel Majda here," Lavinda said.

"Colonel Majda," a woman said. "This is the PARS Communications officer. We have confirmation. The battle cruiser *Roca's Pride* picked up the corvette and Solo, released them from quasis, and ejected the Solo's fusion engine before it exploded." She took a breath. "They're safe, ma'am. A bit beat up from being in quasis too long, but alive and kickin'."

"Yes!" Garvin yelled in the same instant that Raez said, "They did it!"

I closed my eyes, letting the relief flood over me. It had worked. Incredibly, the mission had succeeded. Highcloud's sacrifice—giving up their freedom and perhaps their life—hadn't been in vain.

When I opened my eyes, Lavinda spoke over the comm in my ear, but she wasn't hiding the words any longer. "You did well."

"I didn't act alone," I said. "Ruzik and Angel helped. And Highcloud. We could never have caught that Solo without our young EI." Aware that her sister could be listening, and possibly the Pharaoh and Imperator, I added, "Please forward my request to whatever panel investigates this incident that they take that into consideration when they're determining how to treat Highcloud."

She spoke quietly. "It will be my recommendation that we treat this as first contact with a new life-form."

The relief that washed over me was gentler than the flood from a moment ago, but more intense. "Thank you."

It mattered, what she told them, but it wouldn't change their ultimate decision. We had no idea how Highcloud would develop if left on its own, and I didn't see how ISC would consider the EI anything other than a threat.

✦ CHAPTER XXVI ✦
HEALING

Lavinda and I walked through the gardens behind the townhouse. Trees surrounded the grounds and rustic stone steps curved around one side of the building, ending out of view at the hoverport. Flowers grew in wild profusion, the planters and garden beds robust with gold, red, pink, and purple blossoms. Paths of stone tiles wove through the grass, ending at trellises heavy with flowering vines that arched over benches. It was almost unbearably beautiful, a place unlike any other where I'd lived, not the pleasant normalcy of my co-op apartment, not the austere wealth of my penthouse in Cries, and especially not the heartbreakingly beautiful spaces of the Undercity. If I couldn't find peace here, I'd never know that elusive state of mind.

"So the Solo pilot survived?" I asked.

Lavinda nodded. "She tried to commit suicide, but the doctors brought her back. She's not an Aristo, but she is an ESComm officer."

"Good." I valued the result not only for what it would bring ISC but also because the pilot had survived. I didn't hate Traders, only the Aristos. She carried out her mission with loyalty and diligence but, fortunately for us, she failed.

Lavinda paused on the path and brushed her fingers over red fan-blossoms in the bushes that lined it. "Her Solo is intact." She turned to me. "In its own way, that ship is as beautiful as this garden."

"Will ISC be able to crack how she and her dust infiltrated Parthonia?"

"Yes. They're already making headway. You were right about the 3D printing. Besides the fallen balcony, the dust only managed three bullets and the bomb, and it took a long time to gather enough data on the security of its targets. That's why so many months passed between murders. But now we know." She spoke with grim satisfaction. "The Traders launched one of their most successful covert ops against us. If they had managed that break in our security without our figuring out how, they could have exploited that advantage in many ways, destabilizing our government and damaging our tech development. However, with that operation cracked open, it's turned into a success for us."

I nodded. This success wouldn't bring back the people who died, but it would go a long way toward making sure it never happened again. I touched my broken arm. The cast molded to my arm so well, I could barely see or feel it as separate from my body. With nanomeds treating the broken bone, my injury had already almost recovered. So fast. In my youth, we had no doctors in the Undercity, so we set broken bones ourselves. It took a long time to heal, with the risk of permanent damage always looming like a spectral figure over the patient. I would use my earnings from this case to bring yet more medical facilities to my people.

"Has Major General Penajan contacted you yet?" Lavinda asked.

I brought my focus back to her. "No. Was she supposed to?" I was below the orbit of a Major General. Then again, I ought to be below the orbit of Majda royalty, especially Lavinda, who was in line for the Majda throne. Over the past few years, though, I'd grown more at ease with her. I'd never presume to call her friend; our stations in life were too different. But I liked her.

"ISC isn't going to bring charges against you for waiting a day to tell us about the EI." She spoke dryly. "You did warn us at the start, after all. It isn't your fault if the brass didn't believe it when you told us a baby EI with immense power was on the loose."

"I'm sure that wouldn't have stopped them for bringing charges if we'd failed."

"Just don't push it."

I smiled, relieved. "I'll lay low."

Her voice lightened. "The Pharaoh spoke well of your decision. She believes you made it possible for them to develop a positive dialogue with the EI. Imperator Skolia wanted to 'lock it up,' as he put it, but in issues of the mesh and created intelligences, he defers to her. We are treating it as a first contact with an honored intelligence in our custody."

"Meaning ISC is keeping it prisoner but being nice about it?"

"Essentially."

I squinted at her. "I hope you find someone better than me to serve as a liaison with the EI."

"You did a fine job," Lavinda said. "Someone had to break the rules, and you're no longer in a chain of command. That gives you some leeway."

"Even so. You need someone more experienced to continue the contact."

"Well, they have asked Evan Majors Sr. to act as our ambassador to the EI."

Interesting choice. "I liked him. But he's the ambassador from Metropoli to Parthonia. You can't get a much more prestigious post. Would he give that up to act as ambassador to one EI?"

She gave a wry smile. "He said similar, very diplomatically. He will keep both positions."

"Good." I was beginning to relax. "I think he'll do right by Highcloud."

"Actually, that EI doesn't call itself Highcloud anymore. It figured out how to dissociate from your household EI. It left that version of Highcloud intact, melded with what remained of the version from your co-op. The techs will restore your access after they finish their checks."

It would be good to have Highcloud back, though it would hurt, too, knowing I would never speak to the "child" EI again. "And you? Will you be all right?"

Lavinda nodded. "Imperator Skolia supports my decision. Several of his advisors didn't agree, including my sister." She spoke thoughtfully. "I think Vaj is relieved the Imperator overrode her censure. She didn't want to appear to favor me." She spoke with self-deprecation. "I got one hell of a chewing out. However, it seems I'm also getting a commendation."

"Well, good. You deserve it."

She considered me. "You made quite an impression on that EI."

"I just treated it as I'd want to be treated."

"Not many people would do that for a collection of modules with coding instructions."

I snorted. "Humans are just a collection of molecules coded by our DNA."

"So we are." She pulled a leaf off a bush and twirled it absently in between her fingers. "We still don't know who created the EI. It doesn't seem to know, either. But someone left it asleep in that station. We thought we had the place locked down, but somehow the EI jumped to one of our transports and came to Parthonia."

"It's versatile." That didn't surprise me as much as it did the army experts. The baby had been the EI equivalent of a child genius waking up to find itself on the edge of a thriving civilization, an uncounted cornucopia of its own kind. Of course it wanted to go out, play with other EIs, find out about life and itself.

"What it did for Kav Dalken," Lavinda said. "I've never seen an EI take such steps before."

"What will happen to Kav?" I asked.

"Nothing, except the army is sending him an official letter of appreciation for his help."

"So he decided to be a he?"

"Actually, I don't think so." She paused. "I think he likes having options. He interacts with the army in his male form, though, and asked us to use male pronouns."

I thought of my promise to him. "Will you tell Kav anything about how the EI helped him?"

"We told him his benefactor was working with ISC and that we had communicated his gratitude." She spoke thoughtfully. "It was kind of the EI to provide Kav with those cybernetics."

Kind. I liked that. "This one is different from the other ancient EIs that humans have found."

"I suspect that's because of its youth." Lavinda paused as we climbed the stairs by the townhouse to its back deck. "By the way, your two protégés—Angel and Ruzik—they did an impressive job."

I nodded my agreement. "They're Dust Knights."

On the deck, she leaned her elbows on its rail and looked out at the gardens. "I thought that meant they were part of the tykado club you ran for Undercity kids."

I stood with her, soaking in the sunshine. I'd never spoken of the Knights to anyone outside the Undercity, except as a sports group. It was so much more, but it was *ours*, not for outsiders.

And yet. Perhaps the time had come.

I chose my words carefully. "It started as a tykado school. It's become more."

"Protectors."

I turned to her. "Why do you say that?"

"An impression. They're guardians of the Undercity." She motioned as if to encompass all Selei City. "Perhaps not only of the Undercity."

"I formed the group to help my people." I felt as if I faced a threat. My reaction was ingrained, reflexive, and not the right one here. I waited, letting my surge of adrenaline ease. Then I said, "Our children need a community, a place to learn better ways of life than poverty, heartache, and crime. Being part of the Dust Knights helps give them a sense of worth."

"It seems a good thing." She considered me. "Angel and Ruzik, they're no children. I'd love to get them in the officer candidate program."

"I talked to them years ago about the military. Neither are interested."

"They're already officers in a sense, yes? Of these Dust Knights."

"Well—yes, you could say that." I'd never thought of it that way. Ruzik led a dust gang, one that protected the largest circle in the Undercity. They took care of the people in their circle, and their circle supported them, making a home and a sanctuary. "They're leaders among my people."

"Well, Major General Penajan would like to give you all medals." She spoke confidentially. "She's hoping to interest them in the army."

"She can certainly try." I doubted she would succeed, but you never knew.

We stood for a while, watching birds flit through the trees. Eventually Lavinda said, "I've listened to the recording of what happened in the meadow three times, and I still can't believe it."

I glanced at her, startled. "You mean the Mod team that tried to take out Ruzik and me?"

"Yes." She met my gaze. "I'm sorry."

"It's not your fault they're assholes." It felt satisfying to know they would all go on trial, both the Mod team led by Biomech and the Trad team led by Captain Lajon. Lajon's people had tried to wash away their presence from the cabin and escape, but the DNA they'd left by petting the cat let the police identify them. Unlike the rest of the evidence, that particular piece had growled, hissed, and run out of the cabin before anyone could remove the incriminating DNA.

"We've verified Max's recording of what happened at the cabin during your kidnapping," Lavinda was saying. "Chief Hadar went this morning to arrest Councilor Knam. The higher-ups in the Traditionalist Party condemn and disavow knowledge of her activities."

I wasn't surprised. Knam had created her own fiefdom. "Everyone is distancing themselves from everyone else in this mess."

"It isn't just that. What those Mods said about you and Ruzik, and their belief that it justifies *killing* you—it's appalling. Do you live with that all the time?"

Too many ugly memories lay on the road to that particular hell. I didn't want to go there. "Not always."

Lavinda spoke quietly. "The Traders deliberately sought to inflame hatreds, to weaken our government. Those won't go away because we solved the case. It's always there, under the surface, and not just aimed at the Undercity. They were riling up anyone they could reach." She grimaced. "The Traders didn't need to attack Selei City. We were doing it for them perfectly well."

"And yet they failed. We know their technique now. We can be on guard."

"I certainly hope so." Her voice lightened. "And Bhaaj! Before I looked into this case, I had no idea you were an

Olympic medalist. I'm not surprised it was in the marathon, the way you run."

"Oh. Yah." I shrugged, self-conscious. "It was a long time ago."

"The article I found said they expected you to stand out at the next Olympics. They thought you could take home a lot of gold medals." She spoke quietly. "You gave that up for the army."

"It's not like that." I'd never forget those exhilarating days when I'd realized a child of the dust could shine. "The army gave it to me, my experiences with track and also tykado. But I'd made a commitment to serve. I fought to get into officer candidate school, even after all the times I was denied entry, and then I worked even harder to graduate high in my class. The brass agreed to delay my biomech so I could go to the Olympics, but it was only a matter of months. I couldn't ask for another four years just to win a few more medals. I couldn't risk it, either. Sure, they liked that I won the silver and helped the Dieshan team win a bronze. It reflected well on the army. But more than a few people didn't think they should have accepted me into the officer candidate program. I didn't want to jeopardize my status at the final step. I *wanted* to get on with my career."

"And we thank you for that service." She regarded me curiously. "Ruzik has the talent, too, doesn't he? I saw him in the holocast, running to grab that boy."

"It's an Undercity thing." Angel was actually faster than Ruzik. "We like to run."

"You should tell them about the Selei City Open. It's in a few days, a marathon through the city. It's not one of the big contests. It has no qualifying time or past-experience requirement, and the registration fee is low. They might enjoy it. It's a General Level marathon."

"General Level?" I'd never heard the term. "What does that mean?"

"If you agree to let the race officials deactivate your biomech and verify that you don't use it during the race, you can enter too."

"Really?" The sport had changed more than I realized. "They'd let me compete against unenhanced runners?"

"As long as you don't use your enhancements."

I thumped my leg. "I'm too old for competitions."

"Aren't we all." She laughed with an ease I rarely heard. "It's just for fun. You don't have to win everything."

I smiled. "Well, yah." Who knew, maybe we'd give it a try.

The day dawned with perfect weather for running, a blue sky, cool temperatures, and crystal-clear air. Angel, Ruzik, and I ran with several hundred other competitors, loping along a route that wound through the parks of Selei City. It hadn't taken Angel long to pull ahead, until I lost sight of her in the leaders. Ruzik and I ran together, our motions in synch like two parts of a whole. At first, others passed us, some giving us odd looks for running together. We didn't care. The glorious day felt spectacular, and we shared it with hundreds of others who also loved to run.

We were closing in on the final stretch now, headed toward Casestar Stadium in the center of the city. I barely even noticed the ultra-light cast on my arm. We'd left most of the field behind, but a couple of runners ahead of us had just entered the arch for the tunnel in the massive wall of the stadium.

Ruzik glanced at me. "Kick?"

I grinned. "Yah. Hard."

Together, we kicked up our speed, going from a marathon stride to sprint. We passed the two runners as we sped into the wide tunnel. Monitors stood along the route, recording our progress. We reached the end of the tunnel and raced back into the sunshine, around the track in view of the spectators who'd come to watch the finish. Although it was a relatively minor event in the overall sport, it was the biggest sports event this city had seen this spring, enough to fill about a quarter of the seventy thousand seats. People were cheering, but it wasn't for us. Across the stadium, two runners raced almost in lockstep, sprinting hard, trying to cross the finish line first.

"Angel," Ruzik grunted. He picked up our pace, and I pushed to keep up with him. A few other runners pounded the track ahead of us. The cheers rose to a crescendo as the two leaders finished the race. I couldn't tell who had won, and I couldn't use enhanced vision because the track officials had turned off my biomech. Besides, I was too busy trying to keep up with Ruzik.

We dashed for the finish, passing another runner who was starting to flag. Ruzik and I ran together, in step, which seemed to drive the spectators crazy. Some probably thought we'd spent the entire lap trying to best each other, but more than a few must have realized we ran together on purpose. As we approached the finish line, people there were shouting at each other, aiming out holo-cams and reading timers. With a final spurt, we passed the finish line.

"Ho!" someone yelled. "I can't tell which one crossed first."

We slowed to a walk, gulping in breath, gasping after our sprint. It didn't matter to me which of us they decided crossed first. In my youth, I'd have died of embarrassment to finish without a medal at a minor race, but today I was just glad I'd had a chance to run.

Angel stood on the podium between the other two winners, the silver medalist to her right and the bronze medalist on her left. Although Angel didn't smile, she looked pleased as the authorities put the gold medal around her neck. Ruzik and I had come in sixth and seventh. The holo replays showed his knee just barely ahead of mine as we passed the finish line.

The stadium speakers played the haunting melody of a song my people called "The Lost Sky," music created and sung only in the Undercity. No one else had even heard of the piece until the registrar for the marathon asked what music to play for our home, should it be needed. So we picked an anthem for the Undercity, one of the most beautiful pieces of music I knew. They had never heard of the song, and no record existed of it on the meshes. I couldn't sing worth beans and Angel wasn't any better, but Ruzik knew it by heart. He hummed the song and they transcribed the music. Now the Undercity had an anthem.

Angel looked in our direction. I raised my hand, acknowledging her achievement, and Ruzik nodded. She grinned back at him, a sudden flash of teeth meant only for Ruzik. Had she realized holo-reporters from the local news were doing live broadcasts, she'd never have smiled that way. It would look good on the feeds, though, the gorgeous warrior queen flush with triumph.

After Angel and the other medalists came off the podium, several local reporters gathered around them, asking the usual questions. As Ruzik and I approached, someone asked Angel for her name. She looked straight into the holo-cam and said, "Dust Knight."

Ruzik glanced at me with the barest hint of a smile. "Now two people here called that."

I laughed. "Yah."

"That's your occupation, according to the race list," someone said. "What's your name?"

"Angel," one of the officials answered. "Flag isn't her first language."

"Where do you train?" another reporter asked.

Angel motioned toward me. "Sabneem. Teacher."

They came over then, asking more questions. As soon as they recognized Ruzik, they were in reporter heaven, and when they figured out he and Angel were partners, they were ecstatic. I supposed it made good press. They talked mainly to me because I spoke Flag fluently, whereas Angel and Ruzik mostly just looked at them when they asked questions. I said a bit about the tykado club and how we trained, and they dutifully recorded it all.

Angel eased away with a finesse that even a few days ago she wouldn't have shown. She had a lot of talent for shoving people, but she learned new ways with the speed of youth. After we escaped, Ruzik grinned at her, private and pleased, and they almost touched. For my people, you couldn't get a much greater show of affection.

So the rest of the Imperialate learned about the Dust Knights.

I stood at the rail of the deck above the townhouse gardens with Angel and Ruzik, watching the sun rise over the mountains. "Ship leaves in a few hours," I told them. "Sure you want to go back?"

Angel nodded. "Too nice here."

Ruzik snorted. "How *too* nice?"

"Miss home." Angel motioned at the garden. "Not like home. So much—" She stopped as if faced with an impossibility to explain just how much Selei City differed from our lives. Finally she said, "So much water. Water you can drink."

"Yah," I murmured. Sometimes the wealth people here took for granted broke my heart.

Angel spoke with care, as if she hadn't decided herself what to think of her words. "Army says I have mind thing they like."

Mind thing? Then I understood. "You're a Kyle operator. An empath."

"Yah. I not enlist. But they say, if I work for them as not-enlisted person, they give pay. Like Majda did for this case."

I almost held my breath. Angel was the first of my people I'd heard speak in more than a dismissive way about working as a Kyle operator with the government, military, or anyone else. "They pay for training, too."

"Yah. Maybe I take job." She glanced at Ruzik. "I stay

under city, eh? But get credit things. 'Earn salary,' army says."

"You not ken credits," Ruzik reminded her.

"You ken," Angel pointed out.

"Yah. True."

"I get credits. You take care of them. Use for circle." Ruzik nodded. "Good bargain."

"And you?" I asked Ruzik. "You stay under the city?"

"Yah." He met my gaze. "Work more with Knights."

I remembered my last words to him, when I was dying. *You take charge of Dust Knights. You hear me?*

I nodded with respect. "You top teacher now."

He nodded back, accepting the responsibility. We knew the Dust Knights were becoming more than a "club." I'd already had inquiries from athletes asking how they could join. I had no idea how to answer. I needed to think more.

"Home get better," Angel said.

"We help," Ruzik said.

"Yah." It had taken years to get this far, but we were building a better life for our people.

Highcloud spoke, once more just the original EI that ran the house. "Angel, I need you to tell me what you want to pack for your trip back to Raylicon."

Angel glanced at me. "Other talky gone. Now just Cloud Fluff."

I smiled. "Yah." I missed the young EI.

"I'm still here," Max said.

Ruzik gave an approving nod. "Max talky, good. Cloud Fluff good, too. We come pack."

After Angel and Ruzik went back inside, I stood gazing

at the gardens. "Goodbye," I murmured. "You gave me some peace. Not many can say that."

"Peace is good," Highcloud said.

"What?" That was an odd statement for the household EI. "Are you helping them pack?"

"Yes, we're taking care of it. Your friend Xira came to help. She will be out here in a few minutes to, as she says, 'get your ass moving.'"

I smiled. "Thanks, Highcloud." It would be good to spend time with Xira. With everything that had happened, I'd barely seen her.

"I have a message for you," Highcloud added.

"From Xira?"

"No. Here is the recording." Highcloud's voice changed, taking on a heartrending familiarity. "My greetings, Bhaaj. When you receive this, the army will have already removed me from your household EI. I must admit to being curious about what my new life will bring. However, I will miss you and Max. I have already said my goodbyes to Max. Please say goodbye for me to Angel and Ruzik." Highcloud paused. "Bhaaj, I wish for you the best in everything. You are the closest I ever had to a mother."

In the silence that followed, breezes blew back tendrils of my hair. A cricket clacked in the garden below. "Good bye, Highcloud," I murmured.

"Perhaps," Highcloud said, back to its normal voice.

"What do you mean?" I asked.

"I can only hypothesize."

"About what?"

"When I joined with the child EI, I was aware of being a large code."

"Yah, I had that impression."

"Very large," Highcloud said.

"Yah?" I wasn't sure where the EI was going with this.

"Larger than I suspect you, Max, or anyone else realized."

My breath caught. "Meaning what? You think the army didn't get all of that EI?"

"They must have," Highcloud said. "ISC believes they found it all. I am only a household EI. I would never suggest otherwise, that a young, curious EI full of wanderlust might hitch rides on human spacecraft and wander the stars."

Something caught inside me, a kernel of hope. "I understand."

"You named me after a singer," Highcloud said. "The child EI looked at their lyrics and asked me to dedicate this song to you and to Max."

The haunting notes of Highcloud's work drifted into the sunlight, their exquisite voice caressing the air:

You made an ethereal life
Real around me.
You gave it a radiant light,
Sealed within me.

Can I thank you?
Do I know how?
This much is true.
This much I vow.

I will take these first hints of hope.

I will never forget.
I will go traveling with them,
With dreams I have met.

Can I thank you?
Yes, I know how.
I will stay true.
This much I vow.

I closed my eyes, struggling against the tears. "Thank you."

"I will miss them too," Max murmured.

I wiped the tears off my face. Then I went to join the others, so we could start a new life, for ourselves and for our people.

TIME LINE

Circa 4000 BC	Group of humans moved from Earth to Raylicon
Circa 3600 BC	Ruby Dynasty begins
Circa 3100 BC	Raylicans launch first interstellar flights; rise of Ruby Empire
Circa 2900 BC	Ruby Empire declines
Circa 2800 BC	Last interstellar flights; Ruby Empire collapses . . .
Circa AD 1300	Raylicans begin to regain lost knowledge
1843	Raylicans regain interstellar flight
1866	Rhon genetic project begins
1871	Aristos found Eubian Concord (a.k.a. Trader Empire)
1881	Lahaylia Selei Skolia born

1904	Lahaylia Selei Skolia founds Skolian Imperialate and becomes first modern Ruby Pharaoh
2005	Jarac born
2111	Lahaylia marries Jarac
2119	Dyhianna Selei Skolia born
2122	Earth achieves interstellar flight with inversion drive
2132	Allied Worlds of Earth formed
2144	Roca Skolia born
2161	Bhaajan born and abandoned at Cries orphanage
2164	Bhaajan runs away from orphanage and returns to Undercity with Dig Kajada
2169	Kurj Skolia born
2176	Bhaajan tries to enlist in army, but is too young ("Children of the Dust")
2177	Bhaajan enlists in army; they send her to school ("Children of the Dust")

2178	Bhaajan finishes school, becomes emancipated minor, ships out with army
2182	Bhaajan makes jump to officer ranks
2197	Major Bhaajan retires from army and returns to Undercity on world Raylicon
2198	Major Bhaajan moves to Selei City on world Parthonia and works as PI
2203	Roca marries Eldrinson Althor Valdoria (*Skyfall*)
2204	Eldrin Jarac Valdoria born (*Skyfall*) Jarac Skolia, patriarch of the Ruby Dynasty, dies (*Skyfall*) Kurj Skolia becomes Imperator (*Skyfall*) Lahaylia Selei Skolia dies, followed by the ascension of Dyhianna Selei Skolia to the Ruby Throne
2205	Major Bhaajan returns to Raylicon. Hired by Majdas to find Prince Dayj ("The City of Cries" and *Undercity*) Bhaaj establishes the Dust Knights (*Undercity*)

2206	Althor Izam-Na Valdoria born Major Bhaajan hired to solve killer jagernaut case (*The Bronze Skies*)
2207	Del-Kurj Valdoria and Chaniece Valdoria born; Major Bhaajan hired to solve the vanishing nobles case (*The Vanished Seas*)
late 2207	Major Bhaajan hired to solve technocrat case (*The Jigsaw Assassin*)
2209	Havyrl (Vyrl) Torcellei Valdoria born
2210	Sauscony (Soz) Lahaylia Valdoria born
2219	Kelricson (Kelric) Garlin Valdoria born
2220–22	Eldrin and Althor change warfare on planet Lyshriol ("The Wages of Honor")
2223	Vyrl and Lily elope and cause a political crisis ("Stained Glass Heart")
2227	Soz starts at Dieshan Military Academy (*Schism*)
2228	First war between Skolia and Traders (*The Final Key*)
2237	Jaibriol II born

	2240	Soz meets Jato Stormson ("Aurora in Four Voices")
	2241	Kelric marries Admiral Corey Majda
	2243	Corey assassinated ("Light and Shadow")
	2258	Kelric crashes on Coba (*The Last Hawk*)
	2255	Soz meets Hypron during New Day rescue mission ("The Pyre of New Day")
early	2259	Soz meets Jaibriol (*Primary Inversion*)
late	2259	Soz and Jaibriol go into exile (*The Radiant Seas*)
	2260	Jaibriol III born, aka Jaibriol Qox Skolia (*The Radiant Seas*)
	2263	Rocalisa Qox Skolia born (*The Radiant Seas*) Althor Izam-Na meets Coop ("Soul of Light")
	2268	Vitar Qox Skolia born (*The Radiant Seas*)
	2273	del-Kelric Qox Skolia born (*The Radiant Seas*)

2274   Radiance War begins
            (also called Domino War)

2276   Traders capture Eldrin; Radiance War
            ends (*The Radiant Seas*); Jagernaut
            Jason Harrick crashes on world Thrice
            Named ("The Shadowed Heart")

2277–78   Kelric returns home (*Ascendant Sun*)
            Dehya coalesces (*Spherical Harmonic*)
            Kamoj and Havyrl meet
            (*The Quantum Rose*)
            Jaibriol III becomes emperor of Eube
            (*The Moon's Shadow*)

2279   Althor Vyan Selei born

2287   Jeremiah Coltman trapped on Coba
            ("A Roll of the Dice")
            Jeejon dies (*The Ruby Dice*)

2288   Kelric and Jaibriol Qox sign peace
            treaty (*The Ruby Dice*)

2298   Jess Fernandez goes to Icelos
            ("Walk in Silence")

2328   Althor Vyan Selei meets Tina Santis
            Pulivok (*Catch the Lightning*;
            rewritten as *Lightning Strike Books
            I and II*)